"Very, very funny...Sandlin has a deft touch with characterization and dialogue that keeps the reader right with him from the first page to the last. He's a pleasure to read."

—*Wichita Eagle*

"Tim Sandlin's fourth and most satisfying novel, *Sorrow Floats*, is a little bit Tim Robbins, part Jack Kerouac, and a whole lot of John Irving."

—*Missoulian*

"Hilarious...not since *Lonesome Dove* have I met such an enticing crew of booted misfits between the covers of a book."

—*Greensboro News & Record*

Praise for *Social Blunders*

"A story of grand faux pas and dazzling dysfunction...a wildly satirical look at the absurdities of modern life."

—*New York Times Book Review*

"A weird, funny, raunchy novel that veers wildly from pathos to slapstick and back again, and it's surprisingly effective."

—*Booklist*

"Wild, wonderful, and wickedly funny...Highly recommended."

—*Library Journal*

"Downright superb...wickedly funny...richly rewarding."

—*Milwaukee Journal*

"Sandlin is the only novelist I've read in the last two years whose prose forced me to laugh out loud."

—*Bloomsbury Review*

"Tim Sandlin only gets better. *Social Blunders* is an affecting book, now sprightly, now sad, as his characters experience the common upturnings and downturnings of life. It is fiction to be savoured."

—Larry McMurtry

"Ribald...comic and bawdy...oddly endearing...an effective blend of flippancy and compassion."

—*Publishers Weekly*

Praise for Tim Sandlin and *Skipped Parts*

"Pound for pound, Tim Sandlin's stuff is as tight and funny as anyone doing this comedy novel thing."

—Christopher Moore

"Sandlin can see that there is a kind of gruesome comedy in what happens to us, but the humor is never mean, and he loves his people too much not to understand that their grief and nostalgia and frustration is real."

—Nick Hornby

"There is no more compelling subject than young human males and females coming together in the spring of their lives...A thoughtful, surprising, and delightful entertainment."

—*St. Louis Post-Dispatch*

"A sparkling tale...*Skipped Parts* offers some big helpings of western wit, down-home adult humor, and once-in-a-while sorrowful truths...It's a classic story of the well-read, old-before-his-time young teen and hip mom learning to cope...Excellent."

—*Indianapolis News*

"Wittily told...reminiscent of Larry McMurtry's *The Last Picture Show.*"

—*Library Journal*

"Chock-full of wonderful characters and good writing."

—*Dallas Morning News*

"This witty, often touching portrayal of a dirt-streetwise youth's coming of age sparkles with intelligence."

—*Booklist*

Praise for *Sorrow Floats*

"A raucous, surprisingly original tale."

—*New York Times*

"Unforgettable...*Sorrow Floats* has a multitude of gifts to offer—laughs, real people, high drama, and a crazy cross-country journey that makes it hard to put aside for long, if at all."

—*West Coast Review of Books*

"Sandlin understands that the best black comedy is only a tiny slip away from despair, and he handles this walk without a misstep."

—*Dallas Morning News*

"A zany road trip across America starring an engaging heroine and two AA devotees occupies talented novelist Tim Sandlin in *Sorrow Floats*."

—*Cosmopolitan*

"Able storytelling and an engaging cast of dysfunctional modern American pilgrims animate this winning tale of the road... Sandlin fashions a convincing tale of redemption."

—*Publishers Weekly* (starred review)

"Arousing piece of Americana....rowdy, raunchy...A total delight."

—*Library Journal*

"Funny and poignant...Sandlin's sustaining insight and faith in humanity give the book compassion and hope."

—*Winston-Salem Journal*

"Hold on to your heart, sit on your hat, and give yourself over to a delicious, pothole-filled journey. *Social Blunders* is a sad and savvy coming-of-good-sense novel."

—Shelby Hearon

"A kinder, gentler Tom Robbins and/or Kurt Vonnegut... funny...compelling, sad, a weird brand of black comedy, and important modern fiction."

—*Nashville Life*

"Some writers make you laugh out loud. Tim Sandlin is one."

—*Winston-Salem Journal*

"Hilarious."

—Copley News Service

"The best moments in *Social Blunders* come from Sandlin's sense of the inevitable comedy in even the most tragic situation. But to describe them too fully is to betray their sense of art and delight."

—*Planet*

Praise for Tim Sandlin

"Sandlin is Tom Robbins with a heart."

—*Atlanta Journal-Constitution*

"This man is writing himself into a richly deserved place of honor on all our shelves."

—John Nichols

"Sandlin just keeps getting better and better."

—W. P. Kinsella

"In a region heretofore dominated by Larry McMurtry, Tom McGuane, and Ed Abbey, Tim Sandlin, of Oklahoma and Wyoming, is emerging as a new and wickedly funny talent."

—*Publishers Weekly*

"Tim Sandlin is among the growing coterie of writers who are shaping the fictional territory of the New West."

—*Kansas City Star*

Also by Tim Sandlin

The GroVont Books

Skipped Parts

Sorrow Floats

Social Blunders

And coming in 2011, Tim Sandlin returns to GroVont with Lydia, *available at booksellers everywhere.*

Sex and Sunsets

Western Swing

The Pyms: Unauthorized Tales of Jackson Hole

Honey Don't

Jimi Hendrix Turns Eighty

Rowdy in Paris

Skipped Parts

Tim Sandlin

sourcebooks landmark

Cover design by Jessie Sayward Bright
Cover images © Luis Alvarez/Getty Images

Published by Sourcebooks Landmark, an imprint of Sourcebooks, Inc.
P.O. Box 4410, Naperville, Illinois 60567-4410
(630) 961-3900
Fax: (630) 961-2168
www.sourcebooks.com

Library of Congress Cataloging-in-Publication Data

Sandlin, Tim.
Skipped parts / Tim Sandlin.
p. cm.
1. Teenage boys—Fiction. 2. Divorced mothers—Fiction. 3. Mothers and sons—Fiction. 4. Teenage girls—Fiction. 5. Teenagers—Sexual behavior—Fiction. 6. Adolescence—Fiction. 7. Maturation (Psychology)—Fiction. 8. City and town life—Wyoming—Fiction. I. Title.
PS3569.A517S55 2010
813'.54—dc22

2010020944

Printed and bound in the United States of America.
VP 10 9 8 7 6 5 4 3 2 1

For Carol and Kyle,
Marian, my editor and friend,
and Sally, my sister

Acknowledgments

I COULDN'T LIVE THE WAY I DO WITHOUT A LOT OF HUMORING from the people of Jackson, Wyoming, especially Michael Sellett who owns the *Jackson Hole News* where I work, and the employees of Jedidiah's Original House of Sourdough, the Valley Bookstore, and the Teton County Library who keep me fed and pointed in the right direction. None of the beauty of life in paradise would mean squat without friends like Lisa Bolton, Lisa Flood, Pam Stecki, Hannah Hinchman, Shelley Rubrecht, and Teri Krumdic. Tina Welling read the manuscript and helped immensely.

Although I never met them, Ed Abbey and John Nichols showed me there is no excuse for not living where you want to live or doing what you want to do—a good lesson to learn while you're still young.

We were as twinned lambs that did frisk i' the sun
And bleat the one at the other. What we changed
Was innocence for innocence.

—Polixenes, King of the Bohemians
The Winter's Tale

The two grey kits,
And the grey kits' mother
All went over
The bridge together
The bridge broke down
They all fell in
May the rats go with you
Says Tom Bolin.

—Nursery Rhyme

1

I REMEMBER BEING WAY OUT IN RIGHT FIELD AND MY NOSE hurt. Hurt like king-hell, as if my sinuses were full of chlorine. Now I know that when anyone moves from the South to Wyoming, their nose always hurts like king-hell for two weeks. Has something to do with the humidity, I guess, or the altitude.

But at the time, standing out there in right field pretending to spit in my glove so I could hide my right hand as it pinched my nostrils, I thought Lydia and I were the first Southerners ever lost in Wyoming. I also thought the nose pain meant I had leukemia and would die soon.

"Sam, Sam, can you hear me?"

Sam's eyes fluttered in weak recognition of his grandfather's presence.

"Sam, I'm so sorry you're dying of leukemia, I'm sorry I shipped you and your mom out to the Wilderness when you needed to be home the most."

Sam tried to raise his hand. It was a noble effort.

"Sam, this is your grandfather, can you forgive me before you die?"

The poor boy's lips worked, he made the supreme effort, but no words of forgiveness would escape his mouth. Slowly, painfully, he smiled.

Back then I often had recurring daydreams of people being sorry when I died.

Out in right field, I was keenly aware that people were watching me. Where they watched from, I wasn't certain, but I always know when I'm being watched. It makes my butt itch. I have a feeling this deal goes back to the second grade when Lydia told me not to scratch in public because someone was always watching. Lydia's the kind of mother who would do that to a kid.

Since I couldn't scratch where it itched and my nose hurt like king-hell, I stood out there in right field kind of twitching. I hunched my right shoulder up to rub my ear, then blinked my eyes hard, trying to scratch my sinuses from the inside. I raised up on my toes and tensed my butt cheeks. That didn't help at all, made me feel more watched.

The trouble, of course, was social alienation. I'd always played baseball with gas company conduits behind third base and the Caspar Callahan Carbon Paper plant twenty yards off the first-base foul pole. Now, nothing lay behind third base, only the bare valley floor stretching forever to a line of green along a river, then another forever before the Tetons jumped up two dimensional in the background.

The openness got me. There are no treeless spots in North Carolina—unless someone's fought like king-hell to make them that way. Here, I could see a tree up by the school and a few scraggly little willows we'd call weeds marked the home run fence behind me, but other than that—zip. Zappo. Nothing. I was lost in limbo where the unbaptized babies go when they die.

Off the first-base line was almost as bad. A bunch of rural, shrieking types played pathetic volleyball. They all had their hands over their heads like apes. I could see pit stains from thirty yards. If the wind changed, I'd be in big trouble.

The batter swung wide and missed by a foot. He was tall and gangly. One thing I had to admit about Wyoming, even in the midst of my bad attitude, the kids might be ugly but hardly any of them were fat. Maybe a girl or two, and they were more muscled broad than fat. I spit in my glove again. Somewhere along the line I'd decided spit was good for leather and not to be wasted.

The kid batter swung again and again missed by a mile.

"Sam, you've only been gone from Greensboro a short time, yet you've returned with the demeanor of a cowboy."

Sam tipped his wide-brimmed hat. "Yup."

"You seem so much taller and more enigmatic."

"Yup."

Caspar had banished us before—that's what he did when Lydia pulled one of her classic boners. But that was to Maine or Georgia Sea Island and summertime. This was a mockery. Mars. The inside of a vacuum cleaner bag.

I heard laughter. They weren't just watching, they were laughing at me. I chose to take the high road of the sports hero and ignore them.

The night before—our first night in hell as she called it—Lydia had told me about school. "Sam, honey bunny." The honey-bunny stuff was a nasty habit. "Sam, honey bunny, you're at the worst age possible to be starting a new school. You can handle it one of two ways. You can wallow in superiority, tell yourself everyone's a stupid yahoo but you."

"Yahoo," I said.

"Or you can be nervous as heck that you won't fit in and no one will like you and you can suck up like a puppy dog."

"Neither way sounds fun," I said.

"I advise superiority. It has always stood me well." This conversation took place before 10:30.

"Hey, kid, throw the ball."

I ignored them. I wasn't sure how it had happened, but the gangly kid stood on second and there was a new batter.

"Hey, dummy."

A ranch boy crossed the foul line, walking straight toward me. I concentrated on the new batter who was a spastic or some such. He switched sides of the plate between every pitch.

The boy came up on my left. "You deaf, kid?" He was real skinny and had bad pits on his chin. When he spit a wad of juice, I looked at his swollen cheek in amazement. I'd never seen anyone chew tobacco and this guy couldn't have been more than thirteen, fourteen years old.

"Can I help you?"

The boy wrinkled his nose and mimicked in a high voice. "Can I help you."

"What's the problem?"

"Our volleyball." The boy had about six inches of extra belt hanging off his buckle.

"Your volleyball's the problem?"

"You've got it."

I looked down at the ball at his feet. Same color as Lydia's skin. "I'm sorry, I didn't see it."

"How could you not see it. It's right there." The boy bent down to pick up the ball. "We thought you were foreign. Can't understand American."

From the left side of the plate, the batter drilled a high fly down the right field line and I took off. I'd show the turkeys. Not a kid in Wyoming could make this catch. I pictured myself, at a dead run, reaching out, spearing the ball, then whirling and firing a strike to the cowboy-booted second baseman to nail the gangly base runner.

Almost worked that way.

I flew across the playground, made the jump, snared the ball, and came down with my left foot in a hole. As I started to fall, I caught myself with a straight right leg, stumbled a couple steps, pitched forward, and hung myself on the volleyball-net guy wire. Would have done permanent damage, except the force of the sprawl yanked up the stake holding down the guy wire. As it was, my head jerked back, my feet kept going, and I made a sound like *yerp*. Then I slammed to my back. I rolled into the pole which, without its guy wire, fell across my body, bringing the net down on my face.

Breathing was tough. I lay in silence, staring at the blue above. A black bird circled up near a cloud. Yellowish spots formed at the corners, swelling in front of my eyes. Turning my head carefully, I looked at my left hand. The ball lay tucked in my mitt. It had been worth it.

Way high, a face came into view. She had remarkably well-defined cheekbones, dark hair pulled back, and blue eyes. Black hair and blue eyes, like Hitler.

The eyes blinked once. She opened her pretty mouth and disgust dripped off her voice. "Smooth move, Ex-Lax."

2

I FOUND LYDIA STRETCHED OUT ON THE FAKE COWHIDE COUCH, more or less surrounded by magazines and Dr Pepper bottles. An ashtray overflowed onto a deck of cards on the floor.

"Mom, we can't stay here."

"Mutual trust and respect, Sam, always remember what our relationship is based on. You must never fling in my face the fact that I am a mother."

"These kids are morons, Mom. Lydia. Worse than morons, they're Nazis. I almost killed myself today and they laughed. Can you believe it?"

"Children laugh at pain. It's what makes them children." Lydia lit a cigarette. I don't know what kind. She made it a policy never to smoke two packs of the same brand in a row. She inhaled deeply and blew smoke at a huge stuffed moose head on the wall. When Lydia lifted her chin and squinted her eyes, her long forehead seemed to grow even longer, and her remarkably thin lips puckered into what I took as a pout. Lydia pointed at the moose with her middle finger under the cigarette. "That goes. I won't have the dead passing for art."

I collapsed on the foot end of the couch and kicked off my sneakers. "When we first came in yesterday, I figured out which room was the other side of the wall, and went looking for the rest of the moose."

Lydia watched me through the light blue smoke cloud. "Most people don't catch self-effacement, Sam. Try something else."

I went in the kitchen and returned with two Dr Peppers. Lydia was still staring at the moose. The house had been rented to Caspar as is from a doctor who overemphasized Hemingway, which meant every room had at least one mounted head. Two antelopes flanked the bed in my room. I'd already named them Pushmi and Pullyu after two characters—one character, actually, with two heads—in a Dr. Doolittle book. The antelope on the left had longer horns that bent toward each other. He was Pushmi. I imagined Pullyu was a female.

I opened both bottles with a church key from under the sink. "Look at those nostrils. Each one's big as a hooker's twat."

Lydia reached for her pop. "That's another matter we should speak of. This is Wyoming. Thirteen-year-old boys do not compare objects to a hooker's twat."

"You'd rather me laugh at pain?"

"And how do you know what a hooker's twat looks like?"

"Jesse told me they're like a big, black, chocolate éclair."

Lydia glanced down at herself. "I certainly don't look like a chocolate eclair."

"You're not a hooker."

Lydia propped her feet up on a pile of old *Field & Stream*s. Cigarette in left hand, Dr Pepper in right, she looked considerably more like a bad baby-sitter than anyone's mother. She had the toes of a child. "We must be normal here," she said. "I'm tired of trouble. If these kids are morons, just wonder where Caspar will banish us if we mess this one."

The thought was inconceivable. I plopped into a straight chair with elk gut or something stretched across the back. "Damn, Lydia, what did you do to hack him off so much?"

She waved her hand like brushing away flies. Lydia had the longest, thinnest fingers I had ever seen. "Nothing. I didn't do a thing."

"Look at it from my point of view. You told me about the Cuban guy and the dancer and the strip show on the diving board. If this one's so horrible you can't tell me, think what my imagination is going to imagine."

Lydia smiled. "Oh, fuck you."

I propped my feet up next to hers and drank from the bottle. "Normal, remember. Wyoming women don't use that word in front of their baby boys."

"Fuck Wyoming women too."

I went back to the kitchen, opened the freezer, and pulled out a frozen pizza. "You know how to light the oven?"

"Are you kidding?"

The apprentices' eyes widened in fear. "Chef Callahan," they cried. "The hollandaise sauce is separating."

Sam smiled mysteriously to himself and tapped his two-foot-high chef's hat to a rakish angle. "Let's see the problem, boys."

The apprentices, both of whom were shorter than Chef Callahan, stepped aside as Sam peered into the stainless-steel bowl. "Boys, bring me two egg yolks, a half lemon, and a tennis racket."

"Sam, something's wrong with the television."

I put the pizza back in the freezer and found a pound can of cashews and a half-full jar of pickles. Caspar's doctor friend was big on Mexican condiments. The shelves were packed with four-alarm sauce stuff, dried peppers, and boxes of prefab taco shells, nothing you could make a meal of. Back in the living room, Lydia was sitting up, squinting at a snowy picture on the TV screen.

She slapped the side of the set. "Can you believe this, one channel, if you find this a picture."

I set the cashews and pickles on the end table that had elk horns for legs. "Hope you don't mind a light dinner."

"I thought maybe PBS wouldn't come through, but this is modern America. Everybody gets at least three stations."

We chewed cashews and watched *My Three Sons* as Mike, Rob, and Chip pushed their dad's busted Buick up the street. I wondered what it would be like to have brothers. Or a dad. "Maybe if we put in an antenna."

"I doubt it. We've fallen off the edge of the Earth. My destruction is complete. You want the last pickle?"

I settled into my end of the couch with my knees over Lydia's legs and *A Farewell to Arms* and the *Hardy Boys Mystery of the Haunted Swamp* on my leg. The guy in *Farewell* talked like an idiot, but the war parts were neat. Every time Frederic and Catherine started doing a Punch and Judy act—I love you, Catherine, I love you, Frederic—I switched to a half-hour of the Hardy brothers wholesomely sniffing out clues.

The red phone rang twice. Sam answered, "Yes, Mr. President."

"Callahan, we've got a problem."

"That's what I'm here for, sir."

"The Ruskies are filling Cuba with missiles and I just don't know what to do."

"Blockade them, sir."

"That sounds awfully drastic, Callahan."

"We must be firm, sir. The Red Menace doesn't respect wimps."

There was a long silence. "All right, by golly, we'll try it. You've never let me down yet. Callahan, I have one other question."

"My time is yours, sir."

"Why don't you let your mother and school chums know that you are the principal advisor to the President? Why let them go on believing you're just another kid?"

"It's my way of keeping in touch with the little people, sir."

—

The cabin was so quiet it was noisy. The toilet ran, the refrigerator kicked on and off like a lawn mower, I opened the back door twice before figuring out the water heater knocked. By 9:30 I knew who was hiding in the swamp and what kind of wine went down in an Italian pool hall.

"Mom?"

Lydia ignored me.

"Lydia?"

"Yes, dear."

"How can you go so long without peeing?"

"It's a sign of the upper class."

"You haven't moved except to play with the TV in four hours that I know of. Why don't you go to the bathroom like other people?"

Lydia lit another cigarette, a Lucky Strike this time. "Honey bunny, you read like a guy chasing whiskey with beer."

Both books lay propped open, face up on my chest. "I like reading two books at once."

She blew smoke at the moose. "You're dead," she said.

The moose stayed cool.

Lydia made her version of a sigh, which is more like the sound you get when you stick a knife in a full can of pop. "I've made a decision about this banishment deal, Sam."

"Should I be told?"

"The way I conducted life back home didn't work."

"I'll say."

"I'm calling time out. No more connections for a while. I'm declaring myself a temporary emotional catatonic."

I thought about this. "How's a catatonic supposed to raise a son?"

Lydia looked down at her long fingers. "We'll negotiate an arrangement."

At 10:00 the news came on and we sat watching stories about people in east Idaho. Potatoes were important. Rangers in Grand Teton Park—which GroVont is smack in the middle of—were being plagued by elk poachers. Vice President Johnson was in Vietnam complaining about the food. During the sports, I didn't recognize the names of any of the teams.

"It's ten-thirty."

Lydia smiled. "You mind?"

I went into the kitchen and brought back a pint of Gilbey's gin and a two-ounce shot glass.

"You be all right?"

"Sure, I'm fine. I think I'll sleep out here tonight and start unpacking in the morning."

"I'm going to bed now." I bent over and kissed her forehead. It was cool and slick. Her hand touched the back of my head.

"Your hair needs cutting."

"Any barber around here's going to make me look like one of them."

"I'll do it myself. It'll be like we're pioneers."

I did the shower and toothbrush thing, ate a children's multiple vitamin, snuck one of Lydia's yellow Valiums, and put on my pajamas. I wore pajamas to bed back then. Before I flipped off my light and lay down to wait for the pill to kick in, I stood behind my open door, looking at Lydia through the crack.

She was at the window with the shot glass in her left hand and her right foot propped up on the sill. She stared out a long time. I could see the blank tightness on the side of her face, the twin knots on her neck, and a tiny throb on her temple visible clear across the room. She lifted her right hand and drew something in the fogginess her breath made on the window. I always wonder what she drew.

I had a dream that I was a fox and a bunch of uniformed people on horses chased me through a Southern hardwood forest.

Sam's lungs cried out with the pain of charging headlong down the steep hillside. He tripped over a rotting log and sprawled onto his face. Rolling over quickly, he made it to his knees and crawled through the thick, thorny underbrush and into a weed-choked stream.

He turned west, splashing through the frigid water, using his paws and legs to pull himself upstream. Sam heard the dogs running up and down the bank, baying to each other and their wicked masters. Horses thrashed through the trees. He'd fooled them for the moment. Now to find a safe hole. He waded around a corner and came face to face with the blue-eyed Hitler girl astride a giant, sneering bay. She laughed and raised the rifle to her shoulder.

3

It's a weird school too. There's maybe forty, fifty kids to the grade, so seventh, eighth, and ninth are each divided into two classes, slow and quick. It's a social thing that lasts for life. I got all huffy the first morning because I thought the cowpoke of a principal had slotted me into the slow class, but then I saw the others at lunch hour. I've been to South Carolina; I know cousin crossbreeding when I see it.

So right off the bat before I'm even awake, there's this teacher character with hair he must cut with hedge clippers. I made up a short story in which the guy was drummed out of the Marines for doing something disgusting to a recruit three months ago and his reentry into society hasn't gone well. The people in charge tucked him away in this God-forgotten valley where nothing he could do would matter.

"He machine-gunned his entire English class, sir."
"None of those kids would have ever left Wyoming anyway."

I like to make up short stories; it's what I do.

The man had the face of a haunted Marine—all hollowed-out surfaces around the eyes, below the cheekbones, the temples. His chin had a cleft you could hang a bra over.

I'd hardly settled into the farthest back desk I could find when he marched over and stuck out his hand. "Hi. I'm Howard Stebbins. I'll bet you like football."

"No, sir. I'm from North Carolina."

Howard laughed like I was a real kidder and slapped me on the elbow. I can't stand having male people touch me, especially coaches. I never met one yet didn't like to watch boys take showers.

Along with coaching the junior high team of the season, Stebbins taught seventh-grade English and high school driver's ed. Lots of coaches teach driver's ed. I don't know how he got the English job. Maybe somebody old died.

Howard sat on the corner of his teacher's desk, looking casual while he talked *Huckleberry Finn*. "Mark Twain combined high adventure, slapstick comedy, and moral outrage into one monumental work, probably *the* American novel of the nineteenth century."

I hope nobody tells Moby Dick. I'd never been as jazzed by Huck and the boys as the young reader is supposed to be anyway. For one thing, the ending sucks eggs. We're walking down a road a thousand miles from home and buddy Tom Sawyer pops up. "Hey, Huck." "Hey, Tom."

Get real, Mark.

Mr. Stebbins asked all these leading questions about Negro and white motivations and is the river thematic, and it didn't take but about six minutes to figure out that the Nazi girl and I were the only ones who had actually read the book.

This teased-up and sprayed-down hairdo up front had read as far as chapter four—"The Hair-Ball Oracle"—and got hung up. "He says the hair-ball big as a baseball came out of the fourth stomach of an ox. I never heard of a hair-ball in a cow."

"Well, Charlotte, superstition plays a big part in the book."

"Daddy's seen a gallstone big as a fist, but even a idiot could tell a hair-ball from a gallstone."

Teddy the chewer with the weird belt spoke up. "Maybe it was a coyote. I've seen coyote hair-balls would gag an ox." He was still chewing—right there in class. Had a Maxwell House can to spit into.

"An ox isn't the same as a cow," the Nazi girl said. "It's bigger."

Charlotte couldn't be stopped. "Oxes eat grass so their turds are runny, same as a heifer."

The kid who played third base yesterday held up his hand. His name was Kim Schmidt and that morning before school he'd shown me his one and only God-given talent. He could make a sound exactly, exactly mind you—when Kim showed me the trick he must have said "exactly" six times—exactly the sound a dog makes when it throws up.

"The German shepherd," Kim had said, before his mouth went oval and his throat clicked three times, then he made the sound. I believed him.

"The cowdog," he said. I couldn't tell the difference; guess you'd have to know your barfing dogs.

Anyhow, Stebbins called on Kim who explained that a hair-ball would be in the first stomach of an ox, not the fourth, and that Jim the Nigger, or Mark Twain, had counted backward.

"Ain't no hair-balls in no cows," Charlotte insisted.

Stebbins took a shot at directing the discussion back to theme and character development. "Let's leave hair-balls for the moment—"

"We haven't decided about them yet," Charlotte said.

"—and go on to Twain's brilliant use of Negro dialect." I'm not even sure Stebbins had read the book. That "brilliant use of Negro dialect" smacked of the Classic Comics introduction.

"Maurey," Stebbins asked the Nazi girl. That was her name—Maurey. As in the record-setting base stealer for the Dodgers. "Maurey, what did you think of the way the character spoke?"

Maurey sniffed like the question was beneath her dignity. She was wearing a blue fuzzy thing and her hair came down more on one side than the other, the Jackie Kennedy look. "Nobody really talks that way."

"Why do you think Twain wrote the dialogue in dialect if no one talks like that?"

"He wanted Huck to seem stupid and Jim even stupider. It was a way to put them down for being hicks."

The class seemed to buy the rap. Who was I to publicly disagree with a Nazi?

Stebbins wasn't sure. "So, Maurey, how do you know no one talks the way Twain wrote?"

"I've heard Southern accents on TV and they're nothing like 'I'se gwine ta hyar a gos, Massa Huck.' What dope would talk that way?"

I knew better, but I jumped right in without raising my hand. "Huck is from Missouri which isn't the South, and the book is set before the Civil War. Maybe people back then didn't talk like they're on TV."

She reddened and turned in her seat to stare at me. I've seen disdain—nobody can touch Lydia at true disdain—but I'd never seen such intense disdain aimed right at me. "How do you know how people spoke before the Civil War? You're not a day over eighty."

Some of the kids sniggered and right off I was in the modern equivalent of school bully beating up the new kid at recess just to prove who's toughest.

"I'm not even eighty," I said back in as close to her tone as I could pull off. "I just figure Mark Twain knew more about how Negroes around him every day talked than you do."

Stebbins opened his book, then shut it again. He cleared his throat. "We know Mark Twain was one of the great proponents of equal rights for all. We appreciate that here in the Equality State."

I said, "Yeah, but he couldn't stand a Jew."

Stebbins looked surprised. "Are you sure?"

"Twain blamed every problem he ever had on Jews."

A girl up front I hadn't noticed before spoke up in a semi-Southern accent. "Are you Jewish?"

"No, I'm not Jewish."

"How do you know Mark Twain hated Jews then?"

"I can read."

A general murmur circulated the room. Natives were turning ugly. I might go through this and still get beat up at recess.

Maurey's face had these two white spots on her forehead and her hair bounced when she talked. "How can you say that when you hate Negroes."

"I don't hate Negroes."

Stebbins finally made it to his feet. "But you're from the South."

"So."

"Everyone in the South hates Negroes." That's from the teacher. Can you believe it? For a moment I was struck dumb.

"You can't deny it," Maurey said.

I looked from face to face. They all looked the same. I had an inkling of what a black person sees in a white world. "Have you ever spoken to a Negro?" I asked her.

Maurey didn't answer.

"How can you say anything about Negro speech if you've never spoken to one?" Mr. Stebbins started to say something, but I cut him right off. "Have you ever seen a Negro, Miss Smarty Pants?"

The smarty-pants deal took things too far, but this was junior high war. If I didn't shut her down now, I'd spend the next six years in the coat closet.

"Of course I've seen Negroes," she said.

"Where besides TV?"

Teddy spit in his can. "I seen 'em in Denver when we went down Christmas."

"Did you speak to any?"

Teddy grinned and let juice run down his chin.

The girl up front came to the class rescue. "My daddy knows plenty niggers back home and we hate 'em all."

"Does every Caucasian in the South hate Negroes?" Maurey asked her.

"I don't know 'bout Caucasians, but ever'body in Birmingham does. Daddy moved here 'cause niggers got his job."

Stebbins knew better than to try to control Maurey or me—we were smarter than him—so he tried to pull off some dignity on the little Dixie racist. "We do not call them niggers out West, Florence. They prefer to be known as Negroes."

"Huck Finn calls the guy Nigger Jim."

"That's because Huck is an ignorant hick," Maurey said. "Hicks talk that way."

"They'll always be niggers to me."

"See."

Stebbins shut his book with a pop. "Polite people say Negroes."

I corrected the Marine washout one more time. "Actually, in North Carolina, the younger ones are calling themselves Afro-Americans."

The whole class busted up at this. Don't ask me why. What some people think of as funny has always been a mystery to me. Even Stebbins chuckled. "That's a bit far out, don't you think."

I just shrugged. I snuck a look at Maurey and got the scowl to end all scowls. I crossed my eyes at her. She turned around to face the front.

About then the bell rang. Stebbins shuffled up his papers and books. He stared out at the class—not at me, mind you, just vaguely in the air above the third row—and said, "Sam Callahan, I'd like to see you here after sixth period."

Great. First day of school and I'm being held over to clap erasers.

Next came Miss Flanagan and geography, then Mrs. Hinchman and citizenship. She showed us on the chalkboard how to write a check. I'd been writing checks since the third grade.

At lunch hour I skipped the post-cafeteria baseball game. Figured I'd blown that one yesterday; they'd have stuck me in right field again anyway. Hardly anyone under sixteen can hit to the opposite field, and since there aren't many left-hand batters, right field in junior high is like let's-get-rid-of-this-guy-so-we-can-talk-about-him.

Instead, I sat on the cafeteria steps and watched Maurey play volleyball. She was pretty good. She was the only girl out there who could serve and didn't squeal like a stepped-on cat every time the ball came near. The blue thing I'd seen from the back in Stebbins's class was a pullover-sweater deal. She had on an off-white skirt that came about mid-knee and rose up when she jumped at the net.

Somewhere in there, she realized I was watching. She glanced over a couple of times, then after a bad serve, she turned and stared right back until I looked off at the Tetons.

Sam felt the rock above for a seam, the tiniest crack with which he could pull himself another foot up the sheer face of the mountain. The calf of his left leg began to quiver. Hundreds of feet below, the waterfall crashed down granite walls, roaring like an angry lion hungry for flesh.

Sam had to move. Suddenly, the fingertips of his left hand felt an edge. No wider than a dime, this must be the next line of safety. Groaning, straining, sweating like August in Charleston, Sam pulled himself up higher, ever higher, until finally he stood on the dime-wide ledge.

Okay, next step. A crack slit the rock vertically. If he could work his way into the crack, his feet braced on one side and back on the other, Sam stood a chance of wriggling his way another stage up the impossible north face of the Matterhorn.

His stomach felt the rock give before his ears heard the tearing sound. The thin ledge began to separate from the mountain. It snapped like water dribbled into french-fry grease. With a cry, Sam leapt for the vertical crack. His hands beat against the side of the mountain, his fingernails seemingly digging into the solid stone. Sam froze there for a moment, like in a Roadrunner cartoon when the ledge gives way under the coyote and he hangs suspended in midair just long enough to look at the camera and swallow once.

Then Sam fell to his death. His grandfather would be sorry now.

After lunch came history taught by Miss Barnett who I knew was senile as those old black guys who sit on their porches in Greensboro with Ping-Pong-ball colored eyes and catheters. I supposed they kept her on because she'd been with the school since Wyoming was run by Indians, and no one had the heart to make her stay home.

I didn't concentrate much. Mostly because I didn't have to—everyone in class seemed to be taking naps—but also I was somewhat concerned about this after-school discussion with Howard Stebbins. What if he was weird?

Maybe he was just pissed because I knew more about Mark Twain than he did. Or it could be that thing about Twain blaming his problems on the Jews. Maybe Stebbins was Jewish. We had Jews in North Carolina but you couldn't tell them from anyone else except when they made a big deal out of a holiday or something. Nobody—unless you count a few Klansmen that I don't count—cared anyway. Lydia'd been to New York City to see her mama's mama, and she said there you could tell the difference and it mattered for some reason.

When I was nine or so, I heard Caspar say the government had Jewed him out of something or another. I asked Lydia what that meant and she said they'd circumcised him. I believed her, it wasn't 10:30 yet.

—·—

The Marine washout made a good story, but Howard Stebbins wasn't nearly that interesting. Nobody is as interesting as the stories I give them. In real life, he was a local boy who'd been a valley sports hero back in the mid-fifties. Still owned county records in the 440- and 880-yard runs. He'd captained the only GroVont basketball team to ever make the state finals.

Then old Howard went off to the University of Wyoming and kind of got lost. He kicked around a few years, doing what it took to get a teacher's certificate and filling the third or fourth space on depth charts over at the athletic department. He came back home where he was still somebody, married a local girl, and settled into the life.

The high school coach had exactly the same story only he was ten years older.

Howard told me most of this—and I made up the rest—while I stood quietly next to his cluttered desk, wondering if it had any significance. In a varnished walnut frame next to a gift pencil box, I spotted a woman with ratted and sprayed blonde-white hair and glasses behind two miniature versions of Howard. Same hedge-cutter haircuts. The littlest one had glasses with lenses thick as my thumb.

There were three other photos in the room, up above the chalkboard. Abraham Lincoln, Albert Schweitzer, and Kurt Gowdy.

Stebbins leaned back with his hands behind his head and his feet propped up on an open desk drawer. "You watch out for the Pierce girl."

"I don't know a Pierce girl."

"Maurey Pierce, the one you riled this morning."

I fell back on false bravado. "She better watch out for me."

"She can ride a horse standing on its bare back."

"Is that a reason to watch out for her?"

Stebbins touched himself on the top of his nose, then along the hairline. "GroVont's too small to make enemies."

He was afraid of her. It was my first experience of a grown-up afraid of a kid. Now I think it's fairly common, some grown-ups are afraid of all kids, but up until then I looked at the world as an us-and-them situation, with Lydia kind of straddling the line.

I wondered if Maurey was running a bluff on everyone. She didn't seem that mean. She was pretty in a 1939 movie-vamp way. I'd seen her smile early in the volleyball game. Real earth-eating bitches—such as my mother—don't have fun during sports. They don't really enjoy anything.

Stebbins looked down at something really interesting on the back of his hands. "I saw that catch you made yesterday."

I shrugged, not sure if I was supposed to affect modesty over the catch or contrition about the net deal.

"You've got some athleticism, Sam. Ever play on a team?"

Bing, my bullshit bell sounded. He wanted something from me. My auto response when someone wants something is to politely lie. "No, sir. I never had time, what with my studies and all."

"We've got a pretty decent little football team here at GroVont Junior High."

Football is my least favorite sport to play, as opposed to watch, right down there with soccer and checkers. I like games where you stay upright. I can fake basketball pretty well—no kid comes out of North Carolina who can't—but baseball is where my rocks come off.

When I didn't react, Stebbins stopped the beat-around-the-bush. "I want you at practice tomorrow."

"Gee, I'd like to, sir. But we just moved to town and my mother needs me at home."

He frowned and continued inspecting each knuckle of each finger, starting at the left and working his way across. "It takes twenty-two players to practice and I've only got twenty-one and half of them still suck their mama's tit at night."

"I no longer nurse, sir."

He looked me straight in the eye. "Callahan, I need to explain how I grade in my classes. You know the difference between an A and an F in English?"

Truth is a pain in the butt to face. "Me coming out for football?"

Stebbins slapped me on the shoulder. "See you tomorrow at four."

Lydia was right. All men are fuckers. As I slumped out the door, the king-jerk broke into a whistle—"Ragtime Cowboy Joe"—then he stopped. "Hey, Callahan."

"Yes, sir."

"Did Mark Twain really hate Jews?"

—·—

I had my heart set on making it home without any more incidents—that's one thing I hate, the uncontrolled incident, the completely unplanned demand on my coping abilities—but cities are the place to turn invisible. In GroVont, everyone thinks they have a perfect right to horn in on everybody else's life.

Anyway, I was walking down Alpine, almost to the dirt spot we were supposed to call a yard, when this voice said, "Son, come over here."

Son? There was an instant of taking the thing literally until I saw the guy who'd called. Looked like Khrushchev in overalls. He stood across the street in front of one of those loaf-shaped Airstream trailers, only instead of shiny silver, this one had been painted toe-jam black using a cheap brush so every stroke showed. Sagebrush grew up through two '54 GMC three-quarter-ton trucks, the kind with the oval rear windows, and a king-hell ugly dog stood atop the cab of another '54 GMC three-quarter-ton with an oval window. My guess was the two dead trucks provided parts transplants for the runner. Fairly easy enough guess to make.

"Son," the guy said again. "Come here. See this." He didn't have a shirt on under the overalls so you could see all this wired-out body hair, and he had on huge black rubber boots that came up to his knees. The truck had a plastic stick-on sign that read COUNTY WATER WARDEN.

"What's a water warden?" I asked.

The man spit. "Don't talk down to me, son. My granddad homesteaded this valley, and if it wasn't for him you wouldn't be living here so free and easy."

"Oh." I didn't follow the line at all, but when people don't make sense I've found it better to grunt and not make any eye contact.

"Don't tell me there's no water wardens where you come from."

I looked at the dog. He had black-and-white spots and was shaped like a banana—had a little bitty stub tail. "Does he always ride on top the cab?" I asked.

"Otis likes the wind."

"Otis?"

"He's Otis, I'm Soapley." Soapley was one of those men who have a three-day growth of beard every day.

"Sam Callahan," I said. "Pleased to meet you. How does he ride up there without falling off?"

"Water warden opens the headgates. Makes sure ranches get what they're supposed to and no more. Comes a drought, I run the county."

"Oh."

"In winter I plow the road. I'm important then too. I can say who gets out and who don't."

"I don't think we have headgates or road plows in Greensboro."

"Don't talk down to me. I won't be talked down to." Soapley shifted his weight from one foot to the other—had a stance like he was in the on-deck circle, waiting for his turn at bat. Back and forth, his thumbs kind of twitching.

"I'm not talking down, I just wonder how he stands on the cab while you're driving without falling off."

"Otis."

"That's your dog's name."

"Otis's smart, smarter than you. That's why I invited you over."

"You invited me over?"

"Look at his face and pretend you're a pretty girl."

I looked at his bullet-shaped head. He had a good resemblance to Soapley, especially the forehead part. "I can't pretend I'm a pretty girl."

"Just do it for God's sake."

So I pretended I was Maurey Pierce for a minute, which is a good exercise for a short-story writer.

"Hi, I'm Maurey Pierce."

"The hell you are."

I pretended I hated Sam Callahan and sat down to pee.

The ugly dog's right eye closed and opened.

"He winked at me."

Soapley hit it big with pride. "Smartest dog in Teton County."

"Oh."

Back in my own cabin, I found Mom on the couch. "Lydia, this dog across the street rides on top the truck cab and winks."

She stared at me across her long fingers, through the blue haze of cigarette smoke. "You expect me to show an interest in this?"

"Not especially."

"Then don't muddle the air with details. I don't want any details whatsoever about goings on in this state."

—

As neither one of us still knew how to light the stove, Lydia and I ate in the White Deck Cafe that night. Lydia never was much for cooking anyway.

For food, there was the White Deck Cafe between a barbershop and an art gallery on the town triangle—as opposed to other towns that have a square—and the Tastee Freeze out on the highway by the Forest Service headquarters; except on Sunday nights when the VFW had all the wienies and beans you can eat for a buck.

Anyone celebrating an anniversary or whatever would drive the twenty miles into Jackson where the restaurants had soup-spoons and the cash register wasn't a Dutch Masters box.

The only reason for going to the White Deck was to eat.

After we slid into the booth I started flipping the jukebox wheel while Lydia cleaned silverware with the hem of her shirt. For being a total slob at home, Lydia had remarkably high standards for cleanliness in others.

The waitress called, "Keep your pants zipped, Jack, I'll be there when I get there," as she swept by with three dinner plates on her left arm and one in her right hand. She was in her early thirties, maybe ten pounds overweight, and on the back of her belt in white, square letters, I read the word DOT.

"Her name is Dot," I said to Lydia.

Lydia looked at her teeth reflected in the butter knife. "What kind of woman would name a child Dot. I'd rather be blind than saddled with a name like Dot."

Dot brought the plastic-wrapped menus and two waters all in one hand. "Max told me you're the folks in Doc Wardell's place. The guys paid me a dollar each to find out if you're single."

There were four other booths of customers, four men each in three of the booths, all with their sleeves rolled up, and two ancient geezers looking dead in the corner. Lydia was the only woman, besides Dot, and I was the only kid. No one used the tables or the stools along the counter.

Lydia inspected the water glasses for spots. "Who's Max?"

"He owns the place. Max said Doc Wardell rented his house to your father or grandfather or somebody—"

"Tell them I have five husbands," Lydia said, loud enough for the men to hear for themselves. "Every one of them rich, mean, and jealous. I'll be rotating them through on a weekly basis."

Dot broke up. I love people who laugh so hard they break up. I've never broken up in my life. She went on for a good minute while the men shifted in their booths, suddenly developing a need for salt or mustard, anything to keep their hands moving. One skinny fart with a king-hell Adam's apple stared right at Lydia, like she was in a zoo. I took him for a preacher.

Dot draped her hand across my shoulder and I didn't mind. "That line'll be all over the valley by sundown," she said. "Thirty years from now your name'll come up in conversation and they'll say, 'Did you hear about her first night at the White Deck?'"

Lydia opened her menu. "Just tell them I own a rifle."

I looked up at Dot and she smiled at me.

One thing I've always wondered is whether or not men found Lydia good-looking. It's so hard to be objective on your own mother. Most people tend to look at their own mom as beautiful until you hit seven or so, then you ignore her for a while, then you decide she's an old hag.

I had just turned thirteen then, which would put Lydia at twenty-eight, not all that over the hill, even for a mom. And, as we hung out together most of the time, we'd developed kind of a bitchy husband-and-wife deal. I don't mean Oedipal or anything disgusting like that. When or if she kissed me good night, I always screamed "*Ooooh yech,*" and she screamed right back "*Ooooh yech.*" I just mean I took care of Lydia as much as she took care of me, and we hung around each other a lot, so I felt like we were orphans together, sort of.

She hadn't told me to go to bed or pick something off the floor in eight years—if she told me then.

But back to pretty. Nine men out of ten took one look at Lydia and were afraid of her; the other one was willing to give up wife, job, and reputation to fuck her on the spot. But this effect wasn't from looks. I'd call the deal demeanor. Lydia had demeanor. And a fairly decent set of knockers.

"So what happened in the seventh grade today?" Lydia held her cheeseburger in one hand, peering at it suspiciously.

"Do you really want to hear?"

She turned the cheeseburger around to inspect the other side. Lord knows what she was afraid of. "Of course I want to hear. It's my job. If I don't want to hear, Caspar will take you to Culver Military Academy. We wouldn't want that now, would we?"

"I wouldn't."

Lydia gave me a sharp glance. "Neither would I. Now tell me what happened in school today."

"I think I fell in love."

Lydia was back inspecting the burger. Maybe she expected something to crawl out before the first bite. "That's nice," she said. "How can you tell you're in love?"

"Because there's this girl in class and I can't stand her."

"That's always a good start."

I was eating the Tuesday blue plate—pounded steak with mashed potatoes and brown gravy. "She hates my guts, called me Ex-Lax yesterday."

"Sounds like love to me." Lydia finally took a bite, chewing very slowly. When she swallowed, twelve men in the room exhaled.

The pounded steak desperately cried for ketchup but, for some reason I never understood, Lydia considered ketchup plebeian. If I used a dribble, we'd go into twenty minutes on the sort of people who put ketchup on food—the sort who eat pounded steak in the White Deck if you asked me—and I'd rather try to understand conflicting emotionalism.

"I don't like any of the kids at school because they're all idiots, only I don't like her the most and she's not an idiot. Not liking the others is like not liking grits—big deal. But not liking her is like not liking a water moccasin. When she looks at me it's like I have the flu. My stomach aches." It's hard to explain love at thirteen.

Lydia looked at me with interest. "Better eat fast. That gravy is turning to axle grease."

Maurey said to Sam, "Let us walk through the oak forest along the stream."

He stood and together they strolled up the dirt path. Birds flittered over their heads, deer watched quizzically from the shadows. The forest had no underbrush. Everything was clean. It was a scene from Bambi.

Maurey took Sam's hand in her own. Their fingers entwined, not like shaking hands with a stranger, every pore of her hand touched every pore of his.

At the stream they found a small waterfall tumbling over moss-covered rocks into a deep pool where trout jumped lazily for mayflies.

"Let us sit," Sam said.

"Whatever you want," she murmured, taking off her sneakers.

They kissed, faces pressed together, arms around one another's backs. Maurey smiled at him. "You know why I like you more than the other boys?"

"Because we're the only two in seventh grade who can read?"

She laughed and shook her head no.

"Because I'm a suave big-city Easterner who's been to New York and seen a baseball game at Yankee Stadium?"

"No, silly." She leaned her head on Sam's shoulder. "Because you're so tall."

There was a crash. I lay in the dark, eyes open, hoping it was a one-time deal. Lydia and I'd had contact after 10:30 before and it never was good luck. Something heavy slid across the floor and there was another, smaller crash. What would Beaver Cleaver do if June was so drunk she trashed the living room?

He'd go help her to bed.

As I pulled myself out from between the sheets, a big crash came, followed by Lydia's raised voice. "Cheers. You're dead, Les, and I'm not."

The TV lay on the floor sideways. The big crash had been a couple of book boxes going over—science fiction and Westerns. Lydia stood with her back to me, her head up toward the moose.

"Mom?"

She turned. "Honey bunny?"

"What's up?"

Lydia waved her shot glass in the direction of the moose head. "Les and I were toasting our new relationship."

I looked at the big head mounted on the wall. "Les?"

"Short for Less Like Drinking Alone. That's his name. We're buddies."

I pointed to the television on the floor. "You made a social blunder."

Lydia tried to follow the direction of my point and almost fell. She caught herself with one hand on the end of the couch. "Social blunder, my ass. I knocked over the goddamn TV."

I moved into the room to catch her if she went down. "Any chance of you going to sleep?"

"You're joking your mama, aren't you, sweet prince." Lydia closed one eye to focus on me. Her skin seemed paler than usual and her hair needed washing. Her posture wasn't worth a poop. Her mouth opened and shut before she spoke. "I had you too young."

"Are you sorry about that?"

She took a step back and fell into a sitting position on the couch. Took her a second to recover. "I don't think in those terms."

"You're sending me mixed messages, Lydia. Caspar's shrink said you shouldn't send me mixed messages."

"Oh my God." She slapped her hand over her mouth and spoke through her fingers. "I'm sending my baby mixed fucking messages."

I stood there in my blue-striped pajamas, watching her. "Maybe I'll go back to my room."

Wrong thing to say. Lydia's lower lip quivered and the tears came. I had to go through the arm-around-the-shoulders, patting-her-hair, apologizing-for-the-world deal. She blubbered. "You're all I've got. If he takes you I'm all done."

"He won't take me."

"I'm twenty-eight and everything good that's ever going to happen to me has already happened." She sniffed a couple times. "And I hate myself when I do it, but sometimes I blame that on you."

"Lots of good things might happen to you."

Her face turned to me. "Name one."

I looked at the TV on the floor, then at the moose, Les, then back at Lydia's tear-blotched face. "You might win a contest."

She pouted. "I haven't entered a contest."

"Tomorrow, that's what we'll do, we'll enter a contest. Now's time for sleep."

She jerked away. "No." She held up her index finger, left hand, as if making a point. "I have a chip."

How was I supposed to handle that? "In your nail?"

"Everyone says my hands are my finest feature and I have a chip."

"We'll fix it right up first thing in the morning."

"To hell with you, Mr. Solicitatious to the Drunk. We'll fix it now. I may be stuck in the hell hole of the West, but I will never let myself go." This from a woman who was on the verge of sleeping in the same clothes she'd slept in last night.

Her head nodded at the book boxes spread across the floor. "I was looking for my nail kit."

"And the TV?"

"It slipped." She stood up too quickly and sat back down. Then she stood up again. "The bathroom."

"I'm tired and sleepy, Lydia. Use verbs."

"My nail kit that Mother Callahan gave me is in my overnight bag in the bathroom." Getting out an entire proper sentence must have exhausted her because she sat back down again. "Help me to the John, honey bunny." She held out both arms.

"Nope. If you can't walk on your own you can't play with scissors."

"Bastard."

"What's that make you?"

Lydia bounced off both walls on her way down the hall, then through the open bathroom door. When I got there she was leaning over the sink with her forehead and nose propped against the mirror, staring into her own eyes a half-inch away. Lydia stuck out her tongue and touched the tip of it to the mirror.

I said, "You're licking the mirror."

"I'm making contact."

"With who?"

"Myself."

"You're licking the mirror."

The bathroom was actually the niftiest room in the house, although I tend to think that about any house. It had this claw-foot bathtub and a commode that sat about two inches higher than what I was used to. Made crapping feel awkward until I discovered *The James Beard Cookbook* turned into a footstool brought my body back to the right angle.

A big stump rested next to the toilet, acting as a table or counter space or some such, and Lydia's overnight bag sat on the stump. While Lydia went into close-range self-hypnosis and connected with herself, I decided to sit on the side of the bathtub and watch.

She suddenly turned to me. "Sam, have you ever had a hard-on?"

"Mom."

"I was thinking about the hooker's twats on Les. Have you ever experienced a hooker?"

"I'm thirteen, Mom." That twat talk was all bravado, like most of my off-color language. Women had twats, I was certain of that, but I wasn't certain exactly to the inch where they were located or what they did.

"And I realized I hadn't seen your little thing in years. It was so cute when you were a baby. We had this black speckled basin I used to wash you in, and you'd always pee straight up, then we'd both giggle and have the nicest time." Her cheek was stuck to the mirror now, in the center of the fog circle left by her breath.

"Lydia, don't you know how much it embarrasses kids when their mom talks about cute naked stuff they did as babies."

Her head slid down a notch. "Then you went to grade school and came back a smartass."

I didn't know what to say. I just sat there, hoping this kind of crap wouldn't warp me when I grew up.

Lydia kind of lunged-fell sideways into the overnight bag, and junk exploded all over the place—toothbrushes, combs, curlers,

Vaseline, spray deodorant, my Clearasil, gum, pens, female hygiene objects I'd never seen before—and a bottle of Pepto-Bismol hit the floor and broke. Pink blood oozed under the tub.

Lydia said, "There," and fell to her knees, bopping her forehead a good one on the edge of the sink.

I reach out, but she growled at me—like a cat. "Stay away." She was crouched in sort of a cave under the sink with the toilet on one side and the tub up the wall on the other. By kneeling off to her left, I could see what dear old Mama was up to under there.

The leather fingernail kit lay against a drain pipe, zippered side to the wall. Carefully, Lydia reached out, picked it up, and turned it around counterclockwise. She seemed to take forever pulling the zipper, sliding out the scissors. I touched her shoulder but she growled again.

She bit her lower lip hard as she slow-motion trimmed the fingernail back the thinnest sliver, then slid the scissors back into their slot. File next. Right side first, working her way up the nail, tapering the top just right, then down the left. Pink Pepto-Bismol flowed into view from between her legs. Lydia ignored it.

Her voice was only a whisper. "I didn't let myself go." Then she slid the file back into the case and, as slowly as she'd opened it, zippered the kit shut. Lydia placed the leather case on the floor and, using it as a pillow, fell asleep.

I went back to bed.

4

Caspar looked like a short Mark Twain, which is maybe why I don't care for *Huckleberry Finn*. He did a lot of things I hated to Lydia on purpose and a lot of things I hated to me accidentally, but his one unforgivable sin was being short. That stuff is hereditary as hell.

Caspar had a gray hearing aid that he kept turned down except for when he was talking, and he wore a white suit year round, Southern as all get out. Every day, he stuck a fresh yellow mum in his lapel. I used to think the mum had something to do with Me Maw and he'd once had a heart, but Lydia said it was part of some spiffy self-image thing, and if Caspar ever had a heart, he sure wouldn't advertise the fact.

The day we left Greensboro, after these ape-men-redneck movers piled all our stuff in a truck and went away, Caspar came out on the porch to deliver some sort of farewell to the family. Lydia was sitting sideways in the porch swing, reading *Reflections in a Golden Eye* by Carson McCullers, and painting her fingernails black. I read the book on the drive west and decided not to ride any horses. The black fingernail polish was a Lydia statement to Caspar, but he missed it.

I was on the plank floor sorting baseball cards. It was late in the summer and there'd been a rash of trades before the final pennant drive, which meant I had all kinds of guys in the wrong place. Willie Mays had collapsed in the batter's box the day before we left so his card was out on top.

Caspar drew himself up into what passed for posture. He fingered his hearing aid and gave out a little snort. "The purest treasure mortal times afford is spotless reputation."

I looked at Lydia who shrugged. "You been in the library again, Daddy?"

He hovered over me, looking like an old man pretending to be an even older man. "Do you know why I'm sending you to northwest Wyoming?"

I stared up into his permanently black fingernails. No matter how much Caspar played at Southern gentility, carbon in the cuticles would forever show his roots. "Because Lydia messed up again."

Lydia coughed real ladylike into her hand. Casper wasted a glare on her before going on. "Because I measured in the Rand Atlas and Jackson Hole is farther from a major baseball team than any other spot in the country."

"Oh."

"And you are leaving those cards here."

"Caspar."

"There will be no discussion. In Wyoming you are to mature into a gentleman. You will think carbon paper, not baseball."

Lydia almost stood up to him. "Daddy, don't take it out on Sam. He's innocent."

The old goat actually hooked his thumbs under his suspenders. "Nothing you touch is innocent. One mistake out there and he goes to Culver Military Academy. Are the implications clear?"

"Yes, your daddyship."

Caspar stared down at me. "Carbon paper, Sam. The country turns on carbon paper. Nothing else matters to you."

"Yes, sir."

"Bring your cards to the basement."

When Caspar opened the screen door, I snuck Willie Mays and Gil Hodges into my socks. They're the only two I saved. Caspar incinerated every other player from 1958 through 1963 in the basement coal stove. And he made me watch.

"Gentlemen, on punts we have two men we pop free for the block. First one's the outside rusher, that's you, Callahan. Line up on the side of the line that the kicker's kicking foot is on. Got that?"

I nodded. No reason to go into the Yes Sir mentality until I had to.

"You have a second and a half to move from here to a spot two feet in front of the kicker, and you're being blocked one-on-one so there's no time for anything fancy. Just get around the guy and fly."

Practice hadn't been the irritating grunt I'd expected, mainly due to the pleasant temp. My one shot at September football in Carolina came to drippy sweat and stomach cramps followed by heat prostration and first aid from the student trainer. Here, I did the jumping jacks, touch the toes, ran through a few old tires, and did okay.

Thank God nobody had loads of gung-hohood. I figure Stebbins recruited the whole team the way he got me. We were hundreds of miles from a decent college team and, what with limited TV exposure, there was little instilled pigskin fanaticism. A couple guys tried rolling blocks, but I stepped aside and they ate dirt. Neither one seemed to take it personally.

"Our other punt blocker will be Schmidt here. You line up at middle linebacker. Talbot, you cross-block their guard, blow his ass down the line. Then Schmidt comes through the hole."

Why is it coaches use first names in class like normal teachers and last names on the field? And who started this gentlemen jive? Coaches and cops love to call people they don't like gentlemen.

We lined up and shuffled through four or five punts without using the ball. A kid named Skipper O'Brien stood across the line with his elbows up. I let him bump me a time or two, figuring the poor schlock's ego needed a buildup. He had red hair and an overbite you could open a can with. Red-headed children tend to feel inferior.

When it came to the real drill, our punter was so awful that Stebbins did the kicking himself. He said, "Yup, yup, yup," and everybody took off. I faked O'Brien's jock to the outside and zipped right up the middle. The punt boomed off Stebbins's left foot, traveled maybe nine inches and caught me dead in the lungs.

I rolled over and over, wound up armadilloed on my back. Try breathing when you can't. It's a panic deal. I couldn't see squat, but I could hear, and I felt someone pull me off the ground an inch by a belt loop, then lower me again. God knows why.

Stebbins's voice floated in. "Nice block, Callahan. Get up, we'll try it again."

My mouth and nose felt sealed in Saran Wrap. The thing lasted forever.

More voices. "Think he'll die?"

"Doubt it."

"He don't look like a nigger."

"His mom tried to pick up Ft. Worth at the White Deck last night."

"I heard it other way around."

A toe poked me in the ribs. "He's turning blue."

"Maybe the nigger comes out when he's hurt."

Stebbins's voice again: "He's no nigger, he's not fast enough."

I pretended to pass out.

I got the wind knocked out of me one other time. In North Carolina, I was little, six or seven, and Lydia and I were playing seesaw. She had to scoot way up near the middle so our weights sort of balanced out. It was fun because the air was nice that day and Lydia didn't play outdoors stuff with me too often. About all I could ever get out of her was an occasional game of crazy 8s.

So I'm going up and down, up and down, admiring to myself how pretty Lydia is down the board from me. She had on a gray sleeveless shirt and white shorts. She'd spread a magazine out on the board in front of her so she could amuse herself and me at the same time. Every now and then she'd raise her face to swipe the bangs off her forehead, and she smiled at me kind of absentmindedly, as if she'd forgotten I was there.

Then, while I'm way up a mile high on top of the world, the damn coach of some swim team walks up in his stretchy trunks and rubber thongs. Had a blue whistle on a cord around his neck. I hate coaches.

He cocked his head to one side and banged on the skull bone over his right ear. "Does your little brother know how to swim?"

Lydia marked her spot in the magazine with her finger and turned to stare at the bare-chested coach.

He switched sides of the head and banged some more. "Every young man should know how to swim. It is vital to his safety and the safety of his loved ones."

Lydia looked up the board at me. "Sam, do you know how to swim?"

"No." I wasn't happy about being passed off as a little brother.

She turned to the coach. "No."

"I could teach the little snapper. Maybe you and me should walk over to the ice cream stand and discuss it. My treat, I'll even stand the boy a single cone."

Lydia stared at him a few seconds more, just enough to cause him to stop banging on the sides of his head, then she said, "I do not receive gentlemen without the decency to cover their repellent chest mange," and dignified as all get out, she swung her right leg across the board and got off the seesaw. I couldn't believe it. I didn't breathe for five minutes or stop crying for an hour, not until the stupid swimmer went away.

I was depressed that fall. I'd never been depressed to the point where I knew it before. Depression is like a headache or true love or any of those indefinable concepts. If you've never been there, you don't know what it's like until you're too far in to stop the process.

But I remember coming home from football practice to entire evenings on the couch next to Lydia, neither of us talking or reading or anything. We'd just sit with our eyes glazed, waiting for 10:30.

I figured out the stove deal so we ate frozen pizzas three nights a week and at the White Deck the other four. That's something of an exaggeration. Lydia bought rib eyes every now and then, and I got good with Kraft Macaroni and Cheese in a box. Some Sundays we drove to Jackson for late breakfast at the Wort Hotel.

So far as I can tell, Lydia made good on the emotional catatonia threat. She went a good month without speaking to a human other than me and Dot. Even with Dot, Lydia took to pointing at things on the menu or going through me.

"Tell her this hamburger is overcooked. Your sneakers have more flavor."

I turned to Dot and shrugged.

Dot laughed like we were perfectly pleasant folks making a joke. She had nifty dimples. I had a crush on her that wouldn't let go, and Lydia's attitude caused me some embarrassment.

Once when Lydia left me the money to pay and fluffed out the door, I explained things to Dot at the cash register.

"My mom's kind of high-strung. She doesn't mean anything personal."

Dot looked sad for the first time. "No one should apologize for their mother," she said. "All moms are doing the best they can."

"Are you sure?"

A guy did try to talk to us once. Big, wide fella with a grin, he came slamming through the door and walked straight toward our table, pulled a chair over and straddled it backward with his hands across the top slat. The middle finger on his right hand was missing two joints.

He held the stub out to me. "Look."

I looked but didn't see anything other than a short finger. Lydia didn't look. "It's short," I said.

"Look at the tip."

I shrugged. Seemed like a fingertip to me.

"I lost it in a chain saw and at the hospital they took a skin graft off this arm," he showed me a scar on his left arm, "and stuck it over the tip."

"Why are you telling me this?"

"Look close and see."

I finally figured out that he meant he didn't have a fingerprint so he could commit crimes. I looked so I could say, "Gee, no fingerprint," but then I saw all this wiry hair.

"Your fingertip's hairy."

The big lug's grin showed a flashy gold tooth. "Never seen anything like it, huh? Look, ma'am." He stuck the finger between Lydia's face and her food. I couldn't believe it, the guy had his hand in a pornographic position three inches from her nose, and she was speechless. Normally, Lydia practically spit at anyone who called her "ma'am."

"They shaved the skin off my arm before grafting it, but the hair all grew back. Ever see anything like that?"

He turned his hand sideways into the handshake position. "Ft. Worth Jones, ma'am. I'm more than pleased to meet you."

Lydia stared at the hand a moment, then up at the guy's expansive face.

I said, "I heard your name at football practice."

The gold tooth flashed in the fluorescent light. "Hope they said something good."

"How do you spell *Fort*?"

He looked perplexed by the question. "F-T period. Like the town."

"Oh."

He still had his hand out. "Saturday night's movie night at the VFW, little lady. *The Inspector General.* I'd be pleased if you'd accompany me."

I was sure "little lady" would spark a Lydia volcano, but nothing happened. She just sat there. My theory is Ft. Worth was so far from her frame of reference that Lydia couldn't see him.

Ft. Worth looked at me. "Is she okay?"

"Medication."

He stared intently at Lydia's eyes. "Yeah. Would you tell her I dropped by."

I nodded.

The tall stranger stepped through the White Deck screen door and strode to the counter. "Black coffee and rare beefsteak."

When Dot brought out the stranger's supper, she refilled his coffee cup. "What brings you to town, stranger?"

"Passing through."

Dot was amazed at his calmness. "Honey, nobody passes through Gro Vont. Where you headed?"

"Paris-France." The stranger paused to light a Cuban cigar. "Want to come along?"

Dot looked around to see to whom the stranger was speaking. "You want me to run away to Paris-France?"

"Your considerable beauty and charm are wasted in this king-hell hole. I want to uncover your light and let it shine on the world."

"But I'm overweight."

The stranger studied Dot from her white sneakers to her teased hair. "I like 'em with meat."

As Dot took off her apron and threw her order book in the trashy she asked, "What's your line, mister?"

"I'm God's gift to waitresses."

"And what's your name?"

"Callahan, ma'am. Sam Callahan."

I actually dragged Lydia to a football game. We were playing Victor, Idaho, and I started at split end—even caught a pass, a first for me and the team.

The rodeo grounds east of town had bleachers, but the football field didn't—says something about local priorities. The football field was a flat spot on the valley floor cleared of sagebrush and marked off with lime. Probably the only playing field in America completely surrounded by national park. Spectators backed their trucks up to the sidelines and sat on tailgates, a few even had strap-back lawn chairs. Almost everyone had access to a cooler.

Maurey Pierce was one of the cheerleaders. They wore these really short, considering the temperature, pleated white skirts and red turtleneck sweaters with GV over what would have been the right breast if any of them had had breasts. I took the color scheme as a joke because our football uniforms were tan and brown, like the hills behind the school. We were in camouflage.

As the team ran onto the field, the cheerleaders jumped up and bent their knees and yelled "Go, Badgers," our nickname, and threw their pom-poms in the air. Maurey's pom-pom landed right in front of me and I stepped on it on purpose,

At the bench, as the guys milled around, hitting each other in the shoulder pads and growling, I checked back to see Maurey standing there with a muddy pom-pom in her right hand and a godawful look on her face. Ugly, mean. I guess nobody'd ever stepped on anything of hers before. Her legs were pretty, but the knees stuck in a little.

Lydia parked Caspar's '62 Olds on the south 10-yard marker, way off from everyone else, and kept the engine running and the heater on. I knew that was a mistake, but I was so psyched about my mom being out in front of the whole town, I forgot. You see, this big cottonwood tree stood off that end zone, the only decent-sized tree anywhere near school.

Toward the end of the first quarter, a steady stream of men and boys started drifting up to the cottonwood, then back past the Olds and onto their trucks, lawn chairs, and coolers. Practically every guy waved to Lydia, coming and going.

I caught my pass on the last play of the first half. We were behind, 24-zip with nothing to lose, so Stebbins called for the Hail Mary bomb. Jimmy Crandall, the quarterback, figured out what he meant and showed the rest of us with a stick in the dirt.

The play involves both receivers and all three running backs splitting off to the right side of the line and when Jimmy goes "Yup, yup," we take off hell-bent for downfield, he throws the ball as far as he can, and we see what happens from there.

Jimmy "yupped" and everybody took off but me. I'd watched the Crandall kid throw in practice. Had an arm like a broomstick. So our receivers and all their defenders charge off forty yards downfield and Jimmy launches this wounded duck that wobbles about twelve yards to where I'm waiting—hits me in both hands and the chest, I hang on, the crowd goes wild. About ten potato heads jumped on me, but I didn't fumble and we got our first first down of the half, what would prove to be the only first down of the game.

Ft. Worth and a bunch of those White Deck hoodlums leapt in their trucks and honked horns. Maybe it was sarcasm, hell, I don't know. But I was proud. None of those kids who ate at home every night had caught a pass.

I played it superior when I left the field and passed the cheerleaders, but I snuck a quick glance and a couple of them were watching me. Women always love a football star. Maurey wasn't one of the couple, she was deep in her own superior routine.

I jogged over to the Olds and knocked on the window until Lydia rolled it down. She had the rearview mirror cocked off sideways.

"You see me catch that pass?" I asked.

"What?" Her eyes were stuck on the mirror. A bunch of high school boys waved at her as they walked behind the car toward the cottonwood. "You know what that tree is?" Lydia asked me.

I glanced over and got embarrassed. "It's the pee tree."

"Have you ever used it?"

"A few times during practice."

Lydia's eyes finally came back to look at me. They held that reckless Carolina glitter that I'd both loved and feared before our drive west, before the post-10:30 doldrums set in all day. "Sam, honey bunny, I believe I've seen every penis in GroVont."

I stood up straight and looked across the top of the Olds to the pee tree. It was disgusting. Nobody tried to cup with their hands or anything. And they knew too. The high school boys were nudging each other and giggling and sneaking leers our way.

I said, "I call that sick."

Lydia smiled as she gazed back into the crooked mirror. "I call that hospitality."

The next day, Saturday, it started snowing. I wasn't total hick enough to run into the street hollering, *"Jeeze Louise, what's this white stuff?"* I'd seen snow in Carolina, just not a whole lot. It was still a cold novelty. We both kept it casual—"Look outside, honey bunny, Jack Frost came last night"—but, underneath, Lydia and I were pretty excited.

She stared out the window the same old way, right foot on the sill, Dr Pepper in one hand, cigarette in the other, but something had changed. She wasn't staring into the void or herself or wherever Lydia went when she did her lost-in-space number. She was looking out the window.

"What're those bushes over there?" She pointed with her cigarette across the street behind old Soapley's trailer.

"That's sagebrush."

"Kind of pretty with the snow on it."

We'd been living in a sagebrush ocean for two months. Something, either the snow or the penis parade, had opened the connection between Lydia's eyes and her brain.

"You ever notice those mountains the other side of town?"

"It's the Tetons, Lydia. We live smack in the middle of Grand Teton Park."

"I knew that." Her lips had a near smile, as if she remembered something. Which made me nervous. I wanted Mom to wake up, sure; it's no fun coming home to an emotional slug, but Lydia awake could be a powerful force. The difference between a passive and an aggressive Lydia was like the difference between mononucleosis and a hurricane.

I ripped off Lydia's new book, *Catch-22*, and rode my bike

down to the White Deck. The snow was only an inch or so deep, but I still hit a slush spot and crashed the bike. Right out in front of Dupree's Art Gallery, I slid sideways under a parked GMC. Afforded Dougie Dupree no end of entertainment. I got an earful of cold mud and the right half of my clothes wet. Bent my handlebars.

Added to all that indignity, Dot wasn't even working. Some prissy little bopper hardly older than me bounced over and took my order for peach cobbler and coffee. Only other customers in the joint were two slack-cheeked retirees, named Bill and Oly, arguing over a fish they didn't catch in 1943.

"It was a brown, didn't you see the jump it made."

"Brookie. Biggest damn brookie anyone around here ever saw. Fought like hell when she hit my gray ghost, but she didn't jump. Brookies don't jump."

"Weren't a ghost. Was renegade you rubbed worm all over." I'd hoped Dot would see me reading this fabulously sophisticated novel full of sex and rebellion and think I was interesting. Instead, I dumped four spoons of sugar and a load of cream in the coffee and sat there with *Catch-22* propped open by the napkin box, staring out the window.

Not that the book wasn't a kick. It was the first time I realized death and despair can be funny, depending on how you look at it. All comedy, from *I Love Lucy* to *The Taming of the Shrew*, would be sad if it were true. This idea would eventually grow into my philosophical outlook on life.

But snow was more important than outlooks that day. Since then, an incredible amount of my time has been spent looking at snow, playing in snow, fighting with snow. Like true love, it has caused me hordes of pleasure, pain, and anxiety. From the White Deck window, it appeared soft and harmless. Lydia might seem soft and harmless, seen through a window. Goes to show you.

Two yards either way and Sam Callahan would have missed the dying trapper. As it was, Sam heard the low moan, "Diphtheria," just before he stumbled over a frozen lump in the blizzard.

"Diphtheria," it said again.

Sam brushed snow crystals off the old man's face and held the frozen body in his arms without doing anything that might be misconstrued as latent homosexuality. "What's that, old-timer?"

The man coughed for several minutes, then spoke. "There's diphtheria in Yellowknife."

"I'm not afraid of sickness."

The dying man's eyes were frozen open so he couldn't blink. "The serum. I have the serum in my pack. Those settlers won't die if they get the serum."

Sam made his decision. "I will take the serum to Yellowknife."

"But the blizzard. No one could make it through this blizzard."

"I'll make it, or I'll die trying."

The old man's lower lip quivered. "I did," he whispered, then he was dead.

Maurey Pierce banged through the door followed by LaNell and LaDell Smith, the twins all giggles and flouncing curly hair. Maurey stopped when she saw me and did a narrowing-of-the-eyes number. I narrowed mine right back. Overt hostility hadn't erupted in the first two and a half months of our relationship. I'd call it extreme wariness, at least on my part. Maurey seemed to regard me as a very large, but non-threatening bug.

She dropped into the next booth with her back to me. LaNell and LaDell made a minor scene on who had to sit on the inside. LaNell and LaDell are the kind of twins whose clothes will match their entire lives. From the back, they're kind of cute in a narrow-shoulders, big-hips fashion, but they both squint up their eyes like they just put in new contact lenses and haven't gotten used to them yet.

I'm afraid God only passed out one brain between them.

At first, they made a major point of ignoring me. They all ordered hamburgers with Pepsi and went into this drawn-out debate on Liz Taylor's treatment of Eddie Fisher. Maurey defended Liz. "Maybe she and Richard are in love," which outraged the twins no end.

They cited Debbie Reynolds and Eddie's mother and Burton's wife Sybil or Sydney or something. I didn't give a hoot and I don't think Maurey did either. Nothing that happened to anyone more than fifty miles away could possibly affect GroVont, Wyoming, so it seemed stupid to worry about Liz and Eddie.

Then the bopper waitress, whose name was Laurie, brought me a coffee heater. "Anything else?"

"I'm fine, thanks."

I should never have spoken. Or maybe they'd exhausted Liz talk and they'd have turned on me anyway. LaNell's voice was comparable to cutting a cardboard box with a butter knife. "Hey, Sam, don't you know you're too young to drink coffee."

I gave her the mystery smile I'd been working on just in case I ever found myself in a Western poker parlor.

LaDell came in next. "Your mother should tell you not to button the top button on that kind of shirt. You look like a squirrel." The pair stared at me with their upper lips warped so I could see watermelon-colored gums over their incisors.

I defended my button. "It's cold outside."

"It's cold outside," LaDell mimicked. "Wait'll January."

I wished I could see Maurey's face. Her back hadn't moved so at least she wasn't laughing at me like the retard twins. Maybe she felt an empathetic connection.

LaDell continued. "Hey, Maurey, he's reading a book on a Saturday. Trying to show off and study in public."

"It's not a school book. It's literature."

"Litter tour. Litter tour." What makes people between the ages of eleven and fifteen such mean jerks? I'd rather be ninety-five than thirteen again.

Maurey swung her arm onto the back of the booth and turned her head to look at me. "What literature?"

I showed her the cover of *Catch-22*. "It's new. This book will change the way we look at both the novel and war forever." I stole that from a blurb off the back cover. Then, I added my own, "And sex."

The twins oohed harmoniously. Maurey's eyes never left the book. "What do you know about sex?"

Actually, *Catch-22* had a ridiculously small amount of sex in it. "After I finish this book I'll know a lot more about it than you."

Bill picked up the napkin dispenser and slammed it into Oly's temple. Oly fell sideways out of the booth, his upper plate skittered across the cafe floor and stopped under a stool. After a few moments' disorientation, Oly made it to his knees and began to crawl after his teeth.

Us kids, even Laurie, all pretended we hadn't seen a thing. Young people aren't allowed to notice grown-ups conking each other.

Bill sat there with the napkin dispenser in his hand, watching his friend crawl away. He had the blankest look on his face. He blinked twice and swallowed, then he called to Oly, "Was a brookie."

Joseph Heller knocked on the cabin door. It was opened by a weathered-looking boy of thirteen. "May I see your father?" Joseph Heller asked.

"I have no father."

"Is this not the home of Sam Callahan?"

"I'm Sam Callahan."

Joseph Heller stared at the boy in amazement. "Surely you can't be the Sam Callahan who wrote White Deck Madness, *the greatest American novel since* Moby Dick.*"*

The boy smiled mysteriously. "The New York Times Book Review *rated it higher."*

Joseph Heller could not believe this young man was the same writer who had wrenched his heart out and made it bleed. Yet, as he looked closer, Joseph Heller saw the sadness and depth behind the boy's deep blue eyes.

"Yes," Joseph Heller said. "I believe you are a novelist."

"Thank you, sir."

"May I have your autograph?"

5

WE HAD A-BOMB DRILL FRIDAY IN MRS. HINCHMAN'S CITIZENSHIP class. She said, "Okay, you see a bright flash, now how should you react?" and we all dived under our desks. Viewed from below, my desk was really disgusting.

Why would the Reds bomb a national park anyway?

Lunch was tuna croquettes with lima beans, and this apple crisp stuff that you never find anywhere but institutional cafeterias. I sat with Rodney Cannelioski because we were both outsiders. Rodney's father was a recently transferred soil scientist with the Forest Service and our mutual new-kid-in-school deal fostered a certain us-against-them mentality. Or it would have if Rodney hadn't offered to give me his witness the day we met.

He looked me right in the eye. "Do you know Jesus?"

"Jesus who?"

"I found God on August 22, 1961."

Rodney had also been raised that it is immoral not to clean your plate at every meal. I hate that attitude. As quick as I finished off my apple stuff and stirred the beans once, I stuck my fork upright in the croquette and said see-you-later.

Rodney pointed his fork at my tray. "You'll go to hell if you don't eat all that."

The plate arrangement was artsy, would have made a really sick black-and-white photograph. "Rodney, if a person goes to hell for not eating tuna, I lost salvation awhile back."

Outside, the snow came down lightly in little dandruff-sized flakes. I found Maurey Pierce crying on the cafeteria steps.

In my life, men and boys cry. The women I'd known up to that point—and ever since—did not allow tears. And Maurey seemed so normal there on the steps, bent over, hugging her knees. Since it was Friday, she had on her white pleated cheer skirt and the red sweater. We didn't have a game, but the cheerleaders got off sixth period to practice that day anyway. Her hair was pulled back by a tortoiseshell-colored barrette. There's no one more quickly loved than a tough person turned vulnerable.

I sat on the damp steps next to her and looked off across the schoolyard at the Tetons. In less than a week, the mountains had gone from stark gray to clean white. The wind whipped snow devils off the peaks, but down below, on the cafeteria steps, sound was muffled and dead.

Maurey said, "They killed President Kennedy."

I looked at her face, then away. A pickup truck pulled into the cafeteria loading zone, but no one got out. White exhaust smoke plumed from the tail pipe, then spread and disappeared against the white background. "Are you sure?"

Maurey nodded, not looking at me. "It's on the radio."

Her fists rested one on each knee with the thumbs inside under the fingers. John Kennedy was dead. Dead was an odd word to me. People on television died every night, but that wasn't real. John Kennedy was on television, but he was real. Down by the volleyball poles, some older kids were whooping at each other, making magpie sounds.

"Who killed him?"

Maurey shrugged. "Texans."

Why would Texans kill the president? I thought of Jackie with her little hats and Caroline and John-John. Now he had no father either.

As word spread through the yard, kids gathered in small groups of shallow faces. No one had ever told us how to behave when something happened we couldn't comprehend. At the teachers' parking lot, some kids were singing "Yah, yah, the witch is dead," over and over. Maurey's jaw tightened. I could see each bone along the side of her face.

I wanted to say something to her that would make a difference. I wanted to tell her it wasn't true, President Kennedy was alive, and no one was singing the witch is dead about him.

The kids cheering Kennedy's death ran around the yard, taunting the others, behaving like real twerps. Dothan Talbot led the bunch, followed by his sister Florence and a couple of ranch kids who still wore cowboy boots even in the snow. Dothan was a ninth-grader. His hair was an oily flattop and he was a jerk to play football with, always the guy popping wet towels in the locker room and talking loud about pussy.

Dothan stood facing us with his hands on his hips and his feet spread. "Look at the little lovebirds bawling on the steps. You two crying over the nigger lover?"

I looked from Dothan to Maurey. Her eyes were amazing.

Dothan's teeth showed a gap when he grinned. "Know what Caroline Kennedy asked Santa to bring her at Christmas?"

Florence squealed, "A Jack-in-the-box." Must have been a stock joke around the Talbot house.

Dothan's eyes locked on Maurey's. "Maybe you're a nigger lover too."

Maurey's shoulder caught him belt high, knocking him over backward with her on top. His hand twisted through her dark hair, then pulled her over into the slushy snow. As Dothan sat up, I kicked him in the throat. He caught my foot and pulled me into the pile. Florence started screaming like her teeth were being ripped out.

Did I jump into the fight in anger over Kennedy's senseless death or because I knew it was the way into Maurey's heart and/or pants? Whenever I do something right, I always suspect that I did it for the wrong reason. I couldn't understand why the president was suddenly dead, I hated Dothan's glee, I hated all the ignorant grunts in Wyoming or North Carolina or anywhere else who make things dirty for the rest of us.

Maybe I wasn't simply sucking up to Maurey. Maybe I got myself beat up defending decency. Hell, I don't know.

And beat up is what I got. Within seconds he'd twisted my arm up behind my back and slammed my face into the cold mud. He used his knee to pin me there while he wrestled a flailing Maurey into the same position. Then Dothan held us, each with one ear ground into the earth.

Maurey and I faced each other, nose to nose, maybe eight inches apart. Dothan's hand spread across the side of her head, his nails digging into her cheek. He had me more by the neck. She didn't make a sound so neither did I. The one eye I could see wasn't crying anymore. It was hurt. Not the physical hurt I was in or the shame hurt of having your face rubbed in the snow by a horse's ass. Maurey's was the kind of hurt you get when you discover what an unfair mess of a world we're stuck with and how helpless we are to do a damn thing about it.

Or maybe she was just king-hell pissed. I'm always reading twenty minutes of insight into a glance in someone's eyes.

Sam Callahan came off the ground with a roar. He kicked once and Dothan's knee bent at an impossible angle. Sam caught him with a left to the liver, a right to the mouth, and an elbow in the solar plexus.

Sam picked up a baseball bat and broke it across Dothan's forehead. Then Sam picked him up and threw him through the glass door.

Florence's godawful screaming stopped and I felt the sharp weight lifted off my spine. I rolled sideways, coughing, and looked up to see Coach Stebbins holding Dothan by both arms.

Florence had the voice of a raped goat. "They started it. They started it. They jumped on my brother."

Maurey spit snow. "He was celebrating the fucker who killed Kennedy."

Stebbins stared at us on the ground, then his eyes traveled the circle of kids, Teddy the Chewer, Chuckette Morris, Kim Schmidt. His jaw looked like he'd been hit, not us. He let Dothan go, then turned and walked back into the school.

That Friday in November must be the most analyzed, beat-to-pulp day in history. The day everything got quiet; the day America lost her virginity, or at least her innocence; the day the fifties ended. More strangers spoke to each other that day than any time before or since.

A lot of newspaper and TV guys made their careers that day. An entire industry has grown around trying to figure out what happened. I hate to think we'll never know.

I take it as the day I first talked to Maurey, without which I'd be a different deal.

I've asked a number of people who were ten, eleven, twelve back in 1963, and most of them recall it as the day the grown-ups cried.

"Come on," Maurey said.

"Where?" She was standing up, but I still sat in wet snow. I felt somewhat debased by losing the fight. Dothan wasn't that tough. Maurey's white skirt was a mess. I imagined the guys got some great panty shots, which was probably a bigger deal to them than the death of a president.

"I can't be here anymore."

"That makes sense."

"We can to go my house and watch the news. I want to know what this is about."

I glanced at the school. "Think they'll miss us?"

She held out a hand to help me up. "All the rules are off today, Sam. Nothing we do matters."

How did she know that? Maurey wasn't any older than me. She didn't have any more experience at presidential assassinations. Some people are just born with intuition.

I held on to Maurey's hand after she pulled me upright. She looked at me sharply.

"You said the rules are off today."

"Don't get carried away." She drew her hand free.

The town seemed asleep as we walked by the triangle. A few trucks sat outside the Esso station and the White Deck, and a parked Buick was running next to Kimball's Food Market, but we passed no people, not even a dog, and the snow made everything unreal and quiet. The flag twisted around the pole in front of the Forest Service headquarters. I glanced at Maurey a few times, figuring the implications. Was the truce temporary or had a connection been made? A snowflake landed on her cheek and I counted to four before it melted.

"So all Southerners aren't racist?" she asked.

"Nope."

"Why do they try to make us think they are?"

"Makes a better story, I guess."

We stopped at a yellow house with white trim. "Want to make a bet?" Maurey asked.

"You live here?"

"Mom will have heard about the president and it'll have had no effect on her at all. She'll be baking cookies and waxing the kitchen floor."

"My mother's never baked a cookie in her life." Waxing floors was too much even to deny.

"I wish my mom hadn't."

We found Mrs. Pierce cutting out coupons at a coffee table. She had on a green apron with all these profiled sharp-nosed women on it in silhouette. The dishes were all clean in the drain board. A Santa Claus magnet held a newspaper recipe to the refrigerator. The contrast to Lydia's kitchen was a hoot.

Mrs. Pierce had the same long, long neck, but on Maurey it was pretty and classy, while on her mom it was mostly strings. And Mrs. Pierce's eyes were more a faded, washed-out blue.

She smiled at Maurey. "You're home from school early."

"They let us out on account of the assassination."

"I know, isn't it a shame about Mr. Kennedy." She bent over a Sunday magazine section and scissored with a precision I wouldn't waste on a coupon. "I wonder if Petey's school will let out early too. Let me finish this last one and I'll make us some hot cocoa."

My theory is all thirteen-year-olds are embarrassed no end by their mothers. I mean, I thought Mrs. Pierce's perfect homemaker act was kind of cute, like a Betty Boop cartoon, and cocoa sounded okay. I could use a warm-up after all that snow wallowing. But Maurey's disdain came across like a paper cut.

"The president is dead, Mom. This isn't the time for hot cocoa."

Mrs. Pierce put down her scissors. "It's always time for cocoa. What happened to your skirt?"

"I fell down."

After Maurey changed, she and I sat on a couch in the den to watch history unfold on a black-and-white RCA Victor fourteen-inch. I had trouble with juxtaposition. There was the scene—Maurey and me next to each other in a spotless house in the absolute midst of the Wyoming winter—and there was what we watched—muted, frightened faces, people talking slowly. Death and national tragedy.

My stomach hurt. Maurey chewed her lower lip. Her eyes were a dark blue with gray specks. I guess I'd never seen them close up before. When they were loading the casket into the plane, she put her hand on my arm.

A Dallas policeman was killed. No one knew why. A doctor explained entry wounds. Maps were shown, detailing Dealey Plaza and the route to the hospital. Cameras filmed the fence of the Hyannis Port compound while analysts wondered if they would tell John's grandmother. Somebody interviewed a priest. They made a big deal out of whether the president got last rites before or after he died.

"What do you think happens to people when we die?" Maurey asked.

World's most personal question and she's asking it an hour after our first real words. I guess all the rules were off for the day. I thought of about six answers, but they were all either unacceptable, cute, or weird. "I don't know."

"Why would God care if someone chants magic words over your body before you die. That's an awful stupid thing to base eternity on."

"My grandfather's Episcopal. I think they go to heaven without it."

"All sounds like a crock to me."

When Mrs. Pierce—who introduced herself as Annabel—brought the cocoa, I noticed Maurey didn't turn it down as unbefitting the occasion. It tasted good, none of that instant jive. This stuff was real and wholesome as life gets—even with a marshmallow half-sunk on top. Maurey held her mug with both hands, blew across the steaming surface, and smiled at the first sip. Down a hallway, I heard a vacuum cleaner kick in.

"Who's Petey?"

"My baby brother. He's a brat, Mama's little angel."

"Are you close?"

"Are you kidding?"

A man was arrested in a movie theater. Eyewitnesses to the murder were interviewed. John Connally's press secretary issued a statement. They announced that Lyndon Johnson, a Texan, had been sworn in on the plane. College football games were canceled for the next day. Everything was canceled.

"I wish my dad was here," Maurey said.

"Where is he?"

"We have a little horse ranch ten miles up the hill and they don't plow the road. He stays out there most of the winter."

"He's stuck?"

"Dad snowmobiles out every couple of weeks and for the holidays. In the summer we're mostly out there."

"What's your dad's name?"

"Buddy. I wish he was home today."

The news announcer said the arrested man's name was Lee Henry Oswald. One after another, strange facts came out. He had a Russian wife. He'd been to Cuba. He'd been to Russia. His name was Harvey instead of Henry. They interviewed his landlady downtown.

"What's your dad do?" Maurey asked.

"I don't have a father."

She looked from the TV to me. "Did he die?"

"Lydia won't tell me anything about him. When she's drunk she claims virgin birth, like Mary and Jesus."

Maurey said, "I'd like to see my mom drunk."

"It's not that neat."

We sat in more silence. I held her hand a little while, but

then she took it away. "So you don't have a clue to what your dad was like?"

"Lydia has these pictures hidden in her panty box. They're from different yearbooks, I think. Four photos of five guys in football uniforms. I kind of figure one of them might be my dad because she hides the pictures."

"Panty box?"

"Lydia hasn't unpacked yet. Her stuff is in suitcases and boxes. She won't sleep in her bedroom."

"What were you doing in the panty box?"

I skipped that one. "One of the guys in the pictures is a Negro."

Maurey studied me closely. "I heard the rumor. Is it true?"

I'm not that dark, a little maybe, darker than Lydia for sure, but not that much, and I have curly hair, but it's not kinky or anything. "I guess the odds are one in five. If my father is one of the pictures."

Petey arrived amid much banging and slamming of doors. He clomped into the den from the kitchen, dropped his coat in a heap on the floor, and crossed to the television where he changed the channel.

"Hey," Maurey yelled. "We're watching that."

Petey ignored her. He stood with one hand on the dial, peering suspiciously at the picture. "What's this?"

"It's news. There's nothing on but news. Now change it back to what we were watching."

Petey didn't move. He had these remarkably dark eyebrows, long eyelashes, and a natural pout of a mouth. Would have made a cute girl. Maurey left the couch and advanced on Petey and the television.

"This sucks." He slapped the screen with the flat of his left hand. I mean, the kid was eight, nine years old, way too far along to think you can punch sense into a TV show.

Maurey grabbed his other hand on the channel knob and

Petey let out a scream. She pulled him hard, but he latched on like a snapping turtle, screaming his damn brains out. He tried to hit her with his free hand, but Maurey blocked him with her forearms. Just as Mrs. Pierce charged into the room, Maurey doubled up her fist and decked her brother in the face.

"Maurey." Mrs. Pierce was aghast.

Petey held both hands over his eyes and went right on screaming. I come from two generations of only-child families. This was miles out of my context.

Maurey looked from me to her mom. "I didn't hit him that hard."

Petey made loud snuffling noises. "She won't let me watch Rocky."

Mrs. Pierce gathered the kid into her arms and glared across the top of his head at Maurey. "You know he watches Rocky every afternoon, what's the matter with you?"

"It's not on today. The Texans killed President Kennedy."

Petey howled. "It is so on, she won't let me see it."

"Look, brat." Maurey stepped to the TV and slowly turned the selector knob all the way around the dial.

See, the deal back then was that if a family had a really tall outside antenna they could pick up two Idaho stations, CBS and NBC. No one in northwest Wyoming saw ABC until the cable came in twenty years later. A person without an outside antenna, say Lydia, could only watch a snowy CBS. Not a bad place to raise kids.

Anyhow, Maurey went clear around the dial twice while Petey snuffled into Mrs. Pierce's breasts and she cooed in his ear.

"She's hiding the station," Petey whimpered.

"Why isn't Rocky on?" Mrs. Pierce said.

Maurey was at a peak of exasperation. "The president of the country is dead. Some things are more important than Rocky the Flying Squirrel."

Petey took this as the lie it obviously was, and his mother blinked dubiously. "Come on to the kitchen, baby Pete, I made some Toll House cookies and I'll pour us some fresh milk."

"I hate Toll House cookies."

There's a certain type of mother who calls chocolate chip cookies Toll House, and I've never liked that type. They're the same women who call gravy sauce.

Mrs. Pierce turned to me. "Would you care to stay for dinner, Sam? We're having tuna croquettes." I checked Maurey to see if she caught the bizarre irony, but I guess she'd missed lunch at school. She was glaring at Petey with that same look she used to give me before today.

"No, thank you, ma'am. My mother will be expecting me soon. She'll have supper on by now."

"You could call her and tell her you're eating here."

"We don't have a telephone, ma'am." There's a Southern defense mechanism where whenever someone makes you uncomfortable, you fall back on antebellum politeness. I saw poverty pity in Maurey's mother's eyes, so I figured I better explain the phone deal. "It's not that we're poor, we just don't know anyone to call."

"Why, you've been in town two months. Hasn't your mother met anyone yet?"

"Lydia's not all that outgoing."

Mrs. Pierce gently moved Petey off her lap. He moved back on. "Well, we'll just have to have you and your mother over for dinner soon."

I tried to picture Lydia in this house full of trinkets and dust-free knickknacks. Mrs. Pierce was the sort of woman Lydia always said "Fuck me silly" in front of.

I shook my head. "My mom doesn't get out much. She's having trouble adjusting to the dry air."

"I'll just have to drop in on her with my welcome wagon basket. My baskets are very popular this time of year."

"I'd think awhile before I did that, ma'am."

—·—

All the rules must have been off that day because when I tramped home through the snow, Lydia wasn't there. Surprised the heck out of me. I took advantage of the situation to dump overflowing ashtrays and clean out the Dr Pepper stash beneath the couch. At least Lydia was consistent—two and a half packs of cigarettes, variety of brands, six pops, Dr Pepper, and a pint of gin, Gilbey's, a day. A boy needs consistency in his life.

The Olds 88 sat in the rut that passed for our driveway, which meant Lydia walked away into the storm or somebody came and got her. Either one would be unique unto itself, but presidential assassinations are unique unto themselves and other little uniques tend to spin off their wake. Look at my afternoon with Maurey.

I drank from my own Dr Pepper and sat on the couch reading *Catch-22* and *Marty's Big Season. Marty's Big Season* is about a Little League team whose coach walks out and this kid, Marty, takes over the team and manages them into the Little League World Series in Williamsport, Pennsylvania. A team coached by Marty's hero uses unethical tactics to beat them and Marty learns a lesson about life.

Catch-22 is about despair, death, and the hopelessness of a sane man in an insane world. It's a comedy.

The house was too quiet. I kept glancing up at Les, expecting him to have moved a tiny bit. The refrigerator hummed some, the water heater knocked, but other than that, it was like no one had been around lately. I went into the bathroom and flushed the toilet but didn't jiggle the handle like you had to to make it quit running. Lydia'd told me the sound of running water soothes neurotics and we'd all be calmer if we slept next to a creek. She said TV white noise does the same thing, which is why she always slept on the couch with the television turned all the way up on a dead channel.

A truck pulled up and I checked out the window, but it was only old Soapley coming in from making sure nobody got too much water or plowing roads or whatever he did late every afternoon. Soapley's cowdog Otis still rode standing on the top of the cab, even in winter, and I was afraid he'd fall off someday and die right in front of me.

Lydia's bedroom-turned-closet smelled different from the rest of the house. I don't know what it was—Lysol and woman odors or maybe a mouse died under the empty bureau or something—but it made me want to get in and get out without wasting any time.

The panty box sat right next to the bureau. Why didn't she open a drawer and dump stuff in? I generally took care of the laundry—we had an ancient Whirlpool set off the kitchen—but I left her clothes in a pile for her to fold and put away. Our relationship wasn't that sick. But why shovel them into a cardboard box instead of a drawer next to it? Maybe unpacking would be like admitting we live here. Heck, I don't know. A person could waste weeks tracking down the motivation behind any move Lydia made.

She owned about sixty pairs of panties too. Digging through the box was like swimming. Swimming in panties is how I'd found the photographs in the first place, but I wasn't about to expose that much to Maurey. Rules off or not, the walls had only been down one afternoon.

I took the photos to my room for a mirror comparison between the guys and me.

Two of the guys stood shoulder to shoulder with their hands on their hips. The other three were posed in fake running and passing shots. Their helmets were weird, like somebody had lacquered ear muffs across the top. Only one had a face mask and it was a single bar.

Numbers *72*, *56*, *81*, *11*, and *20*. Tackle, center, end, quarterback, and halfback, unless they'd numbered positions different back then. The tackle and center were the two-in-one picture. They had dark jerseys with horizontal stripes at the shoulders. Seventy-two was a big guy, a king-hell teenage giant. I hoped he was my father because that would mean I might grow one of these days.

The center had a square head and missing teeth, and the end wearing the same dark uniform was a thin character with glasses under the one-bar face mask. I didn't wear glasses so that let him out.

Eleven wore a different uniform, lighter with a squirrelly black stripe around the belly. He had a flattop haircut—racy compared to the other guys' burrs and crewcuts—and his mouth was skewed in a lewd smirk, as if he had recently laid the photographer's sister. Lydia would go for that smirk. I studied his eyes, then my own in the mirror. Mine were wider, but so were Lydia's. You couldn't tell the color in the picture, but they were darker than the other white guys.

The Negro halfback in what looked like a gray sweatshirt and a dull, leather helmet was shorter than the others—great. A short daddy would be a lot harder to handle than black blood—and he was the only one smiling. Short, fast, and happy. None of those were particularly alluring to Lydia, yet I couldn't just rule him out and go back to the leering quarterback. His blackness alone would cause no end of shame to Caspar, and Caspar's shame was all the allure Lydia needed. There'd been a time when Lydia would have cut off her fingers if Caspar told her not to.

This child shrink Caspar slapped on me made a big deal over the

Unknown Father. Her name was Dr. Eleanor and I never knew if that was a first name or last. She wore orange fingernail polish.

"Don't you ever wonder about your father, Sam?"

"Lydia's dad's enough for anyone."

"You aren't intrigued? What if he's rich or famous or a wanted outlaw?"

"What if he's dead?"

"How would you feel if your father were dead?"

"About the way I feel now."

"Where do you think a person goes when he dies, Sam?"

"France." Why are people always asking me that question?

"What would you say to your father if you met him this afternoon?"

I thought about that one awhile, torn between my natural smartassness and a sudden urge to be cooperative. I was only ten when Caspar decided Lydia and I had an unhealthy relationship and we should both be dissected. My particular case was kicked off after I hid myself in the back of Lydia's closet under a pile of her dirty clothes for two days and a night. Smelled nice and warm in there. Police combed the neighborhood while I played out the symbolic womb situation.

"I'd ask him if he can hit a curve ball."

Dr. Eleanor took this as smartassness, but I'd meant it straight. She looked at me with her lips all prim, which made me feel mean to her, so I tried to explain.

"Lydia can do anything a real father can except teach me how to hit a curve. I can't hit a curve worth crap."

Caspar made Lydia go to a shrink too, but she seduced hers and they took off to Atlanta for a week.

The letter came Special Delivery on Sam Callahan's fourteenth birthday. It was from Don Drysdale, the tallest and most powerful pitcher in major league baseball.

Dear Sam, it read,

1) *Study the pitcher.*
2) *Divide the plate into thirds in your mind. Curves break out and few young throwers can start a pitch inside. Only concern yourself with the outside third.*
3) *Keep your head down, your front toe closed, and swing through the ball.*
4) *Try only to make contact. Worry about home runs later.*

By the way, I am your sperm father. Your mom and I thought you should have a normal childhood which I could never have given you. Come to L.A. and I'll buy you a Ford Mustang and introduce you to some Hollywood babes.

Your Dad,
Don Drysdale

P.S. I love you, Son.

Someone pulled into the yard and revved their engine right up to the limit. I took off down the hall into Lydia's room and stuffed the photos back under the panty pile. I wonder if there's a psychological term for a person who owns sixty pairs of panties.

Lydia kicked snow through the front door as I came out of her room. She pulled off her coat, humming a song I'd never heard in my life. "You eat yet?"

She didn't seem to wonder what I'd been up to in her room. I said, "I waited for you." Lydia lit a cigarette. I don't think she noticed the clean ashtrays either. Lydia never was much for noticing changes. She figured stuff just happened without anyone making it happen. "We had a steak in Dubois."

What's this *we* jive? She hadn't used *we* about anyone other than me and her in a long time. I took a shot at sounding nonchalant. "Who's we?"

"Ft. Worth and his friend Hank Elkrunner drove me over to Dubois this afternoon. Hank's part Indian, Blackfoot or Blackfeet, something about feet. He knows all this neat stuff about the forest. We found a badger track."

"You went into the forest? There's snow, and cold."

"They had snowshoes. It was a hoot, Sam. I tried something new."

"What did you try new?"

"Don't look at me like that, honey bunny. I told you—snowshoeing. It was wholesome." She kicked off her shoes and padded barefoot into the kitchen, then came back with a glass of water, which was really weird. The only time Lydia ever touched water was to wash down pills.

This time she drained the whole glass. "I thought I would never do anything new again the rest of my life, but now I did. How about that?"

"How about that."

She came over and gave me a little motherly hug. "Don't be such a grump, Sam. We're in this place. Hell hole or not, we might as well admit it and see what there is to see." I'd been giving her that rap for a month now, but you'd think Lydia was the first person in history to realize it's more satisfying to live where you are than where you aren't.

"Did you hear about President Kennedy?" I asked.

She broke the hug and went over to pat Les on the side of the head. "Isn't it a shame." Lydia stared off into space and I thought she was dwelling on the pitifulness of a national tragedy. Wrong again. "Did you know coyotes and badgers sometimes run together so they can eat whatever the other one kills?"

"Ft. Worth told you all this nature stuff?"

"Hank. He's interesting. His great-grandfather was one of only four Cheyennes killed at Little Big Horn. That's in Montana. Custer bought it there."

"I know about Custer."

"Hank says he had it coming."

"This guy sounds like a mountain of folklore."

"You know that bucking bronco and cowboy on everyone's license plate?"

"The ones you think are so stupid?"

"They have names, Steamboat and Stub Farlow. Steamboat is the horse."

This was too much strangeness all in one day. "Do any of these little items relate to us?"

She snuffed out the cigarette before it was half smoked.

"Sammy, information can be interesting even if it doesn't affect me personally."

"That's not how I was raised."

I headed for the kitchen to boil mac and cheese water, but something bothered me about the setup. "Did those guys come over here and say 'Let's go for a ride'?"

Lydia smiled at me. "I met them at the White Deck. Ft. Worth has a hairy fingertip."

"You went to the White Deck alone?"

"You don't expect me to stay in this living room forever, do you?"

"I thought you expected to."

"Honey bunny, there's a difference between time out and death. Ask Les, he's the one told me to get my head off the wall."

I looked up at Les, wondering if Lydia meant that symbolically or literally. A lot of weird things can happen on a pint of Gilbey's.

She flipped on the TV. A fuzzy image came on of two

people showing the mechanics of a rifle. Lydia went on. "That Dotty's had a fascinating life. She has a little son she hasn't seen in two years and a husband in Asia, or somewhere, in the army."

"You talk to Dot?"

"We have a lot in common."

You think you're on top of the deal, then suddenly you find yourself actually over to the side with the view blocked.

I was more disoriented than ever.

6

Maurey and I discovered a mutual love of reading books. It was like being in Bolivia or someplace foreign and running into the only other person in a thousand miles who speaks English—instant old-home week.

We raved at each other. "Have you read *Have Spacesuit, Will Travel*?"

"God, it was great. Have you read *Stranger in a Strange Land*?"

Sunday, Maurey and I discussed the sex stuff in *Diary of Anne Frank* while Petey played fort with the couch cushions. Neither one of us knew exactly what sleeping together meant, we were only sure it meant more than being asleep at the same time in the same place.

"It's a metaphor," Maurey said.

"A metaphor for what?"

They were showing the procession as John Kennedy's body was moved from the White House to the Capitol. It was real sad and dignified. White horses pulled the casket up the street followed by a black horse with empty boots stuck backward through the stirrups.

"Jeeze, what a horse," Maurey said. "Wouldn't you love to ride him?"

"Who wouldn't?" The horse looked like a man-killer to me.

Petey dragged a bunch of dolls and a beat-to-death bear into his fort and pretended they were customers at a drive-up liquor store. Being from North Carolina, I had no idea what that meant until Maurey explained.

"You sure have led a sheltered life," she said.

"I went to New York City once. I didn't see any drive-up liquor stores there."

The literary sex stuff confused us both. Growing up around Lydia, I'd learned the patter early—the hooker laid the John with a Bo Peep fantasy on a half and half—but I didn't know what went where when the hooker did all this.

Maurey couldn't even follow it that far. "Bo Peep is about doing it?"

I faked sophistication. "Of course."

Maurey had read *Jane Eyre* and D. H. Lawrence's *The Virgin and the Gypsy*. The virgin gets wet and cold in a flood and the gypsy saves her by doing something peculiar.

I told her about the whores in *Catch-22*.

She told me a Hemingway story where an African guide has a double cot and somebody's wife sneaks out for a couple of hours, then the next day she blows her husband's head off.

I told her about *The Catcher in the Rye*, which I read because a teacher told me not to.

We finally found common ground with *Tortilla Flat*, in which Danny drags every woman in the Flat into a gully, drinks three gallons of wine, and dies.

"But what happened in the gully?" Maurey asked.

I shrugged. "Seems like a lot of book people die afterward."

Maurey pointed to the TV. "Here's the killer."

"Who are all those other people?"

Boom. Oswald bought the big one. Right there, live, in front of me and everyone else, one person murdered another one.

"Holy cow," Maurey said.

Annabel brought in a huge bowl of popcorn and stood in the middle of the family room, staring blankly at the Dallas police wrestling Jack Ruby to the concrete floor. She turned to us. "Who's ready for a snack?"

Petey twisted the bear's head until it tore off its body.

That night I had my first wet dream. It was king-hell peculiar. Lydia and I were in this department store to buy me some new Wranglers. She held a pair of 26-28s up to my waist and said, "Looks right if they don't shrink much. Maybe you better try them on."

I went into the changing booth and Annabel Pierce was sitting on this three-legged stool, naked with Kleenex boxes on both feet. She said, "You didn't eat the popcorn."

I couldn't take off my jeans to try on the new ones with her watching, so I just waited there, holding the pants in front of me, embarrassed because Annabel was old and naked.

She stood up and said, "Here's what the gypsy did to the virgin," and she pressed herself against me and kissed me on the lips, a real closed-mouth kiss, felt like kissing the seam on a football.

Lydia banged on the door. "Come on, I want to see the waistline." Then suddenly I was naked from the navel down, except my socks, and something felt really weird and I woke up with this mess on my stomach.

I wiped myself off with a day-old sweat sock and changed pajamas. In the bathroom, I examined my eyes for signs of jaundice. Me Maw died of jaundice caused by cancer and Caspar said it was hereditary. I checked a mole on my right inner thigh, which I'd been told would change color and fall off if I had polio.

No yellow, no rotting moles. I went in, turned off the TV, and woke up Lydia, which I'd never done before.

She still slept on the couch in an askew post-Gilbey's position, but at least she'd graduated to a white flannel nightgown. No more waking up fully dressed. Out the window, dawn turned the snow from gray to a light pink. That meant she'd had several hours to process the gin and Valium and might be somewhere near coherent.

I stuck the gooey sock up close to her face. "What's this?"

Lydia blinked twice, stretched her spine, then made a chewing motion. It was my first experience at watching a woman go from asleep to awake.

"Sammy?"

"Lydia, something weird is going on and I demand an explanation."

Her eyes focused. "You blew your nose on a sock."

"No way in the world did this stuff blow out my nose."

Lydia blinked a couple more times. She touched the goo with her index finger and touched the finger to her tongue. Her eyes woke up. "You jerked off. It's come."

I'd heard come-brains and come in your pants, and knew it was connected to the penis, but I'd vaguely figured it meant peeing on yourself. Jerk-off was a term used in sports to denote a lazy screwup. "I didn't jerk off, Mom. I woke up with this stuff all over me."

Lydia's eyes left the sock and went to my face. "You had a wet dream, honey bunny. It's okay. Boys have them all the time."

"A wet dream?"

"Were you dreaming right before you woke up?"

I nodded.

"Maybe there was a girl in the dream?"

"She was naked."

Lydia smiled. "Did you recognize her?"

Something told me to skip that one. "She kissed me and I felt funny."

Lydia sat up and hugged me. I held the sock out away from her back. "Poor Sammy. It's a natural stage in life. You just moved a step closer to being grown-up."

I couldn't see how gushing pus on my belly made me a grown-up. "Will you get me a Dr Pepper," Lydia asked. "My mouth is all dried out."

Staring into the refrigerator, I thought about the trauma I'd been through. This was just the kind of information that doesn't sneak up on boys with fathers. Back in the living room, Lydia was examining her face in the turned-off television screen.

"Mom, a major fluid is leaking from my body and no one ever mentioned it. Why wasn't I told?"

She drank about half the D.P. in one pull. "Don't boys talk in locker rooms?"

"Dothan Talbot threw a rubber at Kim Schmidt once. I know how it fits over the end."

"Well, that stuff is what the rubber catches. It's not just for show."

Outside, the pink snow was turning a different tinted gray and I could make out the Tetons off across the valley floor. "What exactly is this stuff?"

"Do something with it. Mothers and sons aren't supposed to talk about this with a sock full of come between them on the coffee table."

I carried the gooey sock into my room and set it on the keyboard of my typewriter. Then I went back and re-asked the question. "Talk, Lydia. I bet every kid my age in the world knows about come and they're laughing at me, saying I'm a squirrel."

Lydia made some eye contact with Les. Then she sipped on her bottle. "Come is like sperm in a runny mayonnaise base. It's where babies come from. That's why they call it come."

"You give this stuff to a girl and she makes a baby?"

Lydia thought. "I guess that's one way of putting it."

"Doesn't it get the girl all messy? I don't know of any girl would want runny mayonnaise smeared on her."

Lydia looked at me sadly. I guess ignorance is always sad when it has to be set straight. "The come goes in the girl, honey bunny. You really don't know, do you? It doesn't get on the girl—until she stands up, then it runs down the inside of her legs and feels icky."

I sat down and tried to picture an anatomy I'd never seen. "You stick your dick up where the girl pees? How can millions of people do something they don't let kids know about?"

"It doesn't go up where they pee, there's another tunnel. And sex is practically all anyone talks about."

"I never heard anyone talk about sticking their dick up a tunnel."

Lydia lit her first cigarette of the day and blew smoke at the dawn. "People use vague adult terms the kids can't follow. Make love. Do it. Fuck."

This was as major as discovering color or water or something crucial to life that everyone else knows about but I hadn't dreamed possible. I wasn't sure I liked the idea. "Lydia, this gooey dick and tunnel and sex stuff sounds kind of grotesque."

She blew more smoke. "It's fun once you get the hang of it."

She was sixteen, a cheerleader at a large Southern high school, with long legs, blonde hair, and real breasts. She came to Sam Callahan in the early evening, as the sun dipped behind the Tetons. "I hear you can teach me something."

"Who told you that?"

"Ramona. She says you revolutionized her life."

"Ramona was a quick learner. Are you prepared to trust me?"

"Yes, Sam, teach me the mysteries of adulthood."

"It's not all pleasant. Icky stuff might run down your leg."

"Teach me, Sam Callahan. Teach me everything."

First thing I wanted to do Monday was tell Maurey what happened during the skipped parts of novels. I made Lydia's coffee, ate a donut, and carefully wrapped my gooey sock in Saran Wrap just in case Maurey didn't believe me. I thought about taking it over to the Pierces' as proof—look, come—but it made a lump in my jeans that made me look squirrelly.

Besides, some things I did know instinctively. How to have sex wasn't one of them. Knowing enough not to talk dicks and tunnels in front of Annabel was. Not all mothers are equal.

That day, Monday, Annabel finally took an interest in the national tragedy. She sat in the overstuffed recliner, cross-stitching a Christmas scene all morning. "Look at Jackie. I heard she hasn't cried once all weekend."

On the television, people filed through the Capitol rotunda on each side of the president's body, four abreast. They'd been standing in line all night so they could do this, but what surprised me was the ones who didn't look at the casket. They looked straight ahead or into the network cameras filming them. Why had they waited in line ten hours to do something they weren't doing?

Maurey noticed it too. "It's sad," she whispered. "I don't see the point."

To take a shot at honesty here, by then I was somewhat bored with the assassination aftermath. The television had been droning for four days without a single commercial. No matter how much it affected the rest of our lives, Maurey and I were just too young for sustained somberness. I wanted to go outside and build anatomically correct snowboys and girls so we could figure out this sex thing.

Maurey was more interested in Friday's fight. I wanted to smash Dothan Talbot and his sister in their inbred noses, but Maurey was into forgiveness. "Dothan didn't know what he meant. It's his Southern jerk-racist parents. I bet all he hears at home is, 'I wish Kennedy would kill himself and save us the trouble.' People talk like that and kids buy it."

Forgiveness isn't my deal. "The clown rubbed my face in snow. I want him to die."

"See. You don't mean that literally."

"Yes, I do."

"Besides, Dothan sees people die all the time on television. He doesn't know real death from make-believe."

I glanced at Annabel, checking her attention level on the conversation. Her face was blank newsprint. I tried to remember if her breasts had tits on them last night. The only tits I'd ever seen were in *Playboy* magazine where they looked like bull's eyes on water balloons. Annabel's breasts were way smaller than water balloons, at least as far as I could see, so maybe the bull's eyes would be way smaller too, like little pimples. Imagining Mrs. Pierce's breasts made me nervous, so I turned back to Maurey. Maurey didn't have breasts.

"What are you defending this guy for? He's king-hell stupid and he's stronger than us. I don't like people stronger than me." Too late, I realized I'd said hell in front of Maurey's mother.

Annabel spoke from over her cross-stitch. "The littlest Talbot is a slow, you know."

"A slow what?"

Maurey was leaning back against the end of the couch with her feet between us. Whenever I shifted, one of her bare toes touched my leg. The index toe on her left foot was as long as the big toe.

She said, "You know what a slow is. Every grade is divided into two classes, quick and slow. We're in the quick class."

"You and I are quick, everyone else seems sort of medium."

Maurey smiled, my discovery that the girl was a sucker for a compliment. "Everyone is put in slow or quick by the second grade and that's where they stay."

"No one ever crosses over?"

"Wanda Martinez went from quick to slow," Annabel said.

Maurey kicked my leg. "That's because her daddy rolled their Jeep off the pass and turned Wanda into a retard."

The television was showing old footage of John and Jackie Kennedy at a dignitary ball. She wore a strapless exotic white thing and leaned toward him, fascinated by what he was saying. John Kennedy looked like a fairy-tale prince. They both had a happy, immortal presence, as if they lived in a special bubble. Then the picture went to a speech John had given in West Berlin. The Germans loved him as much as we did.

"It must be very hard on the Talbots to have a slow in the family," Annabel said. "I don't know what your father would have done if you or Petey had turned out slow."

Maurey straightened her right leg so her ankle was draped over my thigh. "Mr. Talbot doesn't care that Pud's a slow. Probably makes him feel like real folks."

I had some trouble following that. "Pud?"

Maurey laughed. "They call him Pud. His real name is Montgomery and he's the stupidest kid in the valley. I saw him in front of Talbot Taxidermy the other day with frozen drool down his shirt."

Dothan, Florence, and Montgomery. I made a connection. "They're all named for towns in Alabama."

Neither Annabel nor Maurey knew that and for a while we were all three silent as they digested the information and I watched Kennedy give his Cuban crisis speech. Actually, Annabel probably digested the information and Maurey moped because I'd known something she didn't know.

I decided it was time to move around. "You want a Coke? We can catch what's happening at the Deck."

Annabel said, "We have pop here."

Maurey stood up. "That's not the point, Mom."

The light was nice as Maurey and I walked the two blocks down Glenwood to Alpine and over to the White Deck. It has to do with altitude or lack of pollution or something—whatever it is, light in Wyoming can be transparent, energetic. It reflects completely, never losing a bit of brightness, especially after new snow. The light in North Carolina is heavy and absorbent, like a paper towel. You can't see something three blocks away as clearly as something in your hand. In Jackson Hole, distance is irrelevant.

The Tetons stood, *bing*, shining against a sky so blue it appeared artificial. Every snow crystal on the ground was separate from every other snow crystal. It's easy to believe in beauty when it batters you over the head.

As we walked along, I gave Maurey the rundown on last night's revelations, leaving out the part where her mother triggers the mess. She nodded and asked questions at pertinent points. "How much goo?"

"Say what?"

"How much goo came out? Two tablespoons? A cup? A quart? Surely it wasn't more than a quart."

"It wasn't more than a quart."

"More than a pint?"

I tried to remember. "It was all spread out, but I'd say less than a third cup."

"Did you taste it?"

"God, no. But Lydia did."

"That may be illegal."

This shocked me, the thought that a biological process might be affected by laws. "It was on a sock. I never heard of anyone getting arrested for tasting come off the end of a sock."

"You never heard of come till this morning."

"I'd heard of come, I just didn't know what it was."

"Knowing a word, but not knowing what it means, is the same as not knowing it." Maurey's face was flushed pink from the cold. There were rose spots above each cheekbone.

She looked down at my zipper. "When your thing is hard, does it point straight out or down?"

"Up."

"Up. Are you sure? Horses' things point down."

"Up. At least mine does. I don't know about anyone else."

We stopped across from the triangle and tried to picture the internal workings of the deal. Maurey's eyes squinched as she thought. She had the advantage over me in that she knew what male things were shaped like and I didn't know squat about females except there was a tunnel involved.

Maurey nodded. "That's about how I had it figured. The horses confused me. I wonder where kissing comes in."

In books people often kissed before things were either skipped or talked about so metaphorically no one knew what was going on. It seemed to be a one, two, three ritual—kiss, skip the weird stuff, fall in love. I thought about kissing Maurey, right there on the street, in hopes that one thing led to another and couldn't be stopped once begun, but she didn't seem interested in the romantic end of the deal. Maurey was into the mechanics.

"Maybe you could show me your thing," Maurey said.

"It's not hard right now."

"How can you make it hard?"

"I don't know. It just happens sometimes. It's not in my control."

We stood on the curb trying to imagine the unimaginable. This seemed like a big deal—like driving a car—only adults could do and kids couldn't. It would involve touching a girl in places you weren't even allowed to look at. How could you touch something you couldn't see?

"Do you think it feels good?" I asked.

Maurey shrugged as we walked on to the White Deck. "People in books usually think so. There must be more to it than making babies."

7

Dot tousled my hair—a nasty habit if ever there was one—and smiled at Maurey. "I thought you two was mortal enemies."

"Where'd you hear that?" I asked. Older women were always touching my hair. They think it's big fun to embarrass kids.

"Same place I hear ever'thing else." Dot pointed at the floor. "GroVont ever gets a newspaper I could be the only reporter."

Maurey turned sideways in the booth and leaned against the wall. "We're experimenting with friendship. We could go back the other way any second."

I couldn't tell if she was joking or not.

Dot laughed like she always does. "Hate is a good way to start being friends. Better than the other way around like those two old farts." She pointed at Bill and Oly who were back in their regular corner booth. They stared into their coffee cups as if they'd done a freeze-frame in that position.

"What's wrong with them?" I asked.

Dot more or less sorted. "They were meat and gravy for thirty years. Had a logging business, you never saw Bill without Oly or Oly without Bill."

"You still don't," Maurey said.

"We used to think maybe they's queer, but who ever heard of a queer logger."

"Must get lonesome in the woods," I said.

Dot grinned real big. "That's why God made sheep," and she went off into a veritable gale of mirth. Maurey and I cut eyes at each other, knowing this had something to do with dicks and tunnels, but not sure how sheep fit in.

"I have to watch them every minute now. Bill's punched out Oly three times this month. Almost broke his nose the other day. Oly don't know what to make of it. He's gotten skittish. The whole cafe is tense."

I studied the two old men nodding over their coffee cups. They didn't appear skittish, they appeared dead. Their hands wrapped around their cups, as if that was the last possible source of warmth. At one point, Bill swallowed and Oly blinked.

I ordered a cheeseburger and coffee. Maurey had a vanilla shake. When Dot brought the food, Maurey went right to the point.

"Dot, do you and your husband have sex?"

Dot's head kind of snapped back an inch. She snuck a quick look around for eavesdroppers, but there were no other customers besides the old men practicing for death. Dot smoothed her apron with her right hand. "Jimmy's been in the army two years, over in Asia the last six months, so there's been a dry spell here just lately."

I smiled sympathetically. Maurey went right on. "But you used to have sex, right, before Jimmy went away?"

Dot's eyes went into a memory mode. "My Jimmy had the appetite. He'd of done it four times a day if I'd let him. I got scared to wash the dishes for fear of him sneaking up behind me."

"Then men like it and women don't?"

"Oh, I loved it, sugar, better than ice cream and chocolate cake."

"Then why were you scared to wash the dishes?"

"I guess I was more a twice-a-dayer than four times, though if Jimmy'd come back tomorrow, I swear I could adapt."

I stared out the window at the sunshine, pretending I had a woman who wanted it twice a day but was willing to go four. I wondered how long each time took. If it was fifteen minutes, that'd mean an hour of fucking a day.

"My mom won't be home for another twenty minutes," Ginger Ann purred. "You want to stick it in?"

"But that'll be five times since school let out this afternoon."

"Sam, it's not romantic to keep score."

Maurey sucked on her shake straw thoughtfully. "How much come did Jimmy put out each time?"

Dot sat down at the table behind her. "Maurey Pierce. There are things people don't compare."

"Why?" I asked.

"Why? Lovemaking is private. We do it but we don't say how much you-know-what came out."

"It's okay to say 'came out' but not okay to say 'come'?"

Dot blinked three times—blap-blap-blap. "That's talking dirty. Kids your age shouldn't talk dirty."

"I don't see how it can be dirty," I said. "Lydia told me sex is an expression of affection and love, theoretically, and good, clean fun, practical-wise. Why is doing it clean, but talking about it dirty?"

Maurey waved her hand as if she were clearing the air. "I just want to know if a third cup is average."

Dot tittered, which is really weird in a woman over twenty-five. "We girls can't talk about it in mixed company." She nodded her head at me.

I scooted out of the booth. "I'm going to the can." To Maurey, I said, "Remember anything she says. I didn't hold out on you."

Dot slid over into the seat I'd just left. "What's he mean 'hold out'?"

In the men's room, I discovered the deal had gotten stiff again, too stiff, and pointed in the wrong direction to pee. Could just talking about the penis make it get bigger? That would be really weird. Within the last year, kinky hair had sprouted down in the ball area. I knew that when a kid got kicked down there it hurt like shit, more than getting kicked in the stomach or butt, so those clumps in the sac must be nerves.

As I gave it a little squeeze it seemed to get even harder, about as hard as an aspen branch, not as hard as an elm. The thing had been stiffening up now and then since I was eleven, could there be a way to blow the goo without being asleep or sticking it in a girl? I couldn't see how. By pinching the end a tad, I could make the slit open and close, like a mouth. I pretended I was a ventriloquist and could throw my voice.

"Hi there, my name is Dicky. I live in your penis. I get big when I want and I squirt when I want." Then I wagged him side to side.

"Jesus Christ," I said back to Dicky.

Never did get a chance to pee.

When I returned to Maurey, I had to walk past Bill and Oly's corner booth. Neither one had moved, but a low growl came from Bill's upper chest, kind of angry grizzly bear-like. I skirted way wide so he couldn't grab me.

Back to my cheeseburger, I asked Maurey, "Dot tell you how it's done?"

Maurey looked disgusted. "She said sex is a wonderful and special experience, but it can never be done right unless the two people are in love."

"Sounds like a crock to me."

"That's what I told her."

A letter arrived from Caspar.

Samuel,

Everyone can master a grief but he that has had it.

Pay attention. This affects the way you live and there is just a possibility that the family brains skipped a generation and you think with more than your organs.

A man in San Bernadino, California, has invented a way of dramatically strengthening tires by blending carbon black with rubber. This means the price of carbon is going to skyrocket, which means you may be forced to find a job someday. Ask your mother if she knows what a job is. I have also heard an ugly rumor of an old retiree in a garage somewhere who has discovered "carbonless" carbon paper, a way to make carbons without discoloration of the fingers. Added to this misery, a company named Xerox may do away with carbon paper completely.

So the Caspar Callahan Carbon Paper Company is searching for a way to expand. I am considering nylons.

Keep all this under your hat, Samuel.

I trust you and your mother are adapting to the weather. I understand the pass you caught against Victor, Idaho, showed resourcefulness and daring. Good work. Did I ever tell you of my days at Culver Military Academy?

Tell your mother that I have a friend in Belgian Congo whose tenant was recently devoured by rabid Negroes.

Your dignity and the Callahan name are your most precious possessions, Samuel. Guard them diligently.

Your grandfather,
Mr. Callahan

I showed the letter to Lydia. "Are we supposed to think he makes these weird quotes up?"

"It's a tone-setter stratagem to make his thoughts relevant. I remember that dignity line from when I was your age," Lydia said. "I told him I'd rather have a T-Bird."

"What's this Belgian Congo deal?"

"Next stop if we embarrass him here."

I studied Caspar's company stationery. He used a red ink pen in a tiny flowing handwriting that got tinier as it approached the right side of the page. Caspar was tiny himself—under five-five, to my everlasting dismay—but he drove his stretch Continental like a tank. Curbs meant nothing to the man. That military academy crack put an ugly feeling in my gut.

"Did you tell him about the pass?" I asked.

"Are you kidding? My conversations with Caspar are limited to 'Where's the check?' 'Don't be a tramp.'"

"How did he find out I caught a pass?"

Lydia laughed. She'd been laughing regularly since the night she came in late. "Someone's on the payroll."

"Caspar has a spy?"

"Of course Caspar has a spy." She took my shoulders in her hands and faced me. "Sam, listen to me. Your grandfather is Santa Claus. He knows every move you make and he will always know every move you make. Nothing can be hidden. A long time ago, I realized my job is to give the spies something to report. Caspar has never done squat. He gets his jollies off by hearing the juice of my adventures."

"Jollies? He's threatening me with Culver again. I know what that means. It means not having my own room and playing lacrosse instead of baseball. Only squirrels play lacrosse."

Lydia scratched Les under the chin. "I promise, Sammy, that old goat will never separate us."

Sounded like a hollow promise to me. The old goat could do anything he pleased so long as he controlled the wallet. "What about the rabid Negroes in Belgian Congo?"

Lydia grinned, showing an intense number of teeth. "Hell, honey bunny, I can handle rabid Negroes."

I took that about six different ways, then gave up.

I forgot to mention earlier that Florence Talbot was not ugly, she was actually semi-pretty, probably the semi-prettiest girl in the seventh grade, next to Maurey. She had a Lesley Gore look, soft reddish-brown hair and brown pencil-drawn eyebrows. Florence could have even given Maurey a run for the title if she'd learned how to smile.

It was when Florence opened her mouth that the beauty flew out the window. Had a voice like a lunch whistle and this west Alabama accent that could curdle milk.

When I showed up at school Tuesday, Florence was standing in a little gaggle of girlhood, blocking the water fountain. Chuckette Morris was there, popping her retainer in and out with her tongue. And one of the LaNell-LaDell twins.

"Excuse me," I said.

"Why?" LaNell-LaDell asked.

"I'd like to get to the water fountain." I wasn't really thirsty, only in a damned-if-that-Florence-Talbot-is-going-to-intimidate-me mood.

Chuckette and a couple others shuffled aside for me. Since the junior high used to be the grade school, the fountain was about a foot and a half off the ground, so I had to bend way over. When my head came back up, Florence's face glared at me from all of eight inches away. I could see pulses next to her eyes. Her Talbot chin jutted at me like a pointing finger.

I hadn't swallowed so when I flashed her a *What, me worry*

grin, water dribbled across my lower lip and down my jaw—the ultimate junior high gross-out maneuver, next to pencils up the nose.

Maurey wore all black to school that day. I asked her why in the hall after citizenship.

"I'm in mourning for the nation," she said.

"You look like the bad guy in a cowboy movie."

"I'm Jane Eyre, bravely going on in the face of tragedy."

"Right."

Dothan razzed me in PE. We were playing dodgeball and he threw at me and missed about eight times. I might not have been strong enough to win a fight, but I was quick and he was stupid. If he looked at my feet he threw at my head, and if he looked at my head he threw at my feet.

"Hey, Sam," Dothan called, "tell us how Maurey Pierce's hooters feel. Are they foam rubber?"

Now I'm faced with one of those universal crises of youth: to respond to a word without anyone knowing you don't know what it means. "Hooters" was beyond me. From Lydia, I knew knockers, twat, ass, tongue, jugs, head, boobs, whanger, and several other terms such as cock and clit that I knew were body parts, I just wasn't sure where or on what sex they were located.

I couldn't possibly admit to sixth-period PE that I didn't know hooters. I had to answer, yet the wrong answer would give away my ignorance. I don't give away ignorance.

Dothan sensed he had me. "Come on, tell us about Pierce's hooters."

"They feel the same as your sister's."

Lydia breezed in late again Wednesday night. She'd been snow-mobiling with Ft. Worth and Hank Elkrunner. The closest Lydia had ever come to outdoor recreation in North Carolina was fetching the newspaper off the front veranda and she wouldn't do that in winter. I was aghast to see my mother with ruddy cheeks.

"Which one of those two jokers are you after?" I asked.

Lydia lit a cigarette, a girl's brand called Tarreyton. "It's time you learned about priorities, Sammy. Which one do you think I'm after?" The gleam was in her eye. Lydia considered herself on top of the situation.

"How should I know. I haven't met Hank yet and all I know about Ft. Worth is his hairy finger."

"Ft. Worth has more money and a new truck and a nice dog and he's lovably charming. Hank doesn't smoke or drink, he's smarter, more sensitive, and seems to have an inner demon that intrigues me. Which should I pick?"

I considered. Normally, I'd opt for the inner demon because I secretly pictured myself with one that I hoped girls would go ape over, but a new truck and a good dog might be more Lydia's speed. She could be dangerous to sensitivity.

"They both sound like clucks to me."

Lydia hit her cigarette hard. "Here's your first lesson on women, Sam. I'll choose the one with the biggest dick."

Lydia didn't come home at all Friday night. I fixed myself an egg sandwich and sat in the living room, watching "Gun-smoke" and reading a *Life* magazine featuring a photo layout of Brigitte Bardot at her villa in France. The story said she slept in the nude. The concept seemed impossible. What if the house caught on fire and you had to run outside. I'd have died of smoke inhalation before I'd run into the street naked.

At 10:30 I turned on the porch light and drank a Dr Pepper along with two aspirins and a Valium. I went in the kitchen and got out Lydia's shot glass and Gilbey's in case she came in after I fell asleep. I even opened the bottle and measured out her first two ounces. It felt kind of strange to be going to sleep in an empty house. I set the TV on a white-noise station and maxed the volume.

I took *Life* to bed with me and fantasized various Brigitte Bardot rendezvous in hopes of enticing up another wet dream—fat chance. I dreamed I was being chased by Lee Harvey Oswald.

Sam Callahan ran down a long, narrow hallway that reached forever. He passed doors on the right and left but whenever Sam tried to open one, he found it locked. Behind him, limping in bandages, came Lee Harvey Oswald with his mail-order Italian rifle. Lee Harvey's eyes were sunk into deep hollows. He never slowed, kept coming and coming.

Panic gripped Sam by the bowels, he pulled at doors, he threw his shoulder into doors, but Lee Harvey kept coming. Sam reached the end of the corridor—another locked door. His brow poured sweat, his hands trembled, he didn't want to die. Sam pounded on the door.

"Help me, please. Don't lock me out."

Lee Harvey kept coming.

Suddenly the door fell open and Jack Ruby faced him. "This is for Jackie and the kids," he said and pulled the trigger.

Sam felt his stomach on fire. He fell back into Lee Harvey Oswald's open arms.

8

FRIDAY WASN'T THE FIRST NIGHT I'D EVER SPENT ALONE IN A house. In Greensboro we lived in an eight-bedroom deal that Lydia called the manor house even though it was in town. Caspar supposedly lived with us, but Me Maw was in and out of the Duke hospital so much he took an apartment in Durham. I think he couldn't face living in the same house as Lydia without Me Maw there too.

For a while we had a live-in maid, but she remarried her ex-husband, and a cook came around in the daytime. Lydia mostly stayed home doing the TV and 10:30 knockout deal, only every few months she'd go social on me and I'd wake up at two in the morning in an empty house. Lydia was basically a binge or starve person when it came to fun.

Just about the earliest memory I have involves waking up in a dark, abandoned house. I must have been four because I remember the Roy Rogers pajamas and I think I outgrew them by the time I hit five. I was asleep in Caspar's bed.

All my early life I slept on whatever bed or couch was closest when I got tired. Sometimes, it was Lydia's bed with her, other times I fell asleep under my own single bed. Then there were the five extra bedrooms. I pretended each was a different planet. Mercury was neat because the bed was round and covered by a curtain.

But this happened before rooms were planets. I wet Caspar's bed and woke up crying. There must have been a dream, I don't remember. Anyhow, I stripped off the Roy Rogers pajama bottoms and hopped down on the cold floor. With all these beds to choose from, no reason to sleep in a wet one.

But the hallway was really dark, dark as death. Normally Lydia left the bathroom light on and the door cracked so the hallway had a soft glow of security. I wasn't used to blackness.

I felt the wall, then the wall on the other side. I sat down and yelled "*Lid-ya*," but no luck. Pitch black and alone, I couldn't believe it. Monsters lived in the dark—and slugs and rats, rats who could see me but I couldn't see them. They would bite my face in a second. Things could take away my arms and legs.

I hollered "*Paw-Paw*," which was Caspar, but I didn't hold out much hope for him. He'd have kicked me out of his bed if he was home.

I crawled down the hall—afraid I'd lose the floor too if I stood—to Lydia's room but it was a cave. I pulled myself up and stood at the door and cried, trying to will her into place. The steps going downstairs were no better. I had to turn around and slide on my front, one step at a time. I heard a sound and peed again. Somewhere along the way, I took off the Roy Rogers pajama top.

A clock glowed in Caspar's library, which had been Me Maw's bedroom the last year when she couldn't do the stair deal. I pulled some books off the shelves and walked head-on into a globe of the world. In the kitchen, I opened the refrigerator and made light and everything wasn't so bad anymore. I ate some grapes from the vegetable bin, then rolled into a ball, using my body to block open the refrigerator, and fell asleep.

Lord knows why I remember that.

—·—

Maurey's knock on the door made me jump like I'd been hit by a rock. In three months we'd had four knocks—two Jehovah's Witnesses, a Girl Scout turning cookies, and a guy looking for Soapley. I'd begun thinking the outside world couldn't touch me while I was at home.

"Let's try it," Maurey said when I opened the door. She was real pretty and brunette standing on the snow. Her eyes had blue sparkles, like she was interested in what she was doing.

"My mom's not home."

"She and eight other drunks rented a motel room in Dubois when the bars closed last night. They're having a party." Maurey let herself in. She had on Levi's and a red parka. "My second cousin Delores is there. Delores's husband told her mom in the hope of getting her dragged out, but it didn't work, and her mom told my mom and I overheard. Delores and Lydia are the only girls at the party."

"I'm making oatmeal. You want some?"

"Funny how news travels in a small town, isn't it. Got some coffee? I want to explain the rules before we do this."

"Do what?"

"Have sex. Why else would I be here?"

I focused on the label on the back of Maurey's jeans as I followed her into the kitchen. Ever since I was a little boy, I'd wanted to have sex with a girl, even though I didn't know what that entailed until recently. The main reason I'd wanted sex was because, as I understood it, you got to see her naked. I couldn't really conceive of a goal loftier than seeing a woman without her clothes. Rubbing myself against one or having one see me naked were somewhat disquieting thoughts that I'd avoided up to that point.

"We're going to perform sex now?" I asked.

"After coffee."

Maurey and I sat across from each other at the kitchen table—a giant wood slab thing with area cow brands burned into the top—and dumped spoonfuls of sugar and about a can of milk into two mugs. I still didn't like coffee that much, only drank it because I felt like I should. All addictive things are distasteful when you first start out. She blew across the steam and sipped. "You already taught me one thing I didn't know, Sam."

"What's that?"

"Coffee. Now we'll teach each other something."

"You think Lydia might come home today?"

She wrinkled her nose and looked closely at the cup. "Doubtful. Ray, that's Delores's husband, he says they just sent out for Chinese food and two cases of Schlitz."

"Where can you get Chinese food at eight-thirty in the morning?"

Maurey dumped more sugar in her mug. "Dubois is a weird place. Think you can get a stiffie?"

I glanced at my lap and thought about Brigitte Bardot. "They seem to come and go. I haven't figured how to control it yet."

"Maybe it'll happen naturally."

"I've heard something about putting it in the girl's mouth."

"I'm not doing anything that might make me sick."

We stared into our nearly white coffee for a while. I was hungry, but I'd turned off the oatmeal and it seemed sacrilegious to turn it back on when I was on the edge of the Great Chasm. This was more important than food. This was what Lydia said grown-ups lived for.

"We're both virgins," Maurey began.

"I never said I was a virgin."

She gave me the evil eye. I bit my thumbnail. "We're both virgins," she began again, "but someday we're going to find ourselves doing it."

That someday confused me. I thought we were going to do it after coffee.

Maurey continued. "When my time happens, I don't want to come off like a squirrel, I want to know what's going on at all times."

"That makes sense." I stared at her fingers on the mug. The mug said Fort Sumter and had a picture of an army base on the side. Maurey had the smallest hands in the world.

"So you and I are going to learn about this thing now while it doesn't matter, so we won't be fools later when it does."

"Today's sex doesn't matter."

She stared me right in the eye. "We're just friends helping each other learn a new skill. Just friends can't really do it. This is practice."

"Will we still be virgins afterwards?"

"I don't know. That's part of what we're going to learn, where the line between virginity and nonvirginity really is."

I'd always understood it as a clearly marked frontier. "What do you think?"

"I think it's either when you stick it all the way in or when the boy squirts. You better not squirt." She looked at me suspiciously, as if I was secretly planning to play a trick and squirt in her.

"I won't squirt. Promise."

"And no kissing. Kissing is mushy, emotional stuff, and we can't do it if you're going to get mushy."

"No mush."

We were silent awhile. The refrigerator kicked on. I could hear the toilet running in the bathroom. Downtown, the volunteer fire siren howled. It would continue for a minute while the firemen rushed to the station, then there'd be ten minutes of truck sirens. It happened once a week or so, whenever creosote built up in somebody's stovepipe and the chimney caught fire.

"I'm not sure you can do it without mush," I said.

"We can do it."

"Dot and Lydia both say it takes emotionalism."

I know Maurey thought I was just trying to trick a kiss out of her, and maybe I was. Unless you count a cheek peck on Janey Silverman in the fourth grade, I'd never kissed a girl. Like seeing one naked, kissing was another goal. It was hard to believe I was going to skip right over all the intermediate thrills and go straight to intercourse.

"You told me your mom had done it with lots of people. It couldn't have been emotional every time."

I shrugged. I didn't know how often and with how many people it was possible to be emotional. "We could try it first without kissing and if it doesn't work we could kiss without meaning it."

Maurey looked even more suspicious. "I've seen horses do it and horses don't kiss."

We went into my room since that seemed to be the place to commit the act. I sat on the side of the bed while Maurey sat in the chair at my desk. She pushed the *w* key on the typewriter down, then let it up, then back down again. She put her finger on the ribbon and made her print blue.

I held my hands in my lap. "I wish we didn't have to be naked."

"I'm sure that's part of doing it." She kicked off her snow boots. "Maybe we could leave our socks on. The floor's kind of cold."

"How about my shirt? I don't see why I need to take off my shirt."

"Why do you get to leave your shirt on but I don't?"

"Women's breasts are important to the deal. It doesn't work if I can't touch your breasts. All the books work that way. Men's breasts are just for show, like a belly button."

"I'm not showing you mine if you don't show me yours."

Five minutes and much futzing over buttons and zippers later, Maurey and I stood facing each other, down to boxer shorts and panties—and socks. Hers were red wool, mine white gym socks.

"You're first," she said.

"You first."

We stared at each other. I went into a paranoia streak—what if it was a Wyoming ritual, as soon as I dropped my boxers she'd laugh and run away, or even worse, everyone in GroVont Junior High would jump from the closet and point at me.

"Oh, Jesus," Maurey said, and she dropped her panties and stepped out. I had to follow. The silence was fairly eerie.

She looked down. "I thought you'd be bigger."

"I'm not stiff yet."

She poked at it. "When a horse gets a stiffie, it's almost as big as his leg."

"Time to stop comparing us to horses, Maurey. None of it seems to carry over." I held out my finger and touched the nipple on the end of her tit. Touching a tit was the outer limit of my fantasy life. All my lurid dreams had come true. I was ready to put our clothes back on and eat some oatmeal. "Are you disappointed it's not like a horse's?"

Maurey brushed her fingertip through the ball area. "I was kind of scared to have you put something big as your leg up me. I couldn't see how it would fit."

As she touched under the ball sac, things perked up. "Holy moley," she said.

I finally looked at the rest of her below the breasts. Maurey was mostly planes and soft colors. She smelled nice. "You've got hair down there."

"So do you, silly." She continued running her' fingernail up and down and I continued to grow.

"I just didn't expect girls to have hair in that spot."

"Does it gross you out?"

It sort of did but I wasn't about to admit it. "No. It's kind of pretty. How do you see to find the tunnel?"

"It's in there, only it doesn't look like a tunnel from the outside."

"A cave?"

"Yeah, I guess so." I liked the area just below Maurey's collarbone. That was the prettiest spot to look at, although the breasts were most exciting. They weren't anything like the *Playboy* girls. Maurey's were little pooches in her chest. The *Playboy* girls looked as if they had football implants.

"Is that as big as it gets?"

"I guess so. How do we put it in the tunnel?"

Maurey kept running her finger around the base. It felt real neat. I was getting used to having a girl see me with my clothes off and I thought this might be something I'd like to do regularly.

"Horses do it standing up with the stallion behind the mare," she said.

"I told you to forget horses."

"You've never seen anything do it."

"I saw Soapley's dog Otis doing it last week."

"Bet he did it standing up from behind."

Maurey turned around. Her hair came down almost to the bottom of her neck. Her back was real pretty, prettier than the front. Her little butt cheeks were like molded from a catcher's mitt. "You have to get up behind me," she said.

I tried but I couldn't decide where my hands went. "This is awkward. I can't see grown-ups basing their lives on this. Maybe you should bend over some."

I knew it was coming, so I said in unison with Maurey, "Horses don't bend over." She laughed at that and the tension wasn't quite so intense. I learned my first lesson about sex. Always make the girl laugh.

"I'm up too high," I said. "Your hole's way down here."

She flinched. "That's the wrong hole."

"Are you sure?"

"Pretty sure. I think. The hole you go in is the bigger one up front."

"I'm supposed to stand behind you and go in a front hole? Maybe if you stood on a chair or something."

"None of the books say anything about the girl standing on a chair."

"None of the books say anything. They skip this part and go straight to how wonderful it was."

"Let's take a break, Sam. Something's not working."

"Go get *Catch-22*. We'll see how they do it."

We sat side by side on the bed and read chapter twenty-three, where Nately gives three whores thirty dollars apiece to go to bed with his friends.

"Go to bed," Maurey said. "That's the key. Humans must do it lying down."

"More comfortable than a girl standing on a chair. But I don't have thirty dollars. You take a check?"

Maurey hit me lightly on the thigh. "That's for whores. Good girls do it for free."

"And bad girls do it for money?"

"Jesus, you're naïve, Sam. This next paragraph Aarphy talks about making the high school girls 'put out.' I wonder what they put out. I always thought stuff came out of the boy's body and went into the girl's."

We tried it lying down on the bedspread, first next to each other with her back to me, then next to each other with her facing me. Faced together, Maurey got the giggles and we had to stop.

"When Otis did it he got stuck."

Maurey stopped giggling. "Jesus."

"They were butt to butt and Otis looked unhappy, but the female was in a lot of pain, made an awful sound."

"Nobody in a book ever got stuck."

"Soapley dumped buckets of water on them, but they didn't unstick for over two hours. Lydia wouldn't leave the house while they were yowling."

"What will we do if we get stuck? There's no one to throw water on us."

I couldn't answer that one. My thing lost most of its stiffness and Maurey had to touch it with two fingers to bring it back.

I was hot and it just wasn't working. "Look. You'll have to spread your legs and I'll have to lay in between them right on the tunnel. It's never going to go any other way."

"On top of me?"

"Sorry."

"How much do you weigh?"

"One-twenty-five," I lied, giving myself an extra ten pounds.

"How can I have a hundred twenty-five pounds on me. You'll break my ribs."

"Can you see any other way to do it?"

"I think you're almost in. Maybe if one of us touched it, gave it a little guidance."

"Oh, Lord."

"Sam, what are you doing?"

"Uh."

"Sam, stop grinding."

"Uh-huh."

"Sam."

"Ugh."

"Oh gross. You promised, Sam. You jerk, what if I have a baby now."

I couldn't answer. My mind had gone void. Maurey shoved me off and sat up. "Look at this gunk. That's nowhere near a third of a cup. You promised you wouldn't squirt and you lied about how much comes out. This is three tablespoons, tops, Sam." She hit my chest. "You're cross-eyed."

I held one arm over my head. "That was fun."

—

"We couldn't have made a baby. None of it went inside."

"I told you—no kissing, no squirting."

"I discovered something, Maurey. The boy can't control his squirt."

"Look at that. How long before it gets stiff again?"

"Beats me, that was my first time. Do you think we lost our virginity?"

"I sure as hell didn't."

—

"This is hurting, Sam."

"You're too tight, are you certain we've got the right hole."

"Your finger's smaller. Try that."

"Are you kidding?"

"Down lower, you're way too high. Hold it, move up. You're poking something."

"This isn't romantic, Maurey."

"Stop grinding for Chrissake."

"That's the only way to force it in."

"You're on my hair."

"It's coming again."

"Oh, hell."

There was a long pause, then a quiet voice. "Smooth move, Ex-Lax."

Maurey and I were back at the kitchen table, playing gin rummy and not speaking, when we heard Lydia charge in the door.

"Dibs on the John," she called.

"Hell with that, honey," another voice said, a raspy female voice. Then we heard a race across the living room followed by the crash of a slamming door and, "Shit. I'm gonna go in the kitchen sink if you're not out in thirty seconds."

"Someone's with her," I said to Maurey.

"Sounds that way."

The voice in the living room muttered, "Crap it all anyway," then a short woman all in white tromped into the kitchen. She stopped at the sight of us. "Maurey."

"Delores. I heard you were on a roll."

Delores was short—I'd say five foot even—and petite, but proportionately, she sported a huge set of breasts, way bigger than Lydia's or Maurey's. I'm talking out there. And she was dressed like a hooker doing a cowgirl fantasy—white pointy-toed boots, white skirt down to her upper thighs, a white fur vest, rabbit or weasel or something, over a white yoked shirt, and a white cowgirl hat with a peacock feather eye in the dead center. The skirt was held up by a black plastic belt and a turquoise rock of a buckle.

She was chewing gum, of course. "Maurey, hon, I won't tell Annabel I saw you if you won't tell her you saw me."

"What's in the bottle?" Maurey asked.

Delores's right hand covered her mouth when she giggled. I'd have given whatever future I possessed to see her naked. "Turpenhydrate and codeine—good drink for when you're ready to stop drinking."

"Your turn." Lydia came around Delores and into the kitchen. Delores whirled and ran.

"Hi, Mom," I said.

"Who?"

"Hi, Lydia. This is my friend Maurey from school. I told you about her before."

Lydia opened the refrigerator and pulled out a Dr Pepper. "So you two are getting along now?"

I glanced at Maurey to see if this was true. Her eyes were on Lydia, I think admiringly. She was probably going through the same comparison-analysis I had when I met Annabel.

Lydia perched on the sink with one foot touching the floor. "Sam tells me your mother cuts the crusts off your sandwiches."

Maurey looked down at the cards in her hand. "Only on holidays, or for company or something."

"That's okay. If my mom had cut off my crusts, things might have turned out better."

There was a short silence that, as the host, I felt obligated to fill. "Things turned out okay anyway. I think. How was your party?"

"Fairly boring. Six drunk yahoos wishing four would go away so they could go manly on Delores and me. Thank goodness for numbers. Wasn't a cowboy in the bunch had a full set of teeth."

Delores tottered back in the room, adjusting something under her skirt. "God, I whizzed like a racehorse. I swear, you don't buy beer, you only rent it."

At the word *horse* Maurey and I exchanged a quick smile. It helped that each of us was related to one of the two drunks.

"Sam," Maurey said, "meet my cousin, Delores. Ray's looking for you."

Delores unscrewed her little medicine bottle. "Hell, he found us. Him and a bunch of his logger buddies." She took a swig. "They come busting in the door of this motel room, I didn't tell you about the motel room, wanting to save my honor and haul me away, but Lydie's friends..."

"Nobody was going to lose any honor in that scene anyway," Lydia said.

"Speak for yourself. 'Nother hour I'd of figured a way."

"Sure."

Delores hit the codeine. "A fight ensued. Lydie and me escaped by the emergency ladies-only exit."

"Bathroom window," Lydia said. She looked very happy, and not really all that drunk. Her face was flushed and her eyes alive—although maybe she'd been at the codeine bottle herself. "That's the fourth, no fifth time I've had to beat retreat out a can, and it's always a blood pounder."

"Always costs me a pair of hose." Delores lifted her leg to show us. The rip in her nylons went right up past the skirt line. Maurey caught me following it up.

"I need a cigarette," Lydia said.

From somewhere on her person, Delores pulled out a pack and tossed it. Lydia held the pack out to show me. They were Montclairs. "Look at this, honey bunny. Something's come out since we left tobacco-land. Some new kind of menthol mixed with cigarettes. Tastes like they soaked the weeds in gasoline."

She'd never said H-B in front of anyone before. I would have given anything for a gun. "They had that stuff before we left Carolina."

"You sure? How could I have missed it?" Lydia lit one and took a long drag. She blew smoke out her nostrils. "What I don't understand," she began, "is how a woman who smokes cigarettes cured in gas and drinks codeine from a bottle could be related to a little girl whose mother cuts the crusts off her sandwiches on holidays."

Since Maurey and I had the only chairs and Lydia held down the counter space, there was nothing left for Delores but a cardboard box full of cookbooks. This gave me a great alley shot, so that, miraculously, Dirty Dick perked up again.

"I'm not related to her mom," Delores said. "Maurey's father—that's Buddy—his father and my grandfather were brothers, weren't they, hon. Her grandpa came here and started a ranch and mine stayed up in Dubois cutting timber. I guess we got the wild hair side and they got the boring. Present company accepted."

Maurey discarded the five of diamonds. "Dad's okay. He's wilder than he looks, he just works all the time."

Delores's legs moved and I know she was way aware of me. "Buddy's more than okay, hon. I'd be kissing cousins with that man any old day of the week."

Lydia smiled at me. "What've you kids been up to all afternoon?"

"Gin rummy. I owe Maurey three dollars and twenty-five cents."

"No, we weren't," Maurey said. "We were trying to have sex, only we couldn't do it."

I had two kings, two aces, and a possible five-card straight in my hand. The straight was all hearts. I could fill it by picking up a six way high in the pile, but that meant possibly eating about ten cards, and Maurey only held three, one step away from rummy. It constituted a tough decision.

"Why were you trying to have sex?" Lydia asked.

"So we won't be dopes later when we're old enough to do it for real. I wanted to know what it feels like before I hit puberty, and I figured Sam would be more popular and get more dates if he could please girls. He hasn't been all that popular so far."

"How about yourself?"

"I don't have to please boys to get dates."

Delores sat up and leaned her elbows on her knees, nipping off my panty shot. "What seemed to be the problem, honey. Wouldn't the little weinie stand up?"

I decided to pick up the pile. Not much to lose at that point.

Maurey wasn't paying attention anyway. "It stood up, but we couldn't figure where he should go in from, then he squirted."

Delores *tsked* with her tongue. "Prematures, I bet. I hate the prematures. Ray used to have them the worst I ever saw. He came in a movie house once when the wind blew up Marilyn Monroe's skirt."

As I discarded one of the kings, I made it a point not to look at Lydia. "Your turn."

Maurey pulled the king and rummied. "Sam didn't come instantly or anything, but he kept grinding down there without going in."

Lydia blew a column of smoke at her. "Your mom and you have little chats like this?"

"My mother thinks I'm still a child, sweet thirteen and never been kissed. She won't even let me use hair spray. If I ever said *sex* in front of her I swear she'd faint."

"Then why are you comfortable talking premature ejaculations in front of me?" Maurey and I stayed quiet. I don't think either of us knew what ejaculation meant.

"Oh, Lydia, give the kids a break," Delores said. "I wish I could have asked my mother questions back then. I'd never have married Ray if I'd known the first thing about doing it."

Maurey looked Lydia in the eye—made me nervous. Neither one of those two were women to be trifled with and I could feel their little bitch-alarm systems kicking into high wail. "Sam told me that you two have great communication and trust because you don't treat him like a kid and he doesn't treat you like a mom."

Lydia stared her right back. "He doesn't stand a chance, does he?"

"Not that I can see."

No one said much, so I shuffled. Then Lydia smiled real big. "I imagine at his age fucking you is worth what he's bound to lose later."

"I like to think so," Maurey said.

I had no idea in hell what had just happened, but whatever it was was over. Something had been decided and Lydia and Maurey both seemed happy with the results.

Delores pointed the codeine bottle at Maurey. "Were you well lubricated?"

"Lubricated?"

"Wet," Lydia said. "Did you get excited and was it nice and wet down there?"

Maurey thought awhile, but I didn't need to. "She was dry as the blanket. Should we have used water?"

Delores snorted. "Water don't make it. The wet comes from within the woman."

"Is that what put out means?"

"More like ooze out."

"Where does it come from?"

Delores looked at Lydia who gave her an eyebrow shrug. I was to learn quickly that even people who have regular sex don't usually know what's going on. Lydia spoke. "When the girl gets excited, this dampness just shows up, then the guy can go in."

Delores said, "Dampness, my ass. When I'm ready you could wring me out like a washrag."

"Don't be crude," Lydia said. "We're teaching the children a beautiful and precious act and it shouldn't be connected to crude ideas."

"My ass," Delores snorted.

"How does the woman get excited?" Maurey asked.

Delores leaned back so her skirt rode up again. "I just think about doing it and I start leaking."

"But I've never done it before so I don't know what to think about."

"I use gin," Lydia said.

Delores considered. "I'll use Vaseline if that's what it takes."

Concepts were flying across the room too fast for me to hold on. "You pour gin up the tunnel?"

"God, no, you drink the gin and get drunk and horny and men think they're taking advantage of you." Lydia lit another Montclair off the butt of the first one. She leaned over and dropped the used butt into the sink. I hated it when she did that.

"The Vaseline goes up there." Delores pointed to what I thought was roughly her navel area.

Lydia finished her Dr Pepper and tossed the empty bottle at the trash can by the back door. It rimmed once and bounced in. "Foreplay is the only romantic way to excite a woman."

"Kissing," I said. "I told her we had to kiss because they always do in the books but Maurey said it could be done without romance."

"It can be done without romance, only it's not that much fun."

Delores said, "I can have a ball with somebody I can't stand."

Lydia looked at Maurey's chest. "You haven't hit puberty yet?"

She shook her head. "Both Smith twins have and they're treating me like a child."

I thought puberty was when you could do it and before puberty was when you couldn't, so none of this made any sense.

"I guess it's safe then." Lydia stood up. "If you're going to play this game, you might as well play it right. Scoot your chair back."

Maurey looked concerned. "Do I have to undress?"

"That'd be too much even for me. I am his mother, after all."

"Sometimes I forget," I said.

Lydia gave me a gruesome look, then she walked to the food cabinet and opened a package of premade taco shells that'd been up there since we moved in. She held it so the slot ran up and down. "Looked like this, right?" she asked me.

"Hairier."

Delores hiccuped. "I can't wait to write this conversation in my diary."

Lydia went over and put the taco shell vertically between Maurey's legs. "Look at this, Sam. Pay attention."

"Yes, ma'am."

She ignored the ma'am. "Down here is where you go in. One of you has to grab it and angle it right. It'll be years before it just slides itself in."

Maurey nodded, taking in every detail.

Lydia pointed to the bridge at the top of the taco shell. "Right here is a little lump called the pleasure dome."

"Pleasure dome," I said.

"Now, don't go poking right at it, you run your fingers or your tongue lightly around and around the dome and the girl gets wet."

"Tongue. I thought the girl used her mouth, not the guy."

"That's a nasty rumor started by men."

Delores *oohed*. "Makes me wet just thinking about your young tongue down there."

I looked at her. "It does?"

Lydia pointed the taco shell at Delores. "Don't even think of giving lessons."

"But..."

"This is for the kids."

"You gonna teach him how to make her come?"

Her come? Jesus, would the revelations never cease. Girls squirted too?

Lydia shook her head. "Sam's bright. He'll figure that one out soon enough. The ability to give orgasms every time is too powerful a weapon for a thirteen-year-old to deal with."

Maurey's eyes hadn't left the taco shell. "Why didn't Jo talk about this in *Little Women*."

"Two things," Lydia said. "First, any sign that Maurey is a woman and you stop the game. Got that?" Lydia glared at us. Maurey nodded.

"What's the first sign she's a woman?" I asked. No one told me.

"The other is a matter of form. You don't talk like this in front of grown-ups. At your age, sex is something you sneak around and hide."

"Why?" I asked.

"Society would fall apart if people were honest about fucking."

I considered that philosophical stance for a moment, but the idea of a secret weapon that I could use to get girls whether they wanted to get got or not was almost too much. Imagine—high school girls, college girls, baton twirlers, car hops at drive-ins, girl models in the nightie section of the Sears catalogue, girls on TV. I could get Hayley Mills from the Disney movies. I could make Hayley Mills come and, while I was at it, see her tits.

"You want to go in my room and read comic books?" I asked Maurey.

She seemed hypnotized by the taco shell. "Sure, comic books sound like fun."

Delores picked the cards off the table. "I love crazy 8s. You play crazy 8s?"

Lydia threw the taco shell in the trash, then turned to me. "I always thought you were a little boy. Guess I should pay more attention."

"Thanks, Mom."

"Who?"

"Thanks, Lydia."

"Go get 'em, tiger."

As I held her hand and led her away to my bed, Maurey said, "Go get 'em, honey bunny."

So, while my mom Lydia and her new friend Delores sat at the kitchen table playing crazy 8s, Maurey and I exchanged lost virginities. Afterward, we all went down to the White Deck for ice cream, Delores's treat.

9

THIS WASN'T THE HAYLEY MILLS FROM *POLLYANNA*. THIS WAS *the older, more aloof Hayley from* The Parent Trap. *In fact, both* The Parent Trap *twins—the long-haired cultured Boston Hayley and the short-haired, perky California Hayley—sat in the spacious backseat of a limousine parked at the Tastee Freeze.*

Sam Callahan walked right up to their Rolls-Royce and leaned in the back window. "Where'd you guys go to school?" he asked.

The Boston Hayley put on her sunglasses. "We never talk to common people."

"Want to see a magic trick?" Sam asked.

"How juvenile," said the California Hayley.

Then, before they could roll up the window, Sam performed his trick.

The Boston Hayley took off her sunglasses. "What can be your pleasure today?"

"Show me your breasts."

The girls did as they were told. With their shirts off and their glamorous breasts facing Sam Callahan, they asked, "What may we do next to help you feel like the king you are?"

Sam touched the left nipple on each girl. "Do you know where Maureen O'Hara lives?"

"I haven't gotten laid in four months." Lydia blew smoke across the table. "My own kid is getting lucky and I can't."

"There is a problem we can fix," Hank Elkrunner said. He was sitting next to Lydia, across from Maurey and me. Maurey and I were playing a game called hangman where you fill in blanks with letters before the other guy draws a hung stick figure. Maurey was in a good mood because she'd aced a test in citizenship that I made a C on. She put a lot more stock in grades than I did.

"You complain of your dry season," Hank said, "but no one feels sympathy. Each man in this room would volunteer to give you cause to stop complaining." I liked Hank. He spoke slowly and looked at his fingers when he talked. He hadn't been at the table five minutes before he told us he didn't smoke or drink alcohol, just the kind of guy Lydia needed. They seemed real relaxed with each other.

Lydia looked around the White Deck, surveying possible volunteers. Most of the eight or nine guys were dude wranglers on welfare, holing up for winter and waiting for tourist season to kick in. A couple worked for the national park. "I'd rather complain than fool around with these peckerheads. Every one of this rabble is afraid of women."

Hank had this low, growl-like laugh. You couldn't really tell he was laughing except his shoulders moved up and down. "They are not afraid of women. They are afraid of you."

"No challenge in that. Not a man here, this table excluded, that Maurey couldn't have shaking in his Tony Lama's in five minutes."

Maurey looked across at Lydia and smiled. In the last four days since our training session they'd gotten real buddy-buddy. Made me nervous.

Hank picked up his iced tea. "I bet Oly could make you walk the ceiling."

"Oly is dead, only around here dead people go on drinking coffee for six days. It's like growing toenails anywhere else."

This four-months-of-no-sex thing came as kind of a surprise. With Lydia, whenever she leaves the house everyone just figures she's up to something immoral.

"Dusty Springfield," Maurey said.

"Heck." She'd guessed my hangman words. I'd been trying to touch her thigh under the table, and she let me for a minute. Then she picked up my hand and put it on my lap and said, "Keep yourself warm." She smiled so I figured it was okay to try again pretty soon.

Maurey drew the spaces and the two-line gallows. It felt comfortable, sitting with her and Hank and Lydia in the White Deck—like we belonged for a change. Nobody was pushy or wanted anything. None of the customers avoided looking at us or quit talking when we started. Lydia and I were part of the scene.

Lydia still cleaned the silverware when we sat down and still called locals peckerheads. She used the word *home* in the context of North Carolina, and thought Wyoming women little better than galley slaves, but I could see a change. Now, she treated locals more like slightly retarded, well-meaning children rather than cossack rapists with drool for brains. Some ironic humor had entered the situation.

Just that morning I'd heard Lydia ask Soapley what he had under his Polaris and she seemed to understand the answer. Which I didn't.

Dot brought over Lydia's hamburger, Maurey's shake, and Hank and my blue plates—Swedish meatballs, noodles, and green beans. Hank asked for ketchup.

"Got a letter from Jimmy today," Dot said. "He'll be home end of the summer."

Lydia was doing the looking at her teeth in the butter knife number. In it, she stretches her lips out flat so her teeth look like fangs. "The kids tell me Jimmy likes it four times a day."

Dot reddened and pinched me on the shoulder. I pointed to Maurey. "Her. She's the rat, I never said a word."

"What's Jimmy doing in Vietnam?" Hank said. Hank was the first nontelevision news person I ever heard use the word *Vietnam*.

Dot propped one hand on her hip. "He says he's teaching one bunch of monkeys how to kill another bunch. Sounds kind of stupid to me. You want more iced tea?"

Lydia scowled while Dot jacked up Hank's glass. Southern iced tea came presugared and Lydia took it as a personal affront that nobody in the West could get it right.

After Dot left, I used Hank's ketchup and caught crap from both the females. "Hank put it on his stuff," I said.

"Hank's an Indian," Maurey said.

"Hank's a clod," Lydia said.

Hank just smiled. I flashed on a futuristic ganging-up process where I could be in big trouble.

Maurey sucked vanilla shake through a paper straw. "Hank can shoot a rifle under a horse's brisket going full blast, just like in the movies."

"So can you," Hank said.

"Yeah, but you hit what you're aiming at."

"Got kicked in the head last time I tried that trick."

Lydia turned to stare at Hank's head. "It shows."

For some reason, I was looking a couple booths down, right at Bill's rock of an Adam's apple. Oly said something I didn't hear, then Bill stood up and fell into the jukebox. He stuck for a moment, then slid down.

Everybody shut up at once. Oly put down his coffee cup and said, "Bill's dead."

Me Maw died when I was five. Sometimes I speculate that Caspar wouldn't have been such a king-hell hard-butt if his wife hadn't got cancer and spent seven years being sad and then died. I don't know. Maybe he was always severe. Maybe that's why she got the cancer in the first place.

I don't remember all that much about Me Maw before she died. She wasn't up much. I remember her smell, a cross between rubbing alcohol and paper matches right after you blow them out. They made me go in the library-turned-sickroom to say good-bye. Her eyes were way in there and waxed paper-looking. When I kissed her on the cheek, she was wet. I was scared I'd get the cancer from touching her.

At her funeral, Caspar, Lydia, and I sat together in front. Neither one of those two showed a lick of emotion. That carved look on their faces was the one I recognize now as the look a kid gets when a coach yells at him for something he thinks he didn't do, like, "You're not going to get to me, you asshole."

I sat with my hands in my lap and watched Me Maw's face in the box, sure she was going to blink or sit up or something that would freak me out. I wondered if she was wearing shoes. Caspar told me to stop moving my legs.

After the cemetery, we went out for ice cream, same as when Maurey and I lost our virginity. Maybe there's a pattern.

That evening Maurey and I lay on my bed and tried to figure out the death thing. We unbuttoned each other's shirts, and I had mine off, but the impetus to keep going petered out about the time I touched her right breast.

"I wonder what it feels like to be dead?" I asked.

Maurey rolled over to face the ceiling and covered her left

breast with her hand. The eye on my side blinked three times. It was kind of funny, her lying on her back with one breast hidden by her hand and the other one hidden by mine. I never could get over how small Maurey's hands were. "Cold, I guess."

I tried to imagine Maurey's tit cold and dead, but I'd only learned what it felt like warm and alive four days ago, so dead was beyond me. With my hand cupped over her chest, you couldn't even tell Maurey had a breast.

Maurey said, "People sure die easily in books. It's not that casual in real life."

"The easiest place to die is in the movies."

Maurey bit her lower lip and turned to look at me. "I think about being dead all the time. I've read every book in the library I can find about girls dying and I can't figure it out."

I moved my hand off her breast and touched her cheek. "It's not like sex, Maurey. The people who write books don't know any more about being dead than we do."

Bill hadn't looked comfortable dead. He fell with one leg doubled under his body and his head at an off-angle. His belt was cinched up on his belly so he looked cramped. His eyes were closed, which surprised me. I thought people died with their eyes open.

Nobody in the White Deck went hysterical or anything. The Park Service guys flipped him over and tried what passed for artificial respiration back then—a push on the back, pull on the elbows useless maneuver. Lydia went and sat next to Oly, but he didn't seem to notice. He just stared at the lump on the floor that used to be his friend. Once, he said it again. "Bill's dead."

Dot called Jackson for an ambulance while Hank felt Bill's neck for a pulse, but anyone could see he was king-hell dead.

Max the owner came out of the kitchen to watch. I'd never seen him in person before. He had hardly any hair and a purple tattoo of a bird and he wore a sleeveless T-shirt. He didn't talk.

Maurey leaned over me to look, then she sat back and held my hand. It took so long for the ambulance that we tried to play hangman awhile, but neither one of us could concentrate on the letters.

He'd died between the jukebox and their private booth, which meant anyone going to the bathroom had to step over the body, which I wasn't about to do. That's what I remember most about my first look at immediate death—having to pee like crazy and not being able to.

—·—

GroVont has a Mormon church that from the outside looks like a Pizza Hut. And, over by the Tetons, the Episcopal chapel in Moose is more in the way of a tourist trap than a real church. It's not open in the winter. Baptists and Catholics go to Jackson to be buried.

Bill's funeral took place in the VFW. I went because Maurey asked me to, and she went because the Pierces and Bill and Oly were connected in some way to do with World War I. Her grandfather served with them in Belgium and, later, when he died in an avalanche, Bill and Oly did the like-a-father gig for Maurey's dad.

Everyone in the valley is either literally related or spiritually attached. One reason Maurey chose me for the sex practice was because, with me, she knew for certain there would be no hint of incest.

"Besides, I like your hair," she said.

"I thought it was my Eastern casual demeanor."

"Fat chance."

I wish someone would do the like-a-father gig for me.

Lydia wouldn't come with us. "I don't do death," she said. "Les is the only formerly animate object I commune with."

"It'll be interesting. Maurey says all the women in town bake things."

"There was enough competitive cooking after Mama's funeral. And the phone company man is coming. Those people don't take excuses."

So I found myself sitting in a folding chair in a VFW hall with Maurey, Petey, and Annabel. Coach Stebbins and his wife filled out our row.

Annabel had on white gloves, if you can buy that, and this little hat shaped like an Alka-Seltzer with a net over the front. She looked fairly disconcerted, as if a cake had fallen unexpectedly. Petey kicked the chair in front of him the whole service.

Maurey's father, Buddy, sat up front next to poor Oly. I found myself looking at the back of Buddy's head, wondering what a guy who spends most of his time alone thinks about death. He had on a brown cowboy hat and a suit I imagined was worn only to this sort of thing. I wondered if he'd be pissed to know I was sticking my thing in his daughter.

The rest of the place was full of old people who go to each other's funerals, and loggers and a few cowboy types, not too many kids. Rodney Cannelioski was there as a representative of God. Dot smiled at me when I walked in. I'd never seen her out of uniform. She was pretty. Each chair had a number on the back in what looked like red nail polish.

"Trade places with me," Maurey said.

"I don't want to sit next to your brother."

"I can't see the body. Trade places."

After we traded she leaned out in the aisle to stare at Bill. "He looks smaller, and almost healthier."

"That's the makeup."

"Wouldn't Bill be embarrassed if he knew he was going to eternity in Max Factor powder base and rouge."

Coach Stebbins said, "*Shh*," which I thought was rude. Petey gave Annabel a running commentary of the deal and nobody *shh*ed him. The brat.

A woman with large breasts and a print dress stood up and sang "Amazing Grace" in a beautiful voice. I was moved. It was nice to think one thing about Bill's death wasn't bland. Maurey told me the woman, Irene Innsbruck, sings at most funerals and weddings in GroVont. She's the town talent.

Then a man in a gray suit went up front and read Bill's war record. It's funny, but when you're young and you see a really old person, you never think of them as having done all kinds of various, creative things when they were young themselves. Bill sat in his booth and nodded over coffee. That's all I ever thought of him if I thought anything at all, but he'd done a lot of stuff in the war and afterward. He saved some Englishmen from a machine gunner once and got a medal. And he traveled across Russia back when the Communists were killing everyone in sight. Later, he came home and started a lumber company with Oly. All that, I thought, just to fall against a jukebox and die.

Buddy stood up and turned around. He was really big—not like a giant or a fat person—his presence took up a lot of room. Even in the suit, he was the kind of man when he stood up everyone paid attention. If you were ever in a room with Maurey's father you'd always know right where he was. If you said anything, you'd wonder what he thought about it.

He told a story about Bill saving his father's life when a tree twisted and fell wrong. The log lay across Buddy's father's legs in such a way one wrong shift would roll it across his body onto his head. Bill had to chainsaw with the steadiness of a doctor cutting with a scalpel. It was a nice story, even though the avalanche got Buddy's father four years later anyway.

As Buddy told it, he looked straight ahead, and his hands didn't twitch a bit. His beard was the blackest bush I'd ever seen. You could hardly see a mouth in there. I looked at Maurey and could tell she was real proud.

She whispered, "I've heard that story a dozen times. Daddy loves it."

At the cemetery, somebody had built a big fire to unfreeze the ground enough to dig a hole. They'd had to use shovels because they couldn't get a backhoe through the snow. The shovels were leaning against other markers.

Maurey and I stood back by a cottonwood tree. She said, "He had a tumor in his head."

"What makes you think that?"

"Dr. Petrov did an autopsy. He told Daddy a tumor the size of a split pea was why Bill had been hitting Oly the last few months and growling at people. Bill didn't have control over those things he did."

"That ought to make Oly feel better."

"Why?"

The day was all blue and sparkly white. Whoever planned the cemetery put it where family and friends could stand and contemplate an amazing view of the Tetons and the mountains off to the south. The trees behind us practically buzzed with joy at being trees, and a raven circled up by the sun. The only man-made thing in sight was the rodeo grounds, and the stands weren't painted or anything so they looked natural as trees.

I guess it's great being buried in a breathtaking spot, but the contrast between looking at the casket and looking around at the world must confuse mourners. It made me feel funny.

Three older guys in uniforms stood in a line and fired a shot into the air. When the gray-suit guy said a prayer I looked around and saw Buddy Pierce had his eyes open in an unfocused gaze toward Yellowstone. Then his eyes shifted and looked at me. I looked down at my feet.

Sam Callahan lay in the plain pine coffin with his hands folded over his sternum, his blood drained away, replaced by a liquid chemical.

One by one, his family and friends walked past his dead form—his mother and grandfather, his coaches and teachers. Each girl placed a single red rose upon his chest. Charlotte Morris, the Smith twins, Hayley Mills, his baby-sitter from Greensboro, the receptionist at Dr. Petrov's in Jackson. Maurey Pierce came last and her rose was white as snow on the Tetons.

Maurey touched his still hand and said, "You were too young to die, Sam Callahan. We all feel a loss."

Then two funeral directors lowered the coffin lid and Sam's face was touched by light for the last time forever.

Oly stood with his hands at his sides, tiny and cracked and completely disoriented in his suit and hat. The entire marriage and funeral system is set up to make men who work hard feel foolish. I mean, not only was Oly's lifelong sidekick going in the dirt, but now he had to dress like a monkey and deal with the hordes.

Poor guy looked like he'd been hit between the eyes with a mallet. He had the slowest blink I've ever seen. After the ceremony, he didn't move, just kept looking into the hole. Buddy stayed right next to him, like a bear protecting a skinny bird.

"I'm not in the mood to go back to the VFW and eat," Maurey said.

"Is that the plan?"

"Why do women always think food helps?"

She went to tell her mom we were walking back to town and she'd be home later. Annabel was over by the cars and trucks talking to Howard Stebbins. While Maurey explained the deal, Stebbins stared at me meanlike. I guess he didn't approve of the friendship, though I couldn't see how it made crap to him. He probably thought of me as the slimy outsider come to stain local girlhood.

I asked Maurey about this as we followed the county service road the half-mile or so into town.

"Is there a gossip line on us yet?"

Maurey was wearing a dark blue dress and black stockings and new snow boots. Though it was a nice day, I think she was cold. "We're children to these people."

"When they see you coming out of Lydia's cabin they don't suspect ugliness?"

"If we were a couple years older they'd be vicious, we're beyond their fantasies so far. Stebbins thinks your mom might offer me a cigarette—be a bad influence."

"Lydia would never do that."

"Mom's afraid I'll go down to the White Deck and be exposed to french fries. She has this idea that grease is only one step from decadence." Maurey raised her arms out wide and turned around to walk backward. "I don't like winter."

"What's that got to do with gossip?"

"We are no longer discussing gossip. We're thinking how nice it will be at the TM Ranch riding horses with Dad this summer."

"I wasn't thinking about that."

"The TM is up that canyon." She pointed to a crack in the hills. "When the snow melts I can ride my bike up in an hour. I have a horse named Frostbite. He's trained for vaulting but he can run barrels like you wouldn't believe."

The terminology was past my grasp. "Vaulting?"

"Tricks, you know, back mounts, reverse croupers, split-kick dismounts; like a gymnast on a vaulting horse, only our horse gallops. It's fun."

"Sounds like a good way to break your neck."

"Frostbite wouldn't do that to me. He's my baby." Her blue eyes had an in-love misty look.

"What color is he?"

Maurey turned back around to go forward again. She did a little dance step that came out klutzy on account of her boots. "He's a skewbald gelding, five years old but he thinks he's a colt."

"Skewbald?"

She turned on me. "You're the most naïve kid I ever met."

Which is one hell of an attitude if you asked me. I guess naïve is someone who doesn't know what you know. Maurey had never seen a live Negro, so in North Carolina she would be naïve. Neither one of us carried a gun, so in New York we'd both have been naïve. I think. At least I knew that naïve is only a matter of place. Maurey still thought there was a standard.

She stopped walking for a second. "Whenever I try to think about how being dead feels I end up wanting to have more sex. Isn't that odd."

"So let's go to my house."

"I want a Fudgsicle first."

On the edge of town Maurey showed me how to cut between the Highway Department plow sheds into an alley, that ran behind the triangle stores. When we came through the Talbot Taxidermy backyard this little snot of a kid was teasing a snot of a dog with a kitten.

The kid held the kitten up over his head while the dog jumped and howled to get at it.

Maurey screamed, "*Pud.*"

The kid looked over at us with no expression. He had burned bacon-colored hair and a holey nylon coat that seemed stuffed with mattress filler. His jeans were all bloodstained, his shoes spotted by pink cat guts. A kitten head lay on the snow under the prancing dog. Other kitten parts were strewn about the yard. I almost threw up.

Maurey started toward Pud and he lowered the kitten to the very top of the dog's jump. "I'll feed Stonewall."

Maurey froze, her fists closed tight, the veins on her neck gone rope. I drifted off toward the porch to get a better angle at the snot.

"Tell your boyfriend to quit sneaking."

Maurey's lips barely moved when she spoke. "You kill that kitten you're gonna wish you hadn't been born."

Pud studied Maurey out of one eye. The dog was going nuts, barking, leaping, drooling blood from the other kittens. Ugly dog, no tail, box of a body, snubby head—everything repugnant in an animal.

The kitten put out a tiny *mew*. I eased in closer.

"Mom told me to kill the kittens."

"Did she tell you to feed them to Stonewall?"

Pud shrugged. "She said drown 'em. What's the difference?"

"Give the kitten to me. That way you won't have to kill it."

"I want to kill it."

"You do and I'll hurt you real bad."

"My kitten. I can kill it if I want."

With each comeback, their voices went louder and more frantic. I kept easing forward like it was a game of red light/green light and not some king-hell jackshit torturing kittens. The kitten head on the ground had been gray. Its eyes were open.

Pud saw me and stepped back. "Don't."

Maurey put her hands on her hips. "Give us the kitten. That way we won't hurt you."

Pud looked from her to me. He glanced back at the taxidermy and made a decision. "*Mama.*"

I jumped as he dropped the kitten and Stonewall snapped.

I came down on the dog's back with my left hand on his throat and my right hand on his lower jaw. As we rolled through the cat guts he bit the holy heck out of my thumb and index finger. Maurey and Pud were yelling their brains out. The dog and I rolled all the way over; I pulled my hand out of his mouth and got him by the ear. My face was in fur so I bit hard as I could. The dog screamed.

Finally we broke loose and he ran over to Pud, turned and faced me, growling. I spit fur at him. Pud and the dog both had the same crappy expressions on their faces—a mixture of surprise, pain, and mean hate. Their lips quivered.

"He's okay," Maurey said.

"I'm not okay. The jerk bit me."

"The kitten is okay."

Maurey held him to her chest with both hands. The kitten chewed on a button of her coat.

Pud reverted to the whiney brat he was. "I'm gonna tell my brother. He'll kick your butt."

That was a possibility. I pulled myself up and held my bleeding hand over the snow. "They'll kill Stonewall to test him for rabies."

Pud's hand went to the dog's back. "Got no rabies."

"He bit me. They'll have to test and the only way to test is to kill him."

Pud had the ugliest complexion, like peed-on snow. "You bit him too."

"You don't tell Dothan or anyone and I won't tell anyone and your dippy dog won't have to die."

Pud didn't say anything so Maurey and I left with the kitten.

10

"THIS DOESN'T MEAN WE'RE GOING STEADY."

"Sure."

"Move your tongue higher. Right there. Now side-to-side."

I adjusted.

"That's not side-to-side. That's up and down. Do it right."

I adjusted again.

"I mean, we're not even dating. Don't think this is dating or anything. Sometimes you act like we are when we're not. This'll never work if you get the wrong idea. Jesus."

"I wonder if Peter Pan and Wendy did it this way?"

"Don't talk. Work."

"It's not supposed to be work. And move Alice. She's digging in."

"She wasn't weaned. She was way too young to give away."

"Nobody gave her away. Are you wet yet?"

"Don't talk. Lick."

"Well, move Alice."

Maurey leaned forward and picked up Alice who took a chunk of me with her.

"Ouch."

"Are you gonna do your job?"

Maurey put the kitten on her chest and rubbed her with her

check. After a bit, the kitten settled into a steady purr which Maurey tried to match but couldn't.

"I wonder when was the last time Mom and Dad did this? They must have once or twice. I'm not adopted."

"I can't picture Buddy with his tongue out."

"Higher up. You're still too hole-oriented."

"You feel plenty wet to me."

"Don't stop. I like this part better than the rest."

"My jaw hurts. I'm coming up."

"Don't disturb Alice."

"Maybe your mom and dad still have sex."

"Sure. Tell me another one."

I feel like I'm the only kid in America who never believed in Santa Claus. Lydia didn't bring up the subject. I heard things in kindergarten—"What's he bringing you?" "I saw him at the Belk store Saturday"—then they brought one in the morning of our party and made us sit on his lap. He smelled like Caspar's closet.

He asked me what I wanted and I didn't know what to say. I looked at everything but him.

When I asked Lydia, she told me Santa Claus was a personification of free stuff, a childish picture of God, and he didn't exist, but I wasn't permitted to tell the other kids.

"People who don't believe in God have an obligation to keep their mouths shut," she said.

Whole thing zinged right over my head. All I could see was the kids who believed in Santa got paid better than I did.

Christmas morning I stumbled and scratched out of my room to find no Lydia on the couch. I said, "Jeeze, on Christmas even. She's gonna warp me yet," then I headed down her hall and ran into Hank Elkrunner coming out of the bathroom.

He smiled kind of shyly, which I took for an Indian thing because I hadn't seen much shy goodwill in my life. "Happy Christmas, Sam," he said.

"Happy Christmas."

Hank glanced at the closed door to Lydia's room. He had on a pair of white boxers and a leather thong thing around his ankle. More Indian stuff, I guess.

I said, "She went into her room."

Hank nodded. "Your mother is something else."

"What else?"

I shouldn't have done that, made him uncomfortable. He seemed somewhat good for Lydia—got her off the couch anyway—and most of her boyfriends hadn't been good for her. They led her astray. Or she led them astray, depending on whose version you bought.

But I'm always a little odd on the boyfriend deal. On the one hand, I get used to me-and-Mom-against-the-world, and that's comfortable, but then I'm always on the scam for a short-term father figure. Not that any of her boyfriends came close. They mostly either patted me on the head or gave me money to disappear. I can't stand being patted on the head.

Hank would never pat me on the head. I shouldn't have razzed him, but your mom is your mom. You can't go buddy up with every joker pops her in the sack.

"I have something," Hank said. He opened Lydia's door, went in, and closed it behind him. I heard her voice from the bed.

I did the toilet trip—pee, brush teeth, check for zits and facial hair. Since Maurey and I had started our whatever we were doing, my piss had been weird. It came in two streams, a main branch and a little arc of a trickle off to the left. I couldn't decide what that meant. Maybe a Maurey hair had gotten stuck up there and was dividing the flow.

Whatever caused it, there was no way in hell to hit the pot with both streams at once and it was probably the major problem of my life that Christmas. I had to pee sitting down like a little boy or mop the floor with toilet paper after every whiz.

After my mop job, I left the John just as Hank came from Lydia's room. We stopped again, smiling and not looking at each other. "It's in the truck," he said.

"What's in the truck?"

"The thing I have."

I hit the kitchen to make coffee and juice. Lydia taught me how to make coffee before she taught me how to tie shoelaces. I think. This may be an exaggeration, only I can't remember a time when I didn't make the morning coffee. As a kid, I remember standing on a chair to spoon in the grounds. I didn't drink it back then.

Panic mews came from the kitchen closet. When I let Alice out, she freaked, mewing and jumping right to wherever I was about to step. After two nights of her sucking on me so much I never slept, I'd taken to locking her and her box in the closet. A kid's got to get his rest.

I poured a little half-and-half in a cereal bowl and she went at it like I'd starved her for a week. Lydia padded barefoot and robed into the kitchen. She yawned and pushed at her hair. "Should have let the mangy dog eat her."

"Merry Christmas, Mom."

She gave me the look, but for a change didn't pursue the mom deal. "Hank says Happy Christmas and Merry New Year instead of the normal way. Do you think that's a Blackfoot trait or is he trying to irritate me?"

Her bathrobe was this white terrycloth thing that came down about midthigh and tied with a blue cord, real sexy-looking, even on her.

"Are you still claiming your dry spell?"

She smiled and came over to warm her hands against the coffeepot. "No, honey bunny, the drought is broken."

"Please don't call me that in front of him."

"The drought is flooded. The drought has been blown into the Atlantic Ocean."

"Are we going to keep him?"

Even though the pot wasn't through perking, Lydia poured herself a weak cup. She never did have any patience with coffeepots. "Don't be ridiculous. He's not a kitten or a sweater."

"I never said he was."

"Besides we won't be here that long."

Hank walked into the kitchen carrying a rifle. For one horrible moment I flashed on a Wyoming ritual I hadn't known before. Sleep with a woman, then shoot her son. Hank two-handed the rifle to me.

"Happy Christmas."

"What is it?"

"Ruger. Twenty-two caliber. Good first gun for a young man."

Lydia went into a frown. "I'm not sure I approve of firearms for children." I wasn't sure either.

"Sam's not a child."

I was glad to hear that. Hank's face was interesting as I took the gun from him. His eyebrows came closer together and his mouth was thinner. Maybe giving a kid his first gun was a big deal to him.

"Is it loaded?"

"No, but always pretend it is. Don't point it at anything you are unwilling to kill."

Lydia blew across her coffee. "That's the only purpose for a gun, to kill things, right?"

Hank kept his eyes on me. "Protection, security, dignity, procurement of meat."

Lydia went on, "And killing is unethical."

I'd never held a gun before. Caspar wasn't into guns. It was heavier than I'd imagined from *Gunsmoke* or *The Rebel.* Those guys tossed rifles around like sticks. I couldn't see where it gave me dignity, but it felt neat. Let's see Dothan Talbot crap at me. I'd take out his kneecaps.

Hank said, "Can't be a real local if you don't have a gun."

Lydia set her cup down with a click. "We have no intention of being real locals."

Lydia kept up the bitching clear through breakfast, but you could tell her heart wasn't in it. Sometimes she'd lose control and smile, and once I saw her brush her hand against Hank's. Since it was Christmas, I made French toast—put some flour and old Kahlua in the batter for flavor. One thing about growing up with a mom who won't cook or do laundry, you won't hit fourteen helpless and woman-needy.

After breakfast, Lydia poured Kahlua in her coffee refill and we trooped out to the living room to open more presents.

I sat in the center of the couch with them on both sides. It was kind of homey if you're into homey. The presents were lined up on the coffee table. A new radio sat on top of a box from Caspar.

"I didn't have time to wrap it," Lydia said, which I thought was interesting since, technically, she didn't do anything.

"It's neat," I said.

"I figured if the TV is useless, we might as well have some music around here."

The big box from Caspar was a white suit straight out of Faulkner. It was an exact duplicate of the one he wore like a uniform, summer and winter. It was like he had a duty to wear that suit to set an example for Lord knows who. Mine even came with a yellow bow tie.

"I'll look like a goose."

Lydia touched the material with her index finger. "Great costume for sipping mint juleps and putting darkies in their place."

"I don't know a darkie."

"Perhaps I could qualify," Hank said.

Lydia did a smirk. "I'm the one to put you in your place." She reached along the couch and pulled on Hank's ear. He blushed and I like to barfed. There's something putrid about your mother being nice to someone.

Caspar had sent Lydia a twenty-volume set, *Dictionary of American Biography*. Postage alone could have fed GroVont for two days. "Oh, good, a table," Lydia said. She stacked them up next to the arm on her end of the couch and set her coffee cup on *Werdin to Zunser*.

I'd gotten her a harmonica. One thing you have to admire about Lydia, she's honest. If she doesn't like something, she doesn't spare anybody's feelings.

"Oh," she said. "How interesting." She blew one squawk note and put it next to her coffee cup. I didn't feel bad. Lydia is impossible to buy things for and I'd gotten over the personal-rejection crush years earlier when I hand-made and varnished a jewelry box out of Popsicle sticks and she accidentally stepped on it.

Since then, I'd been buying her things I wanted.

Hank was new to the deal though. I felt kind of sorry for him when she sniffed at his Indian bead earrings. They were real pretty.

"They're real pretty," she said in a tone like they weren't. Maybe she thought they were. Whenever Lydia says something sincere it comes out sounding like irony. She saves her truth tone for lies to Caspar.

Living around Caspar and Lydia was always tense, but Christmas things got even more tense than usual. Christmas is like an intensifier—good things are real good and bad things are worse; and things at the manor house never were king-hell neat to start with.

Or maybe it was on account of Me Maw being dead. Christmas is the season for missing dead people.

Whatever it was, Caspar got crabbier and Lydia bitchier and I mostly stayed in my room and played with whatever game they'd sprung for that year. Caspar was big on educational stuff—chemistry sets, butterfly nets. When I was young Lydia bought stuff for old kids and when I got older she bought stuff for toddlers.

The year before our banishment, she got me an Etch A Sketch that said right on the package, "For children 4 through 9."

It was a weird Christmas too. Caspar's hearing aid wasn't working—that or he had it turned off—so whenever I thanked him for a gift, he said "What's that?" and I had to thank him over and over.

My main present was a toy construction company. "Build your first plant," Caspar said. "Commerce."

"What's that?" I asked, looking at all the plastic bricks with lock-in nubs on top, and the girders and wheels and stuff. Gave me the same feeling as a snake—I had no desire in the world to touch any of it.

"Commerce," Caspar grunted again. He stood over me with his arms folded and his little yellow mum and bow tie giving him a smug Captain Kangaroo-type glow. I guess him buying me my first industrial plant to build was like Hank giving me a rifle, a tradition deal. I'm not big on tradition deals.

Just as Caspar said "Commerce" the second time, Lydia wandered into the parlor barefoot in a shortie nightie. She liked to go skimpy around the Carolina house because it made Caspar nervous. All that skin flashing ended when we moved to Wyoming.

She walked over by the fake Christmas tree and lit a cigarette. Her legs were knobby. "Talk sentences in front of Sam, Daddy. He'll grow up thinking men snort instead of using speech."

Caspar glared at her. "If you were a union I'd break you in half."

Lydia blew smoke out her nostrils. "I'm not a union, I'm a daughter."

"Nothing but Communists in the unions. I loathe Communists."

The cook, who was Negro and named Flossie Mae, brought me a waffle and a glass of grapefruit juice.

"Paw Paw can't hear today," I said.

He rocked back on his heels and muttered, "Honor sinks where commerce long prevails."

Lydia took my grapefruit juice and drank it. "He can hear when it's convenient. Daddy, I need some money."

Caspar said, "Commerce is America and America is bound together by carbon paper. Without carbon paper there are no records and without records all is chaos and deprivation."

Lydia smiled at Caspar. "Daddy, have you seen my diaphragm? I'll be needing it at the cotillion this afternoon."

Caspar turned and left. Lydia watched while I buttered and syruped the waffle, then she took it away from me. "He can hear fine," she said.

I sat on the floor surrounded by construction blocks and watched her eat the waffle, wondering what diaphragm meant.

Koreans poured off the hill like sweat off a fat man's forehead. Lead flowed freely as champagne after the seventh game of the World Series. Men died easily as cornflakes turn soggy in milk.

The lieutenant grabbed his throat, gurgled once, and fell. The men turned to Sergeant Callahan.

"What do we do now?" they asked.

"We become the vengeful fist of God." Callahan snarled.

Tommy gun at his hip, Callahan stepped from the bunker and began spraying the hillside with the fire of death. Koreans splattered themselves amongst the rocks. Out of ammo, Callahan threw down the tommy gun and picked up a bazooka. Still firing from the hip, he began marching up the ridge, murdering masses of human beings with each stride.

"Want to learn to shoot?" Hank asked.

"Will I have to kill stuff?"

We left Lydia to do whatever Lydia does and drove over to the dump in Hank's truck. The truck was pretty cool, a '47 Dodge panel deal with electrical tape for a passenger window and a mountain of tools and animal horns and tires and stuff piled in the back so whenever he hit the brakes, the whole mess slid *whump* against the cab.

"How old were you when you first fired a rifle?" I asked Hank.

"Four-and-a-half."

"Gee."

"My little brother taught me."

I wasted ten minutes trying to figure if he was kidding. It was stupid. If you don't know anything about people how can you tell when they're exaggerating? With Lydia, her face stays straight but she moves her hands when she lies. You couldn't tell squat from studying Hank.

"What do you do when you aren't at our house?"

Hank slowed down to pass a hawk tearing at a dead lump of fur. I couldn't tell what the fur used to be. "I get by. Unemployment now, peel logs in the spring, fight fires some summers. My family is on the Kiowa roles so a government check comes every few months."

"Lydia said you're a Blackfoot."

He nodded. "No money in Blackfoot blood. My grandfather was wise, he traded a bottle of moonshine to get listed as Kiowa. Wish he'd done the trade with a Navajo. Navajo's the best-paid minority in the West. Get all the girls too."

"Maybe I can be Navajo."

He glanced at me. "You're short enough."

At the dump, we walked around awhile, looking at the neat stuff. It was like mostly garbage with a second-hand store scattered around. Hank told me that people who dumped something usable would set it away from the muck so other folks could take it home. I saw a lamp I could have used, but dump stuff seemed a little weird at the time. It might have had germs or something. There was a perfectly good Christmas tree.

"Why would someone dump a Christmas tree right before Christmas?" I asked.

Hank shrugged. Sometimes Hank talked like a regular person, then all of a sudden he'd catch himself and go back to *Ugh* and placid facial expressions. I think he saw too many cowboy and Indian movies; he thought people expected inscrutability. That would be a big plus in Lydia's eyes. She could babble away without interruption.

The day was way clear, but below zero, which is cold no matter what anyone tells you about humidity and wind chill and all that kind of crap. I had on six layers and a sock hat and I was still cold. Hank wore a jeans jacket over two wool shirts. He kept his hands in his pockets and made me carry the Ruger.

"Where do you live?" I asked.

He pulled a hand from a pocket and pointed north, up the Dubois road.

"In a tipi?"

Hank's shoulders moved up and down in that silent laugh of his. "Twelve-foot Kozy Kamper. Freeze your butt off in a tipi in winter."

"Have you ever lived in a tipi?"

"Slept in a Cheyenne lodge at the Sun Dance couple years ago. Guy owned it got drunk and knocked down a flap pole, filled it with smoke. I crawled out the side and slept on the ground. That won't happen in a Kozy Kamper."

"Do Blackfeet get drunk a lot?"

Hank didn't answer. He stepped across some partly burnt mattresses and picked up a blackened bucket. He carried it to a pile of trash down in a gullylike place and set it on a dead washing machine. "Big target. You won't miss."

"What if somebody comes along?"

"No law against shooting buckets."

"The dump road's back there."

We walked over and looked behind the line of junk at the plowed out road twisting between dump piles. There was an incredible number of dead cars. They were everywhere. It was like an end-of-the-world movie.

"Any misses'll go over a pickup," Hank said.

"What about a dump truck?"

"No dumps on Christmas."

Hank showed me how to pop out the magazine thing and load cartridges. "Butt first, see. Hard to get it wrong."

"Can these kill elk and moose?"

He shook his head. "Squirrels, chiselers, beaver if you're sixty-seventy feet in. People. Kill people dead."

"But not elk."

"Lung shot might do it, but they'd run a ways and be in pain. The harmonious man kills the animal without hurting it."

"Like with the rifles in your gun rack?"

He nodded and snapped in the magazine. He pulled back the bolt, down, up, shoved it forward. "Safety here, red line means it's off."

"It won't fire with the safety on?"

"That is why you call it a safety."

He handed me the rifle. I felt kind of like I did following Maurey into the bedroom the first time. Sort of. I'd fantasized women's breasts often, but I'd never fantasized firearms. Most of my violent daydream short stories involved hand-to-hand battles, although if the other guy deserved it sometimes I'd pick up a baseball bat and pound his head. Only real fights I'd been in were nothing like movies or books—more wrestling, less pounding.

"Shoot the bucket," Hank said. I raised the rifle to my shoulder. The barrel end wouldn't be still.

"Sight down the bottom of the V."

I sighted and pulled the trigger. Nothing happened.

"Safety's on," Hank said. "Remember I told you about the safety."

I lowered the rifle and pushed the safety button.

"Don't point at me," Hank said.

"Sorry."

I raised the rifle again and waited for the bucket to come into the V.

"Squeeze the trigger instead of pulling."

I squeezed, the gun jumped and powed in my ear.

A bad *yelp* came from behind the gully line.

"Shit," Hank said.

I threw down the rifle and ran forward. Soapley's dog, Otis, was on the road, scream-yelping and dragging himself after the truck. Soapley hit the brakes and jumped out. "He never fell off before."

Hank was at my side. "We shot him off."

"You shot my dog?"

"I didn't do it on purpose."

Everything kind of froze up on me. Hank was suddenly at the dog, bending over with his bandana out. Soapley looked at me, then he was there too. I didn't know what to do. I wanted to go back and start the day again. They worked over Otis's back end. Soapley said "Aw, hell" once.

After a few seconds Otis quit yelping and lay there helpless, which was even worse than the noise. I got down and held his head so he wouldn't flounder around. His eyes couldn't understand. They were scared and hurt and trusting and it was my fault.

"Think he's gone?" Soapley asked.

Hank's hand held fur under the right hind armpit. There was a lot of blood. "Vet might save him. Worth a try. It'll cost a lot and you might lose him anyway."

Soapley looked at the head under my hand. "I'm real attached to the old guy."

"My grandfather'll pay any bills it takes to save him," I said, hating myself for saying it. "I'm real sorry."

Soapley's face held what I took as disgust. I don't know, I'd be disgusted if I was a grown-up and some snot-nosed kid shot my dog and said his grandfather would pay to fix it. I was no better than Pud doing it on purpose.

"Let's load him in the truck," Soapley said.

They held arms under Otis and lifted him careful as they could, but he was in pain, you could tell. His tongue was way out and he trembled bad. I ran ahead to open the truck door and help get him in.

I hate it when things happen to me that really matter. I mean, it's so easy to roll through the days, enjoying the irony of a weird mom or a school full of half-wits, exploring growing up with Maurey. The Kennedy-death thing had mattered, but from afar. This thing with Otis was right up close and my fault. I couldn't be cool and slightly above the situation, which was awful.

Otis lay across my lap with his head on my left thigh and his wounded hip on Hank all the way to the vet's. Hank had made a tourniquet out of his bandana, but there was still so much blood. I could see the white bone in the hole and the back side where the bullet came out was ripped and jagged.

But looking at the mess was better than looking at his face. His eyes hurt me. Pain without understanding is torture. Soon his eyes dulled up some and the quivering got worse. Soapley didn't say anything. I wanted him to cuss me, or talk to Otis or something, but he just drove with his eyes forward and his right hand on Otis's neck.

The vet was eating Christmas dinner and I doubt if he was happy to see us. His name was Dr. Brogan, he had a widow's peak hairline and forearms of a wrestler. He was real severe and scared the wadding out of me.

"Who shot him?" Dr. Brogan asked as he bent over Otis in the truck.

"I did," I said. "I didn't mean to."

"It was my fault," Hank said.

"No, it wasn't."

"You two girls can argue over who did it later. Let's get him inside."

Dr. Brogan went to the house and brought back a stiff stretcherlike thing. Hank and Soapley carried Otis into the animal clinic next to the house. That left me to walk in with the vet.

"You do this often," he said.

"Today's the first time I ever fired a gun."

Brogan grunted. I know he hated my guts. I usually don't mind people hating me, it's their choice, but this guy had just cause so it felt really bad.

They lay Otis on the table and raised his right hind leg with a line-and-pulley deal attached to the ceiling. Brogan gave him an injection in the front leg to reduce the pain, then he studied the place where I shot him.

"What a mess. You did this with a twenty-two?"

"Yes, sir." Hank and Soapley were at the end of the table, holding Otis's head and shoulders. His eyes were closed now so at least I didn't have to face that look anymore.

The doctor cleaned and probed and messed around a long time. He clamped off the exposed artery to stop the bleeding. It looked like a thin worm. The muscles were pink and way down in there the shoulder bone glistened white.

Brogan turned to Soapley. "He's lost the leg."

Soapley swallowed but didn't say anything.

Brogan went on. "See here, the bullet took out all the blood vessels and shattered the bone. I can't believe a twenty-two could cause this much damage."

It all looked like gore to me. I'd never seen any real gore before, unless you count the dead kittens, which count I guess. I felt sick and wanted to go out to the truck and lie down. Christmas was wrecked.

"Do it," Soapley said.

Brogan pulled out an electric razor and started shaving Otis's leg above and below the wound. "Dogs don't get near as traumatized losing limbs as people do. They only know what is, so there's no dwelling on what might have been. He'll be up chasing meter readers in three days."

Hank spoke. "Can the boy wait outside while we do it?"

Brogan's eyes were lightning harsh. "He's going to shoot things, he needs to see the consequences."

I watched his fingers working over the exposed flesh. I said, "You're right."

The big upshot of the deal was I never want to shoot a gun again. People can call me wimp or city whuss or whatever, but as I watched all the cutting and sawing and sewing, I knew that I caused this and I didn't want to cause anything like it from now on.

Brogan went two inches or so up from the wound and slit the skin all the way around. He cut through the fatty layer, then the muscles and laid them back in flaps. It looked like cutting a chicken thigh off the breast. When he cut through the joint, the knife made a scraping sound.

"You going to pass out on me?" he said without looking up.

I glanced down at Hank and Soapley. Their faces were blank, although Soapley was sweating some. "No, sir."

Otis's front paws did a digging motion, so Brogan stopped to give him another injection. Then he clamped off three blood vessels and tied them with black thread. After he made the final cut, he handed me the leg.

"Souvenir."

"You don't have to do that," Hank said.

Brogan started sewing the muscle flaps shut. "Yes, I do."

"It was as much my fault as the boy's."

"You two can share it."

Dr. Brogan wanted to keep Otis overnight. Hank and I waited outside while Soapley did a short good-bye thing, then we sat in the truck and rode back to the dump. I had the leg on my lap. It was mostly black with a large white spot near the top and a smaller one down lower. The toenails were black.

At Hank's truck, I wanted to tell Mr. Soapley I was sorry, but I started crying and he only stared out at the mounds of garbage. He wouldn't look at me or say anything. Hank went over and got my rifle and unloaded it. He made me hold it on the ride into town. I went in the house with the rifle in my right hand and Otis's leg in my left.

11

The day after Christmas I took to my bed with no intention of getting up again. I didn't think, I will never get up again, I just didn't think at all. I knew this was it. I would lie there until I rotted from the inside and mold grew across my face and armpits.

You think you're doing fine, zooming along through the day-to-day, more or less above the deal. I'm making out okay in school, learning all this new sexual territory with a pretty girl, going where you're supposed to want to go, Lydia's in a practically human phase, Hank's a nice enough guy, then I go and blow the leg off a dog and *whomp*, nothing means squat anymore.

I wanted to go backward, to before fucking and before I shot anything, back to North Carolina where I was young. Nothing mattered then either but I didn't know it. Christmas Day in Greensboro I would have been playing basketball in Jesse Otake's driveway. He always made me play point guard because he was an inch taller. I would have ridden my three-speed over to Bobby McHenry's garage to watch his older brother with the cigarette pack twisted into the T-shirt sleeve break down the clutch on his '59 Chevy.

I sure wouldn't have spent Christmas at the dump with an Indian. I never saw a dump in Greensboro. You put the trash on the curb Friday morning and it disappeared. Nobody cared where it went. Dogs didn't ride on top of truck cabs. Indians stayed out of sight.

I wanted to see the ground. How could we live in a place with no ground? And no railroad tracks, and no curb markets or McDonald's or car washes or hotel elevators. Hell, no hotels. I woke up every morning and looked at the ceiling and saw two dead animals with giant bug-eyes and horns. That couldn't be a healthy first sight every day for a person.

My thing got stiff and I lay on my side with one eye open and stared at Otis's leg on my desk next to my typewriter.

The nurse checked on the IVs and crept soundlessly from the room. The boy's grandfather waited anxiously in the hall.

"Well?"

"He says he's fed up. He will no longer accept pain."

"It's all my fault."

"That's what he thinks."

"I should have taken him more seriously. I shouldn't have banished him away from his friends and coaches."

"He says he'll never move again until somebody loves him."

"Poor boy."

Early afternoon the need to pee overcame the need to be in a coma, so I padded barefoot across the house and came back by way of the kitchen where Lydia sat in her white nightgown, working a crossword puzzle.

She had a blue spot on the edge of her mouth where she'd been sucking on an ink pen. She held the pen in her hand like a cigarette with her long, thin fingers pointed at the ceiling.

"Ten-letter word for lampoon."

I opened the refrigerator and looked in at a stick of butter, a jar of dill pickles, a bottle of French salad dressing, and five Dr Peppers. *"Satirize."*

She counted out letters on boxes. "Too short."

"Lydia, would you explain to me about women."

She glanced up at me, then back at the puzzle. "Cold enough in here without the fridge open."

I took the pickles over to the table and sat across from her. I could see the puzzle upside down. Lots of answers had been written in and scribbled out so it was hard to figure what was what.

Lydia filled in a couple of letters. "I thought I already told you about girls."

"I don't mean dicks and tunnels and babies. I want to know why they do what they do."

"Come on, Sam. Nobody knows why anybody does anything. Give me one of those."

"Maurey and I perform sex and I feel something odd for her but she keeps telling me we're just friends and nothing mushy is going on."

Lydia took one of my pickles. "So?"

"Isn't sex the definition of mushy?"

"Four-letter word for dessert. *Cake*? *Tart*? *Pies*?" She tried a letter then blacked it out. "You're lucky she's your friend. In all probability, you'll have a lot more lovers than friends in your life. And you're too young for any deep emotional entanglement." She bit the tip off the pickle. "This way you get the fun of love without the heartbreak."

"But what if I like her and get my heart broke anyway?"

She looked back up at me for a second. "Then you're a sucker."

"Maurey's looking forward to going on dates."

"Aren't you?"

"She thinks she can go to the movies with some guy and flirt and neck, then come back here and get in bed with me and tell me about it."

"Wish I had a deal like that."

"I think it's bizarre, even for us."

"Caricature."

"What?"

"Ten-letter word for lampoon—*caricature.*" She stuck her pen tip in her mouth.

"Is Hank a lover or a friend?"

"Don't be impertinent." She switched pen for pickle.

"Impertinent? Lydia, we passed that six years ago when I started fetching your Gilbey's. You can't be a buddy when it's convenient and a mother when it's not."

"You've been reading too many books."

I sat there scarfing pickles and watching her concentrate on something other than me. Even upside down, I knew several of the answers, but I wasn't about to help her.

"Hank is a suitor," Lydia said.

"That's awfully Southern of him."

"He's kind of a Southern boy. You know he feels terrible about yesterday."

"When are we going back to the South, Mom?"

Lydia crunched on her pickle and ignored me.

New Year's Day I went over to the Pierces' to watch the Cotton Bowl on their TV. Buddy was home, leaned back in the recliner, sipping on a beer with a plate of Annabel's snickerdoodles on a tray next to his hand. Maurey and I sat on the couch but she didn't watch the game. She pulled a cushion up against the arm and sat sideways, reading a book in the old lounging position of bare feet up against my leg.

I felt a little strange, what with her touching me in front of her dad—I've never done well with other people's dads—only he didn't seem to care. It was hard to tell since his face was mostly hair, beard, and two black eyes like periods at the end of a sentence nobody could read. I wondered if that was an outdoorsman deal they developed to stalk game or if Buddy was the only one with marble eyes. When Hank's face shut down, it was like a stone slid over his face and he was untouchable, but Buddy's emotionless look was softer, more like Pushmi and Pullyu over my bed at home.

He talked some about a mule deer that scored a 186 on the Boone and Crockette and a shed roof that caved under the snow, a weasel that had crawled into a generator to get warm and fried itself—not much conversation for the three hours I watched the game. Maurey hung on his every word.

It was Navy against Texas for the national championship. Navy had a king-hell hot-stuff quarterback named Roger Staubach. He zipped passes all over the field, kind of the football equivalent of classical guitar. Magic fingers. Even I could spot style.

Unfortunately, Navy's defensive line was outweighed about thirty-five pounds a head, and by the middle of the fourth quarter Texas pretty much had a wrap.

Petey spread a ton of Christmas toys around the floor so whenever Annabel brought in another round of food and drink she had to lift her feet and titter. She said, "Go play in your room, Petey," in a tone of voice that wouldn't move a rabbit off a road.

One of Petey's games looked like fun. It was a table soccer deal with knobs you turned to kick the ball at the goalie. I wanted to get on the floor and play it with him, only Maurey would take that as a sign of immaturity.

The book she was reading was *Lolita* by Vladimir Nabokov. She'd given it to me for Christmas.

"It's about a girl our age coming to terms with her emerging sensuality," she told me before she borrowed it back. She told Annabel it was by the same author who wrote Peter Pan.

My Christmas present to Maurey was a Pro-Line Frisbee. I

found an ad for it in the back of the *Sporting News* and sent off to a place in Ohio. Could well have been the first Frisbee in northwest Wyoming, which isn't saying much.

"We had a boy from North Carolina in my company on Iwo Jima," Buddy said, apropos to diddley. "Had a thick accent the guys made fun of. Lost his leg to a mine. Why don't you have a thick accent?"

"My grandfather was from New York. I guess you talk more like your family than your neighbors."

He eyed me over a snickerdoodle. "Kid's name was Martin Symons. Said his grandmother could heal by faith, she smoothed over scabs with Coca-Cola. Is that something people talk about down there?"

"Not that I've heard."

"I thought Symons's accent was fake until he stepped on a mine he'd set out only ten minutes earlier. He was screaming, 'M'laig, m'laig.'"

"Daddy got a Bronze Star," Maurey said.

"What for?"

Buddy popped the cookie in his mouth and chewed as he talked. "Killing folks. Army put a lot of stock in that talent."

"Oh."

"Lot of things they send you to prison for are considered heroic in the right circumstances."

"Like murder?"

"I'd never let a son of mine join the army."

Petey rolled on his back and did a "*Pow, pow*" bit with his thumb and index finger. I decided Buddy Pierce wasn't such a jerk after all.

Maurey kicked me with her foot. "Let's go for a walk."

"But the game's not over."

She swung her legs off the couch and bent down on a sock search. "I'm hungry."

Wrong thing to say about the time Annabel brought in our third tray of homemade junk food. "I made coconut kisses."

Petey yippied and made a run for the whatever.

Maurey said, "I want a malt. Get up, Sam."

"Navy might pull it out." Texas was up 28-6.

"Sam, this book makes me think of other things." She sent me a heavy-duty meaningful move-it stare and I caught on.

"Yeah, a malt's just what I need."

The sky was the same color as the ground and low clouds hid the Tetons so it made GroVont seem like a town in an envelope. I was getting tired of off-white, maybe because winter in Grotina only lasts two and a half or three months and my body knew time should be up.

"Don't you ever miss dirt?" I asked Maurey as we walked up Alpine.

"Is Lydia home?" Whenever I say something a woman doesn't understand or want to hear, she doesn't hear it. It's not like she ignores me, more like migratory deafness.

"She's down with a killer hangover. Her and Delores went into Jackson last night and she didn't come home till dawn. She'd lost her shoes somewhere and about had frostbite."

"So she's at your house."

"Dead asleep when I left. Hank called a couple times. I think she didn't feel like a wholesome New Year's Eve so they had a spiff."

"Maybe she'll sleep through it."

I knew what "it" was so I shut up. Ft. Worth drove by in his new Ford pickup truck and waved at us. Then Soapley came by. Otis rode inside now, with his two good front feet up on the dash. I'd taken meat scraps to him several times lately and played with him some in the snow. Whenever Otis saw me he would wag his short tail and jump around, which made me feel bad because he didn't know what I'd done. Soapley said it was okay. Otis didn't remember he'd ever had more than three legs.

"Dogs only know how they feel right now," Soapley had said. "They don't know nothing about before or after."

Soapley gave us the Wyoming road wave of four fingers with the thumb under the steering wheel.

"Is the leg still on your desk?" Maurey asked.

"I went to Kimball's for Lydia's cigarettes Friday and it was gone when I came home. I guess either her or Hank got rid of it."

"It looked kind of gross next to the typewriter."

I shrugged. I hadn't seen all that much difference between a leg on a desk and a moose head on the wall. "It was starting to smell some."

Dot drove by on her way to the White Deck. She pulled over and rolled down her window to ask if we wanted a ride. Dot had put on five more pounds since I met her. It was strange that I'd been in GroVont long enough to notice changes. I didn't really like the idea.

"We'd rather walk, it's a nice day," Maurey said, which was a lie. It wasn't a nice day, it was drab, and I'd rather have ridden.

"Chuckette Morris is having a party next Saturday night," Maurey said after Dot moved on down the road. "You're coming to it."

Maurey had on this dark blue parka thing that made her hair look nice, as if her face was in a frame. It had giant caves for pockets and looked warm. Her parents had given it to her for Christmas.

I asked, "Why?"

Maurey glanced at me and smiled. "Chuckette thinks you have a cute nose. Weird, huh?"

"Chuckette told you this?"

"She asked me if you and I liked each other."

"What'd you say?"

"I told her that was silly. Don't look at me that way. She meant 'like,' as in the right way, as in boys and girls."

"You like me but in the wrong way?"

"I like you as a friend."

I thought that was the point. "As a friend is the right way to like somebody."

Maurey put both hands in her parka pockets. "There's two ways I can like, Sam—as a friend or as a boyfriend."

"And the two ways never overlap?"

She laughed. "Of course not. I couldn't talk like this to a boy I liked."

What could I say? I was strung out on the girl I was sleeping with but we weren't allowed to connect except on a deeper friendship level. I'd of had to be a grown-up not to be confused.

Maurey went on as if she didn't know she was addling me. "She's inviting four or five couples. Her mom is making fondue, that's where you dip food into melted stuff."

"I know what fondue is. Who will you be there with?"

She didn't say anything for a few steps so I knew the answer wouldn't be neat.

"Dothan Talbot."

I stopped and she went on a ways, then turned back. "Don't go all freaky on me, it's just a date."

"But he's our mortal enemy."

"He's your mortal enemy."

"Dothan cheered when John Kennedy died. He rubbed our faces in the snow."

"He told me he's sorry. He was jealous when he saw you sitting with me. He's liked me since the fifth grade."

"Do you like him, as in boys and girls the right way."

She came toward me. "That's not the point. Dothan's

sixteen and can drive a car. We could double with you and Chuckette sometime. You need to get out and meet people."

"Me and Chuckette."

"She's got a lot of personality."

—·—

In my room we undressed quietly so as to not wake Lydia.

"You remember when Delores was saying she gets wet just from talking about doing it?" Maurey asked.

"Kim Schmidt tore this T-shirt in gym a couple of weeks ago. Look at that."

"I think I know what she means. I was reading *Lolita* and there was this part where a real old man and a girl went to the edge of doing it."

"Perfectly good shirt. I look like a hobo."

"Then the author skipped like they all do, but now I know what happened next. And I got kind of excited."

"You're wearing a bra."

"Don't make a big deal out of it, Sam. If you make a big deal I'm going home."

"Do you need a bra?"

"A young lady of sexual experience must be aware of certain things."

"If you're doing it, you should wear a bra whether you need one or not?"

"I need one. Or I will soon. Look at that."

"Where?"

"Don't be a doof, Sam."

"Let's stand side by side next to the mirror and see if your chest sticks out more than mine."

We tried and Maurey was right. She did have breasts. The one on the right was a tad bigger than the one on the left. We moved to the bed.

"What's this?" Maurey asked.

"A mole."

"You sure it's not cancer."

"If it turns black and falls off it's cancer. Right now it's just a mole."

"Does it hurt if I touch it?"

"I don't think so. It feels kind of neat."

"Touch me there."

"Can we kiss this time? It seems weird to learn all this stuff about doing it and not learn how to kiss."

"Have you ever kissed a girl? Move your fingers in a circle now."

"Of course I've kissed girls. Loads."

"I bet you haven't. I bet you got screwed before you got kissed."

"I have too kissed girls."

"Let's see if you can kiss. Only no getting syrupy. It's only practice."

I went in for what seemed like a Rock Hudson-Doris Day knock-your-socks-off smacker.

Maurey said, "Open your mouth, for Chrissake."

"Let me try again."

"Stick out your tongue this time."

"Right."

"Not like that. Move it around some. Softer, like a lick, not like you're mad at somebody. Pretend you're down there only the crack goes sideways instead of up and down."

"Where'd you learn so much about kissing?"

"That one was better, only less suction and open your mouth even wider. Try to touch as much of me at once as you can."

"I bet you've kissed Dothan Talbot lots of times."

"It's time for you to make me wet now."

"But I'm enjoying this. Can't you get wet this way?"

"I'm tingly. I want to see what it feels like with your tongue. Try licking your way down."

I did Maurey's neck and the little brown bull's-eye tits, right first, then left. It was kind of fun, like feeding on a pool table. I played in her belly-button hole awhile until she pushed me down lower. Her breathing was different, faster.

"You're gonna be good at this someday," Maurey said.

"I'm good at it now."

When I finally licked down to the taco shell, I went way to the bottom and deep for a few seconds, then up to the top where Mom had shown us the magic spot. By listening to Maurey's breathing, I could tell what was what—when to go up or down or around, when to put on more pressure or less. I must have been at it a good while because I went into a neat Hayley Mills fantasy.

"Oh, Sam, you make me so wet. I'm nothing but a sponge under your lips."

"Oh, Hayley Mills."

"Oh, Sam Callahan."

It sunk in that Maurey's breath had jumped a pitch. Her back was arched against me and her fingers dug at my ears.

"Had enough?" I asked.

"Stop now and I'll kill you."

Then she went louder and moved into audible peeps. I put on some more pressure and Maurey went nuts. Made painful noises and scratched my one ear. Her spine came way up high, banged her magic spot against my teeth, then she fell back deadlike.

I stopped. "Did I hurt you?"

"Holy moley."

"Maurey. I think we did something wrong."

"Holy moley."

"Can you move?"

"Come here, Sammy."

I crawled up the bed and she put her arm around me. I lay in the hollow under her collarbone, next to her little tit. It felt nice, like maybe we were really dating now and not just practicing.

"What happened?" I asked.

"My body blew up."

"That's peculiar."

"I wonder if I messed something up, like maybe I can't have children anymore."

"Maybe it's the other way around, maybe we made you pregnant and that was the baby being made."

Maurey went quiet. I put a hand on her tummy, where I imagined the explosion had created a new kid. "I better go talk to Lydia," she said.

"She's asleep, unless all that noise woke her."

"She can tell me if anything like this ever happened before. Maybe it's normal."

"Maybe all women blow up when they fuck."

"I don't see how what I just did could be normal."

"Mom'll know, she's experienced."

Maurey started to slide off the bed. I sat up and grabbed her arm. "But I haven't put it in yet."

She friend-kissed my cheek and held my thing, "It'll keep."

"I'm ready to get off now."

"This is important, Sam. Your thing will keep."

The special that night at the White Deck was navy beans and hamhock with cornbread. I'd never had beans before we came to Wyoming. Lydia considered beans peasant food and worried about gas. The gas worry might have been for real. Personally, I was a kid, I looked forward to farts, except in class. Anyone who farted in class might as well commit suicide right there for all the bile that was heaped on him.

Lydia had a steak. She was trying to lose weight, although she didn't tell anybody but me, and she'd decided to become a meatatarian. She went over a month on meat, Dr Pepper, and coffee—lost seven pounds, but gained it back again as soon as she returned to normal person's food.

"Did Hank call?" she asked.

"You know he did. He called four times while you were pretending to be asleep."

"I never pretend anything." Lydia inspected her teeth in her knife. She was really paranoid about talking to someone with a chunk of meat hanging out. Dot came by to refill our coffee.

"I hear you're going to Charlotte Morris's party," she said.

Lydia kind of arched an eyebrow at me. She'd never heard of Charlotte Morris.

I looked down at cold beans. "Guess so, I've never been to a party out West. What happens?"

"Same things as a party out East. Records and games where you get flirty with girls other than your date. You'll probably end up in a closet with someone. That always happened to me."

"Never happened to me," Lydia said.

"That's where Jimmy and me kissed the first time, Annabel Watkins's front-hall closet. She's Maurey's mother now. Jimmy kissed me and I like to died. We went steady for seven years, then graduated and got married. You want pie, it's lemon."

I smiled and Dot took that as a yes. Lemon pie is good but I scrape off the meringue. I'm not into meringue.

Dot brought my pie while Lydia sipped on her third cup of coffee. No wonder it took a pint of Gilbey's to put her under at night.

"So you got Maurey off today," Lydia said.

I shaped the meringue into a little snowman with my spoon. "I guess so. We didn't know what it was when it happened."

"It was a female orgasm. Females who don't get them lead sad and cheerless lives."

"It seemed a lot different from a male orgasm."

"As different as ice cream and gin."

"Why do they use the same word?"

As with any question she can't answer, Lydia ignored me. "Maurey's life will never be quite the same again. It's like hearing music for the first time."

"Do you think she'll like me now?"

Lydia did an eye squint at me, then went back to her coffee. "She'll always have a warm spot in her heart when she thinks of you."

"Is that the same as romantic liking?"

"No. Giving orgasms will make you popular, but it won't get you loved. You're lucky. Being popular is more fun."

"I'd rather have her like me."

Lydia lit a Tarreyton. "Here's the deal, Sam. If you sleep with a girl, and afterwards she still likes you as a friend"—Lydia did body language quotation marks with her hands on "as a friend"—"then she's always going to like you as a friend and she's never going to like you as a lover and there's nothing in the hell-bitch world you can do about it."

I considered this over my pie, which really was good, by the way. Good lemon pie goes to those front-of-the-tongue taste buds and dances. It didn't seem fair that there are two ways of liking someone and girls have total control over which way things happened. Why didn't I have a say in the deal? I didn't know if I wanted to grow up and marry Maurey, but I wanted to hold hands with her on the street or buy her a Valentine card or tell the guys in gym class I had a girlfriend.

Unlike the books, fucking or not fucking didn't seem to have any say in which of the two ways a girl liked a boy. Chuckette Morris liked me the right way and we'd never spoken over six words to each other, but Maurey didn't and I'd given her an orgasm.

"What's a female orgasm feel like?" I asked Lydia.

She took a lung-killer hit on her cigarette, as if she fully intended to smoke the whole thing in one big suck. When she exhaled I felt lost in a Hollywood fog machine.

"There are certain things one sex should keep secret from the other."

"Come on, Lydia, Maurey first said her body blew up, then she said it didn't. Is it a spaz thing like mine?"

"It's more like being underwater and your body expands in every direction at once."

"Is this literal or metaphorical?"

Dot came over to drop off the check and Lydia asked her. "Sam wants to know what an orgasm feels like."

Dot went into Jell-O–jiggle laughter. "I swear, I never know what's going to come out of you two's mouths. Ya'll are as entertaining as TV."

Lydia took that as a compliment.

12

Jackie Gleason waddled up to the podium and blew into *the microphone. The immense crowd at the Wyoming State Fair rustled and grew quiet as wind over the prairie. Mr. Gleason turned sideways so he could see the three women and speak into the mike at the same time.*

"Have the judges reached their decision?"

Hayley Mills, Doris Day, and Maurey Pierce all nodded simultaneously.

"The envelope please."

Doris Day stood and handed the paper to Mr. Gleason. Her eyes were glazed and her forehead the most relaxed it had been since babyhood.

Mr. Gleason opened the envelope as he swung back to the crowd. "And the winner of the Wyoming State Fair blue ribbon for orgasming women is," the crowd held its collective breath, "Sam Callahan."

Yea!

As Sam made his modest way to the stage, a band broke into "Semper Fidelis" by John Philip Sousa and the Cheyenne JayCees' fireworks display lit the air. The crowd went wild with enthusiasm.

Sam shook Mr. Gleason's hand and accepted the award. Then he turned to the judges and smiled. At the sight of Sam's tongue, Doris Day passed orgasm again.

—·—

Having never made out or even kissed before Maurey came along, I only knew one way to do it and that caused me some grief at Chuckette's teen party. Grief isn't exactly the word. I didn't care enough for that. More like unpleasantness in an ugly way.

It ended up in the closet just like Dot said it would. Dot comes off as a pleasant ding, but whenever she says something will happen it generally does.

I was about ready to throw up, watching Dothan and Maurey flirt. He came dressed in black corduroys that I wouldn't be caught dead in. He had on this jeans jacket with his shirt not tucked in so the tails flapped around like tabs on the front and back. I hate that. Maurey couldn't say a sentence without touching him and he couldn't say a sentence without her flying off into laughter.

She looked good too. Her eyes were brighter and her breasts seemed to be growing by the day. It was Saturday and every Saturday Annabel drove over to Idaho Falls for the AAUW bridge club, so we'd got in the routine of practicing on Saturday mornings while Lydia was off doing something wholesome on a snowmobile with Hank.

I spent that morning in bed with her but Dothan got the date. What a gyp. Maurey and I about had the practicing thing down. We'd discovered there's more to it than boy-on-top. As long as this stuck to that, you could wander all over the room—the thrill of the odd position. Maurey even got off again, a lot quicker this time. My jaw didn't feel like I'd chewed eight pieces of Topps baseball card gum.

We French kissed a long time afterward and I liked that just fine, better than the actual humping.

"You disappeared," Maurey said.

"I'm right here with you."

"Every now and then your eyes go away and your mind leaves the room. I feel as if I'm somebody else to you."

I rolled off her but stayed where I could see her face. "I make up stories sometimes."

"Like Mark Twain?"

"I guess. If I can't be a baseball player, I'd like to be a writer someday." I'd never told anyone, not even Lydia, that one. I couldn't believe the stuff I exposed to Maurey. I mean, I didn't know her that well outside of the sack.

"When you're with me, you should pay attention."

"Are you really going to this dumb party with Dothan?"

She sat up. "It's impolite to give me a hard time while I'm still glowing from an orgasm."

"Glowing from an orgasm? Where'd you hear that?"

"Redbook. It was a test. And, yes, I'm going with Dothan and you're going with Charlotte. It'll be good for you to watch me with him, keep you from getting attached to me."

"But I'm already attached to you."

"We can't practice anymore if you get attached."

"Okay, I'm not attached. I don't give a hoot for you."

She didn't care either way. "Orgasms make me nauseous. Isn't that weird?"

"Did you ask Lydia about that?"

Maurey leaned back on her shoulders to pull on her panties. "Just don't be squirrelly around Chuckette. This is your big chance to get a girlfriend." Maurey had a beautiful back.

Five hours later we played this idiot game where each girl writes down a name from the first four books of the New Testament and the boys say which one we'd like to be and when there's a match, the guy and girl go in the closet for five minutes of timed fun. Biblical necking.

The damn game was rigged. Every girl there got the boy she'd picked out ahead of time. There were four couples: Kim Schmidt and LaNell Smith, this guy and girl from Jackson named Byron and Sharon, and us. Sharon had long blonde hair and, coming from Jackson, had everyone swamped in the sophistication deal. Chuckette sucked up to her like the Sharon stamp of approval was the last thing in parties. LaNell looked slightly lost without LaDell there to giggle with. She and Kim didn't pass two words with each other outside the closet. I bet nothing happened inside either.

Maurey went first and I said "Luke" because I knew she liked Little Luke on *The Real McCoys*, but Dothan said "John" and got her. They either set it up or she knew he could only remember one book of the Bible. As they were stepping into the closet, Dothan grinned at me and winked—I could have shot his leg off—and as they came out, Maurey smiled at me. God knows why.

In between Chuckette went on about the fondue and 7-Up.

"Try dipping a piece of cauliflower, Sharon. I don't eat hard vegetables on account of my retainer, but I know they're good. We bought the fondue pot in Yellowstone Park." Sharon looked at the cauliflower distastefully without touching it. The fondue pot had a spouting geyser on one side and some little bears following their mother.

Sharon was at least as beautiful as Maurey, who was in the closet. And LaNell wasn't all that bad when she kept her mouth shut. The truth is I was more attracted to every girl at the party than I was to Chuckette, which is kind of sad because when she wasn't sucking up to Sharon she was sucking up to me.

"Want some more 7-Up?" she asked.

"Okay." Out of pity, I dipped some cauliflower in the melted Velveeta. I always feel like crap when I do something out of pity.

"Do you like 'Dominique' by the Singing Nun?" Chuckette asked. "It's number-one on every station."

I nodded and Sharon sniffed. Byron spent the whole party inspecting his boots. Kim and LaNell sat on the couch with paper plates on their laps. Neither one looked at anybody or said anything, except once when Kim did his barfing-dog imitation.

"I think Dion is gross," Sharon said.

Chuckette and I agreed immediately.

"Gross," said Chuckette.

"Gross," I said.

LaNell coughed politely.

Since the whole valley seemed to have me fated for Chuckette Morris, I'd gotten the lowdown from Maurey. Chuckette didn't have a tremendous amount to look forward to after the seventh grade. Her father, Don, worked for the phone company. Jackson already had dial phones and the outlying areas would follow by spring.

Don Morris once sent an entire paycheck to Oral Roberts. The family had to live on Wheaties and potato chips for a month. Chuckette had a younger sister named Sugar, who was destined to take everything Chuckette ever got away from her. Even at the party, Sugar hung around on the periphery of the action, going through the stack of 45 rpm records and telling Chuckette which ones mattered. I wanted to see Sugar naked.

Chuckette's turn at the game came and we both said, "Mark." The last thing I remember before they closed the door was Maurey looking at me from the back of the group. She held her fingers up in an A-Okay sign. Or maybe it was something dirty, I don't know. I'd hoped she might be a little bit jealous.

"Have you ever kissed a girl?" Chuckette asked. Girls are all the time asking me that question. What do I look like anyway?

I nodded but it was way black and she couldn't see my head. A tiny crack of light came under the door, enough so the penny in one of her loafers reflected a brassy color.

"Have you?" I asked.

"Lots. At church camp last summer three boys kissed me in one night. Deacon Saltzer said they would go to hell."

"You told the deacon?"

"I can't lie. If I lied he would have sent me to hell."

"What's hell like?"

"Are you going to kiss me or not? We've only got five minutes."

"I don't want to go to hell."

"I was twelve last summer. I'm thirteen now. It's okay to kiss when you're a teenager."

"Where's your face?"

In the dark, Chuckette's face seemed almost regular. She didn't have pimples or zits or anything weird like that. Those would come later. I took her by the shoulders and kissed. The poor girl had nothing worth squat in her life, and I felt bad because of that, so I gave her a real kiss. Heck, I admit it, I got into the deal some. I'd never kissed anyone except Maurey, and Chuckette's lips felt different. They were stiffer. The only weird part was when I touched the retainer.

Chuckette put out a little scream and bit my tongue. I yelped and jumped back, banging into the door. Voices came from outside the closet.

"What's going on in there?" from LaNell, "Go get 'em, Sammy," from Maurey, and Dothan, "No copping feels."

Chuckette kind of whimpered. "That's disgusting."

"It was a kiss."

"With your tongue out? It's all wet." We were flattened against opposite walls of the closet, as far away from each other as we could possibly be—about ten inches.

"Is that how people kiss back East?" she asked.

"Sure." I didn't know but I had to convince her I was normal and she wasn't.

"Your mouth was open."

"That's how you do it, Charlotte."

"That's not how Southern Baptists do it."

When I leaned to the right, a hanger bonked me in the forehead. My tongue felt stung. I didn't know if I was bleeding or not and I sure couldn't go back to the party with red dribble on my chin. I felt around until I found a coat or something and blotted my face and tongue.

"What're you doing?" she asked.

"Waiting for our five minutes to end."

Chuckette started sniffling, as if she were trying to hold back tears. When I didn't do anything, she sniffled a good honky one.

"What's the matter?"

"The party's ruined."

"The party's ruined because I gave you a French kiss?"

"Is it Eastern or French? Make up your mind." I didn't say anything so she kept talking between sniffles. "Daddy said it would end like this."

"Crying in the closet?"

"He said boys would try to get me passionate so they could make me pregnant and ruin my life and make me go to hell."

"You don't sound passionate to me."

She sniffed a few more times and blew her nose on something. "I wasn't ready that time. Let's try again."

When I came home I found the toaster oven in the front yard. Someone had evidently stood on the porch and heaved it. I picked up the screen deal you put the food on, but left the rest.

The first I noticed when I went inside was a pair of toilet paper tubes up Les's nostrils. Lydia's voice came from the kitchen. "When was the last time you did something spontaneous? Just cut loose regardless of the consequences?"

Hank's voice answered. "Every action has consequences."

"You're an Indian. Indians are supposed to get drunk and be stupid."

"If I'm stupid I go to jail."

I walked in the kitchen to find Lydia sitting at the table, rolling eight or nine eggs under her hands. Evidence of several more were splatted on the floor at Hank's feet. Alice lapped at the mess. I set the screen from the toaster oven in the sink.

"Hi, Mom, I'm home."

She sent me the look and rolled an egg slowly off the side of the table. It went into a slow motion effect as it fell, then it made a *pop* sound and blew up. The yolk didn't break.

Hank sat in the other chair with his hands on the varnished wood tabletop, his thumbs touching each other. "When you're stupid, you get shipped off to live with the common people for a few months. The worst thing that could possibly happen to you is you might lose your trust fund."

Lydia rolled another egg off the edge. *Pop.* I opened the refrigerator and pulled out a Dr Pepper. "Either you guys want one?" They didn't look at me.

"I wish just once you'd do something you hadn't planned to do," Lydia said.

I opened my pop and sat on the milk crate to listen. It took ten minutes of back and forth to figure the situation, but near as I can tell, they'd gone with Delores and Ft. Worth to a new pizza place outside Jackson and Delores and Lydia got in a vicious fight about how many glasses of beer come in a pitcher.

Hank didn't back up Lydia with enough enthusiasm, or maybe he took the what-does-it-matter stance. Anyhow, he'd failed her and Lydia didn't cut slack when men failed her.

"You're passive as wet toast," Lydia said.

"Who sat on her couch for three months, refusing to accept where she was."

"Who lives in a twelve-foot trailer with a kitchen table that makes into a bed."

"I do." Hank's face had gone rock. I was impressed.

"I'm not about to spend my life waiting for free-cheese day at the county extension office," Lydia said.

"Who asked you to?"

"You are beneath my dignity."

Hank reached across the table. I thought he was going to hit her and I think Lydia did too—she paled real quick. Instead, Hank swept all the eggs off in one swoop of the arm.

"Take your dignity and stuff it up your ass."

Lydia's color came back. "How dare you resort to violence in my house."

Hank stood up, knocking his chair back. "You want spontaneous violence?"

"Let's see it, big man."

The distance between me and Hank's head was about six feet. I figured if he lit into her, I could knock him cold with the Dr Pepper bottle before his second punch.

But Hank went indecisive. I saw it in his eyes. He knew she wouldn't respect him if he didn't take action and would hate him if he did. Typical Lydia positioning. He gave me a helpless look and left—didn't even slam the front door. We sat listening as he started his truck and moved off down Alpine. Lydia stared at a spot on the wall.

"Got rid of another one," I said.

She closed her eyes and exhaled. "Go fuck your little girlfriend and leave me alone."

Right before the 10:30 bottle Lydia caught Alice peeing in her panty box. I heard a crash and a yell, then Alice tore through my room and into my closet.

Lydia threw a full-scale temper tantrum. Glass broke, tables turned over, threats rained. I sat at my desk trying to avoid notice. At first she blamed all her personal problems on Alice, but the bile soon turned on me.

"I'm sick of that cat, I'm sick of this town, I'm sick of you. Every time I turn around there's your hurt stare. I can't breathe without you judging me. Well, I'm a whore and a bad mother, okay. You satisfied?"

"No."

"But you, you know what you are? You're pathetic. A pathetic little boy."

What I knew was I had to clean up the glass, and in one hour—half a pint of gin—Lydia would turn on herself; and in two hours—full pint—she would cry and touch me and beg my forgiveness. Say she couldn't live without me, I'm all she's got.

Et cetera. So on. Boring.

The forgiveness part of the deal was harder than the being called pathetic part. I know thousands of kids go through this process every day, but it's still a pain in the butt.

The next day while Lydia slept I washed all sixty pairs of panties, folded them, and put them in her bureau drawer where Alice couldn't pee. I didn't see the pictures of my possible fathers. Lydia must have moved them.

Monday morning was cold at a level you'd never grasp in North Carolina. I woke up to a half-inch of ice along the inside bottom frame of my bedroom window. When I turned on the hot water for my shower, the water heater made knocking noises and the faucet emitted a tiny, pathetic sigh. I brushed my teeth with Dr Pepper.

Lydia had her electric blanket cranked to ten and her head buried.

"Water's frozen up," I said. "No bathing till the thaw."

Her voice came from under the pile. "I cannot survive without a bath each and every day."

"Keep up the pioneer spirit, Lydia."

"To hell with the pioneer spirit. We're going to die in this hell hole and no one civilized will remember our names. The no-neck locals will feed off our bodies."

"I can't make you coffee."

"I shall not be moved from this bed until Caspar sends us two tickets to somewhere warm."

"Coffee would just make you pee anyway and the toilet won't flush. Sensitive as you are, you'd better not open the lid."

Lydia let out a low catlike moan.

I put on about eight layers of sweaters, coats, and scarves and headed for school. The day was an unbelievable clear blue. Humidity froze in the air, making for a sparkly Wonderland atmosphere. Each step caused a loud protesting squeal from the snow. Would have been neat if my cheeks hadn't stung and the mucus in my sinuses hadn't iced up a half-block from home.

The White Deck windows were so frosted over on the inside that I couldn't see who was doing the morning coffee deal. I hadn't run into Hank since the unpleasantness and I wasn't sure how to come across—friendly buddies together against the opposite sex: "They're all bitches, Hank. You can't live with 'em and you can't live without 'em"; or loyal son: "Don't mess with my mama, man."

I try to always plan for every attitude.

The place was packed but, fortunately, Hank wasn't there. I sat at the counter between Ft. Worth and a sheepherder named Lasco. Lasco had an odor. When Dot poured his coffee, he dumped in three spoons of sugar and stirred it with his thumb.

Talk at the counter centered on a how-cold-it-was routine. Some guy said forty-eight below at his place and others doubted it. Ft. Worth claimed it wasn't a degree under thirty-five below zero. They all agreed it'd been a lot colder when they were my age.

Dot set a cup in front of me and said, "You're blue."

I nodded, too frozen to be cool.

She started rubbing my cheekbones with both her hands. It was kind of odd, being touched on the face right in front of the guys and all. My eyes were six inches or so off her bra strap; my nose even closer.

She was rough, but she created warmth and gave me the thrill of the day. "Got to get blood moving to your head. You'll have a frostbite."

I nodded again.

Ft. Worth was blatantly jealous. He said, "Kid'll get more than frostbite from all the heat you got going."

"Keep your pants zipped, Jack," Dot said. She called everyone Jack when they bothered her.

"If I go outside and turn blue-faced will you rub me?"

"You couldn't handle it if I did."

This got a snicker rippling up the counter. Dot was the queen at sliding around flirty rednecks without doing severe damage to their king-hell egos. I never saw her lose a tip by saying no.

Ft. Worth pointed at me with his stub finger. "His little girlfriend's not gonna like you warming his face on your tits."

Girlfriend? My stomach went queasy. So the town knew

about Saturday practice sessions with Maurey. My first thought was that she would stop doing it and I'd never get laid again. I'd lose her. But the second thought was, hell, I deserve some credit here. This would make my junior high reputation, for good or bad, and Maurey would quit sooner or later anyway. Girls liked a guy with know-how. They'd be lined up for orgasms. My third thought was Buddy's going to kill me.

Fourth, fifth, and on down the line thoughts don't matter squat though because the whole process was based on a false assumption.

Dot took her hands away and picked up the coffeepot. "Sam's too good for Charlotte Morris, anyway. He needs a woman like me, someone who'll do him better than to bite his tongue."

I said, "Charlotte Morris?" but the good-old-gang was laughing at Dot's sauciness and no one heard me. Doesn't take much to entertain guys who wear caps indoors.

Lasco didn't laugh. Maybe he only spoke Armenian or whatever language it is that sheepherders speak. His mouth made chewing motions even when there wasn't anything in it, and he tilted his cup so coffee dribbled down the side and ran off the bottom into his saucer. Then he lifted the saucer and, with a disgusting sound, sucked in his coffee.

There's some scientific principle why when you try to pour a little liquid from a cup it dribbles off the bottom instead of the lip. I learned just enough in school to know these things had a cause, but not enough to know what it was.

What's strange in a small town is how you can have a rich, creative sex life with one girl for several months and keep it a secret from everyone, then you go in a closet and kiss someone you don't give a flying hoot about, and suddenly you're the town talk.

I got to Stebbins's class late, just as he was having everyone open *Island of the Blue Dolphins*. Stebbins's eyebrows jumped toward each other in a stare and several guys grinned into their hands. Teddy the Chewer hummed "Here Comes the Bride." Maurey winked at me. She'd been doing a lot of that lately. I didn't look at Chuckette.

Stebbins talked on about animal symbolism—wild dogs, dolphins, cormorants. I didn't see it. The girl fought animals or ate them. Where's the symbolism in fighting and eating?

Stebbins walked up and down the aisles as he called on people. At one point he stopped next to my desk and stood as close to me as he could get. Florence was explaining about wild dogs in Alabama—Lord knows what it had to do with me and my life—while Stebbins hulked above, breathing on my head. I finally looked over to Chuckette and she smiled real sweet. So did LaNell Smith.

When the hall bell rang, I made a beeline for the boy's room and hid out in a stall full of graffiti, waiting for the next class. Wyoming kids were like the apex of innocence back then. Someone had actually taken the time and energy to carve GOL DURN in the door.

I came out of the John to find Maurey bent over the knee-high water fountain. When she stood up, her lips shone from the water and a single drop held on to the edge of her mouth. She was beautiful.

"So you slipped it to chunky Chuckette," she said.

"I kissed her. Wasn't that the point of the game—to go in the closet and kiss."

"Not that kind of kiss. She's saying you got downright passionate."

"You taught me how to kiss. I only know one way."

"Sure, Sam. You just better not ever hurt her. She's a friend of mine."

"How could I hurt Chuckette?"

Maurey undid the top button on my shirt. "Didn't your mother tell you only squirrels button it to the top? I better not talk to you in the halls anymore, Chuck wouldn't like it. If Mom'll let me put, I'll come by tonight after *Dick Van Dyke*."

How, all of a sudden, could Chuckette control who talked to me in the hall? I was like the African explorer who said "Pardon me" to the chief's daughter and suddenly found himself choosing between marriage and having his chest ripped out. We're talking unfair situation.

At lunch—fish sticks and congealed carrots—I sat across from Rodney Cannelioski. He stood up and left, muttering something along the lines of godless hordes. He should have been the one to choose favorite books of the Bible with her. They could have chapter-versed themselves into a fundamentalist orgy.

A tray slid into view and I looked up to see Chuckette Morris's face. In institutional cafeteria light, she wasn't nearly as passable as she'd been in the closet. Her face was flat, like here's her semi-normal head only the front part has been mushed into shape by a dinner plate and all the features kind of stuck in wherever they would fit. She had these tiny bangs about the length of fingernails.

Her voice wasn't so bad, maybe I could spend our time together with my eyes closed.

"What were you talking to Maurey Pierce about?" she asked.

I arranged my fish sticks into the shape of a baseball diamond. "When was that?"

"Florence Talbot saw you guys talking after Stebbins's class. You shouldn't talk to other girls."

I came so close to telling her that Maurey and I had been talking about fucking our eyes out after *Dick Van Dyke* tonight.

So close. I could have nipped several months of trouble bang in the bud.

"She was saying how much fun she had at your party the other night. She especially liked the fondue."

Chuckette's face lit up. It's just too easy to make some people feel good. "My mom got the recipe from the back page of *TV Guide.*"

"It was best with the crackers."

"Sharon liked it that way too. We're doubling with Maurey and Dothan to a movie in Jackson Saturday after next. Be sure and bring enough money to pay my way and buy a Black Whip. I like Black Whips. You should know that about me since we're going steady."

I had to get out of this quick. "Who says we're going steady?"

She looked at me suspiciously. "Everyone. They all know what you did to me at the party."

"Do I get some say in this deal?"

"You wouldn't come into GroVont and put your tongue in just any girl's mouth, would you? Maybe that's how they do things back East, but in Teton County we're moral."

"I thought I was supposed to kiss you in the closet."

"That reminds me, you're supposed to give me your jacket."

Now I was riled. Thirty degrees below zero and this little moon-face wants my coat because I pity-kissed her. I said the most self-righteous thing I could come up with at the moment.

"What?"

"It'll be a letter jacket in the ninth grade, but we'll make do for right now."

I set down my fork. "Charlotte, there is no way I'm giving you my coat."

Tears leapt into her eyes. She wasn't so pitifully helpless after all. "Ever'one'll think you took advantage of me if you don't give me something to seal our love. They'll say I'm cheap." Her lower lip went atremble.

"Jesus," I said.

"Don't you dare take the Lord's name in vain."

"How about a scarf? My grandfather gave me this scarf." Actually I shoplifted it at Sears when I found out we were moving West. "It belonged to my grandmother. Is a scarf good enough?"

She stopped crying like turning off a faucet. "Let me see it."

I handed her the thing. It was green and about a yard long. I figured I could survive the walk home without it.

Chuckette stuffed the scarf in her purse. "It'll do, I guess. You'll have to buy me a gold chain for our anniversary."

"Our anniversary?"

Across the cafeteria, I saw Maurey carrying her tray over to a table of ninth-graders. She had on Dothan's jacket.

"And another thing," Chuckette said. "All touching stays above the neck until we're engaged."

When I came home, Hank's truck was parked in the yard, which I took as a good sign. Lydia's the kind of person who when she's not happy she doesn't want anyone around her happy either. She can be real uncomfortable to live with when she sets her mind on it. A bitch.

Otis hopped across the road and dropped a red ball at my feet, then gazed up at me with those melted chocolate eyes that only a dog can pull off. Thirty below or not, I had to throw the damn thing.

Otis was really fast, when you consider his missing part. The problem—there's always a problem—was the ball was rubber and he'd slobbered on it and the slobber froze to my mitten, so throwing didn't work out well. The ball had a tendency to stick for an instant, then wobble off about ten feet the wrong way. Otis would pounce on it with his front feet and drool some more before getting a good grip.

I finally launched a fairly good throw way up and toward the house. Otis took off like a shaky shot, timing his leap so as to be most impressive. Just as he jumped, the rubber ball hit the wall and shattered into a zillion pieces.

Made me feel like cold crap. Otis hopped around looking for his toy, actually stepping on the shards of frozen rubber. You'd think I'd destroyed his best pal. Maybe I did, hell, dogs can't tell toys from friends.

Inside, the toilet paper rolls were gone from Les's nose and the door to Lydia's room was closed, so I figured we were into a make-up scene. They really did like each other. It's a shame when people who like each other aren't on speaking terms. Goes against the natural order.

I sang "Surfer Joe" which was big on KOMA that week, so they'd know the kid was home from school and to keep it down. Cute couple or not, I wasn't in the mood for moans and screams from my own mother. I fed Alice, popped open a Dr Pepper and dug out some peanut butter cookies, and wandered into the living room.

The thing with Chuckette bothered me, but the thing with Maurey bothered me more. This jacket deal was some kind of a localized social ritual indicating romantic commitment. An anthropologist could go to town on these northern rural types. Maybe in the early days when a warm coat was a matter of survival, giving a woman your jacket was the ultimate love gesture. Anyhow, Maurey was wearing Dothan's tan-and-dirt letter jacket with the GV on the right breast—definitely a sign of bad news.

She'd be coming over later to do things which the letter jacket implied were off-base, but I couldn't very well ask her about it for fear of causing her to feel bad. Maurey might get in a bad mood and stop practice if I said something she didn't want to hear.

In the midst of this daydreaming, I wandered down the hall, stopped to listen at Lydia's door, and, not hearing a sound, I went into the bathroom. Lydia and Hank were in the tub, together, naked.

"Hi, honey bunny," she said.

"Hi, Lydia." Why is it that whenever something interesting happens to my mother it so often revolves around the can? Hank was behind her with his back up against the end of the claw-legged tub and his hands on her hips. Lydia had the toes of her left foot propped on the faucet.

"Hank got the water going," she said. "Give me a sip."

I handed her the Dr Pepper. "What?"

Hank looked embarrassed no end. I think the family weirdness had just crossed his acceptable-level line.

"Hank crawled under the house with a torch and thawed the pipes. Wasn't that nice of him?" Lydia's breasts were a lot bigger than Maurey's but not as big as the girls in Playboy. They kind of pointed down and the nipples were dark. Her stomach had creases where she was bent forward. Casual as I kept it for the purpose of not coming off squirrelly in front of Hank, I wasn't in the habit of nude conversation.

Lydia offered Hank a hit off the pop, but he shook his head without looking at either of us. She handed the bottle back to me. "There's a letter from Caspar on top of the end table."

"What's it say?"

"I wouldn't open mail from him. I may be your mother, but I respect your privacy."

"Right." I took my pop and left.

Sigmund Freud sucked deeply on the opium hookah, raised one eyebrow petulantly, then nodded toward his young friend. He spoke without exhaling. "After careful analysis, Sam Callahan, I find you the most balanced, sane person I've ever had the pleasure to converse with."

"You're drooling, sir. Have a Kleenex."

"The part I cannot fathom is how someone as emotionally relaxed as yourself could have survived a chaotic background filled with mixed signals and backward relationships, not to mention Miss Neurotic America for a mother-image."

"Everyone must survive their mother, Sig."

Sigmund Freud blew an opium smoke ring into the air and turned into the Cheshire cat. "You are a colossus of will over environment, son. Want a hit of this? It will turn the world into ice cream."

"None for me thanks. Fresh air is plenty enough drug for me."

Samuel—

The youth gets together his materials to build a bridge to the moon, or, perchance, a palace or temple on earth, and, at length, the middle-aged man concludes to build a woodshed with them. Think carbon paper, Samuel.

Caspar Callahan

As I read the letter a second time, Lydia came from the bathroom barefoot in her white terrycloth robe. She didn't look any older than I felt.

"What's dear Daddy got to say?" she asked.

"He's been reading again."

"God, I hate it when he does that."

13

"Well, are you going to kiss me or not?"

Chuckette had asked an interesting question. Whenever you can kiss a girl, you should. I knew that. I'd be a fool to pass, but on the screen a horde of girls in bathing suits were running across the sand and although I knew the movies would never let an entire tit pop all the way out, I could always imagine that might happen, and the flesh they showed was interesting—a lot more breast than I was likely to see anytime soon in real life. So it was a question of taking the tangible kiss from a drab girl who couldn't stop playing with her retainer, or waiting on a possible visual tit that I knew would never happen.

The picture was *Gidget Goes Hawaiian* and I was king-hell lost because this was the first sequel I'd ever seen where the main character is somebody else. When I saw *Gidget* in Greensboro, she'd been Sandra Dee, now she was Deborah Walley. I had no idea movies could do that. I'd thought movie people becoming someone else was as impossible—or at least as illegal—as real people turning into someone else. Shows what I knew.

The plot was that Gidget and Moondoggie have a fight and she flies to Hawaii with her parents where, even though she's an outsider, Gidget instantly becomes popular on the local scene.

"Are you?" Chuckette asked again.

"You'll have to take out your gum."

"If I can touch your tongue you can touch my gum." It was Chicklets, three pieces. Her mouth hadn't stopped snapping and popping since we hit Dothan's '59 Ford. I can't stand girls who chew gum; never could. Makes them look stupid.

"I'm not kissing a wad of gum."

"I'm sorry I came with you. You don't give a whit about my feelings." Which was true.

And to make it a whole lot worse, down the end of our row, against the wall, Maurey and Dothan weren't watching Gidget at all. He had his greasy pinhead right in her face. I could see her hand on the back of his neck.

All the way from GroVont Maurey sat in the middle of the front seat up against Dothan. He drove with only his left hand on the wheel, which made me think he was touching her. Chuckette and I sat up against opposite doors in the backseat. I refused to speak more than a grunt. With no explanation, Maurey hadn't come over for practice that afternoon. Left me sitting home like a goofball. I'd been looking forward to it. A boy needs some sex to relax him before a date.

"You win," Chuckette said, "but it'll cost you another Black Whip."

"Win what?"

She made a big deal out of taking out the Chicklet mess and finding a candy wrapper to stick it in. Then she kind of sighed, put both hands in her lap, and turned to me with her flat face tilted up like she was an Episcopalian taking communion against her will.

On the other side of Chuckette, both Maurey's hands showed on Dothan's hair. What could she see in that Southern turd? He had no redeeming qualities at all—just a mean oily rural kid whose teeth would be bad before he turned nineteen.

He would hit her someday. I could feel it.

I leaned sideways and kissed Chuckette, but I didn't touch her with my hands.

"You forget how the French kiss?" she asked.

"I thought you didn't like it that way."

"Once you get used to the spit, it's okay. Besides, it proves you love me."

I thought about denying I loved her, but what was the use. She wouldn't believe me. Gidget and the happy, well-adjusted kids were dancing around a bonfire on the beach. We'd done that once on Ocracoke Island down on the Outer Banks. Lydia had been with a captain or something from the Coast Guard. The jerk patted me on the head and gave me pinball money. There'd been a girl with red braids named Ursula that I watched for hours but never got up the gall to talk to. She'd had on a yellow two-piece bathing suit and if you stared at the fire awhile, then looked quickly at her, she seemed naked. Sort of. I decided to pretend Chuckette was really Ursula. Maybe she'd had a disfiguring accident or something and had plastic surgery only down inside she was still Ursula just as Gidget was still Sandra Dee.

The fantasy worked me up enough to do the tongue deal and even to touch Chuckette's one shoulder. But midway through the kiss I went into a short story and lost track.

Dear Sam Callahan,

You don't know me but my name is Ursula Dee, daughter of Sandra Dee. I caught sight of you a single time at a cast party on the Outer Banks. I didn't have the courage to speak to you then and that has been a regret I will always have to live with.

Ever since that night, I've imagined what it would be like to have your fingers caressing my bare arms and legs. I want you to touch my feet, Sam Callahan. Mom and I will be in your area soon for the filming of Gidget Goes to GroVont, *and I would appreciate it if you would touch me at that time. Mom wants you to touch her also. She said*

Chuckette slapped me. "That's my knee."

"Oh."

"Don't ever touch my knee."

"Is something wrong with it?"

"My body is a temple."

"Doesn't look like a temple."

She sat up stiff. "What's that supposed to mean?"

"Your body looks like a body. Sort of. A temple is a building, some kind of a church."

She thought about this awhile, but couldn't seem to get around the logic. "Time for you to buy me a Black Whip."

Trading kisses for Black Whips didn't seem the way to treat your body like a temple. "But the movie is almost over. We'll get to see which guy she really likes."

"I want my Black Whip."

Gidget was going to really like Moondoggie anyway. He was the tallest.

While I was standing at the candy counter in the lobby, Maurey came out of the theater, her lips swollen from all the necking.

"You didn't come this afternoon," I said.

"You be home tomorrow?"

I hadn't considered tomorrow one way or the other, so I hesitated long enough to keep her off balance, then I said yes.

"I want you and your mom both there."

"Lydia? We don't need her anymore."

"I do. I'll be there after church." Maurey headed across the lobby toward the ladies' room. About halfway across, she turned back to me and said, "He doesn't kiss near as good as you do."

Sunday, Hank decided to show us the valley. "If you're going to live here you might as well see the place," he said.

Lydia blew cigarette smoke in my face. "We live in North Carolina. We're only here for a lost weekend."

Hank grinned and drank coffee. He'd been in a fine mood since Lydia let him come back. I guess he thought he'd won a point because she called him instead of him calling her. I knew better.

Outside had warmed up, if that's the word you use for zero. At least, ear wax no longer froze. Maurey showed up while we were loading the truck with a picnic and enough blankets to avoid death should the Dodge collapse miles from a heat source. She looked at the pile of cardboard boxes in the back of Hank's truck and said, "You're not getting me in one of those."

"What's she mean by that?" Lydia asked. Her breath put out more fog when she talked than the rest of us. I couldn't figure out why.

Hank said, "The boxes are for moving goods."

Maurey reached over the tailgate and scraped a box with her thumbnail. "Why are they waxed, then?"

Hank shrugged and opened the passenger door for us. "Get in."

Lydia was suspicious. "Since when do you open a door for a lady?"

"Since it won't shut from the inside anymore."

Lydia rode next to Hank and Maurey sat on my lap by the door that not only wouldn't shut from the inside but wouldn't open that way either. On account of the truck having electrical tape instead of a passenger window, I felt somewhat trapped, though in a pleasant way. I hadn't been this close to Maurey in several days and I missed it. A person can get used to touching someone.

My head was jammed up against the gun rack, so I kept my

nose in the little dent on the back of her neck for most of the ride. Her hair smelled way clean, not a shampoo smell exactly, more like fresh-snow clean. She didn't have hair spray or any of the other gunk that Chuckette used to make her hair into a helmet. Touching Chuckette's hair was like reaching into a hole not knowing what lives under the surface.

"There's no excuse for civilized people living here," Lydia said. "Not that any do. But look. There's no trees, there's no country lanes lined with two-story colonial homes and pickaninny shanties. There's no pickaninnies. Man should not live without ethnic diversity."

Hank grunted. "What do you think I am?"

"You're just a white guy with a nice tan and too long hair."

Maurey popped me with an elbow. "Stop that."

"Stop what?"

"You're coming over after dinner tonight. Ed Sullivan said this week would be a really big show."

"He always says that."

"Yeah, but someone told Mom at her AAUW bridge club yesterday that this time it would be big. You want to come over, Lydia? Mom would be glad to have company."

"Every time I speak to Annabel she works the conversation around to laundry detergent. I'd rather talk to my moose."

"Mom," I said.

"Look." Hank pointed as we crossed the Snake River. It was an army-green color and gave off the impression of cold. "No rivers like that down South."

"Nonsense," Lydia said. "The South is full of rivers. And concert halls and department stores and porches. Every house has a proper porch. Here they have mud rooms."

Discussion deteriorated into the stock West-versus-South and rural-versus-urban canned lecture that Lydia used to fill time. I think she hated silence and Hank was comfortable with it and she couldn't stand seeing him comfortable when she wasn't. Much as I liked Maurey on my lap, her butt bones were digging into my thighs. I shifted my weight, trying to find a comfortable divot.

She reached behind herself with her right hand and grabbed my penis hard. I yelped.

"What are you whining about now?" Lydia asked.

"Caught the window knob in my rib."

"Well, keep it to yourself."

We started up a steep hill with pine trees on either side. "This is the pass," Hank said. "From the top we can see the four corners of the world."

Lydia lit a cigarette. "What difference does it make?"

Maurey went into this pulsating squeeze action. It felt good, kind of bizarre, but I couldn't block out of my mind the picture of her kissing that grease bag.

Hank said, "I want to be idealistic. I want to believe in things."

"Like what?" I asked, though my voice came out wrong. I could feel Maurey's smile clear through the back of her head.

"Like beauty and the nobility of man. Look over there." We passed a big live moose, Les's cousin maybe. He was up a little gully, belly-deep in snow, chewing on a bush. Maurey squeezed the hell out of me.

Hank went on giving what, for him, was practically a speech.

"You can believe in whatever you want to believe in up here. Look at the snow on that whitebark pine. People in cities can't believe in the nobility of man because they see no evidence of it."

"I love it when he talks like Chief Joseph," Lydia said.

Maurey said in a deep voice, "I will fight no more forever."

I kept up my end of the conversation under the direst circumstances possible. "Easy to believe in people when there's none around."

Hank hit the steering wheel with one hand. "That's what I mean."

Maurey gave a mighty squeeze and I blew in my pants. Coughed like death to cover the sound and clawed at the window handle, which was a waste; you can't roll down a window that isn't there.

"Sam, control yourself," Lydia said.

"I got hot all of a sudden."

She turned to look at me. "It's freezing in here."

Maurey put her hand back in her lap. "Mrs. Callahan, I came to see you on purpose."

"As opposed to accidentally?"

We were moving up the mountain. I went into a fear fantasy where the truck broke down and all that come froze around my pecker and it broke off.

"We tried to save him, but it came off in my hand," the doctor said.

Maurey Pierce cried until rivulets ran across her cheeks.

"He'll never practice again."

Sam Callahan looked at the emptiness between his legs. "Does this mean I'm a girl now?"

Maurey's voice cut through the story. "How can you tell if you're pregnant?"

There's a conversation stopper for you. We rode a quarter mile up the mountain in silence.

Lydia lit a cigarette. "The game was supposed to stop on your first period."

"I've never had a period. Can you get pregnant if you've never had a period?"

Hank rolled the window down a couple of inches. I asked, "What's a period?"

Nobody pays any attention to me in a crisis.

Lydia blew smoke across Hank at the cracked window, then turned back to Maurey. "What exactly makes you think you might be pregnant?"

"My body is way off, has to be pregnancy or cancer. I get sick sometimes and food smells like poop and my tits hurt."

"Get sick mostly in the mornings?"

"Right. And after lunch at school. And my dreams have been really weird lately."

I glanced over at Hank, wondering what he must think of the turn in our Sunday drive. Hank stared out the cracked windshield at the typically majestic terrain. He had on his implacable look that I was starting to take as something of a pain in the ass. I mean, how convenient if in every slightly off-the-norm social situation you could fall back on the Blackfoot stereotype.

"Do you know what cancer feels like?" Maurey asked.

Lydia suddenly scratched her right ear, a very un-Lydia-like thing to do. "I hardly even know what being pregnant feels like. I was only with child once and I was your age, almost. The subject hasn't come up since."

I felt Maurey's stomach through her car coat. Could I have done something to put a little person in there? Lydia's sex lesson hadn't included anything about the pregnancy process—other than it might happen so we had to stop when Maurey became a woman. I didn't know exactly what Maurey and I could have done to cause or not cause a baby.

It was an odd feeling though. A baby, a live piece of me in Maurey.

Hank pulled into a parking area and turned the truck around. "This is the place."

I leaned to look over Maurey's right shoulder. The whole valley stretched off beneath us like a waxed linoleum floor.

Lines of brown marked the creeks with a wider band at the Snake River. Chimney smoke drifted over the towns of Jackson and Wilson. GroVont was around a corner, too far north to see. The whole thing gave the illusion of being above life.

"God, I hate being practical," Lydia said.

Maurey's hair brushed my face when she nodded. "I know what you mean."

"No use getting agitated until we know for sure. Who's your doctor?"

"Dr. Petrov in Jackson, but I can't go to him. He and daddy played football together in high school."

"Everyone in this state played football together in high school. How about Erickson over in Dubois? He's a Valium candy store. Does your daddy know him?"

I couldn't see Maurey's face, but she shook her head no.

"Then if you are pregnant we can talk abort or not to abort."

"I'm just a kid, I can't have a baby."

"That's what I thought."

We sat a minute, staring at the shimmery view and considering the implications. Buddy would castrate me. I'd heard him talk horse castration before and he enjoyed it. Gave me every disgusting detail. Took an "I've got my balls and you don't" attitude. Annabel would be disappointed. Everyone else would get a kick out of the deal because it would give them something to talk about. Wasn't that much to talk about in winter.

Abortion—I knew what that meant, more or less. Meant keep or get rid of and it was king-hell, kick-in-your-door illegal stuff.

Maurey started yanking at the door handle. "How the hell do you escape this monster, I've gotta slide."

Hank popped open his door. "Only works from the outside."

As Hank ran around the back of the truck, Maurey threw her shoulder into the door which didn't budge. "Give me a box, I'm a kid. Kids have fun, dammit, why won't this door do something."

Lydia looked at me. "You following this?"

I held Maurey around her waist. We were going out into the cold and I had a crotch full of goo and a possibly pregnant just-friends friend. Other than that, I was lost as ever.

—·—

Maurey got me in a cardboard box behind her with her arms up on my knees—almost the same position of Hank and Lydia in the bathtub.

"This smacks of suicidal," I said.

"Stay loose if we dump."

By leaning forward I could see way the heck down the mountain. It was like looking down a great, white throat. Hank had every intention of pushing us over the edge and letting us hurtle down the iced-up angle and into the woods. That's why the box was waxed—so we could go fast and not waterlog out halfway down the mountain.

Lydia lit a cigarette. "Looks like spontaneous fun."

Hank looked up at her. "We're next."

"Over my dead body we are."

Maurey's face was a nifty flush-red with white points on the tip-top of her ears. The air wasn't near as cold up high as it had been in the valley. Hank said it was an inversion. "Same thing that causes smog."

"Pollution causes smog," I said.

Maurey's eyes had a nothing-to-lose glint that worried me. "Whatever happens, don't bail out," she said. "You'll break your neck."

"I know we have a problem, but death isn't the answer."

Her head came back with all that beautiful hair in my face and she laughed and I was charmed to no end. It was the laugh of a child, the laugh of king-hell innocence, not pregnancy and orgasms and jacking-off boys in trucks; not even necking with greasers at the picture show. Maurey's laugh belonged to a person who had done none of those things.

I'd of said something about it if Hank hadn't shoved the waxed box and we took off like a cut-loose elevator.

I'm big on control. I like knowing where I am and where I should be next and how to get there and how to escape any situation. Falling is not your control motif. Maurey was hollering into the wind, same note as when she came in my room. My stomach did the up-the-throat thing.

I guess it was no faster than a sled, but the sleds I'd been on were semi-controllable and didn't fly a half-mile down the ramp. The snow had these hollowed-out dips so there was an up sensation in the midst of the down. Tears froze. Then there was a cliff and we were rolling. I grabbed Maurey as we went through the box. Snow crystals stung while we rolled and rolled and I braced myself for the tree that never hit.

We finally slid to a stop with Maurey in laughter hysterics. I did a four-point and threw up. She shoved snow over the mess as fast as I put it out.

I can't stand it when someone has a wonderful time doing the same thing that I hate doing. "Holy cow, that was a gas," she laughed. "You okay?"

I tried to breathe.

"You'd better move fairly quick," Maurey said.

"Why's that?"

"Hank and Lydia are fixing to face plant on that same drop off and they'll land on you."

I looked back up the hill. Forty yards or so up was a five-foot ledge, not a cliff at all. "No way in hell Hank's going to get Lydia in a box," I said.

Famous last words. I heard the scream just before they came flying over the top. It was one of those stop-action memories that freeze in your head and stay there for life, even if you turn senile and can't remember your own phone number. They floated in the air above the box. Lydia had her arms up, reaching for the sun. Her mouth was an O and I could see the tip of her tongue. One of Hank's black boots hovered over her legs and his left hand showed on her shoulder. He seemed to be leaning back, as if the box was still behind him.

They hit and separated. Hank slid on his chest with his face pushing a great mound of snow before him. Lydia rolled end over end, then fell into a baseball hook slide. Neither one slowed down all that much as they went past Maurey and me. The really weird part was that Lydia went by laughing.

I'd never heard my mother laugh before.

Lydia mostly liked to comment on things. She didn't really care to do anything and laughing requires some kind of doing. I didn't know if I liked this turn of events or not.

When the slide finally petered out, she was lying on her back with both arms out in a crucifixion look. Hank slowly stood up and brushed off his face, but Lydia didn't move a muscle. I flashed on paralysis and death. The three of us all made it to her at the same time. I knelt next to her head and touched her limp shoulder. "Can you move?"

Lydia smiled. "Isn't the air pretty."

"Where does it hurt?"

She sat up with her hands around her knees. "I was just admiring the sky. Do you mind?"

"You never admired the sky before. I thought you were crippled."

"Why can't a person admire the sky without their kid calling for an ambulance?"

I looked at Maurey who seemed to know what Lydia was

talking about. They made eye contact. What I thought was the word: *pregnant.*

Lydia struggled to her feet. "That had a high entertainment value. Let's do it again."

—

I wish I could claim that I caught the historical significance of watching *The Ed Sullivan Show* in the Pierces' family room that night. Kennedy day I knew we were involved in something bigger than us, but Beatles night I was considerably more wrapped up in me and the baby thing than any history-unfolding deal.

My brain was stuck on the first joke I ever memorized. Lord only knows how old I was, but I must have been young because I thought you could tell a joke five thousand times and it would still be funny. It's a wonder Lydia and Casper didn't slap me upside the head.

I would stand real straight and recite, "Mary had a little lamb," then I'd hesitate a millisecond before screaming, "*and the doctor fainted.*" I got the biggest kick out of that.

Buddy was home, sitting in his Stratolounger, taking apart the trigger doogie on a thirty-ought-six. He spread all the little pieces on a cloth on a TV tray. Petey played Candy Land and he cheated. I saw him. Maurey lay on her stomach on the floor with a pillow under her chest and her chin propped on both hands.

She raised one foot, then lowered it and raised the other one. I watched her instead of Topo Gigio, the Italian mechanical mouse. I pretended I was the baby in her. It would be dark and hot and wet. Really wet. I imagined the baby as a wet mouse. It would be a girl. We could name her Vanessa or Chadron; or maybe Nancy since we'd both read over thirty Nancy Drew books.

Maurey would marry me if we had a daughter. Buddy would make her.

Buddy dropped a tiny screwdriver and said "Shit," just as Annabel came in the room with a tray of cocoa mugs. Maurey's mother must have been a cocoa junkie and I think it affected Maurey's outlook.

"Don't talk like a cowboy in front of the children," she said.

"I am a cowboy."

Petey jumped to his feet, singing, "Shit-shit-shit, shit-shit-shit," to the tune of "Jingle Bells." He danced around the room in his pajamas, driving everyone right up the wall. If Maurey's and my kid acted like that I would put him in Culver Military Academy.

Buddy raised his arm in a mock backhand and Petey ran screaming to hide behind Annabel's legs. "Don't let Daddy beat me. Don't let Daddy beat me."

"Now look what you've done," Annabel said.

I was always intrigued by the flow of the Pierce family. I think the only way you can act cruddy to a family member is when you deep down inside care for them. Lydia and Caspar were formal and polite because they didn't like each other. Anything approaching honesty at the manor house would have caused bloodshed.

"Shut up," Maurey ordered.

Ed Sullivan is like the American role model. The guy couldn't do anything—couldn't act, sing, draw, throw a ball—absolutely talentless in every way, not to mention he had the posture of a train-station beggar. Yet he was a king-hell big deal. People sucked up to Ed like he was president of the world or something. No wonder kids grow up weird.

I was watching Maurey breathe, trying to see if there was a baby in there, so I missed the first part, but when she said, "Shut up," I looked at Ed hunched over by a curtain.

He said, "And now...the Beatles."

The audience went nuts—you had to be there—as four

guys in wimp clothes with their hair combed forward broke into "All My Loving." I didn't know it was "All My Loving" at the time. Maurey told me the next day at school after Kim Schmidt told her.

"Sissies," Buddy said through his bush of a beard.

"I think they're cute," Annabel said.

Petey threw a Candy Land marker at the screen.

The weird part was the screaming girls. No way could they hear the music; they were making too much noise. The camera blew off the Beatles to focus on these regular high school-looking girls with tears streaming away and their hands up in helpless supplication. I can't stand seeing strong emotions. Makes me nervous.

Maurey's right foot was up in the air going side to side with the song. She held the cocoa with both hands and blew steam toward the television. When the two Beatles on the left leaned into the same microphone, the scream intensity doubled.

"If they're so hot why don't they buy a separate microphone for each guy," I said.

Buddy had an answer. "Cause they like to stand close to each other. England is all boys who like other boys. I was there in the war."

Annabel did a *tsk* action with her tongue.

My mind said "Pregnant, pregnant, pregnant," over and over. I hate that when you get a word in there and it won't go away no matter what you're doing on the outside.

They sang five songs. "She Loves You" was pretty good and the last one, "I Want to Hold Your Hand," was okay. The others were somewhat drippy for me, though it was hard to tell with all the screaming. For sure they were better than the Singing Nun.

The next act was some dogs who wore fu-fu clothes and rode bicycles. They reminded me of Otis, whose leg I shot off.

I'd been in town six months and shot one dog and gotten one girl pregnant.

Maurey got a comb and stood behind me, combing my hair forward like a Beatle. Embarrassed me to no end.

"You'll look cool at school," she said.

"Being from the East causes me enough trash. If I look like an English wimp Coach Stebbins will hate me sure."

"Coach Stebbins hates you?" Annabel asked.

"He thinks I'm an outsider."

"You are," Buddy said. "But you'll get over it." He held up the rifle barrel and sighted through the tube right at me. Gave me a funny feeling in the spine.

Maurey stood back to admire my hair. "This'll drive Chuckette Morris crazy. She'll be all over you in homeroom."

"I don't want Chuckette Morris all over me in homeroom."

"Have to fight 'em off, huh?" Buddy said.

Maurey smiled at me. "With a stick."

Sometime after midnight, I came wide awake. I lay there with my eyes open, trying to piece together the room, where I was, why, when. What had caused me to come to. A coal glowed bright over by my desk, then dimmed. Lydia's head was silhouetted by the window. The coal moved down and she flicked a part of it into my trash can.

"I was so sick the day I found out I was pregnant with you. I've never been so sick. It was worse than I'd dreamed." She inhaled on the cigarette. "The doctor told Caspar first and Caspar came into my room and hit me in the face. The only time he ever hit me. So far."

The coal went bright again. "I fell into my dollhouse and broke the roof."

She was quiet a long time. I was afraid to move—she

seemed so delicate, fragile—as if raising my head could change her. Lydia finally went on. "I was so sick I didn't care that he hit me. I just wanted you out of me so I wouldn't feel sick anymore." Her foot touched the trash can, making a metal sound.

"I would have gone for an abortion if Caspar hadn't tried to make me have one. Why doesn't that man ever figure me out?"

This time the silence stretched the length of a cigarette. She threw the live butt in my trash can and stood up. "I got pregnant to spite my father and I refused an abortion to spite him. I wonder how that makes you feel."

I listened while Lydia made her way across the house and into her bedroom. Then I got up and poured water into the trash can.

14

"If you are pregnant, we could get married and live in an apartment. I'll find a job."

"Oh, Sam, don't be a squirrel."

Being a squirrel was the worst thing that could happen to a boy. Kids would do anything, no matter how bizarre or dangerous, to avoid squirrelhood; all except for the really squirrelly ones like Rodney Cannelioski who didn't know Shinola. I kind of felt sorry for him. He put more salt on his food than anyone I ever saw. We would sit at the cafeteria table and watch him shake salt over his square slab of pizza for five minutes. You could see it caking up on the awful stuff that passed for cheese.

No matter what a chump you think you are, you never have to look far to find someone else in worse shape—only they don't seem to know it. Lydia says it's not nice to make empty, worthless people see themselves in a true light. "They just get angry and nothing changes anyway."

The conversation with Maurey where I suggested marriage took place next to our Oldsmobile on Saturday right before she and Lydia drove over to Dubois to see the doctor. Maurey had been nervous all week and I knew she was scared—pregnancy is a big deal whether you keep the kid or not—but she would never admit it. She seemed somehow mad at me, as if I'd imposed on her.

The closest we came to talking about the baby was Wednesday after geography when I asked her if she felt like coming by for practice that night.

"We practiced enough, Sam. We're through with practice."

"Does that mean we're ready for the real thing?"

"I'm ready to go back to sixth grade. You can go anywhere you want."

Chuckette walked up and did the dirty-look-at-me thing for talking to another girl and Maurey went off to the ladies' room where I knew she got sick between second and third period every morning.

Lydia put a box of Sterno and her toothbrush in the backseat for their drive to Dubois. She was always afraid the car would break down fifteen miles from any people and she'd freeze to death behind the wheel and be discovered dead with bad breath. She hid boxes of matches all over town in case the power failed in a blizzard. And I know for a fact she stashed a spare toothbrush in the silver toilet-paper tube in the women's John at the White Deck.

"Want anything from Dubois?" she asked before they took off.

"Spider-Man comic books."

"Sammy, you are so infantile."

Maurey sat on the passenger side, staring out the window, not looking at me. It occurred to me we hadn't made eye contact, much less love, in a week.

After they left I felt kind of flat, like you do when you've been waiting for something interesting to happen, then it does, and afterward it's the same old same old. Being a father is supposed to change things, but it was still winter and I still had to go to a junior high full of idiot students and wimpy teachers; Lydia had a boyfriend now, but she still killed a pint of Gilbey's every night at 10:30. Other moms fixed their kids grilled cheese sandwiches. Not once in my whole life did Lydia ever fix me a grilled cheese sandwich.

I had one girlfriend I pitied and another friend who was mad at me for squirting in her. Thirteen years old and my sex life was probably over. Baseball season was months away.

I went inside and lay on the couch with my head over the edge and a cushion on my chest. From upside down, Les looked a little like Caspar. I got to wondering what Lydia did to get us sent to Wyoming, which led to wondering about my father, which led to nowhere, so I got up and drank a Dr Pepper and walked uptown.

Ever since the Beatles last Sunday, hair had turned into a major social issue. The longer your hair, the more coaches and principals viewed you as a rebellious snot-nosed troublemaker. I mean, it had only been one week. How could a person grow enough hair to make a statement in one week?

My hair was probably longer than anyone else's in the seventh grade—the curl showed anyway. That had more to do with Lydia being too emotionally tired to trim it than any wild-in-the-streets quirk in me. But Stebbins took offense, and even our principal, Mr. Hondell, stopped me in the hall to ask if I had a buck and a quarter.

"Yes, sir."

"Get your hair cut then. We're not running a dog kennel here."

Stebbins did his bit of king-hell nastiness in front of the whole class. He was big on public humiliation.

He stood at the blackboard, showing us how to diagram a sentence with a subjunctive clause in it. I find the diagramming of sentences morally reprehensible. Who cares? Was Jules Verne any better or worse a writer because he could diagram a sentence? Seventh grade is such a waste of time.

Stebbins had all these lines going horizontal, vertical, and off at a 45-degree angle—even worked in an interjection, Wow!—when he all of a sudden turned around and said, "Sam, stand up."

I was staring at the back of Maurey's head, bored to death with subjunctive clauses and thinking I was kind of happy I'd probably made her pregnant, so I didn't hear Stebbins.

"Sam Callahan, are you defying me?"

"What's that?"

"I will have no back talk here. The one thing I demand in this class is respect. Now, stand up."

I stood up but basically forgot everything I ever knew about the teacher-student relationship. I asked, "How can a person demand respect?"

He was so amazed he didn't speak. Across from me, Teddy spit in his coffee can and I could see Chuckette digging at her retainer. "Respect is an earned and given deal," I went on. "It can't be demanded. Respect is like love. Force it and lose it."

"You think all that hair makes you smart, don't you?"

"No." For the record, my hair touched neither my ears nor my collar. Already, I resented the Beatles.

"What makes you think you're so smart then, Mr. Callahan?"

There's no answer to a question like that so I fell back on silence. Maurey turned in her desk to look at me, but I couldn't see any expression on her face. She had more to worry about than Coach Stebbins suddenly going weird on me and me going weird back at him.

"I will not allow any know-it-all smart guys in my class. You will get a haircut, do you understand, Mr. Callahan?"

"Sure."

I asked Lydia that night to trim it back some but she said she didn't have the energy just then.

The next day in sixth-period PE—which I say should have been basketball practice—Stebbins pulled me, Dothan Talbot, and a kid named Elliot out of the dressing room and gave us licks for having long hair.

"You'll get a lick a day until I can see white skin above your ears," Stebbins said.

I think we should of had a warning day before the actual licks began. I feel strongly about licks from coaches. They're demeaning, and they sting like all hell. I have no fat back there and I don't adapt well to pain.

Elliot went first, shaking like an aspen leaf. I'll never figure out that kid. He had terrible acne and all he cared about was playing the piano. He was like one of those idiot guys who can't tie their own shoe but can tell you what day of the week January 15, 1631, came on.

Dothan was second and he just smiled as if, boy do I love this stuff. I'd heard his dad was big on licks, so I guess the defiant shiteater grin was his defense mechanism. I didn't have a defense mechanism.

Stebbins's paddle was a one-by-four with a carved handle and World's Greatest Dad woodburned in the flat area. He always swung low, below the butt bones and high on your legs, so sometimes he'd leave a red welt that said Dad backward on your leg.

PE licks are as much a tradition in American values as anything, but I hated every minute of it and if they ever make me president I'm going to make the whole ritual illegal.

Walking uptown Saturday, I dawdled a good deal to work out the ethical implications of the haircut. Stebbins was forcing me to do something by means of fear; therefore I shouldn't do it because his means sucked. But I had been intending to get a haircut anyway, and not doing something because a jerk tries to force you to is letting the jerk control your life just as much as doing it would be. I could end up like Lydia who dyed her hair platinum a few years ago after Caspar told her he'd kick her out of the house if she did. Lydia couldn't stand platinum blonde hair and wouldn't leave her bedroom until it grew out.

At Kimball's Food Market I helped Mrs. Barnett carry two bags of groceries to her Buick. She called me young man.

"Thank you, young man," she said, and she pulled this rubber change pouch out of her purse and gave me a nickel. The pouch was shaped like a run-over football with a slit down the center, and if you squeezed the ends the slit opened. Mrs. Barnett came from a generation that thought shiny money was worth more than dull money, so the first nickel laid in my palm wasn't good enough.

She said, "Just a moment, dear," and took it back, and poked around in the rubber pouch until she found a good one. I tried to imagine what Mrs. Barnett had been like when she was a teenager, before her cheeks got floppy. Had she worried about the compromise between wholesomeness and popularity? In her whole life, had the thought of birth control ever crossed her mind?

Zion's Own Hardware store had a window display for National Center Pivot Month. All the pipes, sprayers, nozzles, and general irrigation deals made me feel like spring had to come someday. I mean, somebody expected to see the ground again. The dogwoods would flower in Greensboro in a month, but Maurey had told me Wyoming trees don't ever flower. They molt.

The Ditch Creek Barbershop was a one-chair deal with three cracked-plastic kitchen chairs for people waiting their turn. There was this gumball machine with a sign saying the Jackson Lion's Club took the gumball money and gave it to people who needed cornea transplants. The back wall by the sink was covered by photos of young guys in army uniforms standing next to each other, and all these medals, ribbons, certificates, notices from the American Legion, and a map of the South Pacific with needles stuck in it.

Pud Talbot sat in the chair, getting himself burred, so I almost left but the barber said, "Be just a minute, son." I figured I better wait in spite of Pud's ugly yap. The barber had called me son. He was telling a story about Okinawa, something about piles of dead Japanese bodies across the road from piles of dead Americans and his job was to keep the flies off the American piles.

"I waved a fan over twenty-two GIs for seventeen hours," the barber said. "Not a single fly laid eggs on my buddies."

I picked up a two-year-old *Time* magazine with John Glenn on the cover. There was a story about how Elizabeth Taylor had eaten a can of bad beans on the *Cleopatra* set and gotten food poisoning. I wondered what Lydia would say if I told her Elizabeth Taylor ate canned beans.

As soon as the barber—who said his name was March—got me in the chair, he did something that nobody who cuts hair ought to do. He pointed to this brown, mushroomy thing nailed to the wall with all the photos and said proudly, "That's my ear."

"Oh."

"Cut it off a Jap at Corregidor. He wasn't even dead yet, just lay there with his bottom half blown off by a sub-Thompson. His eyes didn't flinch or nothing when I took the ear."

"Oh."

"Those Japs were tough. Had to give them that, they were tough. Why haven't I seen you before?"

I gave him the general rundown.

"You're son of the woman in Doc Warden's place, huh?"

He'd started clipping away with the scissors, which made me nervous, so I didn't answer for fear of distracting him.

"I hear your mama's a real pistol."

I had no idea what that meant, so again I didn't answer, but March had his speech worked out and anything I said wouldn't have mattered.

Since then, I've discovered there are some people who think one little spot in their life was real and everything else is just meaningless time killing. I've met sports heroes like that, and a couple of women obsessed with late pregnancy and childbirth.

March was that way about World War II. He was in the Twenty-fourth Division in Sydney, Australia, then in New Guinea where he saw Japanese who had been cannibalizing their dead. He spent thirty-one days in a hole with another guy.

"That was on Davao. These officers came along and told us they needed the hole and we had to get out but I said, 'Forget it, sir.' Front lines weren't like Fort Bragg. Officers don't mean nothing up there."

"Leave the back kind of long."

He switched to the electric buzzing razor which at least couldn't draw blood. "Let me give you some advice, son. You're not too old to hear advice, are you?"

"Right now I need all the advice I can get."

"Find yourself a war. Not a police thing like we're piddling with over in Asia, a real war where you can test your mettle and find true men who are true friends."

"I don't know many men."

"There's nothing like lying in the mud next to a guy all night, knowing you'll probably die in the morning, to cement a friendship." He waved the razor in the direction of his picture wall. "Those are my closest relatives. No one who hasn't been in a war knows the meaning of trust."

"Are you leaving some on the back?"

March spun the chair around and stared me in the eye. "You hear me, son."

"Find a war and make friends."

"That's right. Test yourself, son. Life means something when you know it can end with one bullet. Be a man, son."

"Find a war," I said.

"You'll never live till you kill someone who's out to kill you."

"That's true."

Sam Callahan rode his bicycle up Alpine and turned in at the yellow frame house with the neat yard. As he bounded up the porch steps, he reached down to pick up a toy firetruck blocking the door.

"Honey, I'm home."

Maurey Callahan smiled sweetly from behind her ironing board. "How was your day at the office, dear?"

"A rat race, honey, a real rat race."

"Why don't you relax while I fix us some supper."

"Got to check on my little pal first." Sam went into the nursery and lifted Sam Jr. from his playpen. "How's my son today? Did you learn important new skills?"

The world's most strikingly beautiful baby cooed contentedly and reached for his father's thick moustache.

Maurey came up beside her men and put an arm across Sam's shoulders. "He's the perfect baby. I'm so glad you convinced me to have him."

Sam stretched his arm around Maurey's waist and let his hand rest on her round belly, eight months full with the next of their children. "There's nothing like a family."

I started into the White Deck but this scattered-looking, gangly man in glasses charged out of the Dupree Art Gallery and said, "You've been to the Twenty-one Club."

He had on dark slacks instead of blue jeans which, in GroVont, made him stick out like a foreigner. I said, "I'll be fourteen this summer."

"I mean Fifty-seventh Street, the Guggenheim, the Algonquin Hotel, Baghdad on the Hudson. New York City."

"I saw a game at Yankee Stadium once."

"At the very least you are aware of life east of Cheyenne. Come look at my paintings." He pushed his glasses up the ridge of his long nose and stared down at me eagerly. Any grown-up who wanted to talk to a kid had to be desperate, which made me leery of the deal.

"I don't know."

"I'm Dougie Dupree. Perhaps your mother has spoken of me." He held his hand out for a shake.

"You know my mother?"

The stunned-by-Lydia look came in his eyes. "Come see my works."

I shrugged and followed his back into the gallery. A card table in the middle of the room was covered by some kind of board game deal involving black-and-white marbles. Paintings of the mid-size type filled the walls. Almost all Teton pictures in this highly visible light, three or four had cheap margarine-colored sun rays pouring down the canyons. One showed a cowboy trying to lasso a skinny little pinto with its ribs showing. The cowboy and horse both looked fairly pitiful.

"I did that one," Dougie said. The price was $1,300.

"Do you get many customers?"

He pushed up his glasses. "In the summer they move like popcorn. There's no one at all this time of year, but my uncle owns the place. He doesn't understand on-season, off-season, so he makes me stay open."

"Oh."

"He lives in Florida."

"That explains it." I tried to imagine what it would be like to sit in this room all winter wearing slacks instead of jeans and wishing I was in New York. "How do you know Lydia?"

His eyes got all sly. "We've dated casually."

This surprised me. No one likes a mom who keeps secrets, besides, Lydia never does anything casually. I decided Dougie was lying in his teeth.

He sat at the table and looked sadly down at the board game. "You know the difference between me and your mother?"

I wondered why he played with marbles.

"We both feel superior to the provincial hicks of this area, but she enjoys feeling superior and I don't. Lydia probably wouldn't like Manhattan, she couldn't feel superior there."

"She could too."

"I crave intellectual equals, challenging minds. I hate being a snob in this jerkwater outpost of aboriginal quaintness."

"Lydia likes being a snob."

He stared at the marbles a long time, as if he'd forgotten I was there. I suppose he was thinking of some flashy club in New York City where the men wore slacks and the women respected brains. I couldn't decide whether to slip out the door or stay put.

Suddenly, Dougie smiled. "You wouldn't happen to know go, would you?"

I thought he said "no go," which didn't make any more sense than what he did say.

He nodded at the marbles. "Go is an ancient Oriental game which tests the human mind to its very limit—thousands of years older than chess and much more complex."

I didn't even know chess. "No, I don't."

"That was to be expected. I'll teach you."

"I have to eat lunch."

Dougie pushed his glasses up again. "I'll be here when you're ready to learn."

"Thanks for showing me the paintings. I like the one you did best."

Dougie beamed. "Give my regards to your mother."

"Your regards."

The phone rang and Maurey answered. "Callahan residence."

"Good day, madam. I was wondering if you would be interested in a complete set of Golden Book Encyclopedias of the World, twenty volumes in only twelve easy installments?"

"You'll have to wait until my husband comes home from the office and ask him. Sam handles all the details of our life."

15

"You look sad," Dot said. "You're too young to look sad. I'll bet a strawberry shake would fix you right up."

Why do adults think kids don't have a problem in the world that can't be solved by sugar? "I'd rather have a cheeseburger," I said.

Dot settled her body into the booth across from me. "You eat a cheeseburger in here almost every day. Doesn't your mother feed you?"

"I feed her."

Dot had two uniforms. They were both mostly white, only one had lime-green trim and the other had pink. I preferred the pink, which is what she had on then. It went better with her smile. She also had two little matching hat deals she wore on the supper shift.

She didn't show any sign of getting up to turn my cheeseburger order in to Max. "You're too young to be hangdog, Sammy. Start now and think where you'll be when you get his age." She thumb-pointed to Oly who was nodded out in his old booth next to the jukebox. I looked at him and wondered where I would be when I got his age. I could think of loads of places worse than that booth. By the time you were that old, you couldn't have problems anyway, except it would be tough having people look at you and not care you were there.

Oly'd grown a goiter in his neck since Bill died, which made him more unpleasant than ever to look at, but, other than the goiter, his life seemed the same as ever.

"Something happened that I guess I don't mind, only someone else does and it's going to unhappen without any say from me. Did that ever happen to you?"

Dot looked at me awhile. It was nice of her not to treat me my age. "You ought to have a say in what happens," she said.

"I don't mind it not happening so much as nobody asking me what I'd do if it happened to me."

"That is a problem." We sat a few minutes staring into space. I stared at Dot's hands, which were pretty much normal except for the color. They were way pink, pinker than the trim on her uniform, more like the pink of a person's gums.

"Any chance of you telling me what it is we're talking about?" she asked.

I scratched my nose. "I guess Maurey is pregnant. I guess. She thinks maybe she is. Pregnant."

One of Dot's hands flew up around mouth level, but otherwise she took it fairly well. She didn't say anything so I kept going.

"She and Lydia are over in Dubois at the doctor finding out, but it looks kind of like she is."

Dot's hand went from her mouth back to the table. "Those questions weren't just kid curiosity. I thought you two were playing I'll-show-you-mine, you-show-me-yours."

"We took the game another step or two."

"I guess."

"Now she wants an abortion."

I looked up at Dot's face and her ever-present smile was gone. She said, "Isn't it funny how people who don't want it get it and people who do don't."

"Do you and Jimmy want your little boy?"

"Let me turn in your ticket."

Dot went to the kitchen and I sat looking at myself in the napkin box. The shiny sides had a design that made my face all twisted and weird, so it was possible to pretend I was a fetus. I opened my mouth in an O which looked fishy, but then I breathed out and the jaw in the napkin box went milky.

Dot brought us both cups of coffee. I filled mine with sugar and milk; she drank hers black.

"So your mother is helping her?" Dot asked. I nodded and blew across my coffee. "How about Maurey's parents?"

"We'd just as soon not get them involved."

A smile almost flickered onto Dot's dimples. "Buddy'll roast your butt on a branding fire."

I tried not to visualize the image. "What's an abortion feel like?"

Dot drank some coffee. "I wouldn't know, someone told me it's like having your guts and soul sucked away." More visualization. I think Dot was embarrassed about using the word soul in conversation. She flushed and looked back at the kitchen as if she hoped my burger would come up.

"Abortions are illegal," I said.

"There's a place in Rock Springs, a regular clinic during the week, but on Saturdays and Sundays they do those things to women. I hear it's disgusting, they wheel the women through three at a time and you can hear the doctor or whoever does it scraping the woman next to you."

"Scraping?"

"I heard more than one woman on the number-three table freaks out and runs away half-gassed."

I put more sugar in my coffee. What did she mean, "scraping"? And "gassed"? Did they stick a tool up there and pry loose a dead baby?

"How do you know this stuff?" I asked.

"People think waitresses are deaf. Boy, could I write a book if I had the time."

"I'm going to write a book someday."

Once again, Dot didn't treat me my age. "How about I tell you the true stories and you write the book. We'll split the money."

A bell *dinged* and Dot pulled herself out of the booth to go fetch my cheeseburger. After she left, I thought her stories were okay for her, but when I became a writer I was going to make mine up. True stuff isn't fun enough.

I didn't see Maurey the rest of the day, but Lydia told me the doctor had done a test and we'd know for certain Tuesday.

"What's an abortion feel like?" I asked.

She gave me her look. "Feels like cutting your fingernails real short."

I thought about that. "Someone told Dot it's like having your guts and soul sucked out."

"You discussed this with Dot?"

I told her about the clinic in Rock Springs and how the third-table woman can hear scraping on the first-table woman when she's half-gassed.

Lydia went stern. "Sam, as far as Maurey goes, it's getting her fingernails trimmed. You got that?"

"Why?"

"This won't be a lark for her. I'll brook no talk of guts and souls."

"Yes, ma'am."

"Ma'am me one more time and I'll cut off your allowance."

"What allowance?"

16

TUESDAY AFTERNOON WE PLAYED CLUE. HANK WAS PROFESSOR Plum, I was Colonel Mustard, and Maurey was Miss Scarlet. Lydia sat on the milk crate and smoked cigarettes.

She made fun of us. "The butler did it with a shotgun."

Hank held his cards with both hands and concentrated. Maurey was understandably distracted and I watched her. She had on a light blue sweater with little loops on the shoulders. Every time the refrigerator kicked on, she'd give a little jump.

Hank didn't like Clue. "This game takes logical thought and logical thought goes against everything the Blackfeet believe."

Lydia snorted through the smoke. "Whenever Hank feels inadequate he claims his Indian heritage."

"Who mentioned inadequate?"

"You. You can't figure out who killed where with what, so you blame your bloodline."

Hank had been around Lydia enough to know real criticism from exercising her tongue, which is what this was. Explaining people's flaws to them was a habit of hers; somebody had to do it.

Hank made a decision. "Mrs. White with a rope in the conservatory." He looked over at Maurey who showed him a card. "Damn."

It wasn't the rope or the conservatory because I had both those cards, so Maurey must have Mrs. White. Whoever killed the guy did it with the lead pipe, I knew that much, and I guessed the billiard room, but I was a ways from the murderer.

"What's a conservatory?" Maurey asked.

Hank and I looked at each other and shrugged.

"Opposite of a lavoratory," Lydia said.

I looked at the picture of the conservatory on the Clue board. "I think it's a library."

Maurey put her finger on the board. "Here's the library."

"It's a place where people conserve things," Lydia said.

Maurey rolled and came up four. As she moved Miss Scarlet into the library, the phone rang. We froze in this-is-it poses, Maurey staring at the board and me staring at her amazingly blue eyes.

From the living room, I heard Lydia say "Yes" twice and "Thank you" once, which gave the answer because she wouldn't have said thank you if the news was good. Lydia came to the door and leaned on the frame and blew smoke at us.

"Positive."

Hank exhaled, but Maurey and I just sat there. She blinked a couple of times and her eyes glistened. I picked up my Professor Plum piece and turned it over between my fingers.

"Say something," I said.

Maurey blinked twice more, real fast. "Miss Scarlet, lead pipe, library." She was right.

The next day at lunchtime, Teddy and Dothan got in a king-hell fight over whether some droppings in the school yard were moose or elk. It happened so fast, *zoom*, the yard went from boring to violent.

I heard them arguing, but my main attention, if you could call it attention, was on Chuckette's complaint that her sister Sugar was being allowed to do something at the age of eleven that Chuckette hadn't been allowed to do—talk to boys on the phone, I think. Or use hair spray, I don't know. Chuckette was always upset about something Sugar was allowed to do—when Dothan suddenly tackled Teddy and they rolled across the snow.

Dothan came up on top with his knees on Teddy's shoulders. Teddy spit chew juice on Dothan's shirt and neck. By then a bunch of kids circled around, so I had to watch through their legs, but I saw Dothan making Teddy eat whatever kind of droppings were involved.

Maurey stood on the cafeteria steps, watching the fight.

Chuckette caught me watching Maurey. "Maurey Pierce is lucky to have a boyfriend like Dothan."

I almost asked why, but figured it didn't matter anyway. If Maurey liked in the right way a kid who made another kid eat animal shit, she would never really like me.

Chuckette went right on. "I bet I'm the only girl in school who would go steady with you. Everyone says you aren't good enough for me and I'm settling beneath my dignity."

I looked at Chuckette's flat face and my scarf around her neck, and felt depressed. "That's right, Chuckette, I'm not good enough for you."

"Don't pout. I hate it when you pout."

Lydia drove over to Dot's duplex to get the scoop on the Rock Springs deal, then she made several hush-tone phone calls. Maurey was over every evening, only Lydia was her best friend now instead of me. They would sit at the kitchen table and talk quietly while I watched our one station on TV.

Whenever I went in there, they'd shut up and stare at me until I left. At least she didn't run to Dothan Talbot.

I asked Lydia what they talked about and she said, "Girl stuff."

"Why can't I listen?"

"Give her a week, honey bunny. She still needs your friendship. Just wait until we clean up the mess made by your dick."

A front came through Friday night, dumping a few inches of fresh snow, so the drive to Rock Springs the next day was even more tense than the usual drive to an abortionist. We loaded up as soon as Annabel left for her weekly bridge-club deal, all three of us in the front seat with Maurey in the middle, and almost immediately she took my hand in hers, which made me feel good. It wasn't like sexy hand holding—there'd be no jack jobs on this ride—but more like friendship, like she needed to touch someone who liked her. Lydia had never driven on ice before and it took her clear through the Hoback Canyon to realize the brake pedal caused more trouble than it was worth. We slid right through a stop sign, but no one was coming so we didn't crash.

In Pinedale, Lydia said, "Need a pee?"

I said no and Maurey stared out the window at the road ahead.

The route was the same as the last two hundred miles of our trip out from Carolina in September. Where before I'd seen miles of Wyoming nothingness, now I picked up on details—a line of willows sticking from the snow marked where an irrigation ditch would be if spring ever happened, cottonwoods way off meant ranch houses, the bruise-colored mountains to the east followed the Continental Divide.

The problem was that I didn't feel right about this abortion deal. I was torn between reality and wouldn't-it-be-nice. The reality, and I king-hell well knew it, was that seventh-graders are too young to have babies. Maurey was chock-full of potential of doing something in life, and raising a child would make the next few years predictable. She might become Annabel.

Also, Maurey didn't love me so us being a couple, as in family, was out. And unmarried pregnant girls in small mid-American villages come in for vicious abuse; they'd probably kick us out of junior high.

Buddy would roast my butt on a branding fire.

On the wouldn't-it-be-nice side was the baby. I'd always wanted to be needed, and, whenever I looked around at people in grocery stores, it always seemed like being part of a family would be neat. If I couldn't have a father I could be one. It would be a hoot to teach a kid how to lay a bunt down the third-base line.

With a baby, I'd have a connection to Maurey. Even if she didn't love me in the right way, if we had a child together the right way might happen, or at the least, we'd stay in touch. I didn't know true love from Dothan's moose turds, but I was fond of her hair and eyes and little fingers; I didn't want to lose her, whatever part of her I had.

The bottom reality of the whole deal was that whether I felt right about the abortion or not, nobody asked my opinion.

An antelope—Pushmi and Pullyu's cousin—ran along next to the Oldsmobile for a few hundred yards, then crossed the road in front of us. His white bottom made a whoosh blur going over the fence.

"We were moving fifty miles per and he beat us," Lydia said.

"That's fast," I said.

Maurey didn't say anything.

The clinic was a blond-brick box across the street from a Dairy Queen. Same architecture as a Southern Church of Christ, even had one of those Signs on Wheels out front, but where a Church of Christ sign would read MAKE YOUR BED IN

Heaven today for tomorrow there will be no sheets, or some pithy little saying that sounded great but made no sense to anyone, the clinic sign read Red Desert Medical Arts Complex and listed four doctors and an optometrist.

Maurey let go of my hand long enough for us to get out of the car, then she took it back. "Hank says this is a nasty town," Lydia said. "No place for an Indian."

The wind was blowing so hard we had to lean together across the parking lot, and when I opened the clinic door it whipped back and whopped against the rubber doorstop.

Lydia checked her reflection in the glass and corrected some stray hair. "No place for a white woman either."

Maurey's face looked calm, kind of. She wasn't panicking or anything. Her tongue pressed against her lower lip making a little bulge in the hard-set line of her mouth. She had on jeans, and the hand that wasn't holding mine was in her front pocket. Her eyes gave no information.

We stood over by a water fountain while Lydia went to the front desk and talked to a woman with violent orange hair and turquoise jewelry. They studied a sheet of paper and Lydia handed the woman a wad of cash. During the week the clinic was a regular obstetric place for women who wanted babies, so they had this bulletin board covered with snapshots of newborns with each baby's name and weight written on the white border in blue ink.

Maurey and I stood in front of the bulletin board, looking at the babies. At first, they all seemed the same—wrinkled and rose-colored with squished-up eyes—but then I started seeing differences. Amanda Jen Wayne, 6 lbs. 7 oz., had a widow's peak. Cody LaMar Jenkins, 9 lbs. 2 oz., had a furrow in his chin you could run a straw through.

Maurey's hand tightened on mine, but she didn't say anything. Lydia came back from the desk and tried to get us to sit on this cow udder-colored couch, but Maurey wouldn't move from in front of the baby bulletin board.

She said, "I'm fine," which were about the first words she'd said all day.

A door opened behind the desk and a girl not much older than us came through. She smiled. "Come with me and we'll get you ready."

Maurey gripped my hand harder and looked at me, then at Lydia. She said, "This is the shits."

Lydia said, "You'll be okay."

"I know."

I gave her hand a squeeze and let go. The girl pointed to a door off to the right. "The waiting room is through there. She'll be done in a couple of hours." Then she led Maurey away.

Three Negro men in white shoes took Me Maw away. I was in the bedroom with the round bed, under the bed, waiting for her to be dead. Bed springs are pretty cool if you lie on your back and look up at them. They grow fuzz. I heard the hearse pull up on the driveway and the men joking, teasing each other about someone named Sylvinie.

When the doorbell chimed I crawled out from under the bed to look out the second-floor window at the dark blue hearse with little flags on the corners. The back doors were open. Across the street, the Otake kids dashed around in their bathing suits, playing on a Slip 'N' Slide. The whoops and yells that carried across our yard didn't quite fit the action. Jesse sprayed his sister with the hose, but her scream lagged behind her open mouth.

Two Negroes carried Me Maw out under a plastic sheet on a stretcher thing, with the other Negro and Caspar coming behind. When they were finished sliding Me Maw into the hearse, Caspar tipped each one a dollar. I could see the pink in the bald spot on his head, and his hand which was also pink stretching out with the dollars. The Negroes looked down at their white shoes.

After they drove away, Caspar turned and saw me in the window. I ducked down and slid under the bed.

Lydia and I went back out through the wind to the car where she picked up a *Saturday Evening Post*, then we crossed to the Dairy Queen to wait. I had a taco pie, which was this thing like a sloppy joe on a bed of Fritos in a paper boat, and a soft vanilla ice cream dipped in chocolate wax. I imagined all the people who had sat in this very Dairy Queen, eating ice cream and waiting for loved ones to finish abortions so they could go home and get out of the wind.

Three high school girls bent over their soda pops watched us and giggled, *Titter, titter*, like doofy birds. All Rock Springs must know what happened over there on Saturdays. They knew I was the sperm father of a baby who would soon join the city sewer system. I wanted them to stop talking about me. It made me nervous, made my butt itch like king-hell, then my whole back and neck. The woman at the counter knew I'd been in the clinic too. They all knew.

Lydia glanced up from her magazine. "Stop fidgeting."

"I itch."

"Well, go to the restroom and scratch then."

The bathroom was past the boothful of girls who knew, and, much as I needed to pee, I couldn't walk by them. They'd say something—"*Abortion boy*" or "*Where would you be if your mom...*" Something like that. They might even reach out and pinch me.

"I'm going back over and wait in the waiting room."

Lydia looked across her magazine and raised one eyebrow. "Just don't fidget around me."

At the clinic, I found a bathroom without having to ask the red-haired lady at the desk. She would know I was the cause of everything too. After I peed, I stood at the sink running water and studying myself in the mirror. I don't think I'd ever really concentrated on that before. I mean, I knew what I looked like—a short kid with ears that stuck out, a long forehead and a spooky nose. I could have passed for nine—but I tended to forget. I tended to think of myself as sort of neutral-appearing, as if I could slide through life without being noticed, a face on a baseball card.

Back in the reception room, I didn't even look at the desk lady. She was probably pointing a finger at me.

Six or seven people waited in the waiting room, and not a one was happy. An older couple who could have been someone's grandparents sat holding hands. An angry man in a business suit glared at me. A familiar shape with a crewcut stood, facing the door on the other side of the room. He turned and our eyes met and it was Howard Stebbins.

I said, "Coach."

He said, "Callahan."

Time froze up, my mouth went aluminum foil. The implications raced—I was dead meat. Caught. Finished in Wyoming. How had he known? It hit that he hadn't known. His eyes weren't self-righteously hateful. He was pleading. He was the one with the dead meat.

A low scream came from the back of the clinic, then behind Stebbins, Maurey broke through the door in a white hospital gown. Her animal eyes searched the waiting room and found me.

"Let's go."

At her voice, Stebbins turned and Maurey made a gurgle-gasp sound. She ran; he reached out as if to stop her, then she was past him and moving. Everyone could see her full back and butt below the hospital gown strings.

I looked back at Stebbins, and behind him, in the door, stood Maurey's mother in a white gown of her own. Her face was terrified, ugly; her mouth a gash. She called, "Maurey."

I said, "Annabel," and her eyes shifted to me. Then I got out.

17

The first twenty miles north of Rock Springs no one talked. Maurey rode bent over with her face between her knees. At one point she reached up to crank the heater and fan as high as they would go. I looked at her bare back, at the bumpy ridge of the spinal column with the two dips along each side and her thin shoulderblades. There were two strings, one tied around her neck and another that was supposed to tie around her ribs but had come loose.

Lydia glanced at me and narrowed her eyes.

"Her mom was there," I said, "getting an abortion too. And Coach Stebbins was with her."

Lydia let this sink in as the high Wyoming plains swept by. A mail truck passed us going south, and some ravens swooped around a roadkill deer.

Lydia wrinkled her nose. "Annabel Pierce had sex?"

Maurey's head sunk and I heard her say "Daddy," then she was crying. Her back trembled, contracted with sobs. She cried really loud. I'd never heard honest grief before.

Lydia pulled off the side and held Maurey's head, pulling hair out of her face. I put my hand on her shoulder blade, for a second, then took it back. I didn't know if I was part of the problem or the comfort.

The loudness didn't last long, then came gasps like her breath had been knocked out. She sat up and leaned her head back on the seat, staring open-eyed at the car roof.

"A man was shaving me," she said.

"Where?" I asked.

Lydia said, "Shut up."

"He was touching me, down there, and chewing gum and it felt dirty. I wanted to get rid of my skin. I looked to the right at the Negro girl who had already been shaved. Her eyes were closed like she was asleep and I thought, wow, I see my first Negro and get my first abortion on the same day."

Lydia held a Kleenex up to Maurey's nose and said, "Blow." After Maurey blew, Lydia cracked her window and threw out the Kleenex.

Maurey sniffed twice. "I turned my head to the left and she was looking at me. I said, 'Mama, what are you doing here?' then I realized the man was fixing to shave her too. She said, 'Oh, honey.'

"I jerked and the man snapped at me. I was afraid to jump up for fear he'd cut me there, I had to lie still but I couldn't. My own mother . . ." Lydia leaned over and started the car, but didn't put it in gear.

"The nurse gave the Negro girl a shot, and I knew when she gave me one I'd never be able to move. And Mama kept staring at me. That's when I screamed."

Lydia shifted into drive and we eased back onto the highway. The wind blew snow across the road about wheel level so we couldn't see the pavement but everything a foot off the ground was clear. It made for an unreal effect.

I didn't understand. "This is impossible. How could Annabel be getting an abortion at the same time and place as Maurey?"

Maurey blinked when I said "abortion."

Lydia punched the lighter and waited a few seconds, then lit a cigarette, a Kool. "Once you get past the odds of them both being pregnant at the same time, it's not so hard to figure. This is the only clinic doing them for three hundred miles, that I know of, and it only runs on weekends and we had to come today because of Annabel's bridge club."

Maurey still looked at the ceiling. "I bet there never was a bridge club. I bet every Saturday she goes off with Howard Stebbins and fucks all day." Tears flowed again, only this time with no sound. "And while Daddy's up taking care of the horses and being alone all winter, she's naked with Howard on top of her sticking his greasy thing in my mother."

Maurey's voice rose when she said "my mother."

"His filthy thing that just came out of his filthy little wife who gave him those three brats. Annabel Pierce, the perfect home-maker and thing-sucker."

I had trouble with the picture. Annabel would never allow herself to be seen in an unironed blouse. How could she get naked with a coach? And I suddenly realized what part of this whole thing affected me. Was the abortion off or postponed or what? We'd left Lydia's money—Caspar's really—and Maurey's clothes and shoes back in Rock Springs. They owed us an abortion. Were we talking rain check or blow off?

We drove another thirty miles with each of us lost in our thoughts. My fairly boggled thoughts jumped from Buddy to the baby to how this would change homeroom. The sucker would never blackmail me into coming out for football again. No more licks. Maurey took my hand again in one of hers. I was real happy about that. All I ever wanted was to be needed.

Maurey closed her eyes. Lydia chain-smoked Kools. We passed a cluster of three houses, one mobile home, and a post office with a sign out front that said Eden. One of the houses was surrounded by huge cottonwoods. It had recently been painted yellow and looked strange and kept up in the middle of the white on gray on white winter desert.

Lydia's voice broke the silence. I guess she'd been holding it in all these years, wanting to tell the story, but waiting for the right moment. I couldn't follow at first. She held both hands on the wheel and talked with a cigarette balanced in her mouth, smoke trailing over her face. Her voice stayed flat, no emotion.

"The first time they took Mother to the hospital, before the operations, Caspar had to sell some carbon paper in Durham right before Christmas. Christmas Eve he said he'd get back early and we'd have supper together and open presents. I decorated the tree by myself and put on my blue jumper. Every time a car came down the hill I ran to the window. You know the deal. Everyone that's seen a shrink has a story like it. Caspar never showed up."

Lydia paused to blow smoke out her nose. I think she hoped for some poor-little-girl understanding, but I was her kid—she'd pulled the same crap on me as long as I could remember—and Maurey had just caught her mom aborting a coach's baby. Neither one of us exactly bubbled with sympathy.

"About eight o'clock Caspar called to say he had to stay in Durham, but he'd bring me a nice present the next day. I found a piece of flagstone and went into his study and smashed his best pipe. Then I decided to have a party."

The heater was too hot, but to take off my coat, I'd have to let go of Maurey's hand, and I didn't want to do that. Her breathing had gone real steady. I couldn't tell if she was listening or asleep. I was pretty sure she wasn't asleep, but I just couldn't see making her move.

"I called up the big brother of a girl I knew in school, Mimi Rotkeillor. He was a football player I kind of liked. I invited him over, said my daddy was out of town and he should round up any friends wanted to have some fun on Christmas

Eve. They brought oranges and grapefruit that they'd injected vodka in with a hypodermic syringe. Lord knows where they got the syringe."

"How many?" I asked.

She blinked smoke out of her eyes. "How many what?"

"How many people came over?"

Lydia bit her lower lip. "Five football players from around town. They had oranges full of vodka." I remembered the pictures in the panty box and realized where this story was heading. So did Maurey. Her hand tightened on mine and she opened her eyes.

"We ate the oranges and put on a Rosemary Clooney Christmas album and danced. They kept touching me and I thought, Daddy will be sorry now. He didn't know real boys liked me. Someone found his liquor cabinet and we drank something. I was pretty woozy."

Lydia punched fire for another Kool. We drove through Pinedale without a word, as if this was something she couldn't talk about in front of people.

"One guy was kissing me and I felt warm, and then I was on the floor and he was yanking on the blue jumper. I didn't know what was going on. He hurt me, but I was drunk and didn't care. I kept hoping Caspar would walk in and feel bad. Another guy climbed on me and he was big and I started bleeding and got scared. One of them held me down with his knees on my shoulders and his dick right in my face while another one did it to me."

Lydia's voice came faster. I kept seeing boys in the pictures—numbers 72, 56, 81, 11, and 20.

"They squirted on my face and in my mouth. My hair was filthy. They kept grunting on me and when I cried, they poured vodka on my crotch and it stung. When I screamed they hit me, so I shut up and pretended I was unconscious, but they screwed me a couple more times anyway."

Lydia stubbed her cigarette out in the ashtray. Her eyes were hard, and I could see her jawbone tighten in her cheek. She sped the car up some, but her voice stayed even. "After that, they stood in a circle around my body and urinated on me." She looked over at me for the first time. "That's your daddy."

Maurey brought her head off the seat back; I looked out my passenger window. We came to a small river with ice along the edges and clear across where it slowed down for logs.

Lydia rolled down her window which brought in a blast of cold air. "I was so stupid about sex, I didn't even know if you had five fathers or one until a couple years ago."

"How many?" I asked.

"One. Only one sperm from one daddy took hold. The rest was just gooey come and blood."

"Which one gave the come that took hold?"

She rolled her window back up. "How the hell should I know."

18

Lydia decided that since Maurey was barefoot and pregnant in the snow, I should carry her into the Pierces' yellow frame house.

"I can walk," Maurey said.

"She can walk," I said.

Lydia stayed firm. "We've done enough, I don't want pneumonia added to the list."

So I stood next to the car and Maurey slid over to where I could reach one arm under her knees and the other on her back. After she put her right hand around my neck, I counted three and jerk-curled her up. It was neat in that her back and legs where I touched them were naked. I hadn't grabbed flesh in two weeks, so I immediately developed a stiffie and Maurey got the giggles.

"You can't carry me."

"Me Tarzan, you Jane."

"You're gonna drop me on my ass."

I made a Cheetah sound. There's a limit on how much tension kids can handle before they revert.

We staggered up the driveway in a lurch to the right a few steps, lurch to the left motion. Maurey tickled my ears.

"Quit fooling around and take her inside," Lydia said.

"Who's fooling around?"

At the door, Lydia didn't volunteer any help, which made our entrance a Three Stooges routine. I cracked the screen with my right hand, twisted into the opening, then Maurey turned the knob and I backed into the door with a crash that caught Petey in the face.

Petey sat down hard and howled. I dropped Maurey's feet maybe a tenth of a second before her back so at least we avoided the sprawl-on-the-floor thing. She looked down at my jeans and slapped me lightly on the stiffie.

"I told you no more of those."

"I can't control it."

"You better learn."

Petey held his face and screamed. "*I'm half-dead, I'm half-dead.*"

Coming through the door, Lydia observed the scene with her usual disdain. Telling us the truth had made her more superior than ever.

She said, "Shut up, little boy."

Petey's howl stopped like she'd cut it with a knife. He stared in disbelief.

"Get off the floor. You're behaving like a child."

"I am a child."

"Don't brag."

Petey stood up, thought about bratting out on Lydia, but changed his mind and faced Maurey instead. "I'm not supposed to be alone all day."

"You lived." Maurey headed for the back of the house.

"Mama's gonna get you when she comes home. Hey, you're naked in back."

Maurey turned. "So?"

"Mama's gonna get you."

"Fuck Mama." Maurey smiled at us. "Make yourself at home. I'll be right back."

Lydia beelined for the kitchen with a mesmerized Petey in her wake. She'd wanted to criticize Annabel's homemaking ever since she heard about the recipe box full of alphabetized index cards. I figured she was in there making a cleanliness inspection, looking for cracks in Annabel's Lysol defense system, and I didn't really care to watch Lydia probe for character flaws. She does enough of that with me. But standing alone in the living room felt squirrelly, so I eventually followed on in.

Lydia was standing on a chair, running her fingertips across the tops of shelves. She looked at her hand and said, "How could a woman like this get knocked up?"

I'm sure Petey had never seen a grown-up stand on a chair—Annabel had stools. "Mama's gonna be mad at you," he said with no conviction. "She doesn't like people touching her stuff."

Lydia looked way down on Petey. "In the grand scheme of things, little boy, no one in the whole world cares what your mother likes or doesn't like." She stepped down, walked to the refrigerator, and glared inside. "Everything is dated in ink on little strips of masking tape, the leftovers are clearly labeled. I'd die before I'd live like this. Where's the recipe file?"

I pointed to a flowered file box on the cabinet between a pair of crocheted oven mitts and a framed sampler that read, NO MATTER WHERE I SIT MY GUESTS, THEY ALWAYS LIKE MY KITCHEN BEST.

"Don't touch that," Petey yelped, too late.

Lydia dragged the chair back over from the shelves to the linoleum-topped kitchen table. She sat down and pulled out all the index cards. "Look at this—chipped beef and cheese, chocolate pie, Cindy's mother's venison casserole, cornbread, corn pudding—the woman is a maniac."

Lydia divided the stack and shuffled cards like we were waiting to play crazy 8s. "This'll screw her up more than the abortion."

Petey's wide eyes never left Lydia's hands as she shuffled. "What's a bortion?"

"Dirty oven, kid. Like when meatloaf splatters and you have to scrape out the grease." Lydia thinks she's so cute sometimes.

"My mama's oven is never dirty."

"Was today."

Maurey appeared at the door wearing jeans and a black sweater with her hair pulled back in a barrette. She carried a leather-looking suitcase in her right hand and a tan overnight bag in her left. A stuffed bear poked out of her right armpit.

Petey tattled. "The lady touched Mama's stuff."

Maurey looked at Lydia. "Let's go."

"You're not supposed to leave me alone after dark. I might get in trouble."

"Mom will be along in a couple hours. Meantime, burn up the house if you feel like it."

I felt sorry for the kid. All his limits had been shot down and he looked ready to cry. Since Lydia and Maurey were being ugly, I opted for nice. "She's kidding. Don't really burn the house up."

"But I'll be alone."

"Go watch Rocky the Flying Squirrel."

Petey slammed both hands on the table. "Rocky's not on on Saturday afternoon, stupid."

—

Lydia telephoned Hank, who brought over a couple of frozen pizzas—sausage with mushroom and Canadian bacon. It was odd, like *zap*, Maurey was part of the family and always had been. She helped me wash the dishes without being asked. Hank took out the trash. Lydia painted her toenails black.

After supper we all four hung out in the living room, doing whatever we would have done anyway even if Maurey hadn't bumped into her mom at an abortion clinic. I sat in the elk-gut chair with Alice in my lap, reading *The Once and Future King* and *Tom Swift and His Deep-Sea Hydrodrome.* Maurey brought a pillow from our bedroom and sat on it with her back against the couch. Her book was *The Capture of the Golden Stallion* by Rutherford G. Montgomery. Unlike me, Maurey actually made progress in her reading. I sat staring at the same page—96—in both my books, trying to understand sentences with migratory words.

Lydia perched on her feet on the couch, flipping through a *New Yorker,* while next to her Hank watched "Gunsmoke."

"Miss Kitty is frigid," Lydia said.

"She's just white, all white women look frigid."

"She's frigid."

Our bedroom—had a creepy ring to it. I'd never shared a room with anyone. At the manor house I had four bedrooms I thought of as mine. What hacked me off and made the words swim was that no one ever discussed anything. When we drove onto the GroVont Highway, Maurey had said, "Swing by my place and I'll pick up some clothes."

Then we came home and she asked me which drawers were hers. The stuffed bear lay propped against the headboard, so I figured she was sleeping in the bed, but where was I sleeping? Why hadn't anyone said, "Mind if I stay at your house tonight?" "What's Buddy going to do?" "Gee, Maurey, would you like to live in my room?" "I think maybe I'll have the baby after all."

Instead we washed the dishes, left them to dry in the drainboard, went in the living room and plopped down for the evening. Maurey said, "I'm getting a pillow from our bedroom. Want anything while I'm up?"

"No."

At 10:30 I went out to the kitchen for Lydia's Gilbey's and she went to the bathroom for Valium.

"Hold out your hands," Lydia said.

Maurey, Hank, and I held out our hands so Lydia could shake a little yellow pill into each one. She said to Maurey, "We don't do this every night, understand, but today was special."

"A day I won't forget," Maurey said.

The three of us shared a Dr Pepper to wash down our Valiums while Lydia knocked hers off with a shot of gin.

"Don't let the bedbugs bite," she said.

Hank said, "Sleep with your mouth shut or your spirit will fly around the world and might not be back for your awakening."

Maurey went to the bathroom and I put on my pajamas, then sat in the chair in front of my typewriter. By pressing down on all the keys at once I made them stick together up by the ribbon. A few fell back, but if I really slammed down on a key it usually stuck in the bunch. I got every one but three—Q, ;, and 9—jammed.

Getting under the sheets and waiting didn't feel like the thing to do. She might have me planned for the couch, or maybe she thought we'd sleep with our heads at different ends. It wasn't a day to take anything for granted.

Maurey came in wearing a white flannel nightgown. She'd brushed her hair and looked thirteen and beautiful. On account of the pregnancy, her breasts were growing by the day.

She folded the clothes she had been wearing and put them on the dresser. "Which side of the bed do you sleep on?"

I looked at the bed. It had a sky blue spread with thin white lines running lengthwise. "I never thought about it. I just sleep."

"Can I have the outside? Lately, I pee and throw up at strange times of night."

"Sure." I turned back the blankets and got in. We'd been

together in my bed plenty of times, but I always knew what was going to happen before. "Can I see where the man shaved you?"

Maurey pulled her white nightie up above her hips and looked down at herself. Her crotch was a fold in a flat area at the top of a gentle rise. The distance from her navel to the fold was farther than I'd imagined, like one belly above the belly button and one belly below it. You couldn't tell she'd ever had hair there.

"Weird, huh?" Maurey said.

"I don't know, it looks okay." I reached out to touch it, but she dropped her nightie.

"No touching."

"I just wanted to feel the stub."

"You thought you could get me wet and I'd do something I told you I wouldn't do."

"Maurey, I'm surprised you think that."

"Here's the rules. No kissing and no touching the spot. If you try to kiss me it will ruin everything."

I'd been afraid those were the rules. Maybe after the Valium kicked in she would change her mind.

Maurey slid under the covers next to me. We lay on our backs with our shoulders almost together, only I couldn't see her face because the bear was between our heads.

We listened to each other breathe. In the kitchen, the refrigerator kicked on, and with a *mew* Alice jumped on the bed and settled between us at knee level.

"She finally seems weaned," Maurey said.

"Are we going to keep the baby?"

Her back flinched. "I'm not thinking about that tonight."

"What's your dad going to say about you living here?"

"I'm not thinking about anything tonight, okay, Sam. Don't ask me any more questions."

Nobody said anything for a long time. The front of my forehead started to wooze out with the familiar approach-of-Valium feeling.

Maurey giggled.

"What?" I asked.

"I can sleep with you but I don't know if I can sleep with those pajamas."

I'm feeling touching togetherness and she's laughing at my sleep wear. "What's wrong with my pajamas?"

"They're paisley."

"Grandma Callahan bought them for me."

"Don't they give you nightmares?"

She was beginning to sound like Lydia. "Do you want me to get up and change them?"

"I'd sleep better if you did."

I crawled over Maurey and went to the closet and dug out a pair of pajamas the same color as a pack of Doublemint chewing gum. They were meant for summertime and the bottoms were short, which showed my knees. Maurey stared at the ceiling while I undressed and dressed. I know because I took a peek when I was naked to see if she cared and she didn't.

After I changed I crawled across and settled in on my back again. Alice turned around twice to arrange herself. Maurey moved the bear from between us. She rolled over on her stomach, propped up on her elbows, and stared at me.

"Do you think you can keep from kissing me or touching the spot?"

"I think so."

"You better be sure."

"Okay, I'm sure," I said, even though I wasn't.

"Will you hold me then."

That surprised me. I hadn't learned to separate affection from sex yet. I put my right arm under her and my left arm over her and she curled up with both hands balled into fists between our chests. Her hair was up against my nose.

Maurey mumbled. "I'm so tired. I've never been so tired in my life."

Something large and heavy crashed in Lydia's room. Maurey's head came up an inch off my pillow. "What was that?"

"The grown-ups."

Her head went back down. "I wanted to watch the ten-thirty pint thing. You've told me so much about it."

"It's no big deal. Go to sleep now."

"God, I'm tired."

Maurey's hair smelled good as she slept. I listened to her breathe, thinking about how alive she was and our baby was still alive. I wondered about the crash from Lydia's room. It had sounded like a chest of drawers being dropped from several feet above the floor. Tom Swift's hydrodrome was nothing but a diving bell on legs. I could have written a better book. I would someday. I'd write a science fiction book about Indians—Hank on the planet Jupiter.

Pretty soon my right arm went dead as Otis's leg. Then the Valium took hold and I finally went under.

—

The next morning I showered with cold water. We had a two-person water heater which knocked like someone wanted out whenever you turned a hot tap. I woke to the sound of it knocking, went in the kitchen to make coffee, and while I was there, Hank came out of the bathroom and Maurey went in.

Hank's eye was swollen and a flesh-colored Band-Aid—not his flesh color—covered the bridge of his nose. My guess would have been king-hell pool cue across the face, but Lydia didn't own a pool cue.

He walked into the kitchen and grunted.

I pointed to the coffeepot.

"What was in the pill she passed out?" Hank asked.

"Valium, sort of a tranquilizer-sleeping pill."

He poured a cup, put in cream, and stirred with a Bic pen. "Caused me trouble."

I had to pee so I knocked on the bathroom door and went in. Maurey was behind the shower curtain where I couldn't see anything but a blur.

"Don't you knock?" she asked.

"I knocked."

"Knock louder." The shower went off and Maurey's hand reached out for a towel. The problem was that I still peed a mainstream with a 90-degree-angle shooter, which I'd adapted to by holding my left hand off to the side there. The pee ran down my fingers into the toilet, I washed my hands well before leaving the can, and no one was the wiser. Only Maurey was the wiser when she stepped from the shower, toweled armpits to thighs, and caught me peeing into my hand.

"You're pissing on yourself."

"No, I'm not. I'm shy and hiding dick from you."

"You're pissing into your palm."

"Don't be a squirrel, Maurey."

"The kid who catches his own pee calls me a squirrel?"

Lydia pushed through the door in the same wraparound towel getup as Maurey. She had creases on her face and exhausted-looking hair.

Maurey wanted to tell the world. "Sam pees in his hand."

"All men piss on themselves and shit on women. Get out, both of you."

"It's my turn."

"Out."

Didn't take a lot of brains to connect last night's crash,

Hank's Band-Aid, and Lydia's mood. Maurey and I went to our room and shut the door.

She unwrapped the towel and sat on the edge of the bed with her head bent over, drying her hair. "Lydia's unhappy about something."

"We better eat breakfast at the White Deck."

I couldn't get over how completely nonmodest she was about being naked in front of me. She wasn't flirty or shy or anything—like we'd been raised since birth getting dressed together. Guys in a locker room are more body-spooked than Maurey was around me.

I sat in the typing chair watching her. Her rib cage was a lot lighter than mine. The smallpox vaccination bump on her arm was smaller. She twisted the towel around her head in a maneuver males can't do and looked at me. "What are you staring at?"

"You don't look pregnant."

Maurey stood up facing the mirror. From my chair, I saw her real front and her front in the mirror. Pushmi and Pullyu seemed to be staring at her behind, like when the eyes in a painting follow you around.

Maurey reached out and touched her womb area in the mirror. "My boobs hurt, my feet are swollen, I'm nauseous and pee all the time, my mom had an abortion yesterday."

"That's true."

So I took a cold shower and we escaped to the White Deck. We left an ugly silence in the kitchen. Hank stared at the floor and sipped coffee. Lydia stared at Hank and smoked cigarettes. Maurey and I could no more have stayed in that house than we could have taken back yesterday.

First thing, right off, the instant Dot walked up to the table, Maurey blabbed, "Sam pees in his hand."

How would she feel if I said, "Maurey's got a shaved thing."

Dot did the usual spontaneous gale of laughter. "Jimmy does too. He's like a garden hose with a nail hole on one side and a drip off the bottom."

"I don't drip off the bottom."

"Good for you, Sam."

Maurey wanted embarrassment and wasn't getting any. "Peeing on yourself is nothing to be proud of."

There's not an actress in the world who could fake Dot's laugh. If someone made a 45 of her laughing I'd buy it and play it every morning.

"All men pee on themselves," Dot said. "That's why toilets have the sandwich seat that they lift and never put down. Gives them a bigger target."

She poured us coffee and we went to work with the sugar and cream. A fly landed on top of the sugar dispenser and Maurey tried catching it and missed. "My dad doesn't pee on himself."

"They all do," I said, even though I hadn't known up until Dot said so. I never watched anyone urinate. "Even John Wayne pees on his fingers."

"John Wayne never peed on himself."

I tried to remember John Wayne movies while the fly made another attack on the sugar. It crawled up under the flap and down into the glass a little. Maurey grabbed the dispenser and shook it hard. We watched the fly buzz around above his sea of sugar, totally disoriented. I went into an empathetic fantasy where I was the fly who only wanted sugar, but when I got it someone trapped me in glass and shook me to smithereens.

"John Wayne doesn't pee at all," Dot said. She didn't seem disturbed by the fly in her sugar shaker.

Maurey thumped it down. "Everyone pees."

Dot reached over and with her thumb held open the top flap. We watched the fly walk around inside, waiting for him to stumble on the escape door. I couldn't figure where the fly came from in the first place. It was twenty degrees outside. He—or his ancestors—must have spent the whole winter in the White Deck.

Dot said, "John Wayne's made I bet fifty movies, and have you ever seen him take a leak once?"

The fly found the hole and escaped. I felt like I'd survived a trauma. "I never saw anyone in a movie take a leak."

"Don't you wish life was like the movies," Maurey said.

She ordered cinnamon toast and I had pancakes. Cinnamon toast and coffee wasn't the thing for our future child, but we hadn't reached the stage where I could nag, "Think about the baby, dear."

When Dot brought out the plates, she raised an eyebrow and looked at Maurey. "Well?"

"No."

Dot's face lit like the sun. "You didn't go through with it?"

"No."

"I'm so happy."

Maurey sprinkled extra sugar on her toast. "You never told me you'd be happy if I chickened out."

Dot slid into the booth next to me and patted my hand. "Honey, ever'one says, 'Do what you think best, it's your body,' but they're all pulling for you to keep the baby, they're pleased when you do."

"Why is that?"

"That's the way the world is. Life is neater than anything else."

For all her grins and giggles, Dot was a deep thinker too. *Life is neater than anything else.* I could hardly wait to find some paper and write that down.

"So, are you going to keep the baby?" Dot asked.

Funny how virtual strangers can ask about things that would be personal coming from loved ones. Maurey wouldn't give me an answer to that question, but to Dot she shrugged both shoulders and said, "I guess so."

Made me happy. "Yippee."

Maurey swung in the booth. "You're happy I'm going through with it?"

"Sure, I'm ready to be a father."

"Sam, you'll turn fourteen after it's born."

"I'm ready."

"And you've never lived in a small town. Things are liable to get ugly around here come summer."

Dot nodded in agreement.

"I don't care."

"If my boyfriend doesn't break your legs, my dad probably will."

I paused a moment on that one. "You still have a boyfriend?"

"Whose jacket am I wearing?"

"You could give it back?"

"No."

We zipped into intense eye lock until Dot got nervous and slid from the booth. "I'll leave you young parents to yourselves."

"What about me?" I asked.

"We're friends."

19

CASPAR ATTENDED THE CULVER MILITARY ACADEMY WAY back in the Dark Ages. He rode in the Black Horse Troop and he learned all about leadership. I don't have much use for leadership qualities. Caspar talks about Culver with the same gleam as Mr. March the barber on World War II.

"The friendships last a lifetime," he said.

I never saw any of his Culver pals around the manor house.

"It'll make a man out of you. If Lydia had gone there she wouldn't be the mess she is today."

"She'd be a man?"

"She wouldn't be immoral."

There's something odd about being eight, nine years old and being told three times a week your mom is immoral.

"Don't you want to ride ponies with your comrades? Culver has the finest fencing program in the nation."

"Do they play baseball?"

He buried himself in the *Atlanta Constitution*. From behind the pages, he said, "You're going to end up like her."

I didn't want to end up like Lydia or Caspar either one. I wanted to end up like Willie Mays.

Sunday night a consideration kept me awake after Maurey snuggled up with her bear and went under. The next morning I would leave the joys of impending parenthood and return to the seventh grade and Howard Stebbins. English first period wouldn't be so bad; at least my clothes stayed on throughout the entire class. The locker room before and after PE was the vulnerable point. If he caught me in nothing but a jock strap I'd be easy pickings for whatever stance he chose to take. The stance thing worried me. Stebbins and I had never given a holy hoot for each other, only now we had something in common—Buddy Pierce. I'd fucked his daughter, Stebbins fucked his wife. Not just fucked, we'd run rampant through the household impregnating every hole in sight. If he found out, Buddy would be understandably pissed to the point of blood flowing. The man *enjoyed* castration.

This gave Howard and me a common danger and people with a common danger tend to slide into an us-against-the-enemy deal.

I didn't want that. Stebbins was the coach; he was the enemy. Loyalty to Maurey called for despising the thing Howard had done to Buddy while ignoring the fact I'd done almost the same thing. I'd never thought of humping his daughter as doing something to the man. I'd been doing it to her, or, more truthfully, she'd been doing it to me. But, Sunday night, as I lay in bed listening to Maurey sleep, I started checking the deal out from Buddy's point of view.

I—an out-of-stater—had lain lengthwise on his little girl and slid my dick into her body. I induced orgasm in a thirteen-year-old.

Which would piss the cowboy off the most—daughter or wife? That was the crucial question that would tell whether I had power over Howard Stebbins or he had it over me.

All I knew about the cowboy code came from the movies where no Western people had sex except when the Apaches raped women, and Indians always killed the women they came in. John Wayne would kick butt if someone humped his daughter or wife. Daughters would be worse because of the innocence factor, although—lucky me—John Wayne's code didn't allow beating the holy crap out of a little boy.

Another bottom line was that if Maurey had the baby we were a sure bet to get caught anyway. Howard still had a shot at the clean getaway, which meant from a blackmail point of view I had his ass.

Maurey laughed in her sleep. I liked that. Sleeping next to someone was kind of neat.

Right then, I adopted my attitude. Lydia would be my model. Whenever Caspar caught her with her pants in the wrong spot, she whipped herself into self-righteous rage.

"It's your fault. I wouldn't have sucked that carbon salesman if you hadn't been such a bad parent."

Tomorrow, I'd walk up to Howard Stebbins before English class and say, "Coach, I am justified and you're dog poop," and play it by ear from there.

"I am God's gift to horses," John Wayne said.

"Yes sir, but I accidentally squirted into your daughter and now she's pregnant."

John Wayne squinched up his left eye and looked at Sam Callahan. They were both the same height, only Sam Callahan had better posture.

"That's okay by me," John Wayne said. "The gene pool needs more cowboys."

Of course I didn't walk up to Howard Stebbins and say, "I am justified." There's probably not a kid in Wyoming who has ever said "I am justified."

Instead, I sat at my desk four rows behind Maurey and watched the back of her head while Stebbins droned on about *Ivanhoe. Ivanhoe* for Chrissake. The tale of a very polite knight who had to choose between fair Rowena and the brave, deserving Rebecca. He chose Rowena because Rebecca was Jewish. This guy is supposed to be my role model?

Stebbins stood square-shouldered and cleft-jawed against the blackboard, in the same white shirt with the skinny tie he'd worn to school Friday, just as if the weekend hadn't happened. No abortion clinic across from the Dairy Queen, no runaway girl sleeping in my bed; the world had turned upside down and nothing had changed.

"What do you think inspired the Age of Chivalry?" he asked.

"They sound like a bunch of cowboys," Florence Talbot said.

"They controlled women by making them sacred objects," Maurey said.

Stebbins glanced her way for the first time, then went back to Florence. "Why do you think knights were like cowboys?"

Florence's hair was different. She had what looked like a comma plastered to each cheekbone with a point sprayed down the back of her neck. "They both ride horses."

"They believe in the Lord," Chuckette said.

Next to me, Teddy spit tobacco juice into his Maxwell House can,

I have this theory that Sir Walter Scott's books screwed up the South more than *Uncle Tom's Cabin*. All those mint julep–swilling gentlemen confused the spiritual butt rape of other races and sexes with gallantry.

Stebbins slid his eyes across me to ask Kim Schmidt a question concerning fairness. I put on my Hank-face and stared at him. That's how I knew I had the king-hell seducer of housewives. I could look at him and he couldn't look at me.

In Mrs. Hinchman's citizenship class we learned how the responsible person votes. Rodney Cannelioski and Kim Schmidt ran for president. LaDell Smith wanted to but Mrs. Hinchman said no girls. Rodney and Kim gave speeches in which Kim promised better school lunches and Rodney said he would introduce every man, woman, and child in America to God. Kim won 26 to 2.

Chuckette gave me crap in the cafeteria. "You didn't call this weekend."

That seemed evident, so I concentrated on my mulligan stew. In mulligan stew everything is mashed up together; you can't avoid the gross stuff.

"I don't know why I go steady with you. You're supposed to call me at least once a day."

Maurey was sitting over at the ninth-grade table, where some kid had his eyelids turned inside out and a mouthful of milk so when he talked the milk dribbled off his face and made him look like an idiot. Maurey's face lit in delighted disgust and she laughed. I couldn't believe a soon-to-be-mother would fall for the inside-out-eyelids trick.

"Sharon's boyfriend Byron calls her house a dozen times a day and lets the phone ring once, then hangs up, just to let her know he still loves her."

"I bet Sharon's parents enjoy that."

"You have to start telling me you love me more often or my attention will wander. A woman should never be taken for granted."

I'd never once told Chuckette I loved her. "Did you vote for Rodney Cannelioski?"

"We're doubling again with Maurey and Dothan Talbot Saturday night. Bring more money this time."

I poked a fork at my stew. "Wouldn't you rather have a better lunch than meet Jesus?"

"I already know Jesus."

"Then you should have voted for lunch."

As Maurey stood up to carry her tray to the dump window, Dothan reached out and slapped her on the bottom, right in a spot I wasn't allowed to touch. I looked at Chuckette's face and realized I was sleeping with the prettiest girl in school and going steady with the ugliest.

"I love it when you gaze at me like that," Chuckette said.

"Oh."

"Sam, you can be so charming when you try."

Stebbins didn't show up for sixth-period PE. A few slows slid around the gym floor in their socks, heaving a basketball at the backboard, calling each other "douche bag." Douche bag was the in insult of the winter, but I doubt if a one of them knew what a douche bag was. I only knew because I took a drink out of Lydia's once and she yelled at me.

The rest of us slouched in the bleachers playing dot-to-dot pencil games and finger football. Dothan Talbot passed around three black-and-white postcards of naked women. I wasn't impressed. I'd seen both Maurey and Lydia naked and these women were dogs compared to mine. Their breasts hung like baseballs in the toe of a sweat sock and their bellies pooched. The one straddling a bicycle had hickies from her navel to her fuzz.

"Be like sticking your prick in a milking machine with that slut," Dothan said. "Wouldn't stop till you gave two quarts."

I bet he got that from his dad. Rodney Cannelioski went bug-eyed holding the picture of the woman on the bicycle in both hands. A trance situation.

"How'd you like to pork that, Roddy?" Dothan asked.

Rodney flushed out. "Degrading. This is an abomination against the sacredness of Eve."

Everyone started chanting, "Abomination, abomination," and pushing at Rodney.

Dothan stood up. "Let's take his pants off and see if he's stiff."

A couple of guys jumped on Rodney, he screamed, and I left.

Howard Stebbins sat at his desk in homeroom, his eyes scrunched up in concentration over a paperback. From the door, I watched as he licked a finger and turned the page. The tendency was to feel sorry for him—the sports hero who had lost his glory at nineteen. Now, ten years later, he's stuck in a meaningless town with a plain wife and three foreheadless rats for children. Small-town adultery is nothing more than boredom and timing. In his position, I'd have probably screwed Annabel. What else was there to do in winter?

But the situation called for toughness. Look at the jerk through Lydia's eyes. If I walked in with a heart full of pity he'd have me comparing birth-control methods and talking baseball. Never talk baseball with someone you're supposed to hate.

"This," I said to myself, "is the man who once said I was too slow to be a nigger."

He shut the book—Zane Grey, *Wanderer of the Wasteland*—and looked up.

"They're depantsing Rodney in the gym," I said.

Stebbins blinked twice and it came to me that he was at a higher emotional peak over this event than I was.

"New rules," I said.

His eyes were sheeplike, so I stared at that king-hell cleft running up his chin.

"First, no more forcing me out for sports I don't want. I deserve an A in English and you are to give it to me."

He blinked again. The abortion had made him speechless.

"No more licks on Dothan Talbot for not cutting his hair."

"I thought you and Dothan are enemies. He's Maurey's boyfriend."

"The licks are making him a hero."

"I hadn't realized that."

"You hadn't realized a lot. Number three, no more Saturday bridge club. It upsets my friend Maurey."

Stebbins went back to blinking and looking resigned. I'd expected some sort of resistance, maybe a counterthreat. This was too much like cutting off Otis's leg.

"Anything else?" he asked.

"We're done with *Ivanhoe*. He's a bad influence. Starting tomorrow you read the class *Tortilla Flat* by John Steinbeck."

"I don't know where I can lay my hands on a copy," he said.

"I'll find one." I pointed to *Wanderer of the Wasteland*. "In the meantime, try that. Teddy'll love it."

Stebbins turned the book over twice in his hands. "She went through with it. After you took Maurey away, I tried to stop her. I offered to leave my family."

He looked as if he might cry, which was the last thing I could deal with at the moment. Living with Lydia makes you susceptible to vulnerability. I'd reached enough-is-enough. "They'll push Rodney out in the snow with no pants," I said.

Stebbins raised his head. "Maybe I should save him."

"Maybe you should."

20

MAUREY SHOWED ME HOW TO MAKE A TENT OUT OF THE blankets so you can read by flashlight and eat graham crackers without your mother finding out.

"But Lydia doesn't care if we leave the light on and read and eat all night," I said.

"This is how I've always done it. There are certain things you should sneak around to do, even if no one cares."

"Like reading?"

We sat cross-legged, facing each other, with the books and graham cracker box between us. Maurey's book was *The Black Stallion's Filly*. She'd been on a horse-fiction kick ever since the botched abortion. I was working on *Tike and Tiny in the Tetons* by Frances Farnsworth, *Being and Nothingness* by Jean-Paul Sartre, and the back of the graham cracker box.

Hank loaned me *Being and Nothingness*. He said it would help me understand life and Lydia.

"Do you understand Lydia?" I asked.

"I'm better with life."

I spent twenty minutes on the table of contents—"Chapter Three, Knowledge as a Type of Relationship Between the For-Itself and the In-Itself"—and decided I was still a kid after all.

"You're getting crumbs in the sheets," Maurey said.

"I thought we were supposed to get crumbs in the sheets. If we didn't want to crumb the sheets, we'd be in the living room, on the couch."

"You're losing your sense of play, Sam."

"What play?" Maurey was wearing the white nightie and the flashlight light made her new breasts and the undersides of her cheekbones glow while the rest of her stayed shaded.

I wanted to talk more than read. "Is your real name Maureen? Hank said Maurey is short for Maureen."

"Merle."

I flipped the light beam up at her face. "Merle?"

"Short for Merle Oberon. She was a movie star in the thirties or forties or sometime when Dad used to see movies all the time. He thought she was the perfect woman."

"Was she?"

"I've seen photographs; she had a face like Charlotte Morris."

I had trouble with the picture. "You're named after a beautiful woman who looked like Chuckette?"

"Chuckette's pretty."

"If you like a dinner plate with eyes."

Maurey dug in the box for another cracker. "Our TM Ranch is named for a cowboy star named Tom Mix. Dad's his second cousin's son or something like that. He saw Tom Mix once in San Francisco."

This was considerably more interesting than *Being and Nothingness*. "What was Buddy doing in San Francisco?"

"Art school at Stanford." Maurey reached over and with the thumb and forefinger of her left hand, she opened my pajama fly.

I ignored her, but, boy, did I have hopes. "Buddy's a cowboy. He couldn't be in art school."

"Cowboys aren't stupid, Sam. They just like being alone and outdoors." Maurey held the graham cracker in her right hand

and made a fist, then she let the crumbs sift through her fingers into my pubic area. She said, "Now there's a sense of play."

"I'll show you play." I dived on her and she shrieked. We rolled around, all tied up in each other and the blankets while I stuffed crackers down her nightgown and she crumbled into my hair. I got her a good one, right up the nose. Amid the giggling and mock screams, we rolled off the bed and crashed to the floor where I came out on top. She looked at me with crumbs in her eyelashes and smiled.

I stared into her blue eyes for a long time, then dipped in for the kiss.

"No," Maurey said.

"No?"

"We're having fun, Sam. Don't spoil it."

I sat up. "I don't understand. You kiss Dothan Talbot all the time and he's a jerk."

"I kiss him because he's a jerk. I like you. I can't kiss you anymore."

Cracker crumbs trickled down my balls and into my bottom crack. "I'm nice to you, we sleep in the same bed, you're having our baby, but you can't kiss me because you like me?"

"Right."

"And you can kiss Dothan because you don't like him?"

"I like him, in a different way."

I reached over and dusted the cracker crumbs out of her eyebrows. "Do you think the fall hurt the baby?"

Maurey sat up next to me. "I hope not." We sat shoulder to shoulder on the floor, staring at the log wall under my desk. One of the logs had a whorl knot with bark around the outside of the circle. I wondered if Lydia heard the crash. Probably not; it was after midnight.

"Sam," Maurey said. "I'm sorry you want something that I don't. I'd like to give you what you want, but you're important to me now. What with the baby and things all a mess with Dad, I need you too much to risk anything more than friendship."

She put her hand on my knee. After a while, I covered her hand with mine. We laced fingers and she gave me a little squeeze.

"I don't understand," I said.

"I don't either."

"Shit."

"I'm crumby. Want to take a shower?"

Wednesday evening as the three of us walked into the White Deck, Maurey stopped and stared off toward Kimball's Food Market.

She said, "They're going to Jackson to church."

"Who?" I didn't see anything other than a white Chevelle with the engine left running.

"That's Mama's car," Maurey said.

Annabel came out of the grocery store carrying a single brown paper bag, followed by Petey in his dark suit that made him look like a miniature hit man. Annabel was wearing a purple print dress with yellow leaves on it and a hat.

Petey stopped and pointed toward us. I could hear his high-whine voice but not the words. Annabel looked at us a moment, then opened the back door and set in her sack. She said something to Petey as she moved around the Chevelle and got in the driver's side.

"That'll be Dad's beer and this month's *Redbook*," Maurey said. "She always buys that stuff on the way to church."

The passenger door opened from the inside and I could see Annabel gesturing for Petey to get in the car. He pointed one more time, then he climbed in and they drove off away from us.

Maurey stared after them. "How does she dare show herself in church after what she's done?"

Lydia sniffed. "How does she dare show herself in church wearing that dress?"

—

"So Dothan's going to drive over here in his Ford to pick up his date and her roommate?"

"What's the matter with that?"

"Won't he think it squirrelly that you're living at a guy's house?"

"I told him the truth—Mom and I had a fight so I'm staying with you and Lydia."

"And he didn't think that was squirrelly?"

"I didn't ask him if he thought that was squirrelly. I don't care what he thinks it is."

"Well, it's not traditional."

"You think I should wear this yellow sweater Lydia loaned me or the blue shirt with a white dickie?"

"The blue shirt makes your eyes look nice, but I have serious doubts about the dickie."

The eager boy climbed the highest peak in the Tetons to ask a question of the wise, tall one.

"Sam Callahan, why is it I always want to be with one girl and I'm always with another one?"

Sam Callahan scratched his thick beard. "God planned it so everybody likes somebody but no one likes the person who likes them."

"Why?"

"The purpose of our existence is to keep God entertained."

Double-dating is stupid to begin with. It's hard enough to relax with one person without having to keep track of the insecurities and innuendos of a whole other couple. With me and a girl, there's one relationship to be paranoid over. That's plenty. With four people, I count six connections—me and Chuckette, Dothan and Maurey, Maurey and Chuckette, Dothan and me, me and Maurey, and Dothan and Chuckette. Which would be complicated enough even if Dothan's date and I weren't about to have a baby.

We drove into Jackson to a Leap Year Day sock hop at the Mormon Church rec hall. The Mormons had February 29 mixed up with Sadie Hawkins Day from the Li'l Abner comic strip. I think that's because Sadie Hawkins Day is when women can force men to marry them, and Mormons have the same superstition about leap year. Whatever the reason, almost all the kids except us were dressed in Dogpatch clothes. I wasn't into that straw-in-the-hair stuff. Dogpatch was too close to North Carolina.

Down South, Fundamentalists like the Baptists and Church of Christ don't believe in mixed dancing, but Mormons must be different. Or maybe Wyoming is different. Anyhow, the decadence of doing the twist eight feet from your partner in a fluorescent tube-lit room with more chaperones than dancers thrilled Chuckette to the bone.

She said, "Daddy'd die if he saw this."

"So would my mom."

They stacked Pat Boone and Chubby Checker 45s on a Sylvania record player and we danced under a basketball net. Refreshments were lemonade and cookie squares made out of Rice Crispies and melted marshmallows.

"They'll stick to my retainer," Chuckette said.

"I'll eat yours."

This room with walls the same color as Lydia's face was like dancing in a brightly lit Ping-Pong ball. The chaperones made us change partners regularly so no one would feel left out. During a Sam Cooke song about this guy who was an idiot in school—"Don't know much about history, don't know much biology"—I found myself dancing face to face with Maurey. Sam Cooke thought if he made all A's some girl would get hot for his bod and what a wonderful world it would be.

"Having fun, Sam?" Maurey asked.

I was listening as Sam Cooke connected grade-point average to sex appeal. My fantasy life was peanuts next to this guy. "What?"

"Are you having fun?"

"After an hour, the twist is boring."

"Sharon can do the shimmy. Dance with her."

Sharon could do the dirty bird, mashed potatoes, and the itch, only the chaperones stepped in when she did the itch.

"That's disgusting," Maurey said as Sharon dug into herself like a flea-bit dog.

Dothan did a leer. "I'd like to itch her."

Chuckette popped her retainer. "After high school, I'm joining the Peace Corps."

The chaperones kicked a guy out for being from Idaho.

At the end, two Sunday-school teachers held on to opposite ends of a dowel rod and us boys were formed into a limbo line. Girls couldn't do it because they were wearing dresses. We shuffled around to the music, pretending we were Negroes going under a stick. I bombed early on purpose so people would think I was too tall to see how low I could go.

Chuckette gave me this look that said I'd let us down as a couple. I played Hank, which I'd been doing a lot lately.

Dothan made the final three, but this one skinny little cowboy in boots could really get down there. He didn't even take off his hat. When they gave him the prize—*The Pearl of Great Price* in a vest-pocket edition—he said bareback training made him limber.

Except for a fight in the parking lot between the guy from Idaho and a chaperone, the dance was over by ten.

"I should of jumped in the fight," Dothan said.

Maurey shoved over right next to him in the front seat. "Whose side would you have been on?"

"Doesn't matter, I should have jumped in."

"Why fight when you don't care which side's right?" I asked.

Dothan threw a gap-toothed look of disgust over his shoulder. "Only an outsider would have to ask that."

"You're from Alabama."

"After high school, I'm gonna join the Peace Corps," Chuckette said again. She had me backed against the passenger's-side back door. When she talked her retainer made clack sounds in my ear.

Maurey turned on the radio. "I thought you were planning to get married and have three sons after high school?"

"I might do both. Daddy says we can't get married till I'm eighteen."

We? It's like you go on a date with some girl and she construes it as a life-long deal. One movie and a sterile sock hop and it's marry her or break her heart, although breaking Chuckette's heart wouldn't cause that much stress. I could have Lydia do it.

"I should have kicked that guy's ass," Dothan said.

Maurey turned up "Deadman's Curve" by Jan and Dean. "Which guy?"

A plane flew over GroVont and I pretended I was the pilot, looking down. He'd probably miss the whole town, see nothing but moonlight off the snow and mountains. Every building on Alpine was pitch-black. The Forest Service lights were all off, and the Tastee Freeze. A glow came from Kimball's, caused by the refrigeration units, but the White Deck to Chuckette's could have passed for a ghost town.

The kitchen light showed from our cabin, but it was after

10:30, so I figured Lydia was on the couch in the living room. Hank's truck sat parked in the yard. Otis stood next to it, sniffing a tire.

"Kind of pretty when everyone's asleep, isn't it," Maurey said.

"That dog knocks over our trash one more time, I'm gonna shoot it," Dothan said.

As we pulled up in front of the Morrises' house, the porch light came on. "That'll be Daddy," Chuckette said. "He says we can't waste electricity so he stays up until I get home. Mom stays up from worry for fear I'll be in a wreck. She says if I stay out late, she won't get enough sleep and she'll be sick the next day and it'll be my fault."

"Sounds pitiful," I said.

"They're good parents."

"Want me to walk you to the door?"

The Morrises' front porch was the only lit-up spot in GroVont and that's where we stood to say good night. I didn't want to kiss her, but her face bent up toward me seemed to expect it. Sexiness and pity just don't mix. When I leaned in to Chuckette's thin lips, the porch light flashed.

"I'm in trouble now," she said. "Daddy'll make me ask God for forgiveness."

"We didn't do anything."

"I had an impure thought."

"I didn't."

I got back to the Ford to find Dothan and Maurey's faces in a lock. I hopped in the front seat next to them.

"Fun night," I said.

Dothan looked over Maurey's shoulder. "She bite your tongue again?"

Dothan pulled up beside Hank's truck and turned off the engine. We all three sat in silence, staring at the cabin.

"Good night, Sam," Dothan said.

I opened the door, but didn't move. I looked at Maurey. "You coming in?"

"In a minute."

"I can wait. The lock is kind of tricky and we'd be less likely to wake up Lydia if we go in together." Which were lies; the door wasn't locked, and Lydia was either awake and getting laid, or she was already asleep and nothing short of a fire would affect her.

"She'll be in when she comes in," Dothan said.

"I can wait if you guys want to say good night."

"Get out of the car, Sam," Dothan said.

I looked at Maurey. She reached over and patted my hand. "I'll be in in a minute."

"I don't mind waiting."

Dothan said, "Sam."

In the bathroom, I did the introspective mirror deal for a while. I stuck out my tongue to check the white moldy stuff that sometimes grows there. I wondered if Lydia really connected to herself by touching her tongue in the mirror. Seemed kind of stupid, but I guess you do whatever it takes to feel like you and the person in your body are related. I brushed my teeth with Maurey's blue toothbrush, then I shook it as dry as possible and hung it back next to my red one. Maybe the basic way people connect is through the mouth; that would explain the French kiss.

Because the dryer was broken, Lydia had clothes draped all over Les's horns. I tried to picture Les as a noble beast surviving the wilderness, then carried the deal onto some religion where awareness stays with the body after it dies and he was up on the wall knowing full well that a neurotic woman had hung bras and hose around his horns and stuck a

Gilbey's label over each eye. What indignities would fall on my body after I died?

I sat at the kitchen table, staring down at one of Lydia's ever-present half-finished crossword puzzles, drinking a Dr Pepper, and chewing on some of Hank's jerky, which also came from a noble beast of the wilderness. More indignities.

I figured if sex was poker, the order of the winning hands went like this: mouth to mouth, fingers to tits, mouth to tits, fingers to crotch, mouth to crotch, crotch to crotch; although mouth to tits and fingers to crotch might be reversed or equal. Subheads would include fingers to tits through shirt and bra, through bra only, or directly on nipple. Then there was tongue in ear.

Dothan and Maurey would be about stage two by now—fingers to tits, probably below shirt and above bra. Her right tit was a little bigger than the left one. The tip end stuck out farther.

They wouldn't fuck in my driveway, would they? Get sweaty and wet, blow come right in the Ford? There was nothing in the world to stop them. I could flash the porch light like Chuckette's father did, only our porch light was burnt out. That would only piss Maurey off anyway.

Alice jumped on the table and sat on the crossword, mewing. I didn't care what went across or down anyway. I poured a little Dr Pepper in a saucer and watched as she lapped it up. Would he undress her completely or just pull her skirt up? Dothan was the kind of jerk who would expect a blow job and give nothing in return.

I stood in the dark in the living room and peeked through a crack in the curtain. The half-moon gave the snow a dull nickel look and Soapley's trailer could have been a spaceship or a bloated pill. Dothan's car was too steamed to see into, but I imagined movement; I imagined her mouth around his penis and his fingers tangled in her hair.

The Oriental gentleman slid the evil device around Sam Callahan's finger and over his neck, across the soles of his feet to the twin hooks embedded in his testicles.

"The ancients called it the self-starting torture kit," he grinned. "If you ignore it, the pain is small, but if you think about it, if you worry it, if it makes you sad, it will gradually rip your nerves to shreds and tear your balls out. Eh, eh."

Sam Callahan checked the fit. "Sounds like my kind of deal. I'll take one."

—

As an act of rebellion, I put on the paisley pajamas and sat at my typewriter, pretending to read *Being and Nothingness*. I heard Maurey at the front door and in the bathroom. The water heater knocked when she ran hot water. Nobody would ever sneak around and use hot water in my house.

She came in the bedroom and shrugged out of the blue shirt and pulled the white dickie off. I couldn't see any marks on her body.

"You used my toothbrush," she said.

"I deny it."

She slid the white nightie on over her head, then sat on the bed to pull off her shoes and skirt. No panty shot tonight. "We saw you spying at the window."

"Maurey, I do not enjoy these double dates."

Maurey picked up her hairbrush. "You'd rather I go out with him alone while you sit here and wonder?"

"I'd rather you not go out with him."

"Not an option." She talked as she brushed. "If it makes you unhappy, I'll move out. I'm not here to make you unhappy."

"I don't want you to move out. Living with you is neat."

"What do you want then?"

"Within the options?"

"Within the options."

She held her head down to brush up from the back of her neck. The truth of our baby floating around in this little girl zipped in and out of my grasp. I'd never even looked at a baby up close before. Alice hopped in my lap and I sat, petting her and wishing I could touch Maurey and tell her I loved her, but knowing that would be squirrelly. I wished I had a father.

"I want a Fudgsicle. How about you?"

She looked at me and smiled. "Okay."

I made pecan pancakes while Hank walked to Kimball's Food Market and back for the *Rocky Mountain News*. The women padded around in their nightgowns, looking rumpled and beautiful as they waited for the coffee to kick in and the day to start.

Maurey wore my red slippers. Her hair had that clumped-to-one-side look women get when they sleep.

"Sam slept in paisley jammies again last night," she said.

Lydia lit a cigarette. "What a chump; your mother and I should exchange children. Annabel would love a child in paisley pajamas."

"She could iron them every afternoon."

A tiny row of bubbles appeared around the edge of each pancake. I eased the flipper under a corner and checked for golden brownness. On the one hand it was really nice and homey sitting around the kitchen like this, contentedly feeling the night fuzz drop from my brain. I'd always wanted a family.

But on the other hand two women could be lots more than twice as scornful as one. My life might become nothing but the object of snappy banter. I was glad when Hank showed up with the paper.

"Dibs on the funnies," Maurey said.

Lydia affixed herself in Hank's arms and gave him an open-mouthed kiss that lasted like three minutes.

"Ish," I said.

Maurey rolled her eyes up under her eyelids. "I'll never act like that in front of my children."

"Me, either."

Lydia broke off the kiss and went all smug. "You'll never have a sexual technician like mine."

Hank looked more embarrassed than pleased, but I could tell he was somewhat pleased. Not many good lays get public appreciation. I flipped a pancake wrong and batter glomped all over the griddle.

Lydia ate like a hog. Her appetite must be connected by direct wire to her crotch—one orgasm and she turns into Johnny the Lumberjack.

Maurey didn't eat any.

Hank and Lydia got into a fight that just about snuffed the afterglow. Lydia tore a comic page down the middle. "Red Ryder and Little Beaver are ethnic perverts."

"Don't make fun of Little Beaver," Hank said.

"Look at this yellow headband. He's an embarrassment to beavers everywhere."

Hank looked. "I have a headband that color."

"Ethnic pervert."

The sports page was all Boston Celtics and Winter Olympics. Skiing just wasn't my gig.

I was making a second pot of coffee when someone knocked on the door.

Maurey's face went happy. "That'll be Dad."

Hank and I traded a quick guilt glance. Males must be born with a fear of fathers at the door.

I said, "Buddy?"

Maurey set down her mug. "I figured he'd be down from the TM this weekend. Thanks for letting me stay here."

Lydia said, "You're welcome."

Throughout the whole deal, Maurey and Lydia always knew what was going on and they never told me. I didn't find out Maurey was moving in until she was in, and now the same thing was happening on the move out.

The knock came again. As she walked barefoot into the living room, Lydia said, "I've been waiting to meet the fabulous Buddy Pierce."

I looked at Maurey's eyes. "Are we splitting up?"

She was still smiling on account of her dad. "Oh, Sam, we were never together. I'll still be over every couple of days."

"What about the baby?"

She glanced behind me to see if Buddy was in earshot. "We'll name him after he comes."

"Where will she live?"

"We'll know when it happens, no need to worry about stuff like that until he's here." I knew she was lying. I'd bet anything that Maurey and Lydia both knew what sex, what name, where it would live, and what sports it would go out for. In their little brains they'd already planned its life; they just weren't telling me.

Lydia's voice came from the living room. "Would you care for some coffee?"

"No, thanks, I'll pick up my daughter and be gone."

Then they were in the kitchen and everyone was shuffling around being awkward on the deal.

"Hank," Buddy said.

"Buddy," Hank said.

I guess Buddy felt odd about working out a family crisis in front of people he didn't know. "Get your things," he said to Maurey.

"I'm already packed."

Buddy stood next to me, which made me nervous and itchy. I mean, how far had Annabel filled in the details? She couldn't very well say, "Sam fucked our baby," without spilling the disgusting details of Howard Stebbins and Rock Springs. Any hint of truth would disorder the dickens out of her order. But then, the very term "make a clean breast" might appeal to Annabel.

I risked a look up, but he was so close all I could see was a plaid shirt, an unzipped red parka, and that black bush of a beard. He stayed put while Maurey went off to our room to gather up her suitcase and bear. When had she packed anyway? Had to be while I was in the shower, but you'd think I would have noticed when I got dressed.

"Get an elk this year, Hank?" Buddy asked.

"Yes. You?"

"Killed a cow up on Goosewing."

"Goosewing has always been a good location."

Both men were trying to out-stoic the other. Lydia took the pot from my hand and ran water. "Maurey tells us you went to art school at Stanford."

Buddy's beard nodded.

"What kind of art interested you?"

"Bronze."

"I love bronze, don't you, Sam?"

"It's my favorite metal."

After that no one said anything until Maurey came in and stood next to her father. He put a hand on her shoulder. "Thanks for taking care of my daughter. I hope she wasn't trouble."

Lydia smiled at Maurey. "No trouble. You have a fine little girl, Mr. Pierce."

The beard nodded again.

"See you in school, Sam," Maurey said.

Then they were gone and, at thirteen years and six months, I discovered the pain in the ass of a woman walking out the door.

21

Battle Creek, Mich. (UPI)—The C. W. Post Cereal *Company today announced the Grand Prize winner in its "Most Ambitious Boy" contest. Sam Callahan of GroVont, Wyo., was chosen over 2 million other entrants because Sam wants to grow up to lead the Chicago Cubs to victory in the World Series.*

"More boys become president than win a baseball championship in Chicago," Sam Callahan said.

The Grand Prize was a lifetime supply of Post Toasties, which Sam Callahan regretfully declined.

My loved ones and I survived to baseball season. Praise the Lord.

I discovered that if I tipped the radio onto its left side and held my thumb on the speaker I could pick up about every other word of the Dodger games on KFI Los Angeles. The games didn't start till 9:00 and the signal drifted every twenty minutes, but I never missed a one, even though Sandy Koufax pulled a muscle in his pitching arm and the Dodgers dropped ten of their first eleven. It's not who wins or loses in baseball, it's how clean you feel when you play it. Or listen to it.

My hero object went from Don Drysdale, who actually played the games, to Vince Skully, who announced them.

Vince knew more facts about more subjects than anyone else on earth. I counted—he averaged eight facts between each pitch, and when you figure 250 pitches a game, that's 2,000 facts in nine innings. Even if he repeated one every few weeks, you spread 2,000 facts a game over a 162-game season and you've got a hell of a lot of information.

I don't impress easily, but Vince Skully blew me away.

"Listen to this guy," I said to Lydia.

"I liked you better when you read two books at a time."

"Tell Caspar to forget carbon paper, I'm going on the radio. This guy is a genius."

"You want facts, read the encyclopedia. Saying this clown is a genius because he knows facts is like saying the phone book is a great novel because it has a lot of characters."

I tried to explain to her how baseball is the metaphor for life, but she said life isn't even a metaphor for life.

"Snow is the metaphor for life," Lydia said. "You fall, you freeze, you melt, you disappear."

I wouldn't have bet on the snow-disappearing part. The days grew warmer, we never went below zero at night anymore, but the gray-as-far-as-the-eye-can-see deal seemed the same. Maurey told me spring was on the way, and I said, "How can you tell?"

She said, "Open your eyes and look."

So I made an effort, I started paying attention to what I was looking at, and, sure enough, the never-ending drabness was moving. One day I couldn't see the bottom of Soapley's windows and the next day I could. A rake handle popped up next to the driveway. The highway seemed to widen an inch or so. The snow layer was contracting into itself.

Back in late November, I stood on the back porch one night and wrote my name in the snow in pee—SAN. Ran out of power halfway through the *m*. In mid-April I went out on the porch to pick up the mountain of returnable Dr Pepper bottles we'd thrown out the back door all winter, and there it was on what yesterday had been virgin white—SAN.

"Hey, Lydia."

Lydia wasn't impressed. "If my proudest accomplishment of the year was misspelling my name in pee, I'd hang myself right now."

"You can't write your name in the snow."

"A fact that I thank God for each and every day."

I told Maurey I would give all my future prospects to see dirt.

"What's the big deal about dirt?" We were standing in front of the White Deck, trying to decide between going in or walking up to the Tastee Freeze. Neither one of us was hungry, so it didn't much matter. It was one of those Sunday afternoons when nothing you do or don't do much matters.

"I was used to seeing the ground in Greensboro. By now all the dogwoods and pear trees and magnolias are blooming. The grass is green."

"You want grass or you want dirt?"

"I don't care so long as I touch something that isn't snow."

Maurey seemed to be considering the situation as Ft. Worth and a couple of loggers came out of the White Deck. Ft. Worth faked a right hook in my direction and told me not to do anything he wouldn't do. I said he'd do anything, which was the correct response. A conversation with Ft. Worth had all the spontaneity of calisthenics. Dot leaned over a booth next to the window and waved. She was gaining weight at the same rate as Maurey. To me—and to any of the group who knew what was what—Maurey was edging into obvious, although, so far anyway, no gossip had reached Dot, and Dot said that if she didn't hear it, it wasn't there.

"I don't see the big deal, but you want dirt, I'll show you dirt," Maurey said.

"Hank says if we lose contact with the Mother Earth our souls will wither like the chokecherry in autumn."

"Hank talks that way because he thinks he has to. The man couldn't survive without TV dinners."

Maurey led me over to the Forest Service headquarters, which had a big scenic deck on the back. You could see all the way to Yellowstone. We slid under the deck and onto real, honest-to-God dirt—or mud, depending on where you sat. I went into king-hell hog heaven—dug my fingernails into the cool earth, touched it with my cheek.

Maurey sat with her legs out and her back leaning against a support beam. "There'll be mud all over the valley in a few weeks. You better not embarrass me with this discovery-of-dirt stuff in the schoolyard."

"Can I touch your tummy?"

"Sam, you're so damn predictable."

"I just want to touch our baby." Light came through between the slats of the deck, causing a venetian-blind effect. Maurey's eyes were in the dark, but her mouth and forehead were lit yellow.

She said, "I think Farlow kicked yesterday."

"We're naming him Farlow?"

"That's what I call him when I talk to him at night. Stub Farlow is the name of the guy on the horse on our license plates, but I can't see calling him Stub."

"You talk to Farlow at night?"

"I read him horse stories."

She unzipped her Wranglers and lifted her shirt. In the cross-shadows, her stomach bloated out some, enough to hold up the jeans without help from zippers or buttons, but not much more, only her belly button had turned out where it used to be in. I held out my right hand and touched her with my fingertips.

What I wanted, badly, was a sense of someone real in there, someone that Maurey and I had created out of nothing. But I just couldn't make the leap from runny mayonnaise on a sock to a human person who could sing and play baseball and watch TV. The deal wasn't real yet, and I was afraid it never would be.

Maurey gazed down at her belly. "Mom won't say a word, but I can tell she's going nuts to find out if I've still got it. She sneaks in my room when she thinks I'm asleep and stands there staring at me for hours. It's spooky."

"You guys never talked about Rock Springs?"

Maurey put her hand next to mine. "I haven't talked to Mom about anything since then. She cries constantly, like a wet rag. Gets on my nerves. Feel over here, I think this might be his head."

I felt, but not very hard for fear of squashing his temple. "What does your dad say?"

"What can he do? He knows something weird is up with Mom and me, but he's too cowboy to pry."

"Even if his own family is going nuts?"

"He figures we'll come to him when we're ready. Besides, the mares will be foaling soon. Dad doesn't have time to referee a war."

"He's not curious why his daughter and wife won't talk to each other?"

Maurey guided my fingertips across her stomach. "I guess he's curious, but he won't invade our personal problems."

"You're his family."

I thought I felt something, but I wasn't sure. Her skin was harder than it used to be, like a softball, and I was afraid to touch her belly button.

"At least I'm not sick all day and night anymore," Maurey said. "Mrs. Hinchman's perfume about gagged me to death last month."

"Has Dothan figured it out?"

Maurey lowered her shirt but left her jeans unzipped. She brushed the dirt off her fingers onto my knee. "Dothan doesn't know where babies come from. He's as stupid as you are when it comes to that stuff."

"Are you training him?"

Maurey slipped by that one. "The secret won't last forever, so the day after school ends I'm going public. You and Lydia might want to head back to North Carolina about then."

"I'm not heading anywhere. Farlow's as much my baby as he is yours."

"We may have to talk about that some, Sam."

She moved so the light shaft was on her eyes. They looked dark blue and sad. I reached over and took her hand. "Some shit will hit if this baby's not half mine after it's born."

She pulled her hand away a second, then came back. "Lydia's been whining for months to go back home. What happens when your grandfather says okay?"

"I'll stay here with you."

"Be real, Sam."

"Or you can come with us."

"I'm not leaving Wyoming, you think I'm crazy."

This line of thought gave me a creepy feeling. I was still holding out hope that Buddy would make Maurey marry me. I mean, there were laws that said you had to marry a girl if you got her pregnant. All the time I heard people say, "They *had* to get married." *Had* doesn't leave a choice. I'd just never figured where Dothan would fit in.

The Forest Service also provided the only spring baseball diamond in the form of its plowed parking lot. On weekends, when the cars were gone, we'd choose sides and play these thirty-two-inning games that practically always ended in beanball fights. Choosing up sides may be the single most devastating element in the formation of bad self-images in

America. In every neighborhood one poor little bugger is always the last chosen, which in our case was that born loser, Rodney Cannelioski. If he hadn't been a loser, people would have called him Rod.

For Rodney the Religious, it was even worse than your average teenage humiliation because we always shipped him off to baseball no-man's land—right field—and since the Forest Service parking lot was only big enough for the diamond, outfielders stood in knee-deep snow. Cut down on mobility. Balls hit out there stuck like Brer Rabbit's fist in the tar baby.

Add to which, standing in snow is cold and it's no wonder Rodney didn't enjoy himself on weekends.

One Saturday we played from noon till almost dark. I had six home runs and a triple, and Kim Schmidt and I turned a nifty double play on Dothan and somebody's cousin from Dubois. My next time at bat, Dothan threw four fastballs at my head.

"Easier than letting you hit a home run to Rodney," he called as I trotted down to first.

"Right," I said.

I stole second, then when Teddy hit a hard grounder to the shortstop, instead of charging for third, I fielded the ball barehanded and nailed Dothan in the back. *Thock.* What a wonderful sound.

Results were predictable.

On the walk home I held my head forward and low so the blood would still be flowing enough to freak out Lydia. She can be a tough mom to get a response out of.

"There's gravel stuck in your ear," Kim said.

"You know, I'm starting to feel like a local."

"Starting to act like one too."

"Think I'll have a black eye?"

Kim studied my face. "Only thing dark is from asphalt."

"Maybe if I don't wash, it'll look like a black eye." Bruises would impress Maurey; Chuckette might even let me touch her below the neck. I know that goes against what I said earlier about Chuckette, but a tit's a tit and should always be touched, regardless of how ugly the head it goes with.

Soapley and Otis stood by one of the dead GMCs, looking somewhat mournfully over at my place. We walked over so I could show off my blood and Kim could get in his throwing-up-dog imitation.

"The three-legged cowdog," Kim said, then he went into the *ack, ack, morph* routine. Otis wagged his little tail. I was kind of impressed, which shows how long I'd been away from wholesome entertainment.

The left strap of Soapley's overalls was broken. He gummed his toothpick around so it pointed at a Volkswagen bug parked in my front yard next to Lydia's Oldsmobile. "I seen two of them last summer. They had one at the Fina and the little bitty engine was in back. Alcott made a fool of himself looking for it to check the oil."

"Seems like the wind would blow it off the road," Kim said.

Soapley didn't have his teeth in, which was odd for me because I'd never known they came out. His face caved in when he spoke. "One hit a frost heave up by Cooke City and the bubble come right off the wheels, killed a college boy."

"I wonder who's at your house," Kim said.

"Somebody with a Volkswagen," I said. Unknown visitors were not a good sign. In all the years of my short life with Lydia, not a single surprise visitor had turned into a pleasant experience. Scenes ranged from king-hell boring to ugly three-way tensions between Caspar, Lydia, and the visitor, but however it went, the surprise was never pleasant.

"I better go in," I said.

"Better hurry or you'll stop bleeding."

—·—

"Sam's hurt," Delores gushed, then she rushed and I backed against the door. She was so short, with such huge breasts and a tiny waist, it was like being rushed by an ostrich. Or maybe the ostrich feeling came from her pink getup. Every time I saw Delores she was dressed completely in one color—white, silver, turquoise—all the way down to her boots and up to her cowboy hat. Today she was a flash of pink.

A pink fake-silk handkerchief came from somewhere and I found my right ear pinned to one of the monster tits while she jammed blood back up my nose. "He's wounded, Lydie."

"Wounded means shot. Sam looks more punched out." Through the pink haze, I saw Lydia on the couch next to Dougie Dupree. He had on loafers, slacks, and a madras shirt. Lydia was barefoot, as usual, in jeans and a sweatshirt that said DUKE. A half-full bottle sat on the stack of *Dictionary of American Biography* and chunks of lemon were scattered on the coffee table and floor. Obviously, we were chest-deep in an alcohol session.

Dougie spoke through a lemon wedge. "There is one more example of an event that would not occur in New York City."

"They'd slit your throat for a cigarette, but they wouldn't punch you out. Why did someone hit you, Sammy?" Lydia's face held the danger smile, the one that sets off little smoke alarms in my head. Even bent over with my ear up against God's own tit, I knew trouble was courting the Callahan household.

I decided to lie. "A fella said my mom was a tramp so I hit him and he hit me back."

"How noble." Delores clamped me even tighter to her breast. She smelled of Johnson & Johnson's talcum powder and I wanted to turn my mouth more into her, only I was afraid I'd bleed down her pink ruffly blouse.

"Sam's a regular prince," Lydia said. She knew I was lying. Lydia can always tell, somehow, and I can always tell when she's lying, but in spite of this mutual curse we both go on lying to each other on a daily basis.

"You must admit Marlon Brando is the dominant tragedian of our time," Dougie said, I guess resuming something I'd interrupted. Dougie blew my theory that tall men are never full of crap.

"Brando's eyeballs are upside down," Lydia said. "He's like one of those drawings you turn over and they go from happy to sad."

Delores sighed, which made her breast heave into my face. "I'd let Marlon Brando turn me over. Dougie, did you ever do it from the back? Ray won't do it that way, says it's perverse."

I muffle-mumbled. "I can't breathe."

"I bet Sammy likes doing it from the backside. He wouldn't call it perverse."

Lydia looked at me and threw down a shot. "Delores, you relate all subjects to your organs."

"I can't breathe."

When Delores let up, the oxygen rush made me dizzy. "I better clean up."

"Don't dribble on the floor."

Dougie was cutting lemons for another round. "The New York–trained actors are so superior to those who matriculate in Hollywood, there is no comparison whatsoever."

I went to the bathroom to wash off blood, then back to my room to change clothes and look up *matriculate.* As I passed through the living room, Delores was sitting up close to Dougie with her legs crossed so her pink skirt didn't cover much of anything. She touched his elbow when she talked. "*Life* magazine says Picasso caught gonorrhea from an orgy with colored women."

Back in my room, I left the door cracked and sat at my desk listening to the grown-ups kill off their fifth of tequila. Dougie was explaining why Andy Warhol was a cheater when Lydia said, "I want to dance."

"Dance?"

"In Greensboro I used to enjoy dancing."

I'd been working on a short story about an artist who suspends small dead animals in Jell-O molds. It was inspired by this stuff Max made at the White Deck where he'd start the Jell-O setting up, then dump in canned fruit cocktail and all the grapes and whatever fruit is in fruit cocktail would sink part way to the bottom and stop. Max left his Jell-O in the fridge for a week, so if you ordered it Friday the skin was like rubber. I liked that.

Two of the most famous art critics in Paris scratched their chins as they circled Sam Callahan's gelatinized sculpture.

"It's genius," the one murmured.

"I have never looked at a rat with such clarity," said the other. "Observe the terror in her eyes. The struggle of the ears juxtaposed against the strawberry Jell-O."

"I wonder how he makes it so lifelike," murmured the first critic.

Sam put on his Blackfoot smile. Little did the critics know the rat had been alive when dropped into the Jell-O mold.

Lydia's head appeared at the door. Her eyes had the bemused yet reckless glitter of a skydiver about to take his two-hundredth leap. I'd never seen Lydia blasted on tequila before, and I'm not sure she ever had been. Tequila was fairly new to serious drinkers back then; they hadn't realized yet that it's not the same drug as bourbon or gin.

"You stop bleeding?"

"Yeah, I'm doing my homework," I said, even though she hadn't asked why I was sitting at my desk writing on a legal pad.

"We're leaving for Jackson to dance at the Cowboy Bar. Dougie has a new car."

"You're going to ride in a Volkswagen?"

"I'll make Delores sit in back, otherwise she'll make obscene advances at Dougie all the way and they'll sneak off and leave me alone in the Cowboy. I'm not willing to break in new dance talent tonight."

Her forehead was soft but her eyes buzzed and her mouth kind of twitched. She'd looked like this the week she did whatever she did that got us shipped to Wyoming.

"What do I tell Hank when he calls?"

"Tell him Crazy Horse got what he deserved."

The phone woke me from a dream where my teeth rotted from the roots and fell into a cube of mixed-fruit Jell-O and stuck there all cluttered and disorganized. I knocked the alarm clock to the floor, then bent down to discover the time was just after midnight. Drunk Dougie must have driven the bug into a frost heave and killed my mother, left her twisted on the pavement with blood trickling from both ears. If I picked up the phone my new life as an orphan without Lydia would begin.

The phone stopped ringing for about thirty seconds before it started again. Those were a rough thirty seconds. The mental picture of Lydia dead made me sick, struck down with a flu attack. Maybe she wasn't dead but only brainless in a coma. Shoulda-saids and deals with God blitzed through my head, so when the phone rang the second time I went for it.

The voice said, "He that digresseth from the matter to fall upon the person ought to be suppressed by the speaker. No reviling or nipping words must be used."

"Caspar, you scared the doo out of me. I thought Lydia fell in a frost heave."

"Your next assignment is to memorize *Robert's Rules of Order*, Grandson. Life must be order. Business cannot continue without consistency."

"Lydia and I are full of order. What was that about progresseth from the matter and nipping words?"

"The matter is carbon paper."

"Caspar, it's after two o'clock your time. Did you call to read to me about nipping words?"

"I called to speak to your mother."

"Your daughter?"

"I demand an explanation about the Indian."

Lemon peels, juice, and salt lay strewed around the table. A tequila bottle was on its side under the TV. They'd left the front door open so the gas heater was blasting away for nothing. Order was not the Callahan word of the day. "She seems to have moved the Indian along for the moment, but she might listen if you make her dump him permanently. Lydia misses your ultimatums."

"Put her on the phone."

"Well, she isn't home right now. She had a meeting."

"I control the cash flow."

"And I respect that."

There was a short sound of old-man breathing. "Tell me what you think about night and day, Grandson."

"Carbon paper."

"Good lad." Caspar hung up.

I wandered into the kitchen for a Dr Pepper, then into the bathroom to shake the toilet handle. Lydia would let the water run forever if I wasn't around. I stood at the open door, staring at Soapley's junky yard and trailer and the Tetons beyond. There was enough moon to make out mountains over there, but without delineation or substance. Compared to North Carolina, everything I saw was alien. I wondered if North Carolina would be alien when I went back. That would make all places alien and I wouldn't know where I was anywhere.

The flash of a dead Lydia on the pavement had me screwed up. Maurey contemplated death often, which I'd always put down as a waste of time. To me, death was where they put old people. I'd really be alone if Lydia got drunk and killed—more alone than usual. Then someday I'd die and be alone in a box forever.

Whole thing screwed me up so much I drank a second Dr Pepper and ate a Valium. The Valiums were getting to be a regular thing.

Here's how this deal works: one Valium and one Dr Pepper and I sleep peacefully through the night; one Valium and two Dr Peppers and the need to pee cuts through the fog so I wake up in a couple of hours; two Valiums and two Dr Peppers, I sleep through the night but come to scrambling for the commode. I haven't tested the progression past two and two.

Somewhere in there I woke up with the itch. I blinked at the moon through the window, then stepped out of bed onto my alarm clock, said "Shit," and made my way to the bedroom door. Light from the kitchen gave the living room an indirect glow. As I stumbled along considerably more asleep than awake, a sound sunk in—like someone running and a puppy whimpering. It came to me that Dougie Dupree and Lydia were fucking on the couch.

His long, bony body lay on top, stripped except for one brown sock. His mouth was up under Lydia's jaw and the hand on my side was a fist next to her armpit. Lydia had her head thrown back, eyes open, with wet hair stuck to her cheek. She made a sound like she needed air.

I peed without flushing, then went back and stood under

Les, kind of absorbing the scene of watching Mom screw. The sound got to me—three rhythms—the couch going sideways and up and down, Dougie making the puppy noise, and Lydia. Dougie's back had hair across the shoulders and up his thighs right into his butt, with moles and erupted red blemishes making a constellation pattern—Pisces maybe, or Pleiades.

Lydia's skin showed much paler than Dougie's. I couldn't see her tits, only the sides of her legs next to his and her feet. Her toes pointed in at each other.

I was sure I was supposed to feel something here—disgust or jealous or sick, something—but I didn't; all I felt was odd, like you do when you eat too many aspirins, or it rains while you're at a matinee and you come outside to stuff you didn't expect. The three sounds weren't synchronized, no rhythmic relationship. Their bodies were just stuck together.

Dougie made a deeper, less puppylike grunt, rose on his elbows with his eyes squinched together, then collapsed on Mom like a dead man. Her eyes stared right at me and blinked twice before she closed them.

Back in my room I sat in front of the typewriter, looking out the window at a cloud shaped like home plate sliding past the moon. Lydia hadn't gotten off. Is a kid supposed to root for his mom to reach orgasm or is this a no-never-mind? Dougie's sweat was rubbed into her and his squirt dripped through her body. I wondered where they put Delores.

A single headlight turned off Center onto Alpine and eased up the street toward our cabin. When the light shone on Dougie's Volkswagen, Hank's truck slowed down and the form behind the wheel leaned forward. He switched his beam to low, then back, then he drove on toward the Jackson highway.

22

"HANK CAME BY LAST NIGHT," I SAID.

Lydia didn't deign to hear me. She was slumped back against the booth with each hand clutching a glass of tomato juice.

"And Caspar called about midnight, several hours before Hank came by," I added so Lydia would know when Hank came by and what he saw. Her eyes quivered a moment, but the effort to open them was just too much.

"What'd Caspar want?" Maurey asked. She was eating french fries because Dot refused to bring her a chocolate shake.

"You live on coffee and chocolate shakes," Dot had said. "That's no food for a growing baby."

"You're jealous because of your diet, you can't have shakes so you don't want anyone to have them."

"How about a chef's salad?"

They compromised on french fries. Dot was on a diet because Jimmy was coming home this summer and she weighed twenty-five pounds more than she did when he left.

"Jimmy can't stand fat women," she said. "He won't want me anymore. He'll want high school girls that can eat anything and never gain a pound." I wished she'd hurry up and lose the weight, or else give up. Dot on a diet wasn't near as cheerful as Dot fat.

Maurey took a whole fry in one bite and repeated, "What'd Grandpa Caspar want?"

"He demanded an explanation about the Indian."

Lydia moaned real quiet like and got her right eye open. "What did you tell him?"

"I said, 'What Indian?'"

"He meant Hank," Maurey said.

"I know he meant Hank."

"Then why did you say, 'What Indian?'"

Lydia's left eye made it open but the right one fell back shut. "Maurey, you want some advice?"

"From you?"

"Don't wreck your life trying to make your daddy notice you exist."

"My daddy knows I exist."

I'd wondered about this deal. "Is that why we took Hank in, because you thought an Indian would get Caspar's attention?"

Both Lydia's eyes went closed, but her left hand raised its glass and she took a sip of tomato juice. Behind her, in the next booth, a man reading a newspaper cracked a finger joint. Lydia's face paled even more, her hand shook so hard she spilled juice.

Maurey touched the window with her index finger. "It's raining."

I set down my chicken drumstick to stare at the rain. In Greensboro, it rained all the time, so much that mold grew on walls and fungus between your toes. But GroVont had had nothing but snow or clear and cold for six months. I'd known I missed the ground, but until that moment I hadn't realized how much I missed rain.

"I think it's turning to snow," Maurey said.

"It can't be."

"Or hail."

The man behind Lydia cracked another knuckle. This time both eyes opened and she reached for the napkin dispenser. She stood over the man, holding the dispenser over her head as a weapon. "Do that one more time and you're dead."

"Do what?"

"Do not play stupid with me, I'm a desperate woman."

They went into a stare-off that lasted an embarrassingly long time, until Dot noticed and brought the man a coffee refill. He turned a page in the paper and went back to reading. Lydia slumped into the booth. "God, I hate this place."

Dot said, "I'm hungry."

Maurey said, "What's Hank doing?"

Hank pulled his truck into a parking space at Zion's Own Hardware, then he came back fast across the street straight for the White Deck. For an instant it appeared the Dodge would crash through the wall. I jumped up as Maurey slid across the booth.

Dot put both hands up to protect herself. "What's that he's carrying?"

Lydia said, "Les."

"Les?"

"The moose. The moose is Les."

Hank fell from the truck onto the curb. He pulled himself up by the rearview mirror, then moved toward us, keeping both hands on the truck body.

"He's drunker'n a skunk," Dot said.

Maurey stood next to me. "Hank doesn't drink, maybe he's sick."

Hank lowered the tailgate and sat on it, breathing hard, staring through the window at Lydia. Lydia stared back, both hands tight on the napkin dispenser. A trickle of blood dripped down Hank's chin from a cut on his lower lip, all his shirt buttons except the bottom one were unbuttoned.

Hank stood and turned around to drag Les to the back of the truck. Then he lifted the moose above his head and ran toward us. Dot screamed, Lydia fell sideways from the booth, and Les came through the window.

Glass flew all over shit, Maurey said, "Jesus," I took off for the door. I caught Hank as he was climbing back in the truck.

"Hey, asshole."

His head turned to me without much recognition. I saw a Jim Beam bottle and a pistol on the dashboard.

"Maurey's pregnant."

He blinked.

"You could have hurt her, buttface."

Hank blinked twice more. "Don't call me buttface."

"How about drunk fucking Indian."

Hank nodded in agreement. "And your mother's a whore."

"That doesn't give you the right to get drunk and hurt Maurey."

His head kept nodding up and down. When it came up, a drop of blood fell off his chin. "I'm sorry." He pulled himself into the truck and shut the door, then he rolled down the window. "But your mother is still a whore."

I'd come off the initial adrenaline deal of a stuffed moose coming through the window. All I saw now was a pitiful man screwing himself up because he'd put his hopes on Lydia. I said, "Go on home."

Hank drove away nodding.

—

He'd trashed the cabin. Thrown furniture into walls, broken what few dishes we owned, torn up books and scattered the pages. He got into Lydia's panty drawer and knifed the crotch out of all sixty pairs. I found Alice mewing in my closet. Lydia turned the elk-gut chair upright and sat in it with her eyes closed. I set my typewriter back on the desk, then went into the living room and looked down on her. She looked old and skinny. Even her fingernails were a mess.

"Well, Lydia, you messed it up good this time."

She didn't even open her eyes. "Fuck you, Sam."

"Fuck you too, Mom."

23

THE WEEKEND BEFORE SCHOOL LET OUT, THE FIRE SIREN WENT off about four in the morning. I lay in bed, staring at the dark corner of the room where three lines from the walls and ceiling came together. The siren wailed up and down a minute or so, then came silence except for a pickup truck speeding up Center toward the volunteer fire building. One pumper truck siren kicked in and headed north out of town, soon followed by a second.

Whenever the volunteer alarm sounded, especially at night, I got goosebumps wondering whose place was on fire—Maurey's, Hank's, the junior high. A fire siren late at night is about the saddest sound in the world. I pictured the volunteers groaning "Oh, damn," as they crawled from the blankets to pull on their pants. Their sleepy-eyed wives mumbled "Be careful, honey," not knowing if it was a false alarm or their neighbor's children burning up.

That night I closed my eyes to play which-would-you-rather. Which would you rather have happen, 150,000 Chinese die in an earthquake or Lydia die in a car wreck? Maurey have a baby or Maurey marry me? Caspar let us stay in Wyoming or Caspar let us come home? I ended with me dying of cancer or being buried in an avalanche. Cancer would be slow and painful and pitiful, but an avalanche would be heavy and dark; I wouldn't be able to breathe or move my arms. I pretended I couldn't breathe or move my arms and two tons pushed down on my head until I got the king-hell creeps and spent the rest of the night reading this teenage sports fiction book.

—·—

The next day Maurey and I rode our bikes up to the TM Ranch. We're talking sixty degrees, sunny, no ice on the road or snow on the valley floor. We're talking spring.

I wallowed in it. Living without something most of the time means you get a kick when it's there. By late May, the North Carolina spring is old hat. Nobody cares. But Maurey and I were the weather equivalent of let out of prison. She laughed and tied her hair back in a rubber band. I swerved through every mud puddle on the gravel road so I soon had a wet brown stripe up my back.

"What was the siren about last night?" I asked as we coasted side by side down a hill.

Maurey stood on her pedals. "Probably a grease fire. People dribble grease onto a woodstove and it burns."

"At four in the morning?"

"Maybe it was creosote."

"I bet it was worse than that."

She looked over at me. "What do you want me to say, Sam? The alarm was a trailer fire and eight children were found suffocated dead behind a locked door? Not everything has to be dramatic."

"Some things do."

I cut left to scare a squirrel. He stood on his back legs to chew me out.

Maurey giggled. "You and Chuckette were the cutest couple at the sock hop Saturday night. She's been blooming since that thing came out of her mouth."

"I don't want Chuckette to bloom."

"Face it, Sam. Chuckette's in love."

We found Buddy in a pasture below the ranch house, working way off next to a big rock and a small herd of horses. Maurey's face lit up. "There's my Frostbite." She stood on the second rail of the buck-and-rail fence and let out an unbelievable whistle—didn't put her fingers in her mouth or anything. Just blasted like the lunch siren at the carbon paper plant.

All the horses' ears jerked up, but only one came trotting toward us. Maurey jumped over the fence. "He's so beautiful. I get goosebumps every time I see him."

For the record, skewbald means tan-and-white splotches; kind of like Little Joe's horse on *Bonanza*, only with no black. And Frostbite was a lot bigger than Little Joe's horse. He had nostril flares almost the size of Les's hooker twats.

When he was about twenty feet from us, Maurey held up her hand and said, "Stop."

Frostbite stopped, then he turned and faced Buddy and the other horses.

"Let's see what he forgot over the winter," Maurey said. She took off toward the horse.

I said, "Should you run in your condition?"

At full speed Maurey jumped, planted both hands on Frostbite's butt, and flew onto his back—we're talking the classic Cisco Kid maneuver here—and in the same motion, Frostbite leaped into action.

I'd been to the Ringling Bros. Circus, I'd seen every Gene Autrey movie made in my lifetime, but I'd never seen anything as natural as Maurey on her horse. With one hand on his mane and the other on his back, she kicked her legs over and bounced both feet off the ground, first on the right side, then on the left. At the end of the pasture they made a tight turn and came roaring back with Maurey holding herself up by her arms between her legs and her feet straight out to the sides. Her hair flowed like Frostbite's tail. Buddy stopped working to watch.

Maurey rotated, so she was facing the back, then she lifted her body and stood right on her hands.

The girl was almost six months pregnant. I should have been scared to crap for the baby, but I wasn't because of the look on Maurey's face. It was neater than before, during, or after her orgasm. Sex or death or teen pregnancy—none of that stuff meant squat to Maurey right then. I'm really glad I got to see her face as she rode Frostbite. I learned something important.

Maurey finished by standing on his bare back and galloping right up to me. Frostbite dug in all four legs as Maurey flew backward into a flip. She bounced once and landed with both feet together and her arms out wide.

I clapped and cheered. Maurey smiled. Her face was red and excited and her breath came in short gasps so I could see her breasts, sort of.

I hopped off the fence. "You never told me you could do that."

"Yes, I did. Come on, Frostbite, let's go see Dad."

I walked fast to keep up as we crossed the pasture. "I mean, you told me, but you didn't tell me how good at it you are."

"I'm the best around."

As we approached, Buddy put both hands on his hips. "You're gonna break your neck yet," he said, but I could tell he was proud. He had on a white T-shirt, jeans, and big black rubber boots with pointed toes. You couldn't see his mouth for all the beard.

The big rock next to Buddy wasn't a rock at all. It was a brown horse, lying on her side, hyperventilating. Her belly sucked way in so you could see every rib, then it bloated out.

Buddy didn't seem too disturbed by this so I figured it was a normal horse deal.

Maurey knelt by the horse's head and scratched her under the chin. "Has Estelle been down long?"

"I was eating lunch and saw her out the window."

A really odd thing happened. Estelle's belly rippled and two points shot out of her crotch area, then zipped back in.

Buddy knelt on one knee to peer at her womb. "Damndest thing happened with Lauren Bacall. Her foal came out perfect, except she had no eyeballs."

The two points shot out again, only farther this time, and when they zipped back they didn't zip all the way.

"What's that?" I asked.

Maurey rubbed her hands across the horse's shoulder. "The front feet. Neat, huh?"

"Neat."

Estelle's stomach rippled again and most of two legs and a nose popped out, covered by this white-red puss stuff. It was fairly gross, yet all electric at the same time. Even Buddy's eyes had a glitter and this must have been everyday stuff to him. My heart was going nuts.

"What happened to Lauren Bacall's foal?" Maurey asked.

"Had to shoot her. Damndest thing, she had empty eye sockets where the eyeballs should be. Would have been a beautiful horse too." Buddy reached out and held the two front feet, but he didn't pull or anything. He seemed satisfied to watch.

I couldn't take my eyes off the deal. It was amazing, this live thing crawling out of another live thing. I kept thinking about the baby in Maurey, was he in puss, would his feet come out first, would he have eyeballs. Estelle didn't look in much pain. The whites around her pupils bugged some, and cords in her neck tightened. Once she moved her front legs like she wanted to stand up, but Maurey soothed her back down.

Then her crotch made a slurp sound and the foal slid right out—*plop*—all alive. I wanted to applaud. As Buddy pulled the pussy stuff away from its eyes, the colt had the most astounded look on its face, as if birth was one king-hell of an unexpected event.

Buddy smiled at Maurey. "You want to name it?"

Maurey had a hand on her own stomach. I guess she was thinking of the baby too. Her eyes were glisteny. "How about Dad?"

Buddy looked from her to me and back, then down at the foal. "If you call it for oats, I might come."

"Dad's my choice. What sex is it?"

Buddy did a cowboy-type inspection. "Female. Whoever heard of a female named Dad?"

"I did," Maurey said.

Estelle's front feet kicked and she made it upright. The gunk hung from her crotch like she was losing guts. One back leg came up two or three times until she managed to step on the gunk, then she walked forward pulling the stuff out; same technique as when you come out of the John with toilet paper stuck on your shoe and you try to scrape it off before anyone sees.

Maurey scratched her horse on the ridge of his nose. "So how'd Frostbite winter so far?"

Buddy glanced at Frostbite, then his eyes followed Estelle as she nuzzled the colt. "He's a mean bastard, worse than his daddy ever was. Kicked Simon yesterday, like to broke his neck. Petey get over his cold?"

"Petey never had a cold. He was faking to skip school."

Buddy stood with his big hands on his hips. I thought he was about to say something, but he didn't. He looked over at the shiny Tetons for a few seconds, then down at the foal named Dad.

"Who's Simon?" I asked.

"Dog." Buddy's hand went to his beard. "You kids want to come up to the house, have some lemonade?"

"I think we'll walk up Miner Creek a ways. Sam's never seen a beaver dam."

The pasture was all horse turds so you had to look where you stepped. As we walked toward the creek, Hank drove by on the gravel highway. One arm came out of the driver's window in a wave. I waved back, glad to see him and wishing he'd pull over and talk, but he didn't.

"What's Hank doing?" I asked.

"He found irrigation work up at the Bar Double R. They're laying pipe in from the river. He ever start coming around again?"

I shook my head no. "Took a week to put the cabin together and get Les back on the wall. Lydia won't allow his name said in her presence."

Maurey knelt to pick a yellow flower. "Hank didn't do anything wrong."

"I know and so does Lydia, but admitting she screwed up is beyond her scope."

"Lot of things are beyond Lydia's scope."

"We'll never mess up stuff like our parents did."

The beavers had built three dams, each one upstream bigger than the last. They were solid, too. I'd have bet dynamite wouldn't put a hole in any of the dams, except maybe the littlest, bottom one. Maurey said dynamite would cut a hole, but the beavers would only chew down more aspen trees and fix it overnight, so there was no use blowing holes in dams.

"Only way to get rid of a beaver is to kill it," she said.

"Why would you want to get rid of a beaver?"

"They kill trees."

We sat on a log next to the biggest pond, watching the beaver lodge and waiting for one to pop up.

"Beavers mate for life," Maurey said. "If you trap the female, the male will die from sadness."

"People aren't like that," I said.

"People will find someone else to screw. That's why there's more of us than them."

She told me the names of all the flowers around the pond and up the hill behind us—larkspur, balsamroot, cinquefoil, bear-berry. Maurey knew what to call everything she saw. I really envied her for that. I hardly ever knew the name of anything I was looking at, and that wasn't just because I came from North Carolina and didn't know Wyoming. I hadn't known what anything was in Greensboro either. We must have had ten or twelve kinds of trees in our backyard at the manor house, and the only one I knew was post oak and Caspar had a Negro cut it down. It would be such an advantage to know what things are.

"Let's go." Maurey stood up and held out her hand. I tried to hug her, but she didn't buy it. She turned sideways, which left me hugging a shoulder and feeling like a squirrel. The butt on my jeans was wet too, from sitting on the log. Hers wasn't wet and she'd sat right next to me.

"Do you think the baby knows it exists?" she asked.

"How should I know."

"I don't remember anything before I was three, so maybe I didn't know I existed then."

"I knew I existed the first time Lydia blamed me because she couldn't get a date."

—·—

"I want to show you a nice place," Maurey said.

"Like a secret spot?"

She nodded and started upstream.

"Have you shown this spot to Dothan?"

She stopped and looked back at me in blue-eyed exasperation. "You never know when to shut up, do you?"

"I guess not."

"There's a time to give me crap and a time to keep your mouth shut and this is a time to keep your mouth shut."

She headed up the trail. I wondered how I was supposed to know which was which. Girls—Chuckette, Maurey, and Lydia anyway—always knew what I was supposed to be doing, and they expected me to know also. Didn't seem fair.

We came to this log across a ravine kind of thing. The log was big around as my waist, with loose bark on the sides and a few drops of water from spray off the rocks below. Maurey hopped on the log and walked across like it was a sidewalk.

She turned back to me. "This nice place is over here."

The creek went fast, white, and noisy through the ravine. It was only eight or nine feet below the log; I probably wouldn't break my neck on the rocks below, but cracked ribs or a concussion seemed way possible.

"How about if I slide down the bank and wade across?"

"The water will freeze your feet off." She put her hands on her hips—same position as Buddy standing over Estelle. "Come on, Sam. Don't be a chicken."

Chicken, squirrel, every time I turned around she was calling me another animal. Peer pressure is a weird thing. It'll make even a normal kid like me risk his damn neck over something stupid.

"You can do it, Sam," she called. "The nice thing about this nice place is we take our clothes off."

That was interesting. I stood on the log with my hands out for balance. If the log had been on the ground, we'd of had a no-sweat deal, but up high there was a risk involved and risk isn't something I'm comfortable with. I did it right foot forward all the way across. Slide the right foot up a few inches, drag the left foot behind it. Slide the right, drag the left. Took frigging forever.

About three feet from the far side, Maurey held out her hand. I couldn't make my arm reach out and I felt myself going over, so I jumped. Hit the bank and would have fallen backward into the creek if she hadn't caught me.

"That was easy, wasn't it?"

"Yeah."

"Everything is easier than you think it will be."

"Do we have to go back that way?"

Maurey laughed as if I was a funny fellow.

Her spot was a pool circled by clover up against a hill. On the hillside, willows grew right up to the bank. Tiny purple flowers made a carpet from the creek to the pool.

Maurey stepped out of her tennis shoes and peeled off her shirt. She was wearing a bra. "Strip time, Sammy."

I wanted to see her body naked, but, lack of snow or not, it wasn't skinny-dip weather. "Are we going to swim?"

"Feel the water." She sat on a clump of grass and leaned back to pull off her jeans. Without her clothes on, anyone could tell Maurey's belly wasn't just fat.

I knelt to run my fingertips over the water. "Jeeze Louise."

Maurey's arms were behind herself, undoing the bra. "Don't they have hot springs where you come from?"

"I don't think so." I stuck my hand all the way in. Little bubbles rose off the bottom of the pool, filtering up through green fronds, slowly popping on the surface. Small yellow fish darted among the fronds.

Maurey waded into the pool, bent forward so her hands and wrists got wet as her knees did. "I turned goldfish loose in here when I was seven. Can you believe they live all winter?"

What I wanted to know, besides how hot water could come out of the ground, was what this group nudity would lead to. Probably nothing, there'd been no indication of anything more than buddies-having-a-baby in months. But I would never stop hoping.

By the time I undressed and waded in, Maurey had settled back with her head on a rock and the rest of her body stretched out under the semi-see-through surface. The water was way warm, almost as hot as I like a bath. Maurey's face had a light smile. She was looking at my thing which had shrunk up about the size of a boiled Vienna sausage. I sat down quick so she wouldn't laugh at it.

"Has Chuckette touched your peanut yet?" Maurey asked.

Peanut? "Chuckette doesn't even know men have peanuts. She thinks my fingers can make her pregnant. Have you touched Dothan's?"

Maurey ignored that one. Her hair flowed up by her ears. I touched her foot with mine and she didn't pull back. "I kind of enjoy being pregnant," she said, "once you quit being sick. It's so weird. You men will never know how it feels."

"I bet it's like a football in your tummy."

"More like a rotating watermelon."

I slid around until I was right across from her and the soles of both our feet pushed against each other. The bubbles made a neat tickle feeling coming up my back and legs, like farting in the bathtub only without the embarrassment. Lydia and Hank took baths together, which I thought was weird, but this wasn't weird at all.

Maurey leaned back to look at the sky. "I'm floating in hot water and there's hot water in me with a baby floating in it. We're all the same temperature, water and people."

This was the first I'd heard about the baby floating. "What does the baby breathe if you're full of hot water?"

Her look was nothing but disdain. "Sam, how can you expect to be a father when you don't know squat about babies?"

Below me, the bottom felt like wet vinyl. I dipped all the way under to think about her question. No matter how young or old a guy is, he doesn't know about babies until someone tells him. Knowing what babies breathed in the womb isn't a stage of development like walking or pubic hair. I needed to be told.

"When I need to think, this is where I come," Maurey said. "Even Dad doesn't know about this spot. Now, if you need to think, you can come here."

I tried to think of an occasion when I might need to think. "Thanks."

"Isn't being friends better than being girlfriends and boyfriends? If you were my boyfriend, I'd never show you this spot because we might break up and then where would I be. Someone I don't like would know my secret."

"So if you like someone in the right way and then you stop liking them in the right way, you have to stop liking them at all?"

"Right."

"I wouldn't want that."

She nodded. "See. I told you it's better to be your friend than it is to like you in the right way."

"But I still want to fuck with you."

"I can't fuck with someone I don't like in the right way."

I settled into the hot water up to my ears. To keep her, I couldn't make love to her, even though I already had, and if I made love to her we wouldn't be friends anymore. So Dothan got her body and I got the confidences and the secret spot. What a gyp.

The primary question was: Do all girls think like this? If so, every guy would need two.

"Want to see something neat?" Maurey sat up so only below her navel was under water. She held her left nipple with her thumb and index finger and squeezed. "I discovered this yesterday."

"What is it?"

"Look, silly."

I leaned forward to stare at her nipple. A little watery white drip appeared from nowhere. "What is it?"

"Milk. I can make milk from my tit."

"Jesus."

She squeezed until another drop appeared. There wasn't a slit like on the end of a penis. The milk just oozed through the nipple. Maurey touched the drop with her finger, then touched her finger to her tongue—like Lydia had done with my first squirt. "It's warm."

"Can I taste it?"

She looked at me suspiciously. "It won't be foreplay."

"I know, I just want a taste."

Maurey squeezed her other nipple until a drop of milk appeared. "Okay, but only because it's so neat."

I got to my knees and crossed over next to her. She held her hand under her breast to lift it. I leaned over and licked the warm drop off the tip of her nipple. It didn't taste like milk at all, more like warm dishwater.

"You think if I sucked on it, I'd get more than one drop."

She lowered her breast back to the normal position. "The milk is for the baby, Sam. Tasting one drop is neat. Drinking me would be too strange."

"How do you know what's strange?"

Back at the TM, we fooled around with Frostbite and waited for Maurey's hair to dry.

Maurey's hands moved, touching her ears and nose. Her eyebrows rode higher than usual. "I think I'll talk to Dad before I bike back in. You go on without me."

I was kneeling when she said this, searching for the perfect blade of grass to whistle through. I looked up at her face and a tiny chill ran up my spine. Life, once again, was fixing to turn over.

"Any chance you might skip the part on who the father is?"

Maurey smiled right at me. "Let's just say you and Lydia might want to lock your door tonight."

The best thing about riding a bike from the mountains to a town is, except for a few foothills, the trip is almost all downhill. Maurey's red Western Flyer had three speeds, so hills didn't affect her that much, but I'd been in a grunt most of the way coming out. It's a lot easier to consider alternatives when you're coasting than grunting.

Here's how the alternatives lined up: The best, Buddy would make her marry me. The worst, Buddy would sink to violence—castration, death, or, as Dot predicted, he'd brand my butt.

The big problem was that Western culture was as foreign to me as Afghanistan. I mean, how much violence would the townsfolk think Buddy deserved? He couldn't literally kill a little boy, could he? This wasn't South Carolina. All my life I'd had this confusion as to whether castration is cutting off the thing or cutting out the balls below the thing. Either way made me nauseous and shrivelly.

So far, Dot's predictions had all come true. Which meant Buddy would brand my butt, but I didn't know if that meant metaphorically as in "Somebody gonna kick your ass," or literally as in imprintation by a red-hot branding iron. Branding would hurt like hell, only less permanently than castration. It might give me a romantic allure, along the lines of a tattoo or a vivid facial scar.

"I've been there and back, honey. Why once in Singapore six crazed Chinamen burned an Oriental devil sign into my ass. See my ass."

"TM is an Oriental devil sign?"

"You can touch it if you want."

There was one possibility worse than public branding. Buddy might force her back to the abortion place. Maurey was almost six months along, which made me wonder if there is a moment where a fetus becomes a baby and can no longer be flushed down the toilet.

If Buddy tried to make her abort, I would offer to fistfight him. If that didn't do it I would kidnap Maurey and take her to Greensboro and hide her in Caspar's basement. Nobody was flushing my baby now.

At home, Dougie was in the kitchen cooking something called chicken cordon bleu while Lydia sat at the table painting her toenails black cherry. Dougie smoked Tiparillos and puffed smoke straight up at the ceiling. He had fingers like a girl.

"Lydia, Maurey's telling her dad today."

Lydia blew on her foot. "That's interesting."

"If Buddy comes here will you protect me?"

"You must be responsible for your own actions, Sammy. You knocked her up."

"But you taught me how."

"That is irrelevant."

Dougie opened a drawer. "Where can I find the tarragon?"

At 10:30 I fetched Lydia's Gilbey's and locked the doors. Dougie had washed the dishes and gone home in his Volkswagen. The Idaho Falls news, weather, and sports were over and Lydia was into her nightly bitching about the TV not picking up *The Tonight Show*.

"Remember what we were doing a year ago today?" I asked her.

Lydia carefully measured her first two ounces of gin. "I was drinking my gin and watching Joey Bishop. Now I can't watch Joey Bishop."

"Joey's not on *The Tonight Show* anymore, Lydia. He wasn't on *The Tonight Show* a year ago either. You're thinking of when I was eleven."

"Joey Bishop will always be on *The Tonight Show*."

I picked both my books off the couch. "Today is May twenty-fourth, my annual trip to the plant. You think Caspar missed us today?"

"He didn't miss me."

May 24 was the anniversary of Caspar's first roll of carbon paper. We always had waffles for breakfast on May 24, then I would dress in my Sunday suit and Caspar would drag me through the carbon paper factory. It was awful. May 24 often coincided with freedom from school, a day for being outside, not a day to wander through a hot windowless cave full of loud machines and carbon black, reenacting a someday-this-will-all-be-yours ritual.

Who wanted it? I was twelve years old my last trip to the plant, torn between professional baseball and fiery novelist fighting off the adoring girls. Both my career choices leaned heavily on adoring girls. Women would love a golden glove second baseman with the soul of a poet. What they wouldn't love is a pasty-colored carbon paper maker with permanently black fingernails.

Caspar and I put on hardhats so he could conduct me up and down rows of webs, Shriber carbon coaters, slitter rewinders, core cutters, God knows what all, back into the warehouse mountains of paper waiting and paper done. The big treat came when he let me steer the forklift, which had been a kick when I was six, but come on already.

I stood in my wool suit and politely shook hands with Caspar's some-of-my-best-friends-are-Negroes employees. One old guy without a left thumb had been on the same trimmer six days a week for forty-three years. He always grinned like the brain dead in *Body Snatchers* and called me whippersnapper.

"How's the whippersnapper these days?"

"He's raring to go, Tommy," Caspar said every single year. "Can't wait to take your job away from you."

Tommy chuckled and touched my head while I made up stories about how he lost his thumb and what box of carbon paper it surfaced in.

Maurey's thinking about the rotating watermelon reminded me of my least favorite stop on the tour. At the end, right before we went for ice cream, Caspar led me to the ball mill where this huge silver cylinder spun about fourteen rotations a minute. It was king-hell scary standing in front of all that power, made me feel like a mouse in a bowling alley gutter.

Caspar stuck me right in the roar while he explained how ten thousand pounds of ball bearings spun in there smashing the walls of carbon into liquid, nine tons of spinning ball coming right at me—the ultimate second baseman's nightmare.

Caspar's eyes shone like Buddy's when the foal was born. His moustache crinkled. "Sam, you are on the edge of life. I envy the challenges you shall face in the coming years. There's nothing in the free world as exciting as carbon paper."

Way late I was dreaming Dothan Talbot and his sister castrated me with a pair of first-grader safety scissors, when a bang woke me up and Alice shot off the bed. It wasn't a fuzzy yawn wake-up. I went from sound asleep to Apache alertness in a single moment.

The bang came again; I wished I hadn't thrown out all the bullets with Otis's leg. A voice called from the window.

"Sam, wake it up. I'm tired."

"Maurey?"

"No shit, Sherlock."

I turned on the lights and opened the window so she could crawl in, which was awkward on account of her growing belly. Maurey's hair was one tangled mess, her jeans caked with mud.

"Why not knock at the door?"

"You might of thought I was Daddy and been scared."

"I was scared."

Scooting over my desk, she got mud in the typewriter. Her eyes were puffy red. Red and blue makes an odd combination.

"Can I sleep on your couch tonight?" Maurey asked.

"You can sleep in the bed, I'll take the couch."

"I need some water. My mouth tastes like dead stuff."

When I came back from the kitchen with her glass of water, Maurey hadn't moved. She just stood there with her hands at her sides, her shoulders slumped. I'd never seen Maurey with poor posture.

I handed her the water. "How did it go?"

"He said I'm a slut and a whore. He's ashamed to have me for a daughter." I think she'd put a lot of stock in Buddy being understanding. Everyone thinks love changes attitudes, but it doesn't.

"You just surprised him is all. I mean he's a father and he's real old, you can't expect instant faith. He'll think about it awhile and come around."

Maurey collapsed into my desk chair. "No, he won't. Daddy has morals and I don't."

I wanted to touch her, but I couldn't. "What have you been doing since you talked to him?"

She blinked three or four times. "Can I sleep on your couch tonight or not?"

"Of course you can. Do you want more water?" Maurey shook her head no. She hadn't touched what I got her the first time.

"Are you back to stay?" I asked.

She looked at the floor. "I don't know anything, Sam. Please let me sleep before you ask another question."

"I won't ask any more questions."

She patted my knee. "Thanks, pal."

"Do you want a Valium?"

"No."

24

THE EXTENT OF LIFE'S CHANGES DIDN'T TAKE ANY KING-HELL long time in coming down. Eight-thirty A.M., when Maurey and I swept through the front doors of GroVont Junior High, we were met with the same low-key tact they would have used on Martians. Their eyes were like dogs seeing an elephant for the first time.

"I feel like Lee Harvey Oswald," Maurey said.

"Which one is our Jack Ruby?"

The silence was too loud to handle. I wanted to tap dance or yell "*Fire*" or something, anything to get a reaction from the twin lines of kids backed up against their lockers.

"It's like we have the ultimate cooties," Maurey said fairly quietly.

"If I touched LaNell she would scream." LaNell and LaDell stood next to the girl's room, staring as if we were on TV; they could see us but we couldn't see them.

I was torn between intimidated and cocky. I mean, their eyes showed scorn and outrage at what I'd done, I think, but every kid in school also knew I'd seen a girl naked. That was their dream and now they knew I'd done it. No one could ever accuse me of virginity again. "You'd think nobody in the seventh grade ever got pregnant."

Maurey lifted her chin in what I took as a pride move. "They can't bother me."

"Right."

"Let's go to class."

"You think they hate us or envy us?"

"You and I are beyond their comprehension."

"That's what I thought."

Florence Talbot was so angry her ears were white. When Maurey and I walked past, she slammed her locker—sounded like a bomb—and stepped right behind us. Like stupid sheep, the others fell in behind Florence. I could hear her breathing in my ear and everyone else's shuffling loafers, tennis shoes, and cowboy boots. We must have looked like a damn parade.

Chuckette was the only one waiting in homeroom. We're talking pitiful. You'd think God himself stole her charm bracelet. Puffed eyes, mouth a red gash, she hadn't even ratted and sprayed her hair; looked like a nest on top her head. I felt bad for her. Chuckette had been raised in a certain way: boyfriends loved girlfriends, kids who respected each other didn't touch below the neck, motherhood is the highest deal and unmarried motherhood the lowest, and life—make that Maurey and I— had blasted all that moral theory to hell.

I avoided her, but Maurey walked over to her desk and said, "I'm sorry, Charlotte."

Chuckette wouldn't raise her head. From my seat, all I could see were tears dripping off her weak chin.

Stebbins had long ago quit trying to teach us anything. The last couple of months of school, he sat behind his desk reading from whatever book I fed him. Seemed to me the underachiever types would learn more from hearing a story than discussing one they hadn't read. Some of the kids even listened. After *Tortilla Flat*, Teddy went to the Jackson library, checked out *Cannery Row*, and read it on his own time. Nothing like that ever happened in seventh-grade English before.

Because it was the last week of school, the last two days actually since classes ended Tuesday, I'd put Howard Stebbins onto *The Artificial Nigger* by Flannery O'Connor—might as well hit them with something spiffy at the end. I made him change it to *The Artificial Afro-American.*

Normally you'd think unwed pregnancy would be one of those deals where everyone talks behind your back, but, to your face, ignorance reigns. Florence Talbot wasn't normal. Howard Stebbins read about three paragraphs into *The Artificial Afro-American* when she interrupted.

"Is it immoral to knock someone up in junior high?"

Howard looked up from his book.

Florence went on in her razor-cut voice. "I think people who have illegitimate sex should hide at home in shame."

Maurey said, "Go fuck yourself, Florence."

One of the Smith twins gasped, but after that we went into a could-have-heard-a-pin-drop situation. Howard ran his hand over his forehead, wishy-washy written all over his face. He couldn't very well let a student get away with saying fuck in class, nor could he ignore Florence's shame crack, but he wasn't in much of a position for public confrontations. Rock Springs hung over his head like rotten meat.

Howard looked back down at his book and read, "He might have been Vergil summoned in the middle of the night to go to Dante, or better, Raphael, awakened by a blast of God's light to fly to the side of Tobias."

Florence's voice was a screech. "Maurey said a whore word."

I said, "Shut up, Florence."

Chuckette sobbed and ran from the room.

"Now look what you did," LaNell said.

Teddy spit but missed the Maxwell House can and came dangerously close to my sneaker.

Stebbins read, "The only dark spot in the room was Nelson's pallet, underneath the shadow of the window."

LaDell stood up. "I better go see about Charlotte." She faced me. "Her poor heart's broken, there's no telling what she might do."

A girl named Jenny that I hadn't spoken four words to all year burst into tears.

Stebbins read, "Nelson was hunched over on his side, his knees under his chin and his heels under his bottom."

"I can't stay in a room beside white trash," Florence said. "The stench hurts my stomach."

Maurey repeated, "Go fuck yourself."

Florence and LaNell and some more who just wanted to skip class left. The rest of us stared at the floor, listening to Jenny whimper. I wanted to see Maurey's face, to see if she was unhappy or mad or what. Lydia had been coaching her on this moment all along. Attitudes were worked out weeks in advance, to the point where "Go fuck yourself" might turn into Maurey's theme for the next three months.

Stebbins read, "His new suit and hat were in the boxes that they had been sent in and these were on the floor at the foot of the pallet where he could get his hands on them as soon as he woke up."

"Coach," I said. "Nobody cares."

Howard Stebbins stopped reading and looked glass-eyed down at the book. There was nothing he could say. The glory should have been his. He could be the one standing up for his principles, announcing to the town, "We copulated and we are not ashamed." Instead, he was the coward wimp, robbed even of his righteous indignation.

What was left of the class sat there doing a bump-on-a-log routine. Sometimes late at night, I'd wondered what would happen when word spread. Down South, the Klan might visit. In Faulkner or *Peyton Place* there would have been fires, bodies buried in the garden. But this wasn't *Peyton Place*. Besides going into a shun deal or staring—which would give me an itchy butt—there wasn't much the general townfolk could do. Lydia was a master teacher when it came to ignoring hatred from strangers. Buddy, Dothan, or even Caspar might spoil the gig, but the Golden Rule Class at the Baptist Church couldn't touch me. Maurey was right—fuck 'em.

When the bell finally rang and everyone stood up to bustle off to their second period, Stebbins said, "Sam, you mind waiting around a minute?"

I looked at Maurey. She smiled and nodded but I wasn't big on sending her into that hall scene alone.

"I'll see you in citizenship," she said.

"You sure?"

"Why not?"

Howard's desk was all a clutter with about ten new photos of his plucky wife and box-shaped kids—the family bundled up on snow machines, grinning in front of Old Faithful, bathing-suited on a beach. The one of his wife on the beach was unappetizing. She wore a two-piece deal over her paper-doll body, and she smiled so big you could see her gums. If she'd been my wife, and those had been my kids, I'd of screwed Annabel Pierce in a heartbeat.

"So, Coach, what?"

Stebbins rubbed his hands together. "Did she tell on me?"

"Tell on you?"

"Does her father know, about the, you know?"

"Does Buddy know you and his wife shared an abortion?"

He ran his hand over his forehead. I love it when a coach grovels.

"I don't know if Maurey tattled or not, but I doubt it. She likes her dad."

"I haven't spoken to her bitch of a mother since we had our talk. You can tell Maurey that."

"Knocked her up, got her an abortion, then abandoned the woman, huh?"

He almost looked at me. "Wasn't that what I was supposed to do?"

"Don't ask me."

Mrs. Hinchman must have been the only person in Teton County who didn't know she had a pregnant girl in the second row. She stood up by the blackboard, fluttering her hands and droning on about the order in which one should read the daily newspaper, as if any of these kids ever saw a daily paper. Front page, editorial page, letters to the editor, classifieds. She made what she took as a joke about how we probably read the sports and comics before the international news. I bet Mrs. Hinchman read the obits first—see who she'd outlived.

Thank God Florence wasn't in citizenship. As it was, the boys tittered and the girls stared with hostility, which I could cope with. Hostility is okay, the deal I don't like is when girls burst into tears at the sight of me.

The thing I couldn't figure was how word had gotten out. Maurey told her father, but I just couldn't picture Buddy running down the mountain, shouting, "*My daughter is pregnant by an out-of-stater.*"

I asked Maurey about this at lunch. "How did everyone find out?"

We had a table to ourselves, of course. In fact we had our table and an empty buffer-zone table on either side. I know now how lepers and Negroes feel.

"What?" It was hamburger day—square hamburgers on round buns with crinkle-cut potatoes.

"Maybe someone guessed about you from your belly, but they all know about me too."

"Now I've told Dad it doesn't matter who else knows. You going to eat your onion?"

I picked up my onion slice and put it on her meat. "Who did you tell?"

Maurey looked up. "Him."

Dothan Talbot stood over me grinning like he'd found ten dollars on the sidewalk. "Sammy, boy, how's it shaking?"

"About the same."

Dothan laughed. What's funny about about the same? He turned to Maurey. "We still on for Friday night? *Town Without Pity* is on at the picture show in Jackson." He play-socked my shoulder. "You guys ought to love that one."

He was being ironic. Dothan being ironic was almost as weird as Dothan not smashing my face.

He kept going in the big-happy-family vein. "You and Chuckette come too. It's hot enough to go parking after the movie."

"I'll have to ask Chuckette."

He winked at Maurey. "He'll have to ask Chuckette. If this guy gets any funnier, they'll put him on TV." Dothan walked off whistling "Town Without Pity."

One lesson I've learned about life—you can stay awake all night sweating in the sheets and trying to figure what will happen, and what happens is never, ever, what you expect. So you might as well not worry and get yourself a solid eight hours because sleep is more important than planning.

Sam Callahan answered the phone on the third ring.

A woman's voice said, "I once taught a chicken to walk backwards."

"Flannery O'Connor? I can't believe it. You're the best writer anywhere."

"And if I wanted my people to say Afro-American they'd of said Afro-American."

"It's impolite to say nigger nowadays."

"My people are supposed to be impolite."

"Gee."

"And marry that little girl. You don't want a second-generation bastard on your hands."

Chuckette and her father came over after supper. We'd spent the afternoon at the Pierces' loading Maurey's stuff into the Oldsmobile. I don't know where Annabel and Petey were, maybe there was an understanding, as in they would clear out for three hours while Maurey packed, or maybe it was dumb luck her mom wasn't around to watch.

Maurey had a lot of stuff too. This wasn't a one suitcase, one overnight bag, and a stuffed bear runaway deal. She brought a slew of decorative pillows with things like I ♥ U stitched on the front. She carted out fifteen pairs of tennis shoes, ski boots, cross-country boots, snow pacs, cowboy boots (both formal and working), Sunday school high heels, hiking boots, penny loafers, thongs, fuzzy slippers with little rabbit's heads on the toes.

Then came the sweaters. Maurey's grandmother on the Annabel side liked to knit and had time on her hands.

We crammed all this junk into my bedroom with a lot of it ending up on or under my desk. The writing career was on a definite back burner.

Maurey said, "When the baby comes you'll move to the couch."

"Lydia can move to the couch; she likes it there."

Lydia blew smoke at Pushmi and Pullyu. "Fat chance, Waldo."

The telephone rang while I was heating up the third frozen pizza of the week. We'd fallen into this pattern of White Deck, Dougie's cooking, frozen pizza, White Deck, Dougie's cooking, frozen pizza. I always figured a tall guy wouldn't have to cook, but Dougie took pride in the stuff with the French names. He didn't have a heck of a lot else to take pride in, so I guess you go with what you've got.

Lydia came in the kitchen where Maurey was reading *The Fox* by D. H. Lawrence while I puttered with plates and paper towels.

"That was your girlfriend's father. They're on their way over."

"Uh-oh."

"Shouldn't go around breaking hearts," Maurey said.

"I never once said I liked Chuckette, right way or wrong way. How can I be blamed for hurting her?"

"You led her on," Maurey said.

Lydia opened the oven and let out all the heat. "I'll wager this is the one father you hadn't considered."

Neither woman would go to the door when Chuckette and her dad knocked. They had an attitude of make-your-bed, lie-in-it—which pissed me off no end. Maurey was the one who talked me into sex, Lydia the one with the taco shell, Maurey the one who told me to be with Chuckette, Chuckette the one who thought I loved her because I slipped some tongue. All these women controlling my life, then when a daddy shows up at the door, I'm the loneliest guy in town.

Not that I'd rather hide behind the family skirts.

Chuckette's father turned out to be no threat anyway. He

was this little guy, like five-three, with wire-rim glasses and hair parted flat down the middle.

"Here." He held out the green scarf.

"She can keep it," I said.

"There'll be no gifts from your kind in a Christian household."

Chuckette stood behind him and to the right with her head down and her shoulders slumped.

"I'm really sorry, Chuckette," I said. "I didn't plan for this to happen."

Her eyes came up to mine in the saddest, most beseeching deal you ever saw. "You loving me was the only good thing that will ever happen in my life."

"I know."

"At least I can say I was happy once."

Her father flinched. "Charlotte, go to the car."

We both watched as she dragged herself, like a defeated animal, across the yard and into their station wagon. I felt sad for her, but I didn't know what to do. You can't marry everybody who bases their happiness on you.

Her father turned back to me. "You think this is funny, don't you."

"No, sir, I feel bad."

"Don't lie to me. You never for a moment took my daughter seriously."

Wasn't much I could say to that one.

His little nose kind of trembled. "Boy, I may not look mean, but I've got the power of the Lord and a thirty-thirty with a scope, and I'll do what it takes to protect my family."

"I respect that, sir."

I told Maurey what Chuckette said about me loving her was

the only good thing that would ever happen to her, and how I realized that was probably true.

"Oh, bull, Sam. She was going to dump you before church camp this summer anyway. She likes Rodney Cannelioski only she's afraid he won't like her because she's soiled on account of you."

"That's a lie."

"She told half the school today that you're a bad kisser and she only went steady with you because you're so unpopular and she felt sorry for you and thought it was her Christian duty."

"I'm a good kisser."

Maurey shrugged and bit pizza. "She says you slobber."

This didn't make sense. We were ostracized at school, how would Maurey know what Chuckette said to anyone. "Who told you all this?"

"Sam, I'm pregnant, not deaf."

"But no one spoke to me today."

"Maybe Chuckette's right."

After pizza and Chuckette's father, Maurey and I sat on the front step to watch the sun set behind the Tetons. Another thing about GroVont that's different from Greensboro—at one time of year the sun goes down at 9:30, when just a few months ago it disappeared by 4:30. That's a big difference in day length. It disorients everything.

"Nobody up here has a decent porch," I said.

Maurey's hair was in barrettes and her face glowed like Katharine Hepburn in *The Philadelphia Story*, as if the setting sun moved a piece of itself into her skin. She leaned forward on the step. "What's Soapley up to?"

Otis yip-barked while Soapley bent over the bed of his truck, shoving something back toward the tailgate.

"Even the poorest family in North Carolina has a porch big enough for two chairs and a swing. Nobody here takes the time to sit and watch."

"Usually too cold," Maurey said. "Anyhow, you're talking about a mud room. There's no call for nostalgia over a mud room."

"A porch is not a mud room."

"Is when there's mud."

"Does Buddy plan to brand my butt?"

Spires of sunset bent around the peaks and flowed down the canyons. The mountains still had snow, so they came off a soft white, gold, and rose. One thing Wyoming has is nice stuff to look at.

"What makes you think Dad might brand your butt?"

"Dot said he would. She said he'd calf-tie me and sear a red TM in my ass, and if I really pissed him off he'd delouse, dehorn, and castrate me."

"She was kidding; a person can't be dehorned."

Soapley shoved what looked like a fat, limp body off the back of his truck. Otis jumped back and forth across the body, having a fit.

"Bear," Maurey said.

"Maybe I deserve to be branded. Impregnating girls is immoral and deserves punishment."

"Soapley killed a bear."

As we crossed the street, Maurey explained Buddy's policy on teen sex. "Dad thinks a boy gets laid whenever possible regardless of the consequences. He says the boy will trick his way into a girl's jeans any way he can and that's fair, you can't blame the boy any more than you can blame a coyote for stealing a chicken."

"That's a good attitude."

"Not that he wouldn't shoot any coyote caught in the act."

"This is a real bear?"

"It's the girl's responsibility not to get laid. She has a choice the boy doesn't have."

"What's it mean?"

"You're a coyote and I'm a slut."

"Right between the eyes." Soapley pointed with his knife, a wicked-looking blade in a new-moon curved shape.

"Where'd you get him?" Maurey asked.

"He was feeding on a dead horse up Cache Creek."

On his back, the bear looked small and pitiful. He was a reddish brown, darker on his belly, with a black nose and scummed-over eyes. His fur was patchy and one ear torn into two strips. I'd never seen a real bear before; this was somewhat of a disappointment.

I knelt to touch the pad on one of his back feet. "Why was there a dead horse up Cache Creek?"

Soapley stuck the knife into the bear's tunnel and moved his hand down one leg like the bear had a zipper. "Because I shot a horse up Cache Creek. Why'd you think? Horses don't just die where you need bear bait."

"Wasn't Red, was it?" Maurey asked.

Soapley looked at her and nodded. "He was old, not worth much anymore."

Soapley proceeded to skin the bear. I don't know where the guts were, back with old Red, I guess. Under his skin the bear was waxy like a melted candle.

Maurey knelt next to me. "Red sure was a good horse."

"Best I ever had," Soapley said.

Otis bit into the good ear, stiffened all three legs, and tried to pull the bear away. When Soapley backhanded his nose, Otis growled as if this was a tug of war for life. Soapley slapped again and Otis let go long enough to bite him. Where bears are concerned, loyalty among horses, dogs, and men doesn't mean much.

As the sky gradually darkened, Maurey and I stood by the tailgate, watching Soapley work. He did a real efficient job, pausing only now and then to kick Otis off whatever limb he was working on next. Skinned, the bear looked exactly like a hunch-backed boy about my age who'd been dipped in Crisco. The fingers were unnerving—each joint so human you couldn't tell the difference between my hands and the bear's. Soapley cut off the head, leaving it one piece with the hide.

He grinned at me. "Liver's in the truck if you want a taste."

"Raw?"

Maurey nodded. "Animals get scared and shoot adrenaline into themselves right before they die. It goes to the liver so when you eat it your head buzzes. Indians thought eating raw liver gave them the animal's spirit."

"This is way out of my background."

In bed, Maurey snuggled against my ribs with both hands under her chin and her bear down by Alice at our knees. "I'm glad we're just friends. I wouldn't want to be alone tonight."

All afternoon I'd been working on a question, so now I asked it. "Why was Dothan friendly at lunch?"

Her eyes were on my shoulder where I couldn't see them, but I could feel the lashes when she blinked. "I screwed with him last night."

"I knew it."

"I told him we could keep it up so long as he's nice to you."

I sat up. "Dammit, Maurey, I'd lots rather him beat me up than screw you."

She rolled onto her back with an arm over her head. "I would have pretty soon anyway, I guess. He's my boyfriend."

"A person doesn't screw her boyfriend to protect her best friend. That's not how it works." I was all upset. For months I'd imagined them doing it—him on top, her sucking his thing, him licking hers. It about drove me nuts, but now I knew for sure and for some bizarre reason it was my fault.

"Did you have an orgasm?"

She scooted back and sat up next to me. "It was his first time. He squirted quicker than you ever did." We were quiet awhile, each thinking something, hell, I don't know what. I'm finally back in bed with my true love, the mother of my child, and she's been screwing the king-hell creep of North America. His mayonnaise was probably up there right this second, touching my baby.

Maurey seemed to talk to herself. "I like him in the right way and I was looking forward to doing it for the right reason, you know, love, but since I did it for the wrong reason it wasn't any better than doing it with you."

Not exactly what I wanted to hear.

"At least with you I got off. With Dothan all I got was muddy."

This was awful. "Maurey, don't ever fuck with someone to protect me."

She touched my arm above the elbow. "I didn't do it for you. I did it for me. I'm scared and Dad doesn't love me anymore."

She had on her white nightie. I loved her more than I ever had before, I guess because she said she was scared.

She poked her index finger into my stomach. "Look—here's me. Here's my father, here's my boyfriend, and here's my best friend." She was on the belly button with me on the left rib, Dothan on the right rib, and her father at the top of my pubic hair.

"I've lost Dad and I don't want to lose either of you. If Dothan hates you, I'd have to choose between you guys and

I'd be down to only one. I don't think I could have this baby with only one connection."

"Which would you choose?"

"Him, I guess. Except then there'd be nowhere to live. Dothan's parents are grotesque."

At least she couldn't say that about Lydia. "You screwed Dothan so you could live with me?"

"I guess. No. I don't know, Sam. I wish Dad still loved me, then I wouldn't need either of you and I could live at home." On my stomach, she traced the connection between her and Buddy.

"I need you."

Maurey fell back into a lying-down position. "I know, Sam. That just makes everything even weirder."

I picked up Maurey's bear and put it on her chest. "I'm sorry."

She rubbed the bear's head against her cheek. "Being a grown-up is too complicated."

25

1971—ABNER AND WILLOUGHBY REX PLAY IN THE COOL *black dirt under Abner's daddy's house in Carbon Hill, Alabama.*

Willoughby Rex's voice is somewhat whiny. "Come on, I give you Frank Howard for Mickey Mantle."

"Grow up," Abner says.

"How about Willie Mays and my uncle M.L.'s gallstone?"

"I like my Mickey Mantle."

Willoughby Rex furrows his brow and makes a last offer. "Okay, my Sam Callahan card for your Mickey Mantle and your Roger Maris."

"Throw in Sam Callahan's last novel and you got a deal."

In Jackson Hole, one sort of athletically inclined boy goes rabid for mountain climbing—"The cafeteria wall is a five-point-five with a forty-foot exposure"—and the other sort of athletically inclined boy defines himself by rodeo—bullriding if he's short and self-destructive. That doesn't leave much pickings for Little League. The baseball players are mostly kids who would rather waste the summer drinking Kool-Aid and hassling little girls, only their fathers make them do something, and baseball is less stress than climbing mountains or riding bulls.

Skipper O'Brien's dad volunteered to coach the team. He was on workman's disability from falling off the dam and messing up his inner ear, so he didn't have a regular job or anything interesting to do. The first day of practice Mr. O'Brien sent the whole team to the outfield for fungo-catching. He took off his windbreaker, picked up a bat, threw a ball in the air and whiffed. Missed by a foot.

Right then I told Kim Schmidt we were in for a long summer.

Mr. O'Brien was also the kind of coach who prides himself on not giving his own son special attention, which meant that every day we had to stand there and listen to him yell at Skipper.

"You're a sick excuse for a ballplayer. You can't run, you can't catch, you can't hit. You throw like a girl."

Typical junior high-coach child psychology. Made me glad I didn't have a father.

We opened against Jackson East and lost 17-3. Kim and I scored all three runs. Jackson West shut us out 21-zip.

Most nights I listened to the Dodger game on the radio, then crawled into bed next to Maurey and told her the frustrations of my day, just like we were a real couple. "Rodney Cannelioski is disabled, I swear the kid puts his jock strap on backwards. You know what he did at the plate this afternoon?"

"Sam, I don't give a rat's ass what happened at baseball practice today." She would slap her growing belly. "I'm uncomfortable. I miss my horse. For the first summer since I can remember I'm not riding every day. Little League baseball means nothing to me. Do you understand, Sam. Nothing."

"How can baseball mean nothing?"

Sometimes this launched another round of foul-mouthed tirade—Maurey's language went downhill after that day she said *fuck* in class—or other times she'd lie there silently seething. The seething was hard to deal with.

"You're just jealous cause you're too fat to barrel race."

That one got me Alice across the neck.

—·—

Every now and then Maurey was king-hell happy. One afternoon I came in from practice to find her, Dot, and Lydia in total hysterics over baby clothes. Maurey was holding a mint green sunsuit over her head and dancing while Dot slid clear off the couch and onto the floor from laughing so hard, and Lydia smoked two cigarettes at once. I didn't see anything funny about dancing with baby clothes and said so and that set them off all over again. When she tried to get up, Dot hit her head on the coffee table.

Another time I caught Maurey and Lydia comparing my toddler pictures to the five football players. A photographer had set up his camera in J. C. Penney's and Lydia dressed me in this stupid sailor suit with a flat-topped hat with two ribbons off the back. In every picture, I looked embarrassed about to death.

"He's definitely a Negro," Maurey said.

"I think he looks more like Billy-Butch. See that weak chin."

—·—

That was the night Maurey kicked me out of bed for sleeping. Three in the morning, she bit my thumb.

"My God, you bit me."

"Wake up."

"Why did you bite me?"

"I can't sleep and if I can't sleep I'll be damned if you will."

"Look, tooth marks on my thumb."

"This is your fault. 'I won't squirt,' you said. 'No mush,' you said." Maurey did the line attributed to me in a falsetto. "All you wanted was in my pants. You'd have said anything to screw me."

"That's true."

"And now I'll never sleep again." I swear, she started to cry.

"I could get you a Valium."

"Valium's bad for the baby. I can't take Valium."

"Lydia ate lots of Valium when she was pregnant with me."

"Yeah, and look at you." She sniffled a few minutes and wiped her nose on my pajama collar. "You have to sleep on the floor tonight, Sam. I need the whole bed."

"How about if I take the couch in the living room?"

She clutched my shoulder. "I don't want you that far away. I may need you and I want you next to me—on the floor."

"You may need me?"

She pushed me gently off the bed. "God, I wish Dad was here."

I didn't see Buddy all summer, and, so far as I know, neither did Maurey. I guess he stayed up on the TM, delousing and moving water, whatever it is you do for horse maintenance. Whether because of shame or hard work, I don't know, but he didn't come into GroVont. I can't picture Buddy avoiding anything because of shame.

One day in late June we bumped into Annabel in the checkout line at Zion's Own Hardware. I'd found plans in *Boy's Life* for a self-loading goat feeder that I knew could be adapted into a cradle. Maurey made a list of all the boards, nails, and brackets we'd need and gave it to the man at the lumber counter.

He stared down his eagle nose at her and ignored everything I said, the usual treatment, but he found our stuff.

Annabel stood in line second from the cash register and we were fifth. Third and fourth—March and his fat wife—shuffled and scratched their faces before she realized they'd forgotten wood-stove polish and they disappeared back into the hardware aisles.

"Hi," Annabel said. Her face and stringy neck looked like she'd lost more weight than Maurey had gained. I couldn't see the rest of her. Even though it was about seventy-five degrees outside, Annabel had herself wrapped in this puffy blue parka.

"Hi, Mom," Maurey said.

"Good afternoon, Mrs. Pierce," I said. I don't think she saw me.

"Did you brush your teeth today?" Annabel asked.

Maurey nodded.

"And flossed?"

"Yes, I definitely flossed today."

The customer in front of her paid and walked away, but Annabel didn't move. She looked down at her hands which held a box of Hoover vacuum cleaner bags—size F. "Well, I guess you're doing okay then."

"Yes, Mom, I'm okay. How's Dad?"

"He's okay."

"And Petey?"

"He's okay too."

The man at the cash register said "Next." He waited a moment, then he reached across the counter and grabbed Annabel's package. She didn't want to let go at first, but he gradually eased the box of bags away from her. Annabel's empty hand fluttered around her neck area. "I clean your room every day."

Maurey said, "I know."

We ran into Annabel one other time on the mountain road. Lydia had dropped us off at a spot right below the TM fence line where we could play with Maurey's horse awhile, then cut across to the warm spring without being seen. Maurey said the spring calmed the baby and made her body bearable. I liked it because seeing Maurey's wet belly was neat. She was just a little girl, still playing kick the can and four square, not even old enough for zits, and yet here was this shiny bowling ball stomach with a pooched-out navel—impossible to deny when she was naked.

I wanted to say "We're having a child together" over and over until we believed it, but when I started Maurey dunked her head underwater so she couldn't hear.

"Not listening doesn't make it go away," I said.

"Talking about it twenty-four hours a day won't make it more real."

Afterward, we hung out by the road waiting for Lydia, who was late, as always. Maurey goo-gooed over Frostbite while I walked the top pole of the buck-and-rail fence. Weird how it was no sweat walking a fence pole when the log over the rushing creek caused anxiety. Whenever a car came along we hid in the dry irrigation ditch, but somehow the Chevelle snuck up on us.

What happened was we heard a truck and hid, only it was Hank going to town. He had a cowboy shirt and a new straw hat. The driver's door was tied shut with wire, which meant, unless he'd fixed the other side, Hank had crawled in through the window.

After he drove by, I stood up and stared after him, wishing I hadn't hid—Dougie was passable, but barely, and I missed Hank—and while I was wishing, Annabel came down the hill and caught us in the open.

Maurey said, "Oops."

Annabel eased to a stop and rolled down her window. Petey leaned over from the backseat to stare at Maurey. He screamed right in Annabel's ear, "*She's fat.*"

Annabel ignored him. "You need a ride?" She looked thinner than she had in the hardware store. Her eye sockets kind of rose up off her face, and her body was being swallowed whole by the parka.

"No, thanks," Maurey said.

"Why is Maurey so fat?"

Annabel glanced down at Maurey's body. "She's been eating french fries."

"Maurey, you look like a balloon."

Annabel rolled up the window and drove on down the hill.

—·—

Maurey Pierce smiled mysteriously to herself as she fondled Sam Callahan's thing. "I told Dothan pregnant women can't do it after the seventh month. He couldn't make me orgasm anyway, so I had to get rid of him."

Sam Callahan fondly stroked her lush hair. "More tongue there on the bottom."

Maurey Pierce raised her head and gazed at him with glistening eyes. "Sam, some of your fantasies are bullshit."

Lydia met Buddy once at the liquor store in Jackson. She and Dougie were buying tequila.

"What was Dad buying?" Maurey asked later in our kitchen.

"Looked like a pint of Jack Daniel's and a six-pack of Coke. I hope he isn't planning to mix them."

Maurey sat at the table drawing a picture of Frostbite. "Did you say anything to him?"

"I told him only a cad would walk away from his daughter in her time of need."

"You called my father a cad?"

"He didn't deny it."

"What'd he say?"

"He wanted to know what doctor you're going to, are you eating right, usual parent stuff."

Maurey bent over the picture and didn't raise her head when she asked, "Does he miss me?"

"Buddy wants to apologize and bring you back home but

he can't figure what to apologize for since you're the one who got pregnant."

Maurey looked up at Lydia. "He said that?"

"No. I could tell by his eyes."

The one nice thing about being ostracized by a whole town is people don't crowd you. They give you lots of room at the Pioneer Days Rodeo, and I, for one, appreciated it. The weather was king-hell hot—a full 125 degrees hotter than it had been New Year's Eve, right before Maurey's first orgasm. How can people survive in such a spread?

Last winter I would have given everything Caspar owned to feel warmth again, but now all I wanted was shade.

"North Carolina was never this hot," I said to Lydia.

"Sure, it was. We simply didn't attend the rodeo in Greensboro. Civilized humans stayed inside under the air conditioner."

Dougie perked up some at the word *civilized.* His Ban-Lon shirt had the biggest pit stains I'd ever seen and his face was sunburning by the moment.

"You oughta get a hat," I told him. I had on a used straw Stetson Delores had given me that morning. She showed me how to slope the brim into a V so water and snow wouldn't collect and dump when you look down at your hands.

"It'll never snow again," I said.

"That's the spirit."

The Callahan gang sat in a row—Dougie, Lydia, Delores, me, Maurey, and Dothan—at the top of the bleachers with five or six feet of breathing space on all sides. And five or six feet was a lot. Everyone in the county plus a smattering of into-the-local-scene tourists were packed in those bleachers, sweating all over each other. Buddy, Annabel, and Petey sat right off the rail by the bucking chutes with Stebbins and his odd brood three rows behind them. Buddy was big and hairy as ever. If he knew Maurey was nearby he didn't let on any. Annabel had traded in the blue parka for a turtleneck sweater. I couldn't believe it.

Between the two families, a tour group of senior citizens from Omaha, Nebraska, fanned themselves with their Wyoming Activities guides. I counted—thirty-five blue hairs and one bald man.

Maurey saw them too and pointed out the irony to Dothan. "Senior citizen tours are always women. You think men don't live that long or they refuse to ride buses?"

Irony wasted, Dothan grunted and popped open a warm Coors. I wasn't just happy as a lark about his presence in the Callahan gang in the first place. Dot had heard rumors that he was the real father of Maurey's baby; letting him hang out with us would only fuel that kind of disgusting innuendo. I could just see me paying for the baby—or Lydia through Caspar paying for the baby—and me changing diapers, teaching it to read, playing tooth fairy to it, while county lore held that Dothan's sperm produced it.

They'd be calling me the house-virgin. If forced to choose, I'd rather get the kid than the credit, but I deserved both. After all, Dothan got the girl.

Maurey kept bumping her shoulder into him and touching his knee. To make her jealous, I let Delores touch my knee while I leaned over and whispered in her ear, and I laughed way loud when she said I had such pretty hair and ran her fingernails behind my ear.

Delores was into her black look, complete with a black cowhide flask she wore on a thong over her shoulder like a purse. When she leaned toward me I could see her black panties under her short black skirt.

"Mex-cans were right," she said. "Nothing like tequila to take the heat off."

"Let me try some."

The grand entry parade was colorful—lots of flags, and Shriners in tiny cars, and decked-out cowgirls in flashy Western wear. The difference between these healthy girls and the Southern types, besides wide shoulders and competency, was that the cowgirls spent more time grooming their horses' tails than their own hair. You could tell. The girls were pretty, for the most part, but the horses were king-hell amazing. Coats glittered, heads tossed and snorted, front feet pranced for the fun of prancing. That was a proud bunch of animals.

Maurey punched me on the shoulder. "If it wasn't for you, Frostbite and I would be out there." Her voice was friendlylike, so I took it more as a comment than criticism. It was easy to picture Maurey on a showoff horse. She had the perfect posture for cow-girling.

Mom can't stand it when people take something seriously that she thinks is silly. The thought that a cowboy is admired and considered hot stuff because he can rope a calf or stay on a horse makes Lydia gag.

"That man is strutting." She pointed to a skinny bowlegged kid named Neb Larks who'd just been dumped in the dirt by a bareback Appaloosa. "I can't abide strutting. He thinks all eyes are on his crotch and he's proved his manhood."

"All eyes are on his crotch," Delores pointed out.

My eyes were on his jeans flapping off his butt. The kid had no ass at all, just loose jeans with a round Copenhagen-can imprint worn into the right back pocket.

Lydia was on a roll. "The timed riding of a bucking horse is nothing more than competitive sex. Proof that the man can subjugate anything wild and beautiful and free if he can just get it between his legs."

"Isn't the man generally between the woman's legs?" I asked.

Delores's hand squeezed my thigh. "What gets me is they want a belt buckle for lasting eight seconds."

Dougie sniffed. On top of his sunburn, he had bad hay fever. "A real man doesn't have to prove his manhood in public."

"How would you know?" Lydia asked.

She kept up a running commentary on gene pools—"That boy's parents were siblings. Look at his chin, how can they let him out of the house with a chin that cries incest"—and sexual preferences—"Homosexuals, they're all latent homosexuals"—clear through bareback, saddle broncs, and calf roping.

She found the ropers especially disgusting. "They're child molesters. At least the horses outweigh their subjugators. This is baby rape."

"What's a subjugator?" Dothan asked.

I gave him Lydia's Lord-why-do-I-suffer-fools look but he didn't care. He asked Maurey. "How often does she shut up?"

Maurey laughed like this was the pithiest comment she'd heard in days. I decided to ask Delores if I could see her naked later.

When it came time for bulldogging, the P.A. man said the first entry was Hank Elkrunner with Ft. Worth Jones as his hazer. There was a gap of time I used to look out at the cemetery, then the yearling, Hank, and Ft. Worth exploded into the arena. I saw the calf's eyes first, all wet, black and white, bugged in terror, then I saw Hank's hair. It'd always been longer than a white guy's, but now it flowed back in the wind like a black mane.

Hank came off his horse fast and violent, lifted the yearling, shoved in a leg, and slapped it to the ground—*Bam*. Happened so quick, by the time I realized it was over, Hank was swatting dust off his chaps as he walked back to his horse and Ft. Worth was grinning at some girls in Rexburgh, Idaho, letter jackets.

I looked over at Lydia whose face had gone pale blank and said, "Twice I asked Ft. Worth how he spells his first name and both times he said, 'F-T period, like the town,' only you don't spell the town F-T period at all. It's F-O-R-T, Fort."

Lydia ignored me, as usual, so I went on. "You think I should tell him he's been misspelling his name all his life?"

Dougie gingerly touched his shrimp-red neck. "So what perversion do bulldoggers prefer? You've rated everyone else by their choice of competition."

Lydia blinked a couple times and kind of shook herself awake. "They need a hazer, someone to position the woman before they throw her on her back."

"Looked like a stud to me," Delores said.

Lydia finally shut up.

During barrel racing Delores put her hand on my leg. "I need a Coke."

Dougie squinted down the line. "Coca-Cola and tequila don't mix properly. You'll awaken with a hangover."

"I'd think I was sick if I didn't awaken with a hangover. Sam, honey, go get us two Cokes with lots of ice."

"Can I wait till after the girls finish? This is neat."

She dug her fingernails into my thigh. "I want a Coke with lots of ice, now."

At least behind the bleachers was shady. The concession stand consisted of a card table and a cigar box, three coolers of bottled pop floating in water, and a garbage pail full of ice. Chuckette Morris and Rodney Cannelioski sat on stumps behind the card table, going rapturous on each other's eyes.

I said, "Two Cokes, lots of ice."

Chuckette stood up. "My boyfriend and I are in love."

"Congratulations." I meant it.

"Rodney gave me his jacket. He's a gentleman."

"Chuck, it was thirty below zero when you wanted my jacket. Anybody can be a gentleman in July."

"Don't call her Chuck," Rodney said. "I'm the only one allowed to call my girlfriend Chuck."

I couldn't see how any girl could like Rodney over me, even if I didn't want her to like me. "Can I have my Cokes?"

"Only if you apologize," Chuckette said.

"For calling you Chuck?"

"For everything awful you ever did to me."

I wasn't sorry for anything awful I ever did except not nipping that going-steady stuff in the bud, but she was holding Delores's Cokes hostage. "I'm sorry I got Maurey pregnant while I was going steady with you."

Chuckette filled two wax-coated cups with ice. "You better not ever French kiss with my sister."

"I'll never French kiss with Sugar."

"That'll be forty cents."

Back up in the stands, Delores held her fingers across the top of her cup and poured the Coke under the bleachers—got some kids who were crawling around down there looking up at beaver shots right on their faces.

I said, "I thought you were desperate for a Coke."

"I was desperate for ice." She leaned over with her face up against my ear and whispered in a voice that smelled of tequila, "Here's how real Mexican women cool down on a hot day."

Delores dug two fingers into her cup and pulled out an ice cube. Her hand disappeared under the black shiny skirt, moved up and around some, then came back empty. "Ta-da." She opened her palm to show me the empty hand.

I drank about half my Coke in one pull. "Do all women pop ice up their tunnels?"

Delores giggled and touched my hair. "Of course."

Something happened during the bull rides, the upshot of which was to affect my own personal life, although the way things were headed, the upshot was probably only a matter of time. The announcer said Neb Larks had drawn a Brahma named Tetanus, and while Maurey explained tetanus to Dothan, and Lydia said, "The mind boggles at the thought of this boy's sexual preference," they pulled open the chute and cut Tetanus loose.

I plain don't care for sports where it helps to be short and skinny—horse racing, high school wrestling—but at least in those sports there's a reason for staying underweight. My theory is bull riders ride bulls because being small has given them a personality disorder.

Tetanus came out spinning clockwise along the fence, each flying hoof as big as Neb Lark's head. The bull planted his front feet and rag-dolled Neb into the air, where he twisted, bent forward, and came down face first on a rising horn. It was like exploding a blood-gorged water balloon. *Splat.* Red foam sprayed everywhere.

Tetanus's front end soared again and for one remarkable instant Neb lay lengthwise along the bull's back, his runny crimson face aimed at the sun, then Tetanus popped and Neb flew over the fence into Annabel Pierce's lap.

People who love rodeo love this stuff. Petey screamed, Buddy grabbed Neb by the shoulders and pushed a bandana into his face. The clowns came over the fence, half the senior citizens fell back and the other half pressed forward. Only Tetanus and Annabel stayed sedate. The bull wandered across the arena, calm as an Irish moo-cow; Annabel smiled slightly and stared vaguely into space. Her head seemed disengaged from her body where Neb lay gushing blood.

Maurey's hand gripped my arm. "Mom's not going to like this."

"She looks okay."

An ancient, white International Travelall ambulance eased through a gate as Tetanus eased out. The clowns and Buddy propped Neb up to probe under the blood, looking for the hole in his face. The one eye I could see didn't register pain, more like wonderment. They held under his armpits and feet and lifted him back across the fence. Buddy got in the ambulance first and gently pulled while the clowns guided Neb in.

"This is exciting." Lydia's face was flushed and alert. Blood brings that out in her.

"I might ought to see about Mom," Maurey said.

"I'll come with you."

Maurey was too pregnant to see her feet, so she needed help with the bleacher steps. By the time we felt our way to ground level, the ambulance had pulled a U-ey and was blaring across the arena, siren wailing. The siren seemed unnecessary.

All eyes were on the ambulance and no one but Maurey and me saw Annabel dig into her purse and come out with a hand full of Kleenex. She dropped to her knees, spit on the Kleenex, and started scrubbing blood.

She chirped, sing-song-like. "Have to clean this floor before Buddy gets home. A man's work goes from rising to setting sun, but a woman's work is never done. Never had a flow this heavy before. Buddy will be angry, he doesn't want children..."

Maurey knelt, which was a trick, and held one of Annabel's wrists. "Mama, it's okay, leave the floors for later."

"Can't let Buddy see tracks on the linoleum."

"She's nuts." Howard Stebbins stood a row up from me. "She's nuts, ought to be locked up."

Maurey's eyes blazed as she turned on him. "It's your fault."

"No more than you."

"What's she talking about?" Howard's wife asked.

Annabel spotted the blood on her turtleneck. "God, he's back." She was up, tearing the sweater off over her head. Maurey jumped toward her; I saw hands battling each other, then Annabel was on her back tearing her jeans off. She kept yelling, "*My baby, my baby, you can have my baby.*"

Dothan stood on my other side, amazed. "Her pussy's shaved."

Every rib showed; her hips were shovels pushing out skin. Maurey fumbled with Annabel's clothes, trying to force them back on. Petey cried. Everyone else kind of stood there in a semicircle, staring at this emaciated skeleton woman. Now that her clothes were off, all except her bra, Annabel seemed to want her skin off too. She scratched at her thighs, then dug into her crotch. Her panicked face turned from person to person in the crowd, searching for someone, finding Coach Stebbins. "You tore my baby, you killed my baby."

All Stebbins's nightmares came true at once.

His wife whined. "What's she mean, Howie?"

Annabel howled, "*Abortion.*"

As Maurey moved forward into the pool of blood to get hold of her mom, Annabel went into a crouch. "Where's Buddy. I have to find Buddy."

"He went to the hospital," Maurey said.

Annabel put her hand on the top fence rail, vaulted across into the arena, and took off.

Maurey said, "Holy shit."

She'd have looked better totally naked. As it was, in nothing but her bra, she looked pitiful. Private hell had gone public.

Twenty yards into the arena, Hank roped her—caught both feet in the loop and jerked. Then he was by her body, covering it with a horse blanket. Since Maurey couldn't jump the fence, we circled to a gate and crossed in front of the chutes. The crowd around Annabel parted, giving us a straight view of her curled-up body. She lay sniffling, mumbling, with her knees tucked up to her chest and her hands holding the rope behind her legs. Hank held her head up and brushed dirt from her nostrils.

"You didn't have to rope her," Maurey said.

He looked up at us. "You'd rather the whole county chase her like a calf scramble?"

"I guess not."

"I figure the sooner this is over the better."

Annabel put her face up against Hank's shirt and sobbed.

As the junior high cheerleader drew the clean sheet up to cover her developing bosom, sweat steamed off her forehead. "Sam Callahan, you get me so hot I can scarcely stand it."

Sam Callahan left the bed and padded barefoot into the kitchen where he opened the freezer. Back in the bedroom, he set an ice bucket on his night stand. "Here, honey," he said. "I'll show you what the older women do when I make them hot."

Hank and Maurey wrapped Annabel in blankets and got her into Hank's truck. Annabel seemed to have passed through something and come out on the other side dead. She breathed, but that was all. She didn't move or speak or have any expression on her face. Hank had to arrange her feet around the gear shift, then fold her arms over the blankets.

After I helped Maurey into the passenger side—the door Hank had fixed—they followed Buddy's tracks off to the hospital in Jackson, and Lydia, Dougie, and I retreated to the White Deck where half the trucks in the county had gathered. I don't know where Delores and Dothan got off to, I only hoped they hadn't gone off together.

Lydia sent Dougie around to bum the last three empty chairs in the place, but we had to share a table with two Mormon missionaries in white shirts and skinny ties. Lydia hates all forms of purposeful innocence. She looked around the crowded cafe and said, "Who do you have to fuck to get a cup of coffee in this joint?"

One missionary blushed, but he took it. The other one looked down and opened a *Book of Mormon*. Lydia would have to try harder than "fuck" to shake these two.

A bunch of college boys from Montana sat on most of the stools, and I could see tension between them and the two booths that held Ft. Worth and his gang of rednecks. Ft. Worth had talked the Rexburgh girls into sitting with him, and, from the drift, I figured the Idaho girls came to the rodeo with the Montana boys and the Montana boys felt infringed. They didn't say anything out-front ugly, but they acted surly—kept demanding service in loud voices as if they were being put upon.

I decided to help Lydia with the missionaries. "If a girl shaves the curly hair from between her legs, does it always grow back?"

Lydia checked her teeth in the butter knife. "Leg hair comes back faster the more you shave it, but I don't know about crotch, I never shaved mine. Dougie, you ever shave your pubics?"

"No, I never shaved my pubics." Dougie had sissy hands. How could a person go to a rodeo and sweat tremendous pit stains yet still come out with manicured hands? The missionaries had rougher hands than Dougie.

"Maurey's grew back," I said, "but Annabel was smooth today."

Dougie blew his runny nose on a napkin. "And what does Annabel's smooth crotch signify?"

The Montana boys were getting more obnoxious about the lack of service. I hoped for a fight. "When they shaved

Ft. Worth's arm, the hair grew back even though the skin had moved to his finger."

Lydia breathed on the knife and wiped it on the tail of her shirt. "Maybe Annabel's been shaving herself ever since the abortion." She smiled at the missionaries. "Do Mormons shave their groins after abortions?"

The one with the book stood up. "They'll never serve us here, LaMar. Let's go someplace where we can avoid religious persecution."

"I just asked about shaving clitori."

I noticed something. "It's not religious persecution, nobody's been waited on." Not a table in the room even had menus. Ft. Worth stepped behind the counter and helped himself to the coffeepot, much to the indignation of the Montana boys, so his table had coffee, but I hadn't seen anyone who worked at the White Deck since we came in.

I pushed back my chair. "Think I'll go look for the waitress."

Dougie sniffed. "She's probably committing unnatural acts with the cook."

"You just went off my list," I said. Even if he was Lydia's boyfriend, I didn't have to listen to anyone bad-mouth Dot. I'd been considering it for a month, but now I knew the time had come to move Dougie Dupree down the road.

I worked out various ways to handle his expulsion from the family unit as I crossed in front of the cereal pyramid and pushed through the swinging doors, which meant I wasn't all that alert, but right away I felt something weird in the kitchen. Dot sat on a ten-gallon bucket of burger pickles with her head down so I couldn't see her face. Max sat in front of her on a same-size bucket of mayonnaise and a man in a uniform stood by the grill, staring down at a burned steak.

The man said, "I hate my job."

"The restaurant is full of people," I said.

Max ran his hand over his nearly bald scalp. He looked more lost than ever. "We're closed. The people should go home."

My stomach got a real sick feeling. "What's the matter? Dot, what is it?"

When Dot lifted her face, she had a tear track off her right eye. She looked at me and tried to smile but couldn't. "They took my Jimmy."

I sat on the floor. First Annabel and now this, nothing made sense. "Took? Who took Jimmy?"

The man at the grill seemed to be speaking to the steak. "He was killed in action, that's all I know. The officer accompanying the body sometimes has more details. I just notify the kin. In ROTC they never said anything about notification."

"Killed?"

Max reached over and touched Dot on her knuckle. She still stared at me. "What do I do now, Sammy?"

I hadn't even known Jimmy. I was thirteen, about to be a father. I didn't know what she should do now.

Behind me, Lydia burst through the swinging door. "Who do you have to fuck to get a cup of coffee in this joint?"

26

THIS GUY JIMMY WENT TO HIGH SCHOOL WITH PLAYED THE saddest version of "Taps" anyone ever played on the harmonica. You can do that with a harmonica if you really feel bad. King-hell despair dripped off each mournful note till, except for Lydia and Dot's son, there wasn't a dry eye in the cemetery.

"You ever see the movie *Shane*?" Maurey asked. We stood back a ways by the cottonwood tree—same place we'd stood at Bill's funeral. Everything was the same except that was winter and Maurey wasn't eight-months-and-some pregnant when they covered Bill.

Clouds blew around over by the Tetons, but I was hot and itchy from my clip-on tie and suit coat. "Sure. Alan Ladd. The kid hollering '*Shane, come back. Mother wants you.*'"

"That guy played 'Dixie' at a funeral in the movie. They filmed it here in this cemetery."

"Neat." Although it wasn't all that neat. Whenever I see something really emotional, I like to think it's spontaneous and never happened before. This harmonica player had practice at ripping heart strings.

"Who're the old people?" Lydia asked. Lydia had actually come to the thing for Jimmy. She put on this dark, shiny dress and sunglasses and dragged Dougie away from the gallery. I think she was motivated by loyalty to Dot, which showed how much Lydia had changed since we came to Wyoming. She never had time for Southern women.

Maurey wore this top that looked like an open umbrella and a short skirt. From the knees down she looked thirteen and not a bit pregnant. "That's Dot's parents. They used to live here but the Park Service took their house. He sells siding in Moscow, Idaho, now. The shrunk-up old lady is Jimmy's grandma who raised him." The mom kept pulling Dot's son Jacob off the dirt pile, but every time she got him down he scooted right back up. Cute kid, as kids go. Had a lovable chubbiness and dark, dark eyebrows. Reminded me of John-John at Kennedy's TV funeral.

I unbuttoned my top shirt button behind the clip-on tie. "I wonder why Dot's not raising him."

Maurey shrugged. Lydia said, "Cause she's smarter than me."

"You don't mean that," I said, though I wasn't sure. Normal people go all appreciative of live loved ones at these deals, but I think death just scared Lydia into getting tougher.

After the preacher said whatever prayer you say about dead people, a man in a uniform took the flag off the casket and handed one end to the harmonica player. The army casket was silver and smooth, like a miniature Airstream trailer. Soapley's trailer before he painted it. It was nothing like the two caskets I'd seen before in my life.

The uniformed guy and the harmonica player did this folding ritual, then the uniformed guy handed the flag to Dot, who stared at it as if she didn't know what it was.

Dot's face had lost like five pounds in the four days since the rodeo. More than pounds, her light beam had gone under, she'd lost that inner-cheer thing that made her bright and beautiful. Her posture was shot to hell. She reached for Jacob, as if to prove he was there, but he pulled away and scrambled up the grave dirt.

The black clouds piled high behind the Tetons all the way to Yellowstone and big forks flashed every minute or so. After a flash, I counted to twelve before thunder rolled over the cemetery. Dougie blew his hay-fevery nose. "If they don't finish this we'll be struck by lightning and everyone will die at a funeral."

Lydia kind of sighed behind her sunglasses. "Shut up, Doug."

I'd been to one winter funeral and one summer funeral, and if death is inevitable like Maurey keeps telling me, I'd rather die in summer. Nobody should be left underground when the dirt is frozen.

Dot's fingers touched the smooth coffin. Her lips moved awhile, then she took Jacob by the hand and walked around saying thank you to the clusters of people who had come to tell Jimmy good-bye.

That part even moved Lydia. "Jesus," she said. "Only Dot would remember to be courteous at her own husband's funeral."

Maurey said, "I wish I could have the baby this minute."

Dot hugged Hank, then Coach Stebbins who was there without his wife. They'd both been pallbearers, along with four other guys from the only GroVont basketball team who ever made the state finals. Jimmy was the first guy from the team to turn up dead.

Maurey stood with her hands on her extended belly. "Dot's son will never know his daddy. That's kind of sad."

"I never knew my daddy and I'm okay."

Maurey and Lydia both said the same thing at the same time: "Says who?" Even at a grief gathering, my women stayed consistent.

Somebody gave Jacob a Tootsie Pop that he tried to unwrap as Dot led him over to our little group. He pulled free from her to use both hands on the job, which I could tell made Dot insecure. She wanted to touch him at all times.

Dot stood in front of us, looking torn. She was the kind of person who thought she owed the world cheerfulness, as if by not smiling and laughing she was letting down her part of the load. But she couldn't smile now, and I know that embarrassed her.

"Well." Her shoulders went up and down. "How's Annabel doing?"

Maurey shifted her stomach weight from one leg to the other. "Dad's taking her to a hospital in Salt Lake today. She still won't talk or wear clothes."

"When Annabel comes out of the hospital, you forgive her. Hear me, Maurey?"

What could Maurey say? Dot's husband was dead, so she couldn't very well disagree. Bereaved people are supposed to have special insight into what really matters and what doesn't. Besides, Dot was probably right.

No one spoke for an awkward time, then Dot touched Maurey's belly. "And take care of that baby. No milkshakes and coffee for breakfast."

Maurey went into Dot's arms. "Won't you be here to take care of me?"

Dot looked over Maurey's shoulders right into my eyes. I put my hands in my pockets, then took them out. My turn was coming and I didn't know if she'd expect a hug or what. "I'm going to Moscow for a while," Dot said. "All that's left of Jimmy is Jacob and I want to watch him grow up."

She left Maurey to come to me and the hug was natural as water. Her back felt soft under my hands. "The White Deck won't last without you," I said.

"I won't last without Jacob." At the sound of his name, Jacob looked up and grinned a sticky smile.

After Dot hugged Lydia, she stood back with her hands on Mom's shoulders. "If you find a good man, don't ever let him go. Do you know what I mean?"

"Yes."

Dot's head nodded up and down a few times before she continued. "Pride won't keep you warm after you lose him forever."

Lydia repeated, "Yes."

Jacob dropped his Tootsie Pop in the dirt and burst into tears. Dot did another moment of intense eye-lock with Lydia, then she turned and bent over her son. "It's okay, don't cry, we'll wash it off and make it good as new."

Jacob stomped his right foot. "No."

"Look," Dot said. She put the Tootsie Pop in her mouth and drew it out clean. "See. All new. If you don't want to eat it, I will."

"Mine." Crisis over, Dot led Jacob back to where her parents waited. As she passed the casket, she gave it one last pat, then she picked up Jacob and got in a car.

Dougie blew his nose again, sounded like our water heater when you crank the bathtub hot spigot. "What was all that about?"

Lydia bit her lower lip as she stared off at the lightning behind the Tetons. When she goes into one of those thought trances, I can almost see the process in her eyebrows. They scrunch down behind the sunglasses while she faces whatever it is she's suddenly come upon, then, when she makes her decision, they spread wide and calm.

Dougie talked to Maurey and me through his handkerchief. "What was that 'Know what I mean' stuff?"

"Got me," I said.

Lydia's head kind of snapped. She turned to Dougie and took off her sunglasses, her eyebrows at ease. "It means, Dougie, that you're a nice fella, but you're not a good man."

Dougie drew up as tall as possible. "I don't get it."

"It means we had our jollies, the fun is over. It means thanks a lot, it was real." She shook his hand.

"Are we separating?"

"That's one way to put it. People die, Dougie, and I'd hate like hell for you to be my last man. See you around."

Lydia walked over to the basketball team that was still sulking around the grave. Coach Stebbins fiddled with the pulley deal holding the cylinder over the hole while Hank and the others loosened straps. Lydia walked up to Hank, put her hands on both sides of his face, and kissed him. He jerked back and turned around. Lydia followed him around the circle, almost stumbled into the hole. He had to catch her by the arm.

"Hey, this is good," Maurey said. "Think she'll get him?"

"She'll get him."

"Why does she want him?" Dougie asked.

Lydia gestured with her arms, Hank's face went Indian. The other pallbearers, who only moments before had been droopy and depressed, started to smile behind their hands. Even Coach Stebbins didn't look all that miserable. They needed a tension break, and one thing Lydia can provide is comic relief.

"He wrecked her house," Dougie said.

"That's the Blackfoot way of saying I love you," Maurey said.

"I've been dismissed."

"Don't take it personally," I said. "Happens to me all the time."

Hank tried to walk away. He went clear around the casket and hole, then he headed for his truck with Lydia talking away at him the whole time.

Maurey put her arm around my shoulders, which made me feel real good. She popped the silly tie off my shirt. "Can you give us a ride into town, Dougie? I'm not up to walking home after another funeral."

There was a letter from Caspar in the box:

Dear Samuel,

We have before us the fiendishness of business competition and the World War, passion and wrongdoing, antagonism between classes and moral depravity within them, economic tyranny above and the slave spirit below.

Prepare to take your rightful position. The Black Horse Troop awaits.

Your Mentor,
Caspar Callahan

"What's all this?" Maurey asked.

"He steals quotes from books and we're supposed to think it's off-the-cuff wisdom. The Black Horse Troop is a bad sign, means Culver Military Academy."

"Economic tyranny above?"

"That's him if us slave spirits below get out of line."

"Is unwed pregnancy out of line?"

That was the crucial question. "He didn't like it when Lydia got knocked up."

"Do you think he knows about me and my baby?"

I didn't care to dwell on it. Of course Caspar knew. He knew all. And the lack of comment or action had been weird. Lydia and I could make future plans to our ears, but Caspar controlled the cash flow. Like God.

"What will he do?" Maurey asked.

"You want TV dinners for supper or pancakes?"

"Pancakes."

—

Way middle of the night, like 3:30 A.M., Maurey shook me awake. "Farlow's up against my bladder and I have to pee."

I hoped this wasn't headed to another night on the floor. "So pee."

"Listen."

From the other side of the house came giggles, grunts, and sloshes. "Lydia and Hank in the tub?"

Maurey nodded. "And it's really squirrelly."

"What's squirrelly? Lydia likes doing it in water."

"They have the moose in there with them."

I sat up in bed. "Les is in the tub?"

Maurey nodded again, wide-eyed. I found her a quart mason jar to pee in, then we turned on the light and sat on the edge of the bed, imagining where a moose head fit into dicks and tunnels.

The possibilities were endless.

27

Otis's wink delighted Delores to no end. She couldn't get over an ugly, three-legged dog who stared in her eyes and winked.

"Ray used to wink just like that in high school," she said. "Especially in Mrs. Hinchman's class, he'd leer at me across the room all hour and when I finally looked at him Ray'd wink just like that dog. I thought it was the sexiest thing I'd ever seen. Only later I found out winking is the closest Ray ever comes to foreplay."

"You know why women fake orgasms?" Lydia asked.

Soapley went somewhat embarrassed. He wasn't used to our little gang. We only invited him because it was Maurey's birthday and no one else we invited over could come on account of their mothers wouldn't let them. The Callahan house had a reputation for evil.

Soapley's job was to help me cut wienie sticks out of willow fronds while Hank built the fire. Hank got fire duty because he was an Indian. What he did was spray a half-pint of lighter fluid on some kindling and say, "Blackfoot brave start-um heap big fire," then he threw in a lit match.

The birthday girl was cross. "I don't give a hoot why women fake orgasms and I think wienies and marshmallows for breakfast is stupid." Maurey sat on a pillow on the back stoop, big as a beached whale. We were down to the last week and a half and her sense of humor had failed.

All Maurey'd done for days was piss and moan. "You did this to me, you horny little squirrel. I hope you never poke a girl again. If you ever go on a date the rest of your life, I'll be there to tell the girl you can't pull out before you squirt."

"I bet I could now."

"I'll be dead before you get a chance to find out with me."

"Maurey, we're partners."

"Yeah, right."

Lydia leaned back in her lawn chair and blew Lark smoke in Hank's direction. "Women fake orgasms because men fake foreplay."

Nobody laughed—which made me miss Dot. Dot would be rolling on the ground over a joke that bad. She always made a person feel appreciated.

Soapley eyed the perfect point of his wienie stick and said, "What's foreplay?"

The birthday party–wienie roast had been Hank's idea after he discovered I'd never cooked over a fire with sticks.

"You never roasted marshmallows?"

"Lydia thinks marshmallows are plebeian. I've never even been on a picnic."

Hank stared at Lydia. She did her shooshing-flies gesture. "Well, beat the crap out of me. I'm a terrible mother."

Nobody disagreed and a wienie roast was planned for Maurey's big fourteenth.

The guys cooked meat while the women sat in lawn chairs and told us we were doing it all wrong. Delores shook up a Dr Pepper and held her thumb over the end to spray my face. Hank said a cookout wasn't American unless that happened. I don't know, it all seemed ritualistic to me.

"Why do women brag about faking orgasms?" Delores asked.

I was watching Hank's fingers, how slowly he moved them as he spooned relish and onions on his bun. "I do not understand women," he said.

Lydia was automatic. "So what else is new."

"What's the purpose of faking an orgasm if you tell the man later that you faked an orgasm?"

I looked at Maurey and smiled. She sent a cynical prissy smile back. She'd been talking death and discomfort ever since the funeral, to the point where I was ready to get this baby deal done.

Delores talked with her mouth full of wienie. "Sometimes when I have a real orgasm I tell the guy I faked it so he won't be so cocky. I hate a cocky guy."

Delores had gone king-hell ape on the getup—bright red boots, tight pants, and low-cut blouse deal that showed big air between her breasts, even redder scarf around her neck, red dangly earrings, and, to make herself a piece of art, she'd dyed her hair the color of a North Carolina State home-football-game jersey. I mean *red.* Soapley wouldn't look at her. Every time she bent down to feed Otis a marshmallow, Soapley stared at the ground between his feet and talked irrigation. "Not enough water behind the dam. I'll be locking headgates by next week."

Hank had amazing patience with marshmallows. His came out all golden, same tint as his skin. Mine caught fire. Maurey said she liked them black so I burned seven or eight and took them one at a time to her on the steps. She ate them off the end of my willow stick. Two bites—one for the outer charred stuff and one for the inner gooey stuff. She ate with her eyes closed.

"My baby's going to be raised on marshmallows," Maurey said.

Lydia lit a Lucky Strike off the butt of a Kool. Hot dogs and marshmallows were so far beneath her dignity nobody even bothered to ask if she wanted any. "I raised Sam on Dr Pepper."

Right after we sang "Happy Birthday" I got Delores back for the spray in the face. Lydia hadn't had time to bake a cake, naturally, so we stuck a hurricane candle on a marshmallow and had Maurey blow it out.

"Make a wish, honey," Delores said.

"I wish I'd have this baby today," Maurey said, and blew.

While Delores was bent forward toward the candle, I flipped an old gooey cooked marshmallow off the end of my stick into her cleavage. It stuck for a second before falling into the depths of red.

Delores did a high wail and jumped me like a red tornado. I fell over backward; Otis went into a barking frenzy.

Delores giggle-shouted, "Hank, get him."

I fought the pair of them, but Delores sitting on my stomach bent over my face was a fantasy come true of sorts anyhow, so I didn't mind losing. Above my head, Hank knelt with his knees on my shoulders, which pinned my arms, and his hands holding down both ears. I got into some bucking action that basically amounted to a dry hump.

Delores jumped up and down. "Hi, ho, Silver."

Lydia's voice was bored. "Watch it, Delores."

Otis kept barking and Delores kept laughing. "Hold his nose, Hank. I want his mouth open."

I started to say something rude and she stuffed a marshmallow in my mouth, then another and another. Breathing got difficult until Hank let go of my nose, but by then I couldn't close my mouth because of the marshmallows so Delores stuffed in a few more. I tried to bite her and she went up on her knees, then slammed down on my chest, which almost blew my face into an exploding pimple joke.

"Ten's the record," Delores said. "How many more we got to go?"

Hank's voice came from above my head. "Four, but we might have to use his ears for the last two."

"Okay." Delores was smooshing a marshmallow into my right ear when Otis suddenly stopped barking. Hank's knees went off my shoulders. Delores kept cramming for a few seconds, then she quit too. I was shaking my head back and forth and laughing and trying to touch Delores's magic spots, so it took awhile for the silence to sink in.

Time kind of froze up—way too quiet for good-hearted rowdiness. I looked up at Delores's lipstick-smeared face. She was turned, looking at something on the right. I moved my head and saw white wing-tips.

No one in Wyoming would wear white wing-tips.

"Get up, Samuel," Caspar said.

Delores moved off me. I looked over at Lydia who had gone pale. Maurey pulled herself to her feet. So did Hank. Everyone was standing except Lydia.

Caspar repeated himself. "Get up, Samuel."

Same white suit, pencil moustache, ivory-colored hearing aid, yellow mum, and black-lined fingernails; he had the expression of a stern master addressing impertinent darkies. Or God.

I stood, pulling marshmallows out of my mouth. They kept coming like the trick where a magician draws thirty feet of scarf out of his nose.

Caspar held a navy blue jacket and pants on a hanger in his right hand. The jacket had fancy brocade and dark yellow ribbons; the pants had a dark gray stripe on the outside of each leg. Caspar carried a round hat with a bill under his left arm.

"This is your Sunday uniform at Culver Military Academy. As soon as you clean out your ear, you will put it on."

Lydia said, "Daddy."

"Shut up, girl. We are going home now. We will place Samuel at Culver, then proceed to Greensboro."

I swallowed the last marshmallow. "I can't leave, we're having a baby."

Caspar drew up to his full, righteous five-foot-four as he studied Maurey on the steps. Then his gaze swept around at Hank and Delores, Soapley and Otis, finally Lydia and back to me. "You two have done enough here. We are leaving today."

"No."

"When you attain the age of eighteen and have a job and money, you can make your own decisions. Not before."

My eyes met Maurey's. "Who will take care of my baby?"

"I'm sure the young lady has a mother of her own."

Maurey spoke. "Mom's in the nuthouse."

"Be that as it may, you have made your bed, you must lie in it. I will not have my grandson snared by a spider, which is what you are, young lady. And if you think you will ever see a penny of the Callahan fortune, you are sadly, sadly mistaken."

Lydia said, "Maurey is not a spider."

"I told you to be quiet."

She stood up. "I won't. You can't come in here and ruin everything. This is our home now. These people are our family."

Caspar pointed his finger at Lydia. "A floozy, a Kiowa, and a pregnant little girl—which member of your new family will pay next month's rent." He turned on Hank. "Can you afford to keep my daughter in gin?"

Hank said, "Blackfoot."

"And what does that mean?"

"I am Blackfoot, not Kiowa."

"I understand you live in a one-room trailer. Do you think she will be happy there carrying your papooses?"

Hank's hands were fists at his sides. I thought he might hit Caspar and wondered what would happen then. After a minute of tense silence, Lydia said, "Daddy, you are such an asshole."

Caspar broke the stare-down with Hank and turned back on Lydia. "The day you pay your own way you can live anywhere in any disgusting fashion you see fit. Until that day, you do as I dictate." His busy eyebrows swung to me. "Go inside and put on your uniform."

I didn't move. There was no way I could leave Maurey and the baby now. Even if the baby didn't exist, Lydia was right, this was our home. We fit in GroVont, I couldn't go back to annual visits to the carbon paper plant.

Caspar's eyes almost softened. "Samuel, you have no choice. You cannot fight my will."

I said, "No."

"I'm doing this for you, Samuel. You can't be a father at your age. You can't even take care of yourself."

Caspar was right. Lydia and I had built this new life for ourselves. We'd discovered we were capable of mattering in a place, we had friends, but the whole deal was based on a check coming the first of every month. We had no control over ourselves after all.

I folded the uniform over my left arm and held the hat in my right hand. Lydia wouldn't look at me. Hank still stared at Caspar, Delores smiled weakly and I smiled back. As I passed Maurey on the steps, she said loud enough for everyone to hear, "Tell your grandfather to fuck off, Sam."

"I can't."

I went through the kitchen with its sink full of dirty dishes and into the living room and stood under Les, looking up at his great nostrils. I could hear the toilet running. Lydia had told me over and over that life isn't supposed to be fair, never to want anything and you'll never be disappointed, but this was ridiculous. This was a gyp.

Neatly, I set the uniform on the TV and the hat on the uniform, then I walked out the front door. The Tetons were pretty, glistening over there across the valley through air so clear the mountains appeared flat. My one-speed bicycle leaned against the front wall under Lydia's bedroom window. I wheeled it past her Oldsmobile, Delores's Chevy, Hank's truck, and Caspar's Continental with the North Carolina license plate. Then I hopped on and took off.

28

WILD STRAWBERRIES GREW IN THE SHADE BY THE CREEK, AND fireweed blossomed purple on the hill. Juncos flitted through the willows next to the warm spring. I knew the names of things—some things anyway, the stuff Maurey had told me about. I liked knowing what I was looking at. A year ago I wouldn't have seen the juncos, much less known what to call them.

I leaned back with my ears under the warm water and listened to the gurgle of air bubbles entering the spring from the bottom mud. Air coming right out of the earth—it made an odd picture.

The trouble was, I wasn't emotionally old enough to deal with being ripped from my dreams. Maybe it was a breakthrough that I knew I wasn't emotionally old enough. Other people who are immature are so immature they don't know it. Lydia was emotionally younger than I was, but she'd been ripped so often by life, she'd probably accept losing me. Maybe that's all maturity is—being ripped so often you don't care anymore. Caspar was the emotionally oldest person I knew; I wondered how he dealt with losing Me Maw. Maybe jacking around surviving loved ones is a way of dealing.

I'd come up the hill to think, but thinking wasn't happening. The hot water was more soothing than plan-inspiring, but I guess I needed soothing more than I needed a plan. What I needed most was to be held by someone who loved me and told everything would be all right. Hot water is a weak substitute for love.

Maurey wasn't in love with me, not in the right way. If she loved me, we could fight Caspar. We could flee into the mountains and live like a Disney movie. We could go Romeo and Juliet and die.

I closed my eyes and felt the sunshine on my face. Life was so pleasant at individual moments. Why couldn't people cooperate with each other and give me what I wanted?

First choice: Marry Maurey. Second choice: Stay in GroVont with Lydia and raise the baby with Maurey close by. Last resort: Take Maurey and the baby to North Carolina. Culver Military Academy was completely off the list. And leaving the valley before the baby was born was past unthinkable. If Maurey wouldn't flee with me I'd flee by myself, at least until I attained parenthood. I could live on berries.

When I sat up, water rolled off my hair and down my armpits. Two ravens flapped by, heading west. In Greensboro, I didn't even know where west was. I liked it here, dammit. I'd never liked it anywhere else. I loved Maurey, I loved the baby, most of all I loved Lydia, and Culver meant losing her too. Who would take care of her? Who would fetch her 10:30 bottle?

Maurey wobbled across the log with her arms out.

"You're going to fall and break your butt," I said.

"I could cross this creek blindfolded."

"With all that weight you're worse than blindfolded." I guess I'd known she would come.

She stepped from the log onto the moss around the spring.

"Your grandfather isn't happy with that trick you pulled. He's gone to Jackson to find a motel room." Maurey peeled her shirt off over her head, then she reached both arms around her back to undo the bra that she needed now. Her breasts still weren't big as Delores's, but they were heavy and the nipples had spread into this way-wide target deal.

I pushed the water surface with my palms, causing little waves to buckle across the spring. "I'll never put on that uniform."

She had to lie down and arch to get out of her stretchy pants.

"Yes, you will, Sam. You and Lydia are helpless and we all know it."

I watched as Maurey waded into the spring and sat down. She was so big in the middle and so young on both ends. Her hair was longer, but her eyes just as blue and her cheekbones just as childlike as they had been the first day she called me Ex-Lax. "How did you get up the hill?"

She leaned back on her hands. Even in the warm springs, she didn't look that comfortable. "Hank. He's over at the ranch, talking to Dad."

"Buddy washed his hands of you."

Maurey's face looked sad. "Something's got to happen. Farlow is coming whether Dad's here or you and Lydia are here or anybody's here. The reality is me and the kid can't live alone."

"You'll live with me."

"Yeah, sure, Sam." She stretched her legs straight so the soles of her feet came up against mine. That was our favorite talking-in-the-warm-springs position. "It's either Dad come to town for the winter, me and the baby move in with Aunt Isadora, or we go to Mom's parents' retirement villa in Phoenix. Petey has to live somewhere too, Mom won't be out for a while."

"Aunt Isadora?"

"Delores's mother. She thinks I'm a whore and a cunt. Can you see Delores's mother with any room to gossip?"

Maurey was writing me off the possibility list. Like zip, let's get practical here. Sam's a goner.

I couldn't accept being a goner. "Maurey, none of that will happen, I'll take care of you and the baby."

A scowl ran across her eyes. "Sam, you've spent the last six months bragging, 'I'm a daddy, I'm a daddy.' Have you done any research?"

"Research?"

"Can you change a diaper?"

"Well—"

"Do you even know where to buy diapers? GroVont isn't exactly a shopping center."

I guessed. "Kimball's Food Market."

"Wrong, kid. Zion's Own Hardware."

"Why would a hardware store sell diapers?"

"There'll be days I'm at cheerleading practice or on a date with Dothan and won't be able to breast feed. Can you sterilize bottles and make formula?"

She hadn't mentioned dates with Dothan since Jimmy's funeral. I'd hoped she'd forgotten. "No, I can't make formula"—I had no idea what formula was—"but I can learn."

"This whole pregnancy is theoretical to you. 'Gee, won't it be nice to love someone who can't criticize me.' A real human is showing up, probably next week. Theories don't shit and cry, they don't die if you screw up."

"Love someone who can't criticize me?"

"I know what you think of me and Lydia."

I tried sarcasm. "When did you grow up all of a sudden?"

"Next week, pal."

I ran out of anything to say. I hated being young. I hated needing. Why would God give sperm to a person too young to be a father? I tried to picture myself at Culver next week, signing up for lacrosse, being yelled at for dull shoes, taking showers around boys. Yech. Boys smell bad when they're wet. After seeing something that mattered—love, parenthood,

Wyoming—I couldn't go off to a place where people took shoeshines seriously.

Maurey splashed water on my chest. "Don't be sad. No matter how awful everything is, you and I will have a baby. Eighteen is only a little over four years, then you can come back."

Four years was almost half my life. I couldn't conceive of four years.

She flipped warm water into my face. "Wake up. You know who the rat was? Soapley."

"What rat?"

"The rat who's been on the phone to your grandfather once a week since the day you and Lydia hit town. Caspar wrote him a check after you ran off. Soapley apologized to Lydia and she whapped him with a wienie stick."

"Lydia whapped him?"

"Said Otis is an ugly dog and she'd shoot his other hind leg off if she caught him peeing on her property."

I wish I'd seen that. I splashed Maurey back in the breasts area. "Why did Caspar wait so long to fetch us home?"

"The plant won a big order from American Express. He couldn't leave till they shipped."

Water games escalated. Maurey slapped the surface and got me good. I kicked with my legs, churning up a king-hell froth. She was too big to churn so she tried to kick me in the balls, but I twisted and took it in the thigh.

We were kids again in no time.

When Maurey stood, her belly glistened like a huge wet cue ball. Tiny drops of water winked from her regrown crotch hair. "I better go see if Hank talked sense into Dad."

"Hank's not one to talk sense into anybody, but I've only seen him with Lydia and she doesn't let him talk much."

"He's taking the she's-an-immoral-slut-fuckup-but-after-all-she's-your-daughter approach. I doubt it'll work. I talked on the phone to Dad when he put Mom in the hospital and he didn't like me any more than ever."

"Maybe Hank can shame Buddy into caring for you."

"I bet Dad forgot it's my birthday." Maurey bent down with difficulty and reached into the warm spring. I couldn't see her face when she spoke. "You coming up to the house or you going to hide out all night?"

"Think Buddy will hit me?"

Her hand came up with a fistful of mud which she glopped onto my chin. "Sam, you're too little to hit."

As we sat on the moss, dressing, a bug nothing more than a red dot moved up Maurey's belly to a lump under her ribs.

"What's that?" I touched the lump.

Maurey hooked hair behind one ear and looked down at the spot. "A knee, I think. Maybe his head. He moves around and I can never tell where what is. Feel this."

Her lower abdomen was hard as marble, couldn't have been comfortable for her or the baby. I knocked on it like she was wood and I needed good luck. "Think he's trying to crawl out when he moves?"

"More like rolling over to find a new position. Or dreaming." Maurey pulled her pants over the big belly and stood up to fiddle with the bra. I tried to picture what a womb-baby dreams of—baseball glory, blue skies, food? Unless you believe in reincarnation or preexistence or some other odd religion, a baby's dream would have to be pretty abstract.

"You think he knows he's coming out?"

"Of course, silly. He's not about to spend his whole life floating in fluid."

"But does he know that?"

She spoke through her shirt as it came over her head. "My baby knows everything."

When Maurey stood up, she put her hand on top of my head. "Hot water makes me dizzy these days. It never did that before I brought you here."

"You weren't pregnant before you brought me here."

Real friendlylike, she popped the top of my head with her palm. "Next time I get the urge to learn new skills, I'm picking a kid with a brain."

I leaned over to tie my right shoe. Hank taught me to always tie the right shoe before I put on the left sock. Has something to do with luck. "Let's talk about that, Maurey. I've given this a lot of thought, and I think after the baby is born we ought to start practice again."

Maurey laughed at my preposterousness, then she stepped onto the log. I was holding my left sock to my nose to see if it stunk, when a sound made me look up. Maurey's arm jerked, she leaned right, then fell forward across the log and dropped from sight. The sound when she hit was awful—part splash, part crack, a gasp.

I tore down the bank, fell myself, and landed on my hands and knees in the creek. When I scrambled across to her, she lay crumpled on her back in shallow running water with her left leg at an impossible angle, cussing like king-hell shit.

Mostly it revolved around Jesus and fuck. "Christ, it hurts. How did that happen? I can't fall."

"Don't move."

"Something's broke, Sam. Fuck." Her face twisted up with her eyes closed and her teeth showing. I lifted her head and back out of the creek, but when I touched her leg, Maurey screamed. "God-fuck, what are you doing?"

"I need to see this." I turned her sideways so her body was leaning on the steep bank, but her lower legs were still in the water, which was probably for the best. My own feet, especially the bare one, stung for maybe ten seconds before going numb.

When I pulled her pants leg up, she screamed again, only not so loud. There was blood, not a gross amount, but enough. When I bent to check the inside of her leg, a white shin splinter poked through the skin. Reminded me of Otis.

"Your leg's broke, Maurey."

"Tell me something I don't know." She suddenly went white as the bone and gasped. Her eyes concentrated hard on something I couldn't see, then the spasm passed and she was back.

"Something's bad in my guts," Maurey said.

"Around the baby?"

"God, I hope this isn't a miscarriage. I read about miscarriages." She yanked her pants down from the back. Between her legs was running with water and a trickle of blood.

"Is that creek water?"

She touched the rivulet. "It's coming from me. God, I hurt." She bit her lower lip and the tears came. "Crap. I'm going to die before I have the baby."

"Which hurts most, your leg or your belly?"

My stupid question brought her around. "Jesus, Sam, I can't pick between pains."

I took off my shirt and wrapped it around the blood flow from her leg, but when I touched near the bone, she clenched up. Then she breathed real hard and held her belly. After a few seconds, she gradually calmed down.

"What was that?" I asked.

"I'm either losing the baby or having it. I wish I knew the difference. Nobody ever told me shit. Mama's in the nuthouse when I need her, Daddy hates me. My hair's all wet."

That last one scared me. "I'm going after Buddy."

Maurey grabbed my arm hard. "Don't leave me here, Sam. I don't feel good."

"I have to find help, we don't know what to do."

The tears streamed without a crying sound. "But Dad doesn't like me."

"Maurey, I have to get help. There's no choice."

She pushed me away. "Go ahead and leave when I need you. I'll lay here and die alone."

"You won't die. I promise."

"You promised you wouldn't squirt. You promised you wouldn't fall in love. You promised you wouldn't go back to North Carolina. When was the last time you kept a promise?"

"I promise you won't die." After that she stopped talking. I waded into the creek and found a rock to prop her right leg on, but I figured the left one should stay in the water. She probably couldn't feel it by now anyway. Then I checked the flow in her crotch. The water coming from her was bad, but the blood scared me. I couldn't tell if the flow was slowing down or getting worse.

"You comfortable enough?"

She didn't say anything. I changed my mind and decided to pull the broken leg out of the creek after all. She might lose it from freezing.

"If it gets to hurting too much, put it back in the water."

Maurey nodded.

I touched her shoulder, then scrambled up the steep bank. Maurey's voice came small and frightened. "Sam?"

"What, hon?"

"Thanks."

It would have been faster if I'd gone back up the far bank for my left shoe. By the time I reached the ranch, my foot bled like Maurey's leg. The cowdog Simon chased me the last thirty feet up to the ranch house, so knocking on the door was out.

I blew into a room with Buddy and Hank squared off at

a linoleum table, both cradling cups of coffee. Petey shoved trucks off kindling next to the wood stove.

"Maurey fell, she's hurt." I bent over and held my knees.

Hank recovered first. "Where?"

"Up the creek, a quarter mile, a half mile, I don't know. Her leg's broke and her crotch is bleeding."

Buddy was on his feet and moving, gathering rope, sheets, his knife, something from under the sink. Hank ran to his truck and brought back a hatchet. If you ever have an emergency, have it around cowboys.

"Exactly where is she?" Buddy asked.

"She fell off a log over the creek, past the third beaver dam."

"The warm springs?"

I nodded. "Maurey said you didn't know about it."

"How bad's the bleeding?"

"Not much blood, but lots of clear stuff."

Hank glanced at Buddy. "She broke her water."

Buddy's bushy head went up and down. "Sounds like a tear in the placenta. Watch Petey while we're gone." He threw some towels in a day pack and they left.

—

Lydia did thirty-nine hours of labor before I was born. "It was Nazi torture," she told me. "Ninety-seven degrees and Deep South humidity. Contractions for days. The nurses hated me for being young and rich. I turned into a cat, spitting on them whenever they touched me."

"Nurses are supposed to be compassionate."

Lydia made a forceful "*Huh*" sound. "These dykes laughed at me, said I was a sissy little girl. I called one an evil iron-cunt and she said I was an unwed bitch who didn't deserve pain-killers, that I wouldn't be so quick to seduce Southern boys again if I was punished."

"Sounds like a confrontation."

"I screamed for eight hours. They tied my arms down but I bit the iron-cunt in the shoulder blade. The Negro orderly slapped me till I let go."

Lydia said the doctor gassed her about three centimeters too soon just to shut her up, then he and Caspar went out for barbecue and one of the nurses delivered me.

"That slimey-balled doctor charged full price for delivery and he wasn't even there. He was off licking his fingers with Daddy."

"But after all that agony, look what you have now," I said.

"What?"

"Me, aren't I worth it?"

"Sam, nobody is worth giving birth."

Shannon was born at 1:45 the next morning. I'll never figure where Maurey came up with the name Shannon, but it's pretty and Shannon herself is beautiful as sunshine.

Buddy and I sat on bruised peach-colored plastic chairs in the waiting room playing Chinese checkers. The nurses hadn't known exactly what stance to take where I was concerned. Little girls had had babies in the Jackson hospital before, only not with little-boy fathers doing the pace thing outside with the little girl's father, especially little-boy fathers wearing no shirt and only one shoe. Someone found an orderly smock-looking shirt small enough to more or less fit, but I ended up taking off my right shoe and sock so my feet would match. The left foot was a cut and bruised mess that no one offered to fix. I guess if you aren't a patient they don't worry with you.

About midnight, one of the nurses brought out a box of toys they kept for kids getting their tonsils out. I'd read both lobby

Reader's Digests—"I am Joe's Thyroid"—and concentration had flown off.

The interesting thing about Chinese checkers was watching Buddy handle the marbles. He was so big, and his fingers were even bigger and rougher proportionally than Buddy, it was hard to picture him being concerned with something small as a marble. The man needed large concepts—stallions, freedom, wilderness—not trivialities. Although he did play a mean Chinese checkers. Once I explained the rules, the man was unstoppable.

At first, Buddy hadn't wanted me at the hospital. He and Hank carried Maurey into the ranch house with her leg in a splint and a wad of towels between her thighs. She was drained white, silent, smiling weakly when she looked at me but not looking at me much.

The plan was for Hank to take Petey to Aunt What's-Her-Name's while Buddy drove Maurey to Jackson in the Chevelle. Good thing Annabel was in the nuthouse or they'd of had to cram Maurey into a truck cab.

After they fit her in the backseat, I hopped in to hold her steady on the dirt road.

Buddy said, "You go to town with Hank."

"I'm staying."

He stared at me for about five seconds, which made me jumpy, so I tucked a Hudson Bay blanket around Maurey's waist and good leg and pretended it was a done deal and staring at me with black-bead eyes didn't matter.

Finally, he said, "Okay." Maurey didn't indicate what she wanted from me. She was going into shock.

Halfway between GroVont and Jackson, moving eighty miles an hour, Buddy said, "When I was your age I wouldn't have passed it up either."

I glanced at his beard in the rearview mirror. "I love her, Mr. Pierce."

He swallowed. "I had to be a father; it was my job."

"She understands."

Maurey's hand squeezed mine real hard as another spasm came on. Sweat trickled from her hairline, down her face, and disappeared behind her neck. Her blue eyes stared up at the ceiling. I tried to count between blinks, but gave up at forty-five.

—

The first twenty minutes at the hospital were frenzied with efficient people running in and out of the emergency room. A man hooked Maurey up to a bag of blood while a woman gave her a pain shot in the rear. When it came time to set her leg, the doctor kicked me out. I said, "No, Maurey needs me," but the doctor growled like a big dog so I left.

After that, we're talking seven hours of vacuum time, waiting on the outside, climbing walls on the inside. Buddy talked to me some. He told me about the army and art school and Annabel crying every minute of the drive to the hospital in Salt Lake.

"I can't comprehend anyone that I love," Buddy said.

"I know what you mean."

It's amazing what people will say in crises—even cowboys.

Sitting in that stupid puke-colored chair, staring at "Humor in Uniform" for an hour without getting any of the jokes, I made a conscious effort to think like a person who doesn't put himself at the head of the universe.

Caspar had control and he had a right to control. He took the stern-hand-on-a-naughty-child approach because Lydia and I had done nothing but screw up since before I was born. Let's face the truth here: to a person of Caspar's generation, knocking up a thirteen-year-old is irresponsible behavior no matter how much love is involved.

The way to be near Maurey wasn't kicking and screaming as Caspar dragged me off to military school. The cool course was to give up what I wanted for a while so I could grow up and come back later and have it. Maybe Maurey would learn to love me if I wasn't around. Lots of people are easier to love if you don't actually look at them every day.

Much as adult thinking rankled, not to mention flying in the face of everything Lydia ever taught me, I decided that if Maurey came out okay and the baby came out okay and they let me hold it once, I would leave quietly with Caspar. There wasn't any choice so I might as well go with dignity.

Dignity is a tough concept when your fourteenth birthday is almost a month away.

"Would you like some toys to play with?" the nurse asked.

"I'd rather have a Valium."

29

I WISH THE NURSE HAD SAID, "SAM CALLAHAN, YOU HAVE A daughter." That would have been a hoot. What she said was, "Buddy, you have a granddaughter."

He said, "Thank you, Caroline," which meant they knew each other. Probably went to high school together, everybody else in the state did.

We left the Chinese checkers to follow Caroline the nurse down a well-lit hallway to a glass window looking in on the nursery thing. One wall had nine stethoscopes hanging from a rack and a cut-out picture of Yosemite Sam aiming two pistols at the daddies and people at the windows. Two babies lay swaddled in blue blankets in side-by-side cribs. The one I knew right away was mine had her little slit-eyes open, ears you could almost see through, and black cirrus-cloud hair. A light purple wedge ran from the bridge of her nose to the top of her forehead.

I stared at her so hard my breath fogged the glass and made her look all wispy.

Caroline went into the nursery to bring the baby over to the window and present her like a guy in New York did when Caspar ordered a bottle of wine. Even though I'd rehearsed this moment ever since we left Rock Springs, I didn't know what to feel. I'd expected fatherly instincts to wash over like surf. Instead, I found myself trying to connect this little live person with unfocused eyes and tiny, tiny fingers to runny mayonnaise dripping off my sock. How had one led to the other? It was a big leap.

I said, "I thought blue blankets mean boys."

"She said it's a granddaughter." Buddy leaned forward. "I didn't plan it to be this way."

"But she's so beautiful."

He touched the glass with two fingers. "She is beautiful."

My butt was safe from branding after all.

I slept in my clothes in one of the ugly chairs and the room was way hot so I sweat and stuck to the plastic. Rolling over was like pulling off a giant Band-Aid. Made for bizarre dreams.

The North Carolina basketball team held Sam Callahan on the cross while his grandfather hammered nails through each hand, then fastened his ankles to the upright with barbed wire. Someone stuck a dish sponge in hot Dr Pepper and held it to Sam Callahan's parched mouth. His grandfather moved through the crowd, giving dollar tips to smartly dressed Negroes.

Sam looked across the valley to the cool snow on the Tetons. He allowed a single tear to drop from his newly grown moustache. As blood flowed into his eyes, Sam Callahan groaned aloud. "Forgive my grandfather, for he knows not what he is about."

The women rent themselves and tore their garments. The men wrote poetry.

I woke up to Hank standing over me holding a folded T-shirt and my second best sneakers.

"Morning, Dad." He grinned and his shoulders went up and down in that silent laughter of his. "You are sleeping too long. Don't you know fathers have responsibilities."

I unstuck myself from the chair. "It's a girl."

"The valley is abuzzing with the news—Lydia is a grandma."

I hadn't thought in those terms yet. "Have you got fifteen cents, I need a Coke."

We bought a Coke and an Orange Crush and started back down the hall to visit Maurey. An old lady slept in a wheelchair in front of the nursery window. She wore a floral pink nightgown and a matching bathrobe with drool down the collar. As Hank and I walked past, her head jerked awake and she called me Frederick.

"Frederick, don't drive so fast, you'll kill us all."

"Morning, Mrs. Barton," Hank said, but she was back asleep.

A nurse with her hair all ratted up and sprayed down like she was in a beauty pageant blocked the new mothers' door with her hands on her hips and her tits in my face.

"Where do you think you're going?"

I didn't say anything on account of I figured she was talking to Hank. Grown-ups don't ask strange kids questions.

"Maurey Pierce," Hank said.

"You can see her, but the boy stays." She pointed to a black-on-yellow sign with eight sides like a Stop sign. NO VISITORS UNDER 16 ALLOWED IN MATERNITY WARD.

"But I'm the father."

She looked at me through spider eyebrows. "I don't care if you're the Pope."

Hank raised a hand toward her arm, but he didn't quite touch her. "Susie, the baby is his. Bend the rules and let him in."

"I can't do that, Elkrunner."

I'd had it. "Listen, lady, I'm being carted off to military school this afternoon. If you don't let me see Maurey and the baby, I won't see them for years."

Her hands came off her hips and crossed her chest.

"Susie," Hank said.

"He's not sixteen."

Enough adult behavior. I wasn't leaving Wyoming without seeing my daughter. Time to revert to childish. "I'll howl like a coyote and wake up all the sick people."

Susie's red lips split into a sneer. I'd of given anything for a thirty-four-ounce Louisville Slugger.

I closed my eyes and howled—*owwww*. After a few seconds, Hank joined in, only his was way louder—*OWWWW*. They must train Indians in that stuff. Behind the nurse, a baby wailed with us, and a door opened.

"What's this?" Buddy stood there like a bear who hadn't slept.

Her voice was a whine. "Under-sixteen-year-olds aren't allowed in the maternity ward, Mr. Pierce. They're germy."

Buddy's black eyes went from Susie to me to Hank. Hank was smiling. Howling in a hospital must have given him a charge.

"Sam is sixteen," Buddy said.

"And I'm Gina Lollobrigida."

"Who will you be in trouble with if you let him in?" Behind Buddy, the crying stopped as suddenly as it had started.

"Dr. Petrov will put me on report."

"Tell Dr. Petrov that I said Sam is sixteen. He knows I would never tell a lie." I knew what was coming next so certainly I could have said it myself. "We played football together in high school."

Susie gave up and stalked away. Another crisis averted, I went in the room alone.

Maurey reached for my Coke and drained it. "They shaved me again."

"I thought that was only for abortions."

"Doctors must shave every time they poke around down there. I might as well start shaving myself like Mama, save them the trouble."

Maurey looked awfully chipper, considering yesterday. Her hair was brushed shiny and her eyes glittered blue with interest at the baby stuck to her breast. The surf of love I'd expected last night rolled over me, only more for Maurey than the baby. The baby was still a little abstract.

She held out a Bic pen. "Want to sign my cast?"

Her left leg encased to the thigh hung by the same pulley-and-hook deal the vet used on Otis. Her toes were gray.

"Does it hurt?"

"Itches like king-hell, but doesn't hurt."

"You never said king-hell before."

Maurey smiled, which was neat. "You're rubbing off on me."

"Holy moley." I signed up her leg from Buddy—*Yer pal, Sam Callahan.*

"Is the baby eating breakfast?"

Maurey parted the hospital gown to give me a better view of the baby's mouth clamped to her nipple. She looked asleep. "Her name is Shannon."

"That's pretty, I never heard it before."

Shannon's cheeks sucked in and out and the eye I could see opened, then closed slowly, like a tortoise.

"Can I touch her?"

Maurey looked worried for a second. "Okay, but be gentle. Babies aren't footballs."

"They don't travel as far when you kick 'em."

Maurey didn't like my joke a bit. For a moment I thought I'd blown the chance to touch my baby. We hemmed around and I apologized and Maurey asked me when was the last time I'd had a bath, which she knew full well was the warm springs.

"That water was probably full of cooties."

"You didn't mind it yesterday."

"Yesterday I was different."

Finally, I sat on the end of the bed and touched Shannon on the back of her leg, above the plastic I.D. anklet thing. She was soft as a bubble gum bubble and, I imagined, just as delicate. I had created this. The whole deal was so neat I started hyperventilating and had to stand up.

"I hope she grows up to have my looks and Dad's brains," Maurey said.

"How about me?"

"She'll have your hair."

Sometimes I feel sorry for Petey. He was the only one who lived with Annabel from the abortion to the nuthouse. That period had to have an effect on the kid.

While we waited for Buddy and Hank to haul Maurey out of the woods Petey told me his mother was dead.

"My mama's dead."

"No, she's not." I poured their coffee dregs together into the same cup and took a drink.

"And Maurey's going to be dead too. I'll get her room."

It was cowboy coffee and the grounds hadn't settled all that well. "What makes you think your mother is dead?"

"Cause Daddy said she went away to the hospital. Jason's dad said his mom went away to the hospital and she was dead. Grown-ups say went away when they mean dead."

When Me Maw died Lydia found me under the round bed and pulled me out. She sat me in a chair and looked me right in the face and said, "Me Maw is dead. We won't see her anymore." None of that gone-to-a-better-place jive.

"You want to go outside and pet the horses?" I asked.

"Ever' time somebody dies or gets a bortion or fat or anything, I have to go out and pet the horses. I hate horses. I'm tired of petting horses."

—·—

Hank drove me to Jackson Drug where we bought a box of nickel cigars. He said this was part of the process, I had to give a cigar to everyone I met all day. I didn't know if the deal was Indian or Wyoming or maybe people all over America bought cigars when they had babies. The druggist said, "Congratulations."

"Thank you, sir."

Hank and I each lit a cigar for the ride to GroVont. I was really tired from the excitement of Maurey breaking her leg and having a baby, and I hadn't slept much on the sticky chair, so right off the cigar made me sick. Not so much barf sick, though nausea was a factor, as exhaustion-in-every-internal-organ sick.

Everything was over—I was a father, *yea*, I'd seen Maurey and touched the little baby, all the stuff I'd looked forward to for months had happened and I felt like I'd missed it.

Nothing was left but a long, long trip clear across the country—with the worst driver I'd ever seen.

Hank puffed and sucked and caused a cloud he could have sent signals with. As I got sicker, he started humming the song from "Bonanza." *Bum-ba-ba-bum ba-ba-bum ba-ba-bum-bum.*

"What are you happy about?" I asked. "You're losing a girlfriend."

Hank took the cigar from between his lips. "Your mother has the heart of a mountain lion. The will of a buffalo."

"Lydia?"

"She shall never be daunted by a man."

"Until the first check doesn't show up."

Hank bent forward to look up through the cracked windshield at two hawks wheeling in the west. His foot came off the accelerator and we coasted down the highway while he admired, or studied, or whatever he did. They were kind of pretty.

"I got a winter job," Hank said. "Winter jobs are rarer than girlfriends in these mountains."

I didn't ask what the winter job was—I didn't care—but he told me anyway. "Buddy hired me to feed stock a couple weeks a month while he's in town with the kids."

I felt blue-green. "Mind stopping the truck for a second?"

As throwing up goes, this one was fairly normal—wet heaves, dry heaves, fear of death. Hank handed me a bandana and kept talking.

"We worked it out yesterday before you came screaming in the back door. I hadn't mentioned you two being in the neighborhood, must have been a surprise for Buddy."

"I wasn't screaming."

Hank blew smoke at me. "Try to miss the truck, Sam."

I climbed back in and leaned against the door using the taped-up window as a pillow. "Life's not all the Hardy Boys built it up to be, Hank."

"Beats the alternative." Hank shifted gears and moved back onto the asphalt. I'd never felt so awful.

"All I want is to go home and sleep till Halloween."

"We have to drop by the White Deck first. You haven't had your breakfast."

"Food makes me puke."

"Breakfast is important for a boy."

"I want to go home."

"After we eat."

Caspar's Continental was parked in the line of five or six pickups outside the White Deck.

"I can't go in there, he'll kidnap me."

"Your grandfather will not kidnap you."

"He'll take me straight from breakfast to Culver. I won't be allowed to tell Les good-bye. And Alice, I'm not leaving Wyoming without Alice."

Hank dropped his butt into the near-empty Orange Crush bottle where it sent out a low hiss. "I will not let him take you without saying good-bye to Les and Alice."

"I'm sick, Hank. Let's go home."

He slid toward me because his door was wired shut. "Breakfast, Sam."

Caspar sat in one of the booths with Ft. Worth. They were both examining Ft. Worth's finger when I slid in next to Caspar. Hank took the other side.

"Have you seen this?" Caspar nodded at the hairy fingertip. "Man has an uncanny ability to adapt. Biology is a fascinating subject."

I looked down at my lap. Handcuffs would have been appropriate.

Ft. Worth's voice boomed. "Congrats, Sammy. You're going to love fatherhood. I know I do."

"You have kids?"

Hank reached for the menu in front of Ft. Worth. "He has two sons, but he has not seen them in years or paid a cent for their upkeep. No wonder he loves being a father."

Ft. Worth's lower lip puckered. "I think about 'em all the time."

"How old are they and when are their birth dates?"

Ft. Worth knew the ages, but couldn't quite recall the births. Since I was sitting next to Caspar, I didn't have to look at him, but I could feel the waves of disapproval and disappointment as he sketched the feed plan of a carbon coater on a napkin for Ft. Worth to admire.

"It is all a matter of tension," Caspar said.

"Did you bring in the cigars?" Hank asked.

"I forgot."

"I'll get them." He moved from the booth and stood up. "If that lazy-ass waitress shows her face, order me a donut."

I looked up at Hank who was grinning like an idiot. "Lazy-ass" seemed way out of character for him. While I stared, he went on in a loud voice. "Who do you have to fuck to get a cup of coffee in this joint?"

"Keep your pants zipped, Jack."

Lydia came up behind me and put a hand on my shoulder. She carried a coffeepot in the other hand. The white uniform with the lime green trim was large in the bust and hips, but the little hat was cute.

"Mom?"

"Mutual trust and respect, Sam. Always remember what our relationship is based on. I may be a grandmother, but I'm not thirty yet."

"You can't work, Lydia."

"Watch me." She poured coffee in my cup. Didn't leave room for the cream and sugar, but at least there was no spill.

Caspar made a snort sound with his nose. "Never last a month. The first time she breaks a fingernail she'll be pleading for money."

"Fat chance, Daddy. Didn't you always scream at me to get a job?"

"This is colored work."

"I'm colored as anyone in town."

The cigar and baby had made me dizzy—now I was king-hell confused. "Does this mean I don't go to Culver?"

Lydia leaned over me to freshen Caspar's cup. "Long as we pay for ourselves the old goat can't force us anywhere."

"You will never make rent on tips," Caspar said.

"Dot did."

"I'm moving in too," Hank said. "Selling the trailer and coming to town."

"What about the winter job?"

"That's only two weeks a month. Maurey and I have to live somewhere while Buddy is up the mountain."

"Maurey's living with us?"

"Part-time," Lydia said. "Now what can I get you? Haven't got all day to chitchat with the rabble."

—·—

As I ate bacon, eggs over easy, wheat toast with those crappy little cafe jelly things, and frozen hash browns, Caspar explained the carbon paper industry to Ft. Worth and Hank. He about had Ft. Worth ready to move to Greensboro.

"Are there lots of women down in North Carolina?" Ft. Worth asked.

"A hundred-fold more than here."

"Are they all like Lydia?"

That thought caused a dark cloud to fall across the table as we four considered an entire Southern state full of Lydias.

"Would be a Vision Nightmare come true," Hank said.

I looked across the room to where she was browbeating some tourists whose kids had talked with food in their mouths—"Don't you people in Utah know how to raise children?"—and shuddered.

While I tried to decide what you tip your mother, Caspar fiddled with his hearing aid and drummed his black-lined fingernails on the table. "Samuel, I plan to be in the area a few days."

"You can't make me leave with you."

"I have no wish to make you leave yet. Colored work or not, I have dreamed of the day my daughter would choose to find a job. If fear of losing you frightens her into arising off her backside, then so be it, I won't remove the motivating factor."

"Me?"

"Exactly."

I'd been reduced from grandson to motivating factor, but that was okay. I had a home and a family.

Caspar went on in his tobacco-baron tone. "What I was taking into consideration is whether or not you would accompany me into Jackson. I'd like to see my great-granddaughter."

"Her name is Shannon."

"That won't do at all."

"It's her name."

His moustache twitched as he thought a few moments. "I would like to view her with you before I go."

30

Sam Callahan sat on his front porch with his cane on *his lap and watched sunbeams caress the mountain bluebells and* Lonicera *alongside the gurgling creek. A sage hen strutted over by the outhouse. Two deer wandered into the yard, heads dipping to the grass, then rising to look with velvet eyes at Sam.*

"Maurey," he said. "The deer are back."

Maurey Callahan brought a steaming peach pie and a glass of cold buttermilk to Sam on the porch. "Aren't they beautiful. I wish they'd come closer. I can't see like I could fifty years ago when you married me."

"But your blue eyes are more beautiful than ever," Sam said.

The eyes in question twinkled. "Mr. Callahan, you always were a charmer." As they ate pie, Maurey filled her mate in on the events of the day. "Shannon is bringing all six grandkids out this afternoon. She promised them you'd tell the story about when you wrote the great Wyoming novel between innings of the pennant drive."

Sam smiled to himself, remembering the fall he won a Pulitzer and a World Series. "I sure am glad she had those kids without any help from male people."

"I wonder how she did that," Maurey said.

"In dreams, all daughters are pure and all hits are doubles into the left-field fence."

—·—

Dothan came by the house a week later to take Maurey for a drive in his Ford. I was glad to see her go off with him. I mean, her leg was in a cast and she had stitches down there from where Dr. Petrov did something creepy to help the baby out. Maurey wasn't likely to get wet anytime soon.

She'd shown me the stitches; looked as if he'd used garden loppers to connect the front and back holes. *Ish.* I'd hate to be a girl, always being shaved and cut and poked at, half the population scheming, drooling, lying constantly just to stick a foreign object in your body. The female orgasm must be pretty amazing to make all the crap they go through worth it.

Dothan came in wearing a torn T-shirt and black sneakers without socks or laces. He looked at Shannon for about five seconds. "What's wrong with her head?"

I held the door open and stood by in case Maurey crashed while crutching down the steps.

"Don't wake up Shannon," she said.

"Of course not."

"Her next feeding's in two hours and I'll be back, but if I'm not, you understand what to do."

"I know what to do." I'd learned a lot in a week. I knew what formula is and how to shake warm drops out on my arm and everything else you need to raise a kid.

"You have the White Deck phone number in case you need Lydia?"

"I won't need Lydia."

I helped Maurey into the backseat while Dothan revved the engine. "Bye, kids." I waved. "Have fun."

First time alone with the baby; I'd waited all week for this. She lay sleeping on her stomach with her head turned toward Les. I held my mirror in front of her little nostrils to see if she was still alive—a trick I'd learned on her fourth day—and her breath made the neatest fog heart pattern on the glass.

Then I lifted her from the bassinet and carried her to the new rocking chair. Bassinet, rocker, and the cute pink sleeper she wore all came from Caspar.

At least eight times while we were shopping in Jackson, he stopped to snort out that hairy nose of his. "None of my kindness is for Lydia, you understand that, Samuel? Lydia shall never get a dime from me. This is for that baby."

"Shannon."

"No reason to punish the little one simply because her parents and grandparents are all immoral, shameless hellhounds. The baby is still innocent."

"Thanks for all the stuff, Paw Paw." I know he got a kick out of being called Paw Paw again.

We drove to the Western Union to send a telegram to Caspar's own mother who lived in New York City. I think he was afraid to call her on the phone. Intimidation now ran through five generations of Callahans.

Alice jumped on my lap to sniff Shannon's breath on the front of my shirt. The three of us rocked a long time, Shannon sleeping, Alice purring, me rocking and watching. Shannon was so small I had to hold her head up. Her upper lip was the tiniest, prettiest thing I'd ever seen. The father-love deal crept into the room, not so much like Carolina surf, more on the scale of mountain air.

As we rocked, I started talking to Shannon. I told her the importance of knowing the names of what you looked at and how Caspar hadn't really meant to burn my baseball cards. I explained what she could learn from books, not to ever trust men, and don't take Lydia seriously.

"Mom loves us, she can't help it, only love scares her so she thinks it's a weakness."

Shannon's mouth puckered in her sleep. I traced the pink wedge on her forehead with my finger. Lydia had said it would go away and I wanted to remember it.

"Shannon, your life will be interesting. Wonderful and sad things will happen, you'll feel hordes of emotions and sometimes they won't make sense. Just watch out for coaches and cowboys and you'll be happy." I touched her tiny nose, then the midpoint of her mouth. "You're a lucky girl, Shannon."

She slept. Alice hopped to the floor and bent to lick herself under the armpit. Above it all, Les stayed cool.

I rocked awhile and looked out the window at Soapley's trailer where Otis was digging a hole in the shade of a dead GMC truck. I felt a bit bored.

"Well, Shannon," I said. "What should we do next?"

About the Author

Rebecca Stern

Reviewers have variously compared Tim Sandlin to Jack Kerouac, Tom Robbins, Larry McMurtry, Joseph Heller, John Irving, Kurt Vonnegut, Carl Hiaasen, and a few other writers you've probably heard of. He has published eight novels and a book of columns. He wrote eleven screenplays for hire; two of which have been made into movies. He turned forty with no phone, TV, or flush toilet and spent more time talking to the characters in his head than the people around him. He now has seven phone lines, four TVs he doesn't watch, three flush toilets, and a two-headed shower. He lives happily (indoors) with his family (wife, Carol; son, Kyle; daughter, Leila) in Jackson, Wyoming.

Coming in 2011, Tim Sandlin returns to GroVont with Lydia,
available at booksellers everywhere.

1

My mother, Lydia Callahan, walked out of the Dublin, California, federal women's penitentiary at noon on Mother's Day, 1993, a free woman, with nothing but the clothes on her back and a Land's End fanny pack full of credit cards. She took a taxi to the Holiday Inn in Walnut Creek where she checked in as Lydia Elkrunner and gave her address as hell. Then she washed her hair in complimentary Pert and fell asleep. Lydia was fifty-eight years old; in her dreams she was twenty.

The next night, she telephoned my daughter Shannon in Greensboro, North Carolina.

Lydia said, "I'm out of stir."

Shannon said, "Stir?"

"Prison. They let me go."

"That's wonderful, Lydia. I can't wait to see you."

"I want you to pick me up at the airport Thursday afternoon. I don't know what flight I'll be on, so you'll have to meet them all."

"Which airport is this where you want me to meet every flight?"

"Jackson Hole. I want you to be the one waiting when I come home. No one else."

"Lydia, Dad lives right there, almost next door to that airport, and I live two thousand miles away."

"Are you going to do this for me or not?"

Shannon said, "I was being practical." Then there was silence. In the past, before going underground, Lydia would have flown into a tirade at the suggestion that practicality might take precedence over her will. But prison had taught her the power of silence. Noisy intimidation works on men; women respond to a quieter approach.

After twenty seconds, Shannon said, "I'll be there."

Lydia said, "I would also like you to organize a community get-together. No use sneaking back into town."

"You want a welcome home party?"

"Put up a notice at the GroVont post office. Tell them chicken wings and shitty beer for all. That'll bring the yokels out."

"Anything else, Grandma?"

"What?"

"Lydia."

"Dress nice. This is my triumphant return. I don't need to come off the airplane and see a slob."

—

Lydia's phone call came while Shannon was in the process of breaking up with her tenth boyfriend in ten years. This one's name was Tanner. They had made love with a device Tanner bought for seventy-five cents from a machine in the truckers-only washroom at the Dixie Land Service Center near Highpoint. Tanner was proud of his device, and, in his mind, he had just given Shannon the sensual experience of the epoch.

Tanner kissed her left breast and said, "My God, that was great."

Shannon rolled over on her back to face the ceiling. "I don't feel the way you're supposed to feel when you're in love."

Tanner said, "Yeah, but the orgasm makes up the difference."

"There's more to love than orgasms."

Tanner was confused. His belief system was based on the concept that sexual prowess and popularity go hand-in-hand. "What the hell does that have to do with us?"

"I do not love you, Tanner. You're interchangeable with others."

"But I'm here now."

Shannon rolled back to look at Tanner, who had a little scar on his chin she was fond of. She realized the scar was why she had chosen him in the first place. It lent Tanner a sense of vulnerable danger, but vulnerable danger is not enough in the long haul. "Tonight was fun," she said. "I want you to move out tomorrow."

He said, "No."

At that point, the phone rang.

Tanner pouted throughout Shannon's conversation with Lydia. After they said their good-byes and hung up, he said he was sorry he wasted his youth on a woman with the emotional capacity of a mud flap. He asked her if their time together meant nothing to her, and she said, "That's right." He asked her if she was made of stone. Shannon realized Tanner would not leave her until tears flowed and glass shattered. She would have to make him believe the break-up was his idea, and at the moment she simply didn't have the energy. Instead, she telephoned her father, Sam. This is where I enter the story.